PRAISE FOR THE PETER SAVAGE NOVELS

"I would follow Peter Savage into any firefight."
–James Rollins, *New York Times* bestseller of *The Demon Crown*

"Edlund is right at home with his bestselling brethren, Brad Thor and Brad Taylor."
–Jon Land, *USA Today* bestselling author of the *Caitlin Strong* series

"This **compulsively readable** thriller boasts a whiplash pace, a topical plot, and **nonstop action.** Edlund fans won't be disappointed."
–*Publisher's Weekly*
Praise for *Lethal Savage*

"a near-perfect international thriller"
–*Foreword Reviews*
Praise for *Guarding Savage*

"With **a hero full of grit and determination,** this action-packed, timely tale is **required reading** for any thriller aficionado."
–Steve Berry, *New York Times* bestselling author,
Praise for *Hunting Savage*

"**Crackling action**, brisk pace, timely topic…"
–*Kirkus Reviews*
Praise for *Deadly Savage*

VALIANT
SAVAGE

A PETER SAVAGE NOVEL

VALIANT SAVAGE

A PETER SAVAGE NOVEL

DAVE EDLUND

 Light Messages

Durham, NC

Published 2020, by Light Messages
www.lightmessages.com
Durham, NC 27713
SAN: 920-9298

Paperback ISBN: 978-1-61153-362-0
Ebook ISBN: 978-1-61153-363-7
Library of Congress Control Number: 2020943724

*This is a work of fiction. All characters, organizations, and
events portrayed in this novel are either products of the author's
imagination or are used fictitiously.*

For my good buddy Gary, aka Gary Porter.
You've made me laugh;
you've had my back;
and you've inspired me to dream big.

ACKNOWLEDGEMENTS

THERE IS A SAYING, "May you live in interesting times." Some sources attribute it to an ancient Chinese proverb. Others claim it is Arabic in origin. Regardless of the source, the double entendre has never been more meaningful. As I write this, I have just completed the last twenty thousand words of *Valiant Savage* in imposed solitude, under quarantine (or house arrest, as I prefer to think of it) in Guangzhou, China.

I must admit, the past week has been exceedingly productive. And yet I've not missed the irony. For me, solitude is good when I'm drafting the manuscript. But the follow-on phases of producing a book require the opposite—a high degree of interaction with many talented individuals, whom I want to acknowledge and thank.

First off, I'm very grateful to Light Messages Publishing for partnering with me to bring these adventures to life. This will be the seventh Peter Savage novel, an achievement that could not have been realized without the talent and generous support of Betty and Wally, and from my editor Elizabeth, and copy editor Ashley Connor. It has truly been a joy to work with you, but more than that, to count you as my friends.

In particular, the assistance and direction Elizabeth has provided through the editing process has made every one of these novels so much better than the manuscript that left my desk. I'd like to think that the editing process is akin to cutting a finished gem from a rough diamond. But in reality, I think it's more alchemy, converting lead to gold. Thank you, Elizabeth, for doing your magic and making me look good.

A key part of every book production is the cover. Since I have the artistic talent of a toddler, I am always amazed at the wonderful covers on the Peter Savage novels. But I am especially excited about the cover on this book for two reasons. One, it is bang-on in capturing the essences of this novel. And two, my wonderful daughter, Mackenzie Edlund, pulled together the concept design within a few hours. Thank you so much, Mac.

The legal technical aspects of this novel could not have come together without the help of my good friend Alex Gardner. As former District Attorney for Lane County, Oregon, and now the Director of the Oregon State Police Forensic Services Division, Alex spent hours helping me to understand the nuances of the Federal Appellate Court system, as well as the organizational structure of the Oregon State Police. Thank you, buddy.

Every author I know finds promotion and marketing difficult, if not positively distasteful. I'm no exception. And so the fantastic work from my publicist, Rebecca Schriner, is hugely appreciated. Thank you for the eye-popping graphics, as well as outreach to media (social and traditional), bookstores, and prominent members of the thriller community. You have no idea how much angst you have spared me.

Speaking of members of the thriller community, I want to thank the International Thriller Writers for welcoming me into your midst. I am privileged to have the opportunity to learn from such an esteemed and selfless group of highly accomplished authors. In particular, I want to offer my heartfelt appreciation and most sincere thanks to Steve Berry, James Rollins, Jon Land, K.J. Howe, Grant Blackwood, and David Morrell for your generous advice and encouragement.

Last but far from least, thank you to the fans of Peter Savage and his canine companion Diesel. Without an audience to read these novels, there would be no reason to write them. Please continue to share your comments and post reviews on Amazon, Goodreads, and other social media sites. And if you want to reach me directly, I'd love to hear from you, either through the contact page on my website, www.PeterSavageNovels.com, or via email at dedlund@LightMessages.com.

AUTHOR'S NOTES

A LOT HAS HAPPENED since *Lethal Savage* was released, and Peter Savage and Todd Steed have been busy. Not content to limit their small-arms product line to the magnetic impulse technology, Peter has invented a pulsed-energy weapon with funding from the Defense Advanced Research Projects Agency (DARPA). The design employs a microsecond pulse of laser energy.

How realistic is this? Understandably, this field of physics is veiled in secrecy, although there is some information in the public domain which hints at what is possible, perhaps even probable.

Lasers are commonly used in industry for cutting and welding. In particular, neodymium YAG lasers and other types of fiber optic and solid-state lasers have the necessary qualities for a battlefield weapon, including durability, compact size, and high-power efficiency. In particular, the proliferation of drone technology and the threat presented by drone swarms has driven arms developers to invent new defenses, and laser weapons are playing a prominent role.

Naturally, the U.S. military has been active in developing

laser weapons. In 2014, the Navy tested a high-powered laser from the deck of the USS Ponce, and in 2020, from the deck of the USS Portland. Designated the LaWS (Laser Weapon System), the trials were deemed a success. The Army has also fielded functional laser weapons, and in 2019, a 30-kW laser was successfully fired from the bed of a truck (some sources claim the power output was 50 kW). Not to be left out, the Air Force is also developing an airborne laser, and the Marine Corps has successfully demonstrated a compact laser weapons system (CLaWS).

In public statements, all branches of the military claim the development of laser weapons is for antimissile and anti-drone defenses. The high power reported for the Army test would support this stated position.

Certainly, the actual state of military development is more advanced than what is publicly reported. How advanced? Are we on the verge of shoulder-fired lasers? The truth is no doubt locked in DARPA vaults, but we may be close.

The secret to the capability of a laser to burn through metal is that the energy is focused on a tiny spot. Think of a magnifying glass to focus the light from the sun on a tiny spot—same idea. In designing the pulsed-energy weapon, Peter has considered that the weapon would be antipersonnel, rather than antimateriel (for reasons he discusses with his DARPA program manager), and therefore the laser energy would be absorbed by human tissue. Since flesh is largely water, he reasoned that the energy would heat and vaporize the water. His non-classified calculations are shared in the following pages for those who are interested in a deeper technical understanding.

Further details on the design and materials of construction are unlikely to be declassified any time soon. But who knows? Maybe a backyard inventor will cobble together something resembling Peter's brass board prototype. Maybe the blasters of *Star Wars* fame are just around the corner.

—DE

PROLOGUE

THE APTLY NAMED WEST BEACH RESORT gave the impression of being isolated, although it was only a couple miles from Eastsound, the island's major town. The family-run business comprised a general store at one end of a long pier, several moorings, and a dozen small cabins arranged in a line along the beach. In front of each cabin was a firepit, and weather permitting, visitors could enjoy a spectacular view across Presidents Channel to Waldron Island. At the end of a day of hunting for unique locally made pottery, or hiking the many trails in Moran State Park, it was common practice to watch the sun set from a chair on the pebble-strewn beach.

West Beach had a loyal following of visitors who came to enjoy the natural beauty at a leisurely pace, maybe read a book or two, or take slow walks along the beach or the inland walking paths through dense evergreen forests.

Although the day had dawned with teasing glimpses of sunshine, by late afternoon a heavy fog had settled in along with chilly temperatures. Still, it wasn't enough to push everyone indoors, and the hardiest guests were gathered around their firepits, flames repelling the chill and dampness.

With the muffled purr of a well-tuned engine, a fifty-three-foot Beneteau yacht materialized from the fog like an apparition. It was larger than most boats that moored at West Beach Resort. With bumpers out, it slowly motored toward the end of the pier, its sails furled. As it drew closer, the black hull seemed to merge with the still water, adding to the illusion that the boat was a specter.

The man at the wheel looked to be in his mid-fifties, with graying sideburns that at one time were black. He wore a navy-blue Greek fisherman's cap and rain parka with the collar turned up. He squinted through eyes the color of blue aventurine, one hand on the engine throttle and the other on the helm. With a gentle bump, two crewmen hopped onto the low wood platform and tied off the fore and aft lines.

"Very professional, Mister Brenner," said a younger muscular man with short blond hair, wearing John Lennon eyeglasses.

He had a distinctive scar across his left cheek, extending down to his cleft chin.

Brenner ignored the comment and continued with shutting down the engines and making sure the boat was tied to the dock.

When he was satisfied all was in order, he turned to the blond man. "Now what?"

"Now we walk down the dock to the general store and pay for the moorage."

The cold, dreary weather was encouragement enough for guests to stay close to their campfires or within their warm cottages, and no one was at the general store, although it would remain open for another hour.

"Just remember," the blond man said, "my gun will be pointed at you. If you make any effort to communicate with the store clerk that you need help, or to call the police, I'll put a bullet in you and the cashier. Am I clear?" He moved his right hand into his jacket pocket, where Brenner had seen him place a compact semiauto pistol.

"I've done everything you told me to do. I just want to get this done and see you leave so I can have my life back."

"Good. Just keep doing that, and soon I'll be out of your hair."

Blondie opened the door, and a brass bell hanging above the door jingled. A few seconds later, a woman came out from a back room.

"May I help you?"

Neither man spoke right away, and the blond man discretely nudged Brenner.

He cleared his throat. "Yes. I just motored in and tied up at the end of the pier. I'd like to stay the night and sail on tomorrow morning."

She smiled and glanced over his shoulder, through the large picture window facing west.

"That's a nice yacht you have. We don't normally see them that large."

Brenner returned the smile.

"Have you been to the San Juan Islands before?"

"No. First time."

"Spring isn't the best time—weather's rather fickle, if you know what I mean. You should visit again in summer. Where's your boat normally docked?"

"Uh…" He was afraid if he told her the truth, that he usually sailed out of Phuket, Thailand, the blond man would slay him and the clerk.

"San Francisco," Blondie said. "I think we'll also get some food and beer."

"Sure. We charge based on the size of the boat up to fifty feet. Flat rate for anything larger than that."

"She's fifty-three feet," Brenner said.

The clerk referred to a list taped to the side of the cash register and quoted a price. Brenner pulled his wallet out and started to remove a credit card, but Blondie produced two crisp hundred-dollar bills to cover the charge. While she was writing up the receipt, the two men filled a shopping cart with a selection of packaged food and a case of beer, which Blondie also paid for with cash.

"Thank you, and enjoy your stay tonight."

The men loaded the goods into a wheelbarrow, which Brenner pushed, with Blondie a step behind him. A row of seagulls eyed the pair suspiciously from their perch on the weathered wood railing along the side of the pier.

At the end of the pier, a set of stairs extended down to the floating dock where the Beneteau was tied. Three rough-looking men were standing in a loose group, each watching in a different direction. All were wearing puffy jackets hiding their sidearms from view.

Brenner parked the wheelbarrow at the head of the stairs and handed down the beer and bags of food to the three men who formed a line, handing the goods from one to the next.

"What should I do with the wheelbarrow?" Brenner said to the blond man.

"Leave it."

Brenner descended to the dock and then carried the food onboard, where he stowed it in a cabinet in the galley. The men each popped open a can of beer and chugged most of it down before coming back for air.

"Take it easy," Blondie said. "We still have work to do. Any man who gets drunk or screws this up will get a bullet in his head."

"Sure, boss." One of them poured out the remainder of the beer and motioned for the others to follow him back onto the yacht.

Two men stayed topside while the third man accompanied Blondie down the stairs to the relative warmth of the saloon.

Within the hour the sun had set, turning the gloomy gray into pitch blackness. The two men stationed in the cockpit of the yacht donned first generation civilian night-vision goggles. The devices, which looked like a pair of small binoculars fixed to a head strap, included an infrared illuminator. Although infrared is invisible to the unaided eye, the NVGs were designed to see in the IR band. In essence, the IR illuminator was like a flashlight, but only to those wearing the night vision devices.

The fog seemed to thicken, enveloping everything like a damp blanket. It wasn't long before the campfires in front of the cabins along the beach went out one by one, like so many candles being snuffed out, the muted voices and laughter also dying with the flames.

The guards stationed on the deck of the sailboat were left in near complete silence, save for the gentle lapping of water against the barnacle-encrusted pilings.

With Brenner locked in one of the guest staterooms, the blond man made final preparations.

"Let me have the bag of coke," he said to one of the men.

He then used a razor blade to slit open the small bag and empty the contents onto the polished teak coffee table.

"Seems like a waste of good coke, if you ask me," the man said, while watching his boss.

"I didn't. Besides, this needs to look like a drug deal gone bad. So stop complaining and start hauling the cases up top. And when you get all of them up the ladder, quietly walk down the pier and unscrew the bulb in the porch light at the general store, then get back here."

Stacked on the bed in the second guest stateroom were two olive drab hard-side containers, each about four feet long and half that in width. Stenciled on the cover was *FIM-92*. Given the size and weight of each case, it took two men to haul them up the ladder to the cockpit. There were also two smaller metal cases of dissimilar size, also drab green. Both were heavy.

With the containers staged topside, the guards all came down to the saloon. The blonde man checked his watch once more. It was 3:00 am.

"Okay, it's time," he said to the assembled men, all wearing NVGs. "Remember, no talking. Hand signals only. No one should be up, much less be walking around outside, but we're not taking any chances. Got it?"

All four nodded.

"Two men to each of the Stinger cases, and watch your step. I don't want anyone dragging a container or dropping one— remember, no noise."

"And once we get all the cases in a pile outside the store?" one of the men said. "Then what?"

"Two black Suburbans are there right now, waiting to have the gear loaded. Put the Stingers in one of the Suburbans, and the mortar and shells in the other. And make certain the loads are completely covered. I don't want anyone peeking through the window and calling the cops. We all ride to the ferry terminal, and shortly after sunrise catch the first boat to Anacortes. You okay with that?"

Another nod.

"Now if no one else has any questions, let's get to work. I'll be right behind you, but I have to clean up first."

The blond man spent fifteen minutes wiping down every surface they might have touched. Then he unlocked the stateroom and opened the door. He expected Brenner to be asleep, but he was sitting up, no doubt listening to the previous conversation.

"We'll be leaving now. I thought you'd like to know. You can have your boat back." He stood to the side and motioned for Brenner to enter the saloon. "Go ahead and take a look around. You'll see we didn't damage anything."

Brenner took two hesitant steps forward and looked around from the galley to the dining table to the sofa.

He noticed the white powder on the coffee table. "What's that? You said no drugs—" He gurgled.

From behind, Blondie slipped a thin wire over Brenner's head and pulled back sharply while pressing his knee into the man's back. He applied more pressure until the garrote cut deep into Brenner's neck, closing his trachea.

Brenner struggled, alternating between clawing at his neck, desperate to get his fingers beneath the piano wire, and reaching back, attempting in vain to grasp the blond man's face or hair. The struggling depleted his oxygen faster, and before long he fell to his knees.

Blondie used his knee to push Brenner onto his face, and he was able to apply even more force to the garrote. Blood was oozing from the thin line where the wire had buried into flesh.

Even after Brenner went limp, the blond man continued applying force for another minute, just to be sure. He left the assassin's weapon in place, grisly proof of the crime, but took a few moments to remove prints from the hand grips. Then he climbed the ladder and wiped down the cockpit as well, before striding down the pier to join his team.

The two Suburbans were loaded by the time he arrived. He scanned the area once again, and failing to see any activity, opened the door and eased into the passenger seat.

⊕

It was late afternoon when the local sheriff deputy arrived at West Beach. He was led to the Beneteau still tied to the dock.

"Hello?" he called out.

No reply.

He stepped onto the boat deck and crossed to the ladder leading down to the saloon. The door was closed.

He knocked twice and called out again, "Hello? Sheriff department. I'd like to ask a few questions."

Still no reply.

He checked the door latch. Unlocked. He unclasped the strap on his holster and wrapped his hand around the pistol grip. With his left hand, he slid the cabin door open.

He took the steps of the ladder down into the cabin. His gaze was drawn to the body lying face down, a puddle of blood spread under the neck. The deputy drew his weapon, holding it with both hands as he entered. Searching the three staterooms and two heads didn't take long, and once he was convinced there was no one else onboard, he holstered his weapon and radioed dispatch.

"Make sure the sheriff knows right away. He may want to get the state police involved, too. From the looks of the crime scene, it might be a drug deal that went south."

When the deputy emerged on the dock, he was greeted by the store clerk who'd been working when the yacht arrived.

"Did you convince them to leave or pay for another day?" she said.

The deputy frowned and looped his thumbs in his belt. "You checked them in yesterday?"

"Yes."

"Can you describe them?"

"Sure. There were two men." She proceeded to give a description of each to the deputy. "They said they were going to leave this morning, and they only paid for one night. Is something wrong?"

"Based on your descriptions, I'd bet one of the men is in the cabin, dead. The other guy isn't on the boat."

She placed a hand over her mouth in shock.

"Did you see anyone leave this morning? Maybe by car?"

She shook her head. "No, nothing."

⊕

The two Suburbans drove south after disembarking the ferry in Anacortes. They picked up Interstate 90 east from Seattle, and stopped for gas in Ellensburg. Just after crossing the Columbia River, they turned onto State Route 26, and then south on Route 195, bypassing Pullman. They drove the SUVs hard, making few stops other than for fuel and changing drivers every few hours. As they traveled farther south in western Idaho, the roads became secondary two-lane strips of aged asphalt, and their average speed dropped to less than fifty miles per hour.

South of the Nez Perce Reservation, the two-vehicle convoy picked up a gravel forest service road. Originally cut for logging, the road was still maintained and well-graded. It wasn't long before they reached a gate blocking access to a side road. The lead driver exited the vehicle, unlocked and opened the gate, then passed through. The driver of the second SUV closed and locked the gate. They had been told that the gate marked the boundary to the general's ranch, all ninety-eight thousand acres.

After another hour of driving, they reached a two-story log cabin. It was large and appeared opulent in a rustic sense, more like a designer lodge than a primitive structure.

The Suburbans coasted to a stop under the porte-cochère, the tires rumbling as they rolled over the cobblestone surface. Weary from the marathon drive, the drivers and passengers alike bailed and stretched their legs, milling about the SUVs.

The entrance door, a massive timber construction held together with straps of black iron, opened and a lanky pale man with red hair and freckles stood on the stone landing, looking down on the guests. Only the blond man with the wire-frame glasses and scar recognized him.

He called to his friend. "Parker! Long time, no see."

The man smiled and held his arms out. "Walker!"

As Walker began to advance to the porch, one of the men held out his hand and stopped him.

"Who's the new guy?"

"Relax. You're too suspicious." Walker strode to his friend and embraced him in a bear hug.

"How was the mission?" Parker said.

"Like clockwork. Unloading the merchandise from the boat was flawless. On the other hand, the drive was long. Had to endure hours of bitching. Where should we unload the crates?"

"Have your men drive around back. There's a shop next to the garage. They can stack the cases in there. The general will be very pleased. Every step makes a footprint."

Walker turned to the men still standing beside the Suburbans. "You heard him. Get the crates unloaded."

"I'm ready for a hot shower," one of the men grumbled.

"And something to drink," said another. "Do you think they have a bottle of tequila inside?"

Walker tuned out the chatter and placed his arm on Parker's shoulder. "You know I don't understand when you speak in crazy metaphors."

The tall man laughed. He had studied Buddhism and other Asian religions in college, and it was a subject he still followed.

"I said, when we work steadily, we make solid progress."

"Oh. Why didn't you just say so?"

And side by side they entered the house.

CHAPTER 1

THE WEAPON, IF YOU COULD CALL IT THAT at this early stage, was spread over the table, a cluster of parts and pieces with interconnecting wires and fiber-optic cable. The chaos more closely resembled a half-completed science project than a cutting-edge marvel of electro-optical machinery.

With a screwdriver in hand, Peter Savage squinted his steel-gray eyes as he leaned in close and adjusted the voltage setting on a power supply. Satisfied, he stood, straightening his frame to its full six-foot height. He ran a hand through his brown hair and sighed. Although the wiring was a mess, he knew from experience that a kludged assembly often yielded valuable information.

An inverter hummed softly as he made one final check, followed by a measured nudge to the target to ensure it was in the proper alignment. A portable stand next to the table supported a PC for data acquisition, a single thick cable stretching from a USB port on the PC to an oscilloscope at the table edge.

"Well, looks ready," he mumbled to himself.

After mentally running through the checklist one last time, he depressed a small black button affixed to the work surface. The target exploded in a mist of water vapor and pale green pulp, accompanied by a *pop!*, like a firecracker.

The destruction of the target, although anticipated, wasn't the result of impact by a high-velocity projectile silently spit from the business end of a MK-9 magnetic impulse gun—the hallmark of EJ Enterprises. Instead, the target—a fresh cucumber purchased that morning from the local grocery store—was destroyed by a millisecond-burst of ultraviolet laser radiation.

"I'd call that a positive result," Todd said dryly, arms folded across his chest.

He sported a chocolate-brown goatee and short-cropped hair of the same color. He cracked a rare smile, signaling his satisfaction with the results. As the Chief Engineer at EJ Enterprises, Todd Steed, working from Peter's designs, had been largely responsible for assembling the crude prototype weapon, a responsibility he took seriously.

Although the company was small, with less than ten employees, EJ Enterprises had made a name in the firearms industry for its innovative research. Their principle product was the MK-9 sidearm. Sold exclusively to the United States Department of Defense, the MK-9 was a single-shot weapon that closely resembled a conventional pistol with a long barrel. But unlike conventional firearms, the magnetic projectile was not propelled by an explosion of gunpowder, but by a unique arrangement of solenoid rings generating timed and alternating magnetic fields. It was silent when fired with subsonic ammunition, making it the go-to weapon for Special Forces operators in need of maximum stealth.

A graduate of the University of Oregon, Peter had an

entrepreneurial spirit that rivaled his love for science and engineering. And as an avid outdoorsman, he was at home in the wilderness and enjoyed target shooting and hunting. So it came as no surprise to his close friends when Peter announced that he was going to take firearms development into the twenty-first century. After many false starts, his breakthrough invention was the MK-9, and the success it brought allowed him to expand his business and hire a talented team of designers and fabricators.

Under Peter's creative direction, the engineering team at EJ Enterprises had recently developed a multi-shot version of the MK-9 that looked something like a revolver. With growing sales and a market too small to attract competition, the company provided a comfortable living for its dedicated employees. Revenue from sales of weapons and their unique magnetic projectiles generated enough profit for Peter to turn his attention to a new challenge.

Being a hunter, he understood the challenges of extreme long-distance shooting and had set his mind to come up with a better solution. Only those military marksmen who were gifted and well-trained had learned to compensate for the effects of gravity and wind as a bullet traversed distances greater than a thousand yards. He understood the problem was with the bullet itself, an extremely effective, albeit limited, tool for delivering kinetic energy to the target.

A paradigm shift was needed.

Peter and Todd had already tested and proven the individual components—principally the magnetic inverter, flash tube, and nanomatrix lasing tube. But the brass board assembly distributed across an orange rubber mat on the worktable was the first time all the components were interconnected and functionally tested as a complete system.

Peter punched a couple keys on the laptop, causing a graph

to appear on the display.

"Pulse-duration time is good, right at two milliseconds."

"How about energy?" Todd said.

"The energy peaked at seventeen joules and was constant for the duration of the pulse," Peter pointed to a red line graphed on the display, "which coincides with the strobe flash that initiated lasing. The continuous power draw from the DC supply is steady at about one hundred thirty watts."

"That's about what you estimated it would be."

Peter nodded. "Pretty close. This firing cycle spanned one hundred eighty milliseconds, but we may be able to shorten that a bit as we combine these components and refine the circuit integration. Still, that's a substantial power pulse, so the weapon will have to be energized by a capacitor discharge."

Todd nodded. "That's easy with a standard battery pack. Assuming five shots per second, we'll need to charge the capacitor in a tenth of a second. Might be a bit fast for a single capacitor, but we can get that by using a bank of them."

"Good idea. I need you to stay focused on this." Peter waved his hand over the brass board assembly. "This looks too much like a half-finished concept rather than a functional weapon. As it stands, we can't demo this to any Department of Defense folks. It needs to be packaged into something resembling a conventional firearm. Right now I'd settle for a configuration the size of a submachine gun."

"And no heavier. When do you need to demo it?"

"I have a scheduled call with the program manager at DARPA, Tim McMullen, in thirty minutes. After I share today's results, I plan to invite him for a meeting here in two weeks."

"Okay. I'll get right on it. The machining load is light right now, so I'll reserve one of the CNCs for prototyping parts."

"Thanks. Don't worry about the power supply now. We can figure that out later. Besides, McMullen will likely have opinions on the degree of flexibility to accommodate various batteries already in the supply chain."

"Just don't let him talk you into a four-pack of double As."

Peter grinned. "Yeah, or a pair of button cells. For now, use a lithium-ion battery for the primary power. I don't care if it's big. We should have something in the stockroom that will work."

Peter and Todd had spent most of the previous two months working fifty-hour weeks to get to this point, and they knew there was still a lot of hard work ahead of them. Although DARPA had initially exhibited considerable interest in the concept for the pulsed-energy weapon when first proposed by Peter a year earlier, that enthusiasm soon waned. Objections about how the soldier would know if the laser pulses were off target due to misalignment of the scope, since the ultraviolet photon pulse was invisible to the naked eye, only served to distract the conversation and raise doubts. Some DARPA technicians requested that every third laser pulse be in the visible spectrum, like a tracer round. Another concern raised by several desk-bound officers, who'd never been in combat, related to the lack of effectiveness of the proposed weapon system against steel armor.

"It's designed to be a shoulder-fired antipersonnel small arm," Peter had said, at least a dozen times. "The Army and Navy are already testing much larger laser weapons for taking down aircraft and missiles. Those weapon systems require an enormous amount of power. As such, they are restricted to being mounted on vehicles like small trucks and warships. That's not the job my team is addressing."

However logical, his protestations never elicited more than a grunt or empty stare from the desk jockeys.

Peter patted Todd on the shoulder. "I'm going to get ready for my call. Let me know if you need anything."

Settled in behind his desk, with notes at hand, Peter dialed McMullen. They used a commercial-grade encryption software—not as hard to hack as the military software, but in all probability good enough for their purposes.

McMullen picked up on the second ring. After a few pleasantries, Peter got down to business.

"Before I share our most recent results, do you have any questions from the previous reports I've sent to you?"

With a thick New England brogue, McMullen said, "No. Not for now, anyway. I understand that you've completed the weapon design, and even tested the major subsystems, passing all challenges. I'm most interested to learn if this device will function fully assembled, how well it will function, and what compelling advantages it offers the modern warrior. Obviously it has to be rugged and portable as well. Our soldiers, especially the Spec Ops guys, are already burdened with up to a hundred pounds of gear when they go out on a mission."

Peter had spoken with McMullen on several occasions, and always found him to be direct.

"Fair enough. We operated the fully assembled system in what is best described as a brass board configuration."

"You mean the components were laid out and connected, but not in the finale packaging arrangement?"

"Yes, that's correct. The test was a complete success, and now we are proceeding with a small, self-contained layout in what I think will resemble a carbine."

"You *think*? Meaning, the final packaging has not been nailed down yet?"

Peter was expecting this question. "Not yet. But we're confident we can achieve a product design that has the look and feel of a conventional carbine."

"I like your conviction, but I want to see the data first. If your claims are justified, this could be the most significant breakthrough in small arms since the invention of gunpowder."

Peter was encouraged with the enthusiasm expressed by the program manager.

"I'll encrypt the data files and send them to you later today."

The rest of the call was spent discussing the details of the experiment and the type of testing Peter envisioned for the prototype. There would have to be a determination of effective range under varying environmental conditions, including fog and rain, dust storms and snowfall, which were expected to absorb and scatter the ultraviolet photons and decrease the lethality at distance. And durability of the prototype weapons could only be assessed through realistic handling in exercises conducted in environments ranging from hot, dusty deserts to frigid snow-covered mountains. The test protocol would take months, maybe years, to work through, and cutting corners wouldn't be tolerated.

Near the end of the conversation, McMullen had one final question.

"How did you decide to handle the fire indication?"

Peter was surprised he hadn't asked earlier.

Fire indication, or the physical response of the weapon to being fired, had been the source of innumerable debates with just about everyone at DARPA who was involved in the program. With traditional guns, fire indication was two-fold— the sharp recoil from the gun combined with the audible report. Both were the unavoidable product of the principle physics.

"The solution," Peter replied, "turned out to be far easier than we had imagined. We simply engineered a spring-loaded striker inside the grip. When the shooter depresses the trigger, initially there is resistance, as with a normal gun. Once the trigger breaks, it activates the firing mechanism, and also the striker hits a plate, sending a vibration throughout the stock. The shooter feels this and knows the weapon has been fired."

"Sound?" McMullen said.

"Minimal. It's about as loud as breaking a wooden matchstick. We opted to avoid anything louder. I think you'd agree that fewer detectable signatures are better."

"I'll have to see it, of course. But I like what I'm hearing. Tell your team they've done a good job."

"Thank you. I expect to demo the first prototype in two weeks. Can you visit EJ Enterprises then?"

Following a short pause, McMullen said, "Let me review the data files first. Then I'll get back to you to confirm the schedule. This could be big. I think my boss, Major Hardwick, will also be interested. If you're right—if you can achieve what you claim you can—we're talking about a quantum leap in firearms technology. It's conceivable, perhaps even probable, that a few trained men armed with this weapon system could defeat an opposing force twenty times their number. It would be hard to overstate the impact such a weapon would have on the battlefield—and beyond."

CHAPTER 2

BILLY WAS RUNNING HARD, following a zigzag path that led from one point of cover to the next—a lichen-covered boulder, a large tree trunk, a weathered stump. Just ahead was his destination, a shallow bowl where once a tall pine had stood, the large root ball still adjacent the depression. Soil and several rocks, each as big as a basketball, were lodged between roots the size of his arm.

Feet first, he slid to a stop, securing his rifle to keep it out of the sandy soil. He rolled to his side, then crawled to the edge and planted the two short bipod legs on the earthen lip. Stretching before him for nine hundred yards was an open meadow.

He took several deep breaths, and soon his pulse slowed. Billy was a big powerful man, built like his father. Yet the dash through the forest, carrying a forty-pound backpack and a scoped hunting rifle, had left him winded. His curly black hair, cut in a mullet, was held down with a thin knit skullcap. A short-trimmed beard, angular cheek bones, narrow pointed nose, and chiseled jaw gave him a rugged masculine appearance. The product of a biracial marriage—his father Caucasian and his mother African American—he was often confused as Hispanic or Middle Eastern.

A glance at his wristwatch told him his time was good—nearly thirty seconds faster than his best time. He flipped open the scope covers and completed a preliminary survey of the meadow. In short order, he spotted three targets, but he had to be sure before he fired. He removed his eye from the scope and turned his head side to side, taking it all in. Not seeing anything else noteworthy, he peered again through the optics set at ten-power magnification.

The three targets, each a man-shaped silhouette two-and-a-half-feet tall, were cut from plate steel and set on a stand, like a sandwich board, such that the target could swing forward and backward. He used the size in relation to graduation marks on the cross hairs of the scope to estimate distance. From this crucial information, he would judge the holdover to compensate for bullet drop. The wind was light, almost nonexistent. Perfect conditions.

One minute had passed since he'd slid into the hole.

Imagining the targets were flesh and blood, and out to get him, Billy recalled the strategy employed by Sergeant Alvin York. During WWI, York had shot a half-dozen advancing German soldiers with his .45 ACP by aiming for the farthest of them, thereby not affording the advancing soldiers the opportunity to know they were being picked off as they charged his position.

Billy set the crosshairs on the most distant of the three plate-steel targets, six hundred forty yards out. He applied steady pressure to the trigger and sent the first bullet downrange. He was cycling the bolt even before the strike. Moments later, he heard the metallic clang as the jacketed round splattered upon the hard steel. Already he had the next target in sight… and fired.

Clang!

At only one hundred fifty yards distance, the third and closest target was an easy shot.

Billy nailed it, then ejected the spent cartridge case and scoped the meadow, a prudent practice to make a habit of.

"Not bad." The voice came from behind Billy, startling him.

He rolled to his side and turned his head to face the older man he knew only by his last name—Swanson. Clad in a camouflage Army combat uniform identical to what Billy was wearing, the man was older than him by twenty years, yet he remained physically fit, lacking the bulging belly far too common on middle-aged men. His salt-and-pepper hair was long and shaggy, in line with his unkept beard. With the exception of his clean and fitting ACU, he could easily pass for a drifter.

Almost as a reflex, Billy surreptitiously drew in a breath through his nose and registered the lack of any fetid aroma that enveloped the homeless like a cruel aura, forever signaling that here goes a looser, someone who can't make it in the real world. Or worse, chooses not to, preferring to mooch off society.

Billy knew this firsthand. Not so long ago, he'd wandered the streets—huddled in stoops to avoid the rain, crouched against the side of a building under a sheet of cardboard to ward off the worst of the night chill. He understood the constant fear of assault. And he'd witnesses how readily a life could be sacrificed for a bag of empty cans and bottles.

And all the while, the ever-present stench was like a beacon warning passersby to break eye contact and give a wide berth.

Swanson stepped forward while looking at the stopwatch in his hand. High-power binoculars where hanging from a padded strap around his neck.

"Three aimed shots in eleven seconds. All three solid hits—one head shot, and two about the middle of the torso. I score it as three kills."

Billy's face was devoid of expression. "Thank you, sir." After a pause, "Been practicing a lot lately."

The older man nodded. "What are you shooting?

Billy rose to his feet. Cradling the rifle against his chest, he opened the bolt and ejected the last round. Caught it in his left hand. With the bolt open, he climbed out of the depression and proudly extended the rifle. Swanson grasped the weapon and eyed it admiringly.

"Kimber makes fine rifles." He shouldered it and lowered his gaze to the Leopold scope. "So I hear, anyway. I could never afford a weapon of this quality." He lowered it and studied the cartridge marking stamped on the barrel. "Big cartridge."

"Yes, sir," Billy said. "The three hundred Winchester magnum is used by Army snipers. I'm shooting my own reloads, and this gun does well with a one-hundred-ninety-grain bullet. It took some time to find the most accurate load. Did a lot of experimenting."

Swanson handed the rifle back to Billy. "I don't get it. Most of the men in our organization struggle to earn a steady paycheck, myself included. Hell, it's pretty hard some months just to make it out for field training. But not you. How is that?"

Billy shrugged as he took the rifle back. "Got a settlement from the government when I was only seventeen."

"Must've been a boatload of cash. From the Feds?"

"No." Billy downturned his mouth. "From the City of Portland." He turned to the side, staring across the open meadow, hiding his features from the older man's view.

Billy's memories were still vivid, even though it had all transpired several years ago. He'd just returned from the recycle center after turning in a bag full of empty cans and bottles he'd collected from garbage cans. His mother had taken the twelve dollars and change…said she was going to the corner market to buy something to eat.

He'd stretched out on the tattered sofa, which doubled as his bed in the one-bedroom apartment, and opened a well-used textbook on world history. He spent as many days out of school as he did in the classroom, but not because he wasn't interested in learning. History and mathematics were his favorite subjects. His mother worked long hours cleaning offices, and there was never enough money. She was proud and wouldn't accept handouts. She'd always told Billy that no matter how hard his life was, there was always someone else with even greater struggles.

So Billy pitched in as often as he could. When he was lucky, he'd get pickup work. It was never the same—sometimes moving furniture, other times clearing junk from a building site, or maybe loading a stock room. The only commonality was that it was always menial labor. The pay was below minimum wage, but it was cash, and it was more than he made by scrounging empty bottles.

His father had died in prison serving a long sentence for possession of marijuana. It was his third conviction, and the judge—a blonde, middle-age woman with the right family connections and strong political ambitions—threw down the maximum sentence. Maybe it was because Billy's father had a barrel chest and thick arms covered in tattoos. Or maybe it was because she was up for re-election and wanted to send a message that she was tough on crime. The reason didn't matter.

Billy's father had made many mistakes—nearly all involving drugs. Never anything hardcore, and he never sold drugs. But a history of convictions for possession placed him in the Oregon State Penitentiary. Wanting only to mind his own business and be a model prisoner, he refused to play along with the inmate politics. The day after he declined to join the white supremacist's gang, he was shanked in the shower. Someone had ground a five-inch length of hard plastic into a dagger that left a ragged laceration, cutting his liver in two. He bled out on the tile floor as the water washed his blood down the drain.

To Billy, it seemed like the world was conspiring against him at every turn. It certainly was that night when his mother walked three blocks to the local convenience store. He was sure she was going to spend most of the money he'd given her on a bottle of the cheapest red wine they had, and then buy a couple cans of beans and maybe some Ramen noodles. He was so tired of noodles. All he wanted was a hot, juicy cheeseburger. He couldn't even remember how long it had been since he'd had a McDonald's burger, or any fast food, for that matter. And the idea of a steak dinner with asparagus and baked potato was as foreign as a new pair of shoes...or a clean jacket that fit.

After an hour, Billy wondered why his mother hadn't returned, but soon he resumed his reading. Another hour passed, and there was a knock on the door. The small apartment he and his mother called home was rundown and in a poor neighborhood. Crime was commonplace, and the door had three deadbolts and a chain.

He looked through the peephole. Two uniformed Portland police officers were in the hall. Oddly, they didn't look threatening, or even concerned. He'd seen the police come to other apartments on the same floor, usually to question a suspect or witness, sometimes to make an arrest. The officers always appeared on edge because they knew violence could erupt quickly.

But not these two policemen. They looked bored—no, that wasn't it. Not bored. They looked like they really didn't want to be there, but not because they were in fear for their safety.

What could they want? His heart was racing.

Then one of the officers rapped the door again. Louder this time, insistent.

Billy slipped off the chain and clicked the locks open. He edged the door, enough to peak one eye through the gap.

"Mister Reed?" one of the officers said.

"If you're looking for my father, he's dead."

The two officers exchange a curious glance. "Are you related to Latoya Reed?"

"Yeah, she's my mother. I'm Billy Reed."

The officer frowned. "We'd like to speak with you. Can we come in?"

Over the next ten minutes, the two officers explained how Billy's mother had been taken hostage by a gunman intent on robbing the store. Police had just arrived as the thug was trying to exit. It was dark, and Billy's mom was used as shield by the gunman.

A patrol officer ordered the man to drop his gun, but he didn't. The officer fired, killing the robber, and in the process, Billy's mother. They were sorry, they'd said. And then they left the apartment.

For the first time in his life, Billy cried. He was alone and had no idea what to do. He had no money, and his mother had no savings. Billy was forced into a hard world, with no clue what to do.

The city was supposed to send a social worker to visit Billy, but they never showed up. After a month, he was evicted from the apartment. He lived on and off the street, staying in shelters when he could. Occasionally he'd find his way to the high school, but since he had been absent so much, he didn't fit in. It was there—on the streets—that he met several veterans and learned about fighting and knives and guns. After seven months of living day to day, a social worker found him and shared the news that the City of Portland had a six-figure check for him.

"Why?"

"Wrongful death," she had replied, matter-of-factly. "The policeman was negligent in shooting your mother. He's been fired." Then she turned and walked away, on to the next task in a busy day.

Now eighteen and legally an adult, Billy walked into a bank for the first time in his life. The attractive twenty-something teller scrunched her nose when Billy handed over the check and announced he wanted to open an account. But after she read the amount and noticed that it was issued by the city government, she composed herself and directed Billy to a have a seat at a nearby desk.

He didn't have to wait long before the manager joined him. Billy noticed how groomed the man was, and the pleasant scent of his cologne. The contrast to Billy's dress and state of personal hygiene was stark.

The man asked for his identification. Fortunately, Billy still had his student ID card. Although it was expired, the manager reluctantly accepted it, all the while avoiding eye contact with his new customer. When asked for his residence and mailing address, Billy lied, recalling the old apartment where he had lived with his mother. Later, he'd get a post office box and then update the information with the bank.

With a couple signatures, the manager announced with a forced smile that he would grant Billy a savings account. Under the circumstances, the manager explained, that was the best he could do. A checking account or credit card was simply not possible for someone without credit, like Billy.

"I hope you understand, Billy," he'd said, concluding the distasteful transaction.

And Billy did. He understood, having lived his life constantly spurned by the very society that proclaimed at every opportunity that it was doing all that was possible to help the less fortunate, the under-privileged.

He left the bank with a pocketful of twenties, more money than he'd ever held. He went on to get a driver license, and then he bought a used pickup. When the engine started, it coughed out a cloud of blue smoke, but it ran—most of the time.

The settlement wasn't a fortune, but it was a nice nest egg and could have put Billy through four years of college, and he still would have had enough left over for a year's worth of living expenses.

But Billy didn't want a college education. He had a different goal in mind. One that would hardly be served by a higher education.

His second major purchase was a small used RV trailer that he lived in. It wasn't much, but he didn't need much. His lifelong lesson had been to live frugally, and his windfall wasn't going to change that. With only a post office box and no permanent residence, no credit, no job, Billy became anonymous. And that suited him just fine.

After listening to Billy's story, Swanson whistled. "You're one lucky guy to walk into a bunch of money that easy."

Billy looked back, his eyes hard and cold. "Easy? Is that what you think? That police officer fired fifteen rounds. Five struck my mother. She was dead before the paramedics arrived."

Swanson took a deep breath. "Hey, sorry man. Really. I didn't mean…"

"Don't matter much. It's all history now."

Swanson cleared his throat. "You spend all your time loading ammo and shooting?"

"Yep, pretty much." He didn't know how much he could trust the older man, so he wasn't going to let on that he poached, mostly deer, whenever he needed meat, and moved from campsite to campsite, always staying away from popular recreational locations and state-run campgrounds and parks. The more he could avoid people the better. He had no friends.

Swanson narrowed his eyes. "Why are you with us? What's your game?"

Billy closed the bolt on the rifle and slipped his arm through the sling.

"Game?" He raised his gaze to meet Swanson's stare.

"Yeah. What are you after? No one puts in the amount of time and effort you have without being motivated."

Billy paused as he assessed the older man, as if meeting him for the first time.

"I thought it would be obvious."

"Maybe I'm just slow. So why don't you help me out."

"Pretty simple, actually. I have a score to settle with the system that took my parents from me and dumped me out on the streets."

Swanson smiled. "Is that so?" With a twinkle in his eye, he said, "Well, we may be able to help you out. Come with me. I want to introduce you to someone. Someone important."

CHAPTER 3

LOCATED IN AN OLD BRICK BUILDING that used to be a powerhouse, EJ Enterprises occupied coveted real estate in the upscale Old Mill District of Bend. Marked by three towering chimneys, the exterior of the historic building had been preserved and reinforced, while the interior was gutted and repurposed as a combination of residential and industrial space. Peter's company was located on the ground floor, while the upper two floors served as his loft residence.

The living space was dominated by a large great room. The floor was wide-plank pine with an aged honey patina. All the walls were brick—floor to ceiling, and the ceiling had to be twenty feet high. There was a large fireplace centered along one wall. The mantle above the hearth was a massive, aged timber reclaimed from the original construction. The hearth was six-feet wide and nearly that tall. Consistent with the masculine décor, the furniture was overstuffed and upholstered in tobacco-colored leather.

On the opposite wall stood a bookcase that spanned from

corner to corner, floor to ceiling. The bookcase was natural-finish oak, with an oak library ladder to provide access to the upper shelves. In the center of the wall, surrounded by the bookcase, was an oversized arched passage that led to the kitchen and dining area.

Extending off the west-facing wall separating the fireplace from the bookcase was a rustic deck built from wood and steel, the metal having taken on an orange patina. With access through two pairs of French doors, the deck offered breathtaking views of the Cascade Mountains.

Peter still loved his home, but as an empty nester the memories associated with his surroundings were often bittersweet. His two children were adults and living independent lives. His son, Ethan, was a student at the University of Oregon, his father's alma mater, while Joanna was an interior decorator with her own business in Bend. His wife, Maggie, had died several years ago in a car accident on an ice-covered road. Despite the passage of time, he was still haunted by her memory.

Now, Peter's only housemate was his beloved pit bull, Diesel. Occasionally his girlfriend, Kate Simpson, would visit. But Kate had not been able—or wasn't willing?—to fully accept Peter's lifestyle, which included far too much adventure and near-death experiences. Although they still dated, Peter wondered if they could ever learn to love each other. Maybe the barriers were too great to overcome? And when he was honest with himself, he wondered if his love for Maggie was still too strong to allow him to move on.

With a banal personal life, Peter poured his energy into his work. He needed the excitement of a new challenge to give purpose to his existence. And so it was not at all surprising to his colleagues, especially to Todd, that Peter had been so energized as the pulsed-energy carbine took shape.

⊕

Peter held the door open while his visitors filed in and found chairs around the conference table. For security reasons, the meeting room at EJ Enterprises had no windows, relying instead on ample overhead lighting. With everyone seated, Peter cleared his throat before speaking.

"The governor's office phoned and said she's running about thirty minutes late. But if you don't mind, I'd like to begin and cover some of the more technical details that will probably be of little interest to Governor Bingham."

Major Hardwick leaned forward, resting his arms on the polished cherrywood table.

"Sure. Fine with me." He cast a glance to Tim McMullen, sitting on his left.

A lean man of average height, and with short brown hair, McMullen had left a promising career at the Idaho National Laboratory to join DARPA. His pasty complexion, black-rimmed glasses, slacks, and bulky sweater with the sleeves pushed up to his elbows gave him a sophisticated, nerdish appearance. And while his area of expertise, high-powered lasers, was undoubtedly fascinating to physicists, it was unlikely to generate a throng of rapt socialites at a cocktail party.

Major Matthew Hardwick, on the other hand, could have been plucked from any commercial fishing community along the Northwest coast. His full, round face with ruddy cheeks, and nose covered with a spider web of bluish veins, suggested years of practice in small-town watering holes. His thinning hair was mostly gray, with matching bushy eyebrows that would do Andy Rooney proud. No one would mistake the major for a man who pursued demanding physical activity. The buttons on his plaid shirt strained when he sat, the overlapping layers of cloth pulling enough to show the white T-shirt beneath. Even his fingers and lower arms looked chubby rather than lean and muscular.

As he sat there, Peter imagined that the major could be intimidating—gruff and coarse, ill-refined. That is, until he spoke. Although Peter had only previously shared a couple of phone conversations with Hardwick, his pleasant tone and polite, respectful approach to conversation had left a positive impression. And now Peter noticed the friendly demeanor and sparkle in his eyes as he addressed the others, characteristics of someone who advanced in leadership because of their skill to influence others.

Across the table sat Commander James Nicolaou. As director of the Strategic Global Intervention Team, or SGIT, he straddled the worlds of military intelligence and strike team leader. Jim had been recruited from the SEALs to lead the fledgling organization, and over the intervening years he'd succeeded in building the most capable covert organization within the operational jurisdiction of the Department of Defense.

True to his Greek heritage, his head was covered with a thick mane of jet-black hair. He sported a bushy mustache that stretched to the corners of his mouth, but avoided the full beard so common among special forces operators. At about two hundred pounds and five-feet-eight-inches tall, he was a powerful man without an ounce of fat.

Although Peter and Jim maintained a professional relationship, they also shared a strong bond of friendship that began when they attended high school together in Sacramento. Their lives followed different paths until a few years earlier when Jim reached out to Peter for help with a case involving Russia and alternative energy research. Since then, they'd work together on several missions, and Peter had become a welcome, albeit unofficial, member of SGIT.

Jim leaned back in the padded leather chair, his lightweight windbreaker unzipped to reveal a tan turtleneck underneath.

"It's your call, Major," he said. "I'm just along for the ride."

Hardwick smiled. "Oh, you're being too modest commander. If the demonstration today goes as well as I think it will, then your organization will be tapped to carry out field trials of the..." he checked his notes, "of the pulsed-energy rifle."

Jim faced Peter, and Hardwick and McMullen followed suit.

"Okay," Peter said, "you've all been briefed on this project, but I'd like to review some of the most significant—and unique—features of the PEAP weapon system. PEAP stands for pulsed-energy antipersonnel. It is a scoped shoulder-fired small arm, and most resembles a carbine in physical dimensions and weight. As the name implies, this weapon is designed to neutralize enemy combatants. It is not designed as an antimateriel weapon."

"Why?" Major Hardwick said. "I mean, why is the PEAP rifle ineffective against trucks and lightly armored vehicles?"

"Good question. The answer is important to understand. You see, the weapon fires a millisecond high-intensity pulse of ultraviolet laser radiation. So anything made of metal will reflect a portion, maybe even most, of that radiation. If the laser pulse is not absorbed, it can't do any damage."

Jim squinted and tried to recall what he'd learned about industrial lasers. "But I thought infrared and ultraviolet lasers were used for various manufacturing processes, from etching to cutting and welding. Why is this different?"

"Fundamentally, the same physics apply. But the difference here is time. Or more specifically, the duration of the energy pulse. Because the pulse duration from the PEAP is only two milliseconds, the heat produced by absorption of the radiation is quickly conducted away by metals. Industrial processes are conducted such that the laser energy is continuous, or close to it, so that the heat is localized."

"Two milliseconds is not very long," said Major Hardwick.

"What kind of damage will this do against human tissue?"

"A lot. Because living tissue is a poor thermal conductor, the energy from the laser pulse remains localized in a tiny volume. The result is instantaneous vaporization of water in the underlying muscle and fat cells. This vaporized water is further superheated by the pulse, causing an extremely energetic expansion. It's like a small explosion at the point of impact."

"What do you know of the terminal ballistics?" Jim said.

The term *terminal ballistics* typically referred to the transfer of kinetic energy from a bullet to the object struck by the bullet. It was a sterile term for the massive damage done when a high-velocity bullet impacted the human body.

"Not a lot," Peter replied. "We've only conducted limited experiments. Mostly against fruit and vegetables. But we did two tests on meat—pork shoulder roasts, actually. In both cases, the slab of meat and bone was covered in two layers of denim."

Hardwick pinched his eyebrows. "Denim?"

"Yes. I cut off the legs from an old pair of blue jeans and tied it around the pork roast. Then we shot it. In one test, from a distance of fifty yards. In the second test, from a distance of three hundred yards."

"Why not body armor?"

"Two reasons. First, I don't have easy access to the latest military body armor. And—"

"You could've requested samples," Tim McMullen said. "I'd have made certain you received what you needed."

"I'm sure you would have. But it would've taken time, and I'm running against a tight schedule. I have no doubt that there will be plenty of opportunity for a wide range of testing later. Assuming we pass this gate review."

Everyone nodded.

"And the second reason is that with pinpoint accuracy, the shooter would aim for exposed or lightly clothed areas of the body."

"Like the head," McMullen said.

"Exactly."

"And what was the effect on the roasts?" Jim said.

Peter dimmed the lights and turned on a projector. Two side-by-side photos appeared on the large screen.

"This was the chunk of meat shot at three hundred yards. The results were similar at fifty yards."

The major whistled. McMullen and Jim eased back in their chairs, eyes wide, mouths agape.

With a green laser pointer, Peter drew their attention to the leftmost photo, showing a small charred hole in the blue denim fabric.

"This is where the laser pulse burned through the fabric. And to the right, you can see the effect on the muscle tissue."

The cloth had been removed to expose a gory image. The pinkish-gray tissue was pulverized, revealing a deep hole, as if blasted away by a hidden charge inserted into the meat. At the base of the hole was the white bone.

"Looks like it penetrated at least two inches of muscle," Jim said.

"Three and a half, to be exact. It was a big roast."

"There's no question that would be lethal on a headshot," Jim said. "And if the target was hit in the arm or leg, bleeding would be massive. It's possible the limb might even be blown off. No doubt in my mind as to the potential lethality of this weapon."

"There's more to it than that," Hardwick said. "We need to put the PEAP carbine through the paces. Make sure it's effective in the hands of trained soldiers under simulated battlefield conditions. That's where you come in." He pointed across the table.

Jim cracked a lopsided grin. "My operators would love to get their hands on this hardware." He shifted his gaze to Peter.

"No guarantees they won't break it."

"If they do, then we'll know what has to be beefed up. What works…what doesn't…features your men like and dislike. It's all valuable information."

There was a knock on the door.

Peter said, "Come in."

It was his receptionist, Nancy, who'd been with EJ Enterprises since day one.

"The governor's car is just pulling up out front."

"Thank you, Nancy. We'll be right there."

"Also, Colleen Wilson from KTVZ news is here with a cameraman. They're asking if they can film the meeting between you and Governor Bingham."

Peter shook his head. "No. Explain to them that what we do here is confidential and classified for military purposes. They can video the governor in the lobby, but that's as far as they go."

She closed the door and hurried back to her desk. They didn't get many dignitaries as visitors, and she wanted to present a professional and inviting image. Besides, it wasn't every day that she had the opportunity to shake hands with the governor of Oregon.

"Well, gentlemen," Peter said, "if you don't mind, let's greet Governor Bingham and then carryout a simple demonstration in the laboratory."

CHAPTER 4

AT JUST SHORT OF SIXTY-FEET long by fifteen-feet wide, the room was oddly shaped for a laboratory. It had more in common with a bowling alley than a research facility. The entry doors were located at one end, near a cluster of tables and a shooting bench which included a forked stand to support the fore stock of a rifle. Oscilloscopes, data acquisition computers, and other sophisticated electronic equipment rested upon the tables. A bundled cluster of heavy-gauge wires—yellow, gray, and black—lay along the floor and stretched from the electronics to the far end of the narrow room.

The walls were constructed of cement block and covered with dense foam panels shaped liked pyramids to absorb sound. These panels even covered the ceiling. The material was often used in anechoic chambers.

At the far end of the room, the wall was covered in layers of heavy rubber mats designed to absorb bullets and prevent ricochets. A small stand supported the target—a cantaloupe melon.

Peter held the door open and invited the governor and his DoD visitors to enter. They formed a semicircle around the tables, casting curious glances to the far end of the space, no doubt questioning the presence of fresh produce siting alone on the stand. They stood on thick black rubber flooring, squishing under their shoes, which extended wall to wall.

Although Peter had seen the governor many times in televised interviews, he hadn't expected her to be so short, causing him to tilt his head down as he greeted her. Her handshake felt practiced, not a genuine greeting. Her makeup was subtle and gave the appearance of a woman in her late forties. But her hands told a different story, the age marks and wrinkles suggesting she was at least ten years older.

She took in the unfamiliar items arranged throughout the laboratory. Her gaze finally settled on the futuristic-looking gun resting on the bench before her. Of course, she knew she would be visiting an ultra-high-tech arms manufacturing firm, and that a demonstration was scheduled, yet her expression seemed to convey a mix of curiosity and apprehension.

Governor Kathrine Bingham was under political siege. She'd inherited the office when the former governor resigned amid mounting allegations of self-dealing to financially benefit close friends and family members. Being a close political ally of the former governor, she was also tainted by his corrupt practices, but none of the allegations were ever proven. She'd thought the scandal had been put to rest when she won re-election in a hotly contested race. But now, two years into her term, she was dogged by allegations she was using her official expense account for personal purchases—clothing, meals at fancy restaurants, exotic vacations.

Although she'd always paid the money back, accusations of unethical, and possibly illegal, conduct persisted. It didn't help that her office had not fully cooperated with an official audit. Every time a previously unreported and suspicious transaction came to light, the allegations flared anew.

She accepted the importance of getting out of Salem, and the downward spiral of political fighting. Her most trusted advisors had urged her to travel around the state and make new headlines. Ones that would cross the political divide and draw attention away from her political liabilities.

Although she didn't want to be at EJ Enterprises for some silly, macho demonstration of a new military weapon, she also understood that she needed to make appearances on the eastern side of the Cascade mountains, in the heart of conservative country. And conveying support for both the military and a successful small business would be a good showing.

As a bonus, President Taylor was scheduled to visit Redmond in a few days to spend time golfing with a close friend from his university years. Governor Bingham had managed to garner a coveted invitation to have a thirty-minute sit-down meeting with the president while he was in Central Oregon, to discuss issues important to the Northwest. The governors of Washington and Idaho had also been invited to participate. Top of the list was the growing number of politically oriented paramilitary groups, and the case presently before the Tenth Circuit Court related to a lawsuit brought by one of those militia groups—one that was especially well-financed—claiming that the former Oregon Country was illegally annexed by the United States in the early part of the 19th century.

Bingham considered herself fortunate to have this political windfall. She knew the meeting would not result in anything of substance—no policy changes, no funding proposals, no commitments of support—but it would be a huge boon to her political prestige, and could even serve as a steppingstone to the U.S. Senate. Or just maybe even a successful run for the presidency. Maybe not in the next election, but the following one?

With an ever-present and charming smile, Kathrine

Bingham waited, looking forward to completing this appearance so she could get on to the next item on her agenda, a meeting with the mayor and city council. More smiles and handshakes, another soundbite for the television news, more vague policy statements and feel-good promises. Later she'd have a steak dinner at the Blacksmith Restaurant, and then retire to her suite at the Oxford Hotel. Depending on how she felt, she might even get a spa visit before checking out in the morning.

Her bodyguard, a seasoned Oregon State Police officer and member of the Dignitary Protection Unit, stood silently at her side, hands folded behind his back, his military training easy to read in his body language. Occasionally his service weapon, snugged securely in a black holster on his right hip, peaked from beneath his lightweight jacket.

Peter closed the doors and completed introductions, then motioned toward the PEAP weapon.

"This is the first prototype of a revolutionary new small arm. Although it looks reminiscent of a conventional carbine, it fires a millisecond burst of laser energy instead of metal bullets."

He suspected Governor Bingham would happily skip the technojargon, and since he'd already briefed his other visitors, he moved on to the demonstration.

Peter picked up the weapon and pointed to the major features while describing each.

"The barrel, really an antiquated term now, is machined from an anodized aluminum billet and houses the lasing matrix. As you can see, it's significantly larger in diameter than a normal gun barrel. But there's no reason to make it any longer than what you see here, about fifteen inches."

"Why is that?" McMullen said.

"Because that's the maximum length of the ceramic matrix that generates the laser pulse."

The project manager nodded.

Peter continued. "All the electronics are conformally coated, making them impervious to dust and moisture, and embedded within this portion of the stock where the receiver is found on rifles. The solid stock shown in this sample could be replaced with a skeleton or wire folding stock." He pointed to the top of the gun. "Finally, we've mounted a high-magnification optical sight. When fired, the laser pulse will remain parallel to the line of sight through the scope. Unlike bullets, lasers are not affected by gravity or wind."

"So what makes it work?" Governor Bingham said.

"A battery pack. It doesn't take a lot of power. We placed the battery in the pistol hand grip, but it could be located in another spot. That will be a discussion we have with Mister McMullen and Major Hardwick after they've completed field trials."

"Do you know where these field trials will take place?" she said.

"That's up to Major Hardwick."

The major faced Bingham. "It's too early to say."

"Well, speaking for all Oregonians, I hope you'll find reason to conduct at least a portion of the trials here in our beautiful state. After all, this is the birthplace of this fascinating technology. It would only be fitting that it would be tested here, too."

With a diplomatic smile, Hardwick said, "I'll see what I can arrange."

"So," Peter said, "we've arranged a simple demonstration."

He sat on a stool fixed to the rear of the shooting bench and rested the PEAP carbine on the forked rest. Sighting through the scope, he held the crosshairs just an inch above the center of the melon, drew in a breath, and squeezed the trigger.

The pop and explosion of the cantaloupe caused Governor Bingham to jump, but she managed to stifle a yelp.

Still with his eye to the scope, Peter identified a small

fragment of melon atop the stand. He squeezed the trigger, and a second pop announced the destruction of the piece of melon rind.

After engaging the safety, he stood and faced his audience. All eyes were glued to the weapon.

McMullen stood opposite Peter, at the edge of the shooting bench. "That's it? Just flip the safety off and keep shooting?"

"There's also a master power switch located here." Peter pointed to a button underneath the buttstock. "And an LED gauge is here, next to the power switch. It indicates remaining battery power. Presently it's green, meaning the battery has plenty of charge. Yellow means it's time to change the battery. But yes, that's essentially it. The gun fires semiauto, as fast as the operator pulls the trigger."

Jim and Major Hardwick were listening attentively, and even the governor and her bodyguard seemed fascinated.

"How is the weight?" McMullen held out both hands.

Peter offered the weapon. "Here, see for yourself."

The project manager hefted it and nodded.

He looked at his boss. "Lighter than I expected. Without the weight of a magazine loaded with lead bullets, I think this weighs less than most carbines, and maybe even less than most submachine guns."

Peter allowed a faint smile, and Jim turned to Major Hardwick, looking for a response, but the major remained non-committal.

"Mighty fine," McMullen said, more to himself than to Peter. "I need one of these." He paused, hefting the weapon, scanning up and down its length. "I'll take this one." Then he raised his head. "You don't mind, do you?"

"Actually, I do. This is the first prototype. We haven't completed all the documentation yet and will need this sample as a reference. We'd be happy to assemble additional PEAP carbines for your testing."

McMullen frowned and shook his head. "No, that won't do. I need this one."

Peter stared back.

Hardwick said, "Look Tim, it's going to take several weeks to work out the testing protocol. There's no reason to rush the samples. Besides, we're going to need more than one for testing anyway."

McMullen rammed the weapon forward, smashing Peter across the bridge of his nose and forehead. Dazed, Peter stumbled backward. His heel caught on a seam in the rubber flooring, and he tumbled backwards, his arms flailing out to the side. Jim reached out for his friend, but he was too far away to arrest Peter's fall. As he fell, his head cracked against the edge of a table before he slumped to the floor.

The State Police bodyguard was already in motion and had a hand on his pistol. He'd taken a step to move in front of the governor, when McMullen spun and pointed the carbine at him. He fired three shots, all striking the bodyguard at the base of his neck. The explosive force of the energy bursts vaporizing tissue yielded three sharp cracks, themselves like gunshots. The resulting carnage nearly severed his head. His lifeless body collapsed to the floor, and blood pooled around the hideous wound.

Governor Bingham screamed. Hardwick was frozen in shock, unwilling to believe what had just happened, that one of his employees had just murdered a man in cold blood.

Jim reached inside his jacket for the small of his back. He wrapped his fingers around the grip of his Super Hawg .45.

"That's enough." McMullen pointed the barrel of the laser gun at Jim. "I suspect that's a pistol you have your hand on. Ease it out. Slowly. You don't want to end up like the bodyguard."

With deliberate motion, Jim eased the large pistol out and

placed it on the shooting bench before McMullen.

"You won't get away with this."

"I think I will. And you're going to help me."

"Like hell I will. Might as well kill me now. You won't get my cooperation."

McMullen reached for the pistol without allowing the barrel of the laser carbine to waver from Jim's face.

"I don't want to be argumentative, Commander, but I believe you will cooperate." Then he pointed the .45 caliber pistol at Governor Bingham.

"You're bluffing," Jim said.

"We could continue this back-and-forth, but I doubt my words will convince you."

Jim stared back in silence, his heart was beating strong and fast, adrenaline flowing through his body, muscles ready to respond.

Without shifting his gaze from Jim, McMullen aimed the gun at Hardwick and pulled the trigger. The explosion was deafening in the confined space, the sound only slightly attenuated by the anechoic lining throughout the room.

Governor Bingham screamed again and brought her hands to her face, unwilling to watch the body of Major Hardwick as he slumped first to his knees, and then lay prone, dead.

"Sometimes actions speak louder than words. Wouldn't you agree, Commander?"

Jim was no stranger to killing. He was a veteran of too many battles to remember, many up close and personal. He'd watched as both enemy and fellow soldier fell to violent death. It was an inevitable outcome, a fact of armed conflict that he accepted. But the destruction of innocent lives was far from acceptable. It violated every moral directive he subscribed to.

"You made your point," he said, through clenched teeth.

"Good. Now we are all going to walk out and leave in my car."

"Where are we going?"

McMullen smiled. "In due time." He motioned with the pistol, for the door. "You first, Commander."

Jim shuffled toward the door. The project manager took a step back to ensure a buffer between himself and Commander Nicolaou. As Jim opened the door, McMullen placed the pistol low, barrel against the side of the visibly distraught governor. Side by side, they followed Jim out the door, leaving Peter lying unconscious on the floor.

They had to cross the manufacturing space to reach the hallway leading to the exit. Todd Steed was consulting with another machinist nearby. He'd been waiting for Peter and the visitors to exit. Although he'd heard muted reverberations from the gunshots, the sound insulation doing its job, he had no reason to suspect anything untoward had come down. But he was Peter's friend and was always watching, ready to help if needed.

Todd noticed McMullen was carrying the PEAP carbine. "That's strange. Why would he have the prototype?"

The machinist raised his head. "He shouldn't be taking that, should he?"

"Hey! Everything okay?" Todd called, as the trio strode toward the exit.

Now he also realized that the State Police bodyguard was not with the governor.

His question went unanswered, serving to further raise his concern.

He started marching toward them. "Where's Peter?"

Jim turned, but kept his pace toward the door. "Get an ambulance. Peter needs help."

Todd narrowed his eyes and slowed enough to grab a hammer from a toolbox, before increasing his pace, aiming to cutoff McMullen before he reached the door.

"Don't!" Jim shouted, and raised his hands, fingers splayed. "Stand down! Now is not the time."

"What the hell is going on," Todd stopped his advance.

He knew Jim Nicolaou reasonably well. Well enough, anyway, to take heed of his urgent command.

McMullen never missed a step as he urged the governor to the door and then onto the sidewalk. Jim followed.

The TV news team was loitering outside, planning to catch the governor as she exited following the meeting. They were surprised at her sudden appearance and hasty departure, working frantically to get the camera positioned and turned on. But the trio had already passed by the time the time the cameraman started to record.

It was a short walk to the car, a four-door silver Malibu. It was unlikely to attract any attention, and spotting it in traffic would also prove difficult.

"You drive, Commander." McMullen tossed the keys from six feet away.

"Let the governor go. You have me."

"Oh, she's not outlived her usefulness. Not yet."

Jim opened the rear door. McMullen tossed the energy weapon onto the back seat, then urged Governor Bingham in, never relaxing his aim.

In contrast to the KTVZ news team, who managed to get only a few seconds of video, the security camera above the entrance to EJ Enterprises caught it all.

CHAPTER 5

TODD DROPPED THE HAMMER and ran back to the laboratory. He pushed the door open to a ghastly sight. Two men lay on the floor, presumably dead from the amount of blood pooled around their bodies and the obvious wounds. Then he heard a moan, and circled the shooting bench to find Peter just coming to.

"Take it easy." Todd placed a hand against Peter's shoulder and held him down.

The bleeding from his nose and forehead had coagulated.

"My head," Peter croaked.

"Just stay still. I'm calling an ambulance." Todd made the call to 911 and kept his phone on, but rested it on the floor while he conducted a cursory examination of his friend's head.

Peter's eyes were open and appeared normally dilated. Then Todd ran a hand across his friend's scalp. It came back bloodied.

"Looks like your head came in contact with something hard."

Slowly, Peter rose to a seated position, drawing in several deep breaths. "I think I clipped the edge of the table as I fell backwards."

"What happened to your face?" Todd said.

"McMullen. The bastard rapped me with the PEAP carbine." Peter looked around the room, noticed the two bodies. "Did he take it?"

"Yeah. I'm afraid so."

⊕

Peter sat in his office. The EMTs had cleaned the superficial wounds to his face and the back of his head, and placed an adhesive bandage over the worst of the gashes across the bridge of his nose. He chased down four ibuprofen tablets with a glass of water. Through the open door, he watched as each body, covered in a white sheet, was wheeled out on a gurney.

The City of Bend Police arrived soon after Todd's 911 call. Once it was clear the governor had been kidnapped, the Oregon State Police and FBI soon followed. All the employees were sequestered, and each was questioned separately in an empty office.

A knock at his door jostled Peter from his thoughts. He looked up and felt a renewed throb of pain in his head.

"Detective Colson. How nice to see you again." The words were thick with sarcasm.

"I wish I could say the feeling was mutual. Trouble always seems to find you, doesn't it?"

Peter knew she didn't expect an answer.

Detective Ruth Colson was dressed in dark indigo jeans, a lightweight green hooded pullover, and neon green Oregon Duck sneakers. Her hair was naturally gray, on the way to silver, and she wore it short, exposing her ears. She was old school, right down to her pen and paper notepad. Smart, experienced, and tenacious, she was the lead detective within the Bend Police Department and handled the more complicated and sensational investigations, especially if murder was involved.

The detective and Peter had history, and it was the kind

that wasn't likely to lead to a lasting friendship. A few years earlier, when Peter had been implicated for a murder he'd not committed, it was Detective Colson who handled the case. And more recently, the detective was the lead investigator when a stranger, who was trying to kill Peter, was shot dead in the Old Mill District, right in front of Peter. It was still an open case.

For her part, Colson had learned to associate trouble with Peter Savage. She'd never been able to pin any illegal activities to him, but there was also a significant portion of his file that had been redacted, leaving her to wonder who he was connected to and what he was really up to.

"I already gave a statement to one of your officers," he said.

"How are you feeling?" She noticed his complexion had already turned bluish across his nose and under both eyes.

"Pretty good for someone who just had a carbine slammed into his face."

"We're going to need the video from your security camera out front above the door."

"Sure. Nancy can provide what you need."

"The receptionist?"

Peter nodded. "She also handles our IT."

"Any other cameras? Maybe inside the shop? Anything could be useful."

"No. Only the one. There's a good security system covering the doors and windows. Given the classified nature of the work we do here, video recordings inside the shop isn't a good idea."

"Any idea why Tim McMullen would want to kidnap Governor Bingham?"

"No."

"Did he share anything that might indicate where he's taking the governor?"

"No."

Colson consulted her notes. "Did you see who shot Major Hardwick?"

"It had to be McMullen, unless you think the governor pulled the trigger."

"Doubtful, but we're looking at all possibilities. Why McMullen? Why not Commander Nicolaou? He was also present in the room, right?"

"Jim would—"

"Jim? You know him well?"

"I do. But I'm sure you already know that."

"Go on. Why do you believe your friend could not have shot Major Hardwick?"

"Because it's not the kind of man he is. He could never murder someone in cold blood."

"The state police have already requested a copy of Commander Nicolaou's personnel record from the Defense Department. I suspect they'll find he's an experienced veteran. Am I right?"

"So?"

"Well, I'd wager he has a history of killing people."

Peter didn't try to hide his annoyance. "Killing in combat, when the enemy is trying to kill you, is not the same as murdering an unarmed man."

"But you didn't actually witness who killed Hardwick?"

"No. I was unconscious on the floor after McMullen hit me with the carbine."

"You're referring to this advanced prototype weapon? What's it called, a PEAP?"

"Yeah, that's right."

"To which part?" she said, earning an annoyed glare from Peter.

"Both parts. He hit me. I fell backwards, and I guess I struck my head. Lights out. When I came to, Todd was leaning over me, and the state trooper and Hardwick were both dead."

"Did you see McMullen shoot the state police officer?"

Peter shook his head. "No."

"That weapon of yours damn near took his head off."

"I know." He averted his gaze to the blotter on his desktop.

"Of course you do. After all, that's your business, right? You know, everyone says you're a real smart guy. A genius. So why is it you choose to apply that brain power to coming up with better ways of killing? Isn't humankind good enough at that already?"

After several moments of silence, Detective Colson turned and left Peter alone with his thoughts.

CHAPTER 6

THE CLEAR WATERS OF THE SALMON RIVER bubbled and splashed as they rushed over boulders only a mile east of the confluence with the Snake River. Billy Reed followed Swanson as they rode quad ATVs miles through the steep forested terrain, following a charted path logged into Swanson's handheld GPS unit. Billy had the distinct impression that the older man had ridden this course before, but not recently enough, or often enough, to have the path committed to memory.

As they coasted down the final slope, the trees parted to reveal an encampment near the flowing water. The wall tent was the type used by outfitters, complete with a metal chimney poking through the canvas roof, evidence of a small wood stove inside for warding off the chilly nighttime temperatures.

Once the two ATVs coasted to a stop and the engines shut down, a tall man exited the tent. To Billy, the gray beard, long hair held back in a ponytail, and heavily creased face suggested his better years were behind him. He stood ten feet away, arms folded across his chest, scrutinizing every move Billy made as he dismounted from the seat and stowed his helmet and goggles.

"This is Billy Reed," Swanson said. "He's the guy I told you about."

The man nodded, his coal-black gaze drifting from Billy's face, down to the pistol holstered on his hip, then back up again.

"I've been told you're good with a rifle," he said.

His voice was a deep baritone that reminded Billy of James Earl Jones.

"Yes, that's right." Billy strode forward, closing the gap in two steps, and offered his hand.

The man accepted it, his grip firmer than expected given his sunken cheeks and sallow complexion. Although the man had a sickly pallor, Billy notice his hands were callused and accustomed to hard work.

"My name's Denson. Stuart Denson."

"General Denson has overall authority over the movement," Swanson said.

"General? You were in the Army?" Billy said.

"I was. Discharged after the first Gulf War. But my rank here has more to do with the fact that I founded the Cascadia Independence Movement. It's convenient to borrow military ranks—helps everyone understand their place, as well as the chain of authority. Isn't that right, Captain?"

"Yes, sir."

Denson's focus was still on Billy. "Bring your rifle?"

Billy motioned with his thumb over his shoulder. "I did. In the scabbard on the ATV. Figured you might want a demonstration."

The general forced a smile. "Actions do speak louder than words." He turned his head and placed two fingers to his lips, then emitted a shrill whistle.

Five men dressed in camouflage materialized from the tree line around the camp.

To the nearest man, Denson said, "Take Captain Swanson's ATV and drive out to the far side of the clearing. Place your canteen on a rock or log so our sniper here has a clear view, then come on back." Then to Billy, he said, "It's about five hundred yards. Paced it off myself earlier this morning. If that doesn't suit you, I can have him place the target a bit closer."

"It suits me fine," Billy said.

The ground alongside the river sloped away gently, and it was sparsely covered by grass. Billy watched as the rider found a boulder rising more than a foot above the gravelly dirt. He balanced his olive drab canteen on the top of the rock, then rode back, leaving a trail of dust in his wake.

"Twenty bucks says you miss your first shot," the man said, as Billy lay prone on the dirt and nestled his arms into a comfortable shooting position.

Billy didn't look at the man. "Only twenty? If you were confident, you'd bet a hundred."

With his rifle resting on an integral bipod, and clear view across the intervening terrain to the canteen, he cranked up the variable-power scope to maximum magnification, and sighted on the target. The MIL reticle markings in the scope consisted of a number of horizontal lines in the lower half of his field of view. The canteen was only a little smaller than a human head, and these horizontal lines fed back critical information to Billy, allowing him to accurately hold the cross hairs above the bullet's point of impact. Although it was late in the morning, the air was still calm, so there was no need to estimate windage.

Billy drew a breath and relaxed his body, focusing only on the target. In his mind's eye, he saw the bullet leaving a supersonic wake in the air, then exploding the canteen. There was no sound, no push from the rifle stock. He replayed the image over and over, each time his pulse slowing, and his respiration becoming deeper and less frequent.

With the world around him shut out from his consciousness, he applied increasing pressure to the trigger. His trained touch was such that just before the trigger would break, he paused, timed his pulse, then completed the shot.

The .300 Winchester round barked with authority, and the rifle smacked into Billy's shoulder. An instant later, the canteen was replaced by a violent splash of water as the bullet hit its mark.

Chagrinned at losing the bet, the man dug a ten dollar bill out of his pocket.

"The bet was twenty." Billy slung his rifle over his shoulder.

"Yeah, but you just shredded my canteen. It'll cost me ten to replace it. So I figure we're even."

Billy pocketed the money, then turned to General Denson and Captain Swanson.

"Now what? I assume we didn't all gather out here this morning just to shoot up each other's gear."

"Captain," Denson said.

Swanson dispersed the five soldiers back into the tree line.

"Follow me." The general motioned with a sweep of his hand, toward the wall tent. "We'll be more comfortable inside."

With the flap held open, Billy entered the canvas shelter. The fabric walls seemed to glow wherever the sunlight touched them. Additional lighting came from a gas lantern hissing on a table surrounded by four chairs.

"Have a seat," Denson said.

Billy unslung his rifle and leaned it into a corner before joining the other two at the table.

"So what's all this about?" he said.

Denson leaned back. "Before I go into that, let me ask you a couple questions, if you don't mind."

Billy shrugged.

"Why did you join the Movement?"

"I like to shoot."

"You can do that in a lot of places, and you don't have to be a member of any organization, either."

"Well, as I explained to Captain Swanson a while ago, I don't have any use for the government or the justice system."

"I understand you lived in Portland most of your life. Sounds like it was pretty rough."

"No one did us any favors. And the government...they killed my parents. I didn't have any other family."

General Denson nodded. He'd heard the whole story of Billy's life from Swanson. It's why he'd requested this meeting with the young sharpshooter.

"Do you know where you are?" Denson said.

"Sure. Western Idaho, along the banks of the Salmon River."

"That's right. This is private land. My ancestral home. For generations, my family has worked this land. First it was homesteaded. The cattle were ranged here. My grandfather grew the business, growing the ranch to ninety-eight thousand acres, and became one of the wealthiest men between Seattle and Boise. It's now my land, handed down to me by my father. We still run a few head of cattle. Truth is, I can do pretty much whatever I want to here."

Billy shrugged again. "So?"

"So that makes this land an ideal location for weapons testing and training."

Billy stood and pushed his chair back. "Look, I really don't know why you asked me out here. You've got a nice ranch, General. Now I'll be on my way."

Swanson said, "Have you ever connected with a target at five thousand yards?"

"Yeah, right." Billy chortled. "No one can shoot out that far.

Not even with a Barrett. The longest confirmed kill shot was by a Canadian dude, Spec Ops, and that was three thousand four hundred fifty meters."

Swanson smiled. "And if I told you we will soon have a rifle—a new weapon, a prototype—that will enable a skilled shooter to reach out and touch the enemy at five thousand yards, would you be interested?"

Slowly, Billy sat.

After several moments of silence, he said, "That must be a monster cartridge. Maybe a boat-tail bullet in forty or forty-one caliber, and with a high ballistic coefficient?"

"Let's save the details for later. After all, if you're not interested in working with us, what's the point?"

General Denson folded his hands and cast a steely glare at Billy, his eyes taking on the appearance of black marbles.

"What do you know about the Cascadia Independence Movement?" he said.

Billy frowned. "I'm a newbie, and I mind my own business. I know the basics."

"Really?" Denson raised an eyebrow.

"I know you're trying to split off part of the Northwest as a new state or something."

"Not a new state, a new country. Independent of the United States. My aim, our aim," Denson extended his left hand toward Swanson, "is to carve out all the land from the Cascade Mountains on the west, to the Continental Divide on the east, as Nova Albion. That's the name Sir Francis Drake gave to this region of North America when he claimed it in the name of Britain in 1579."

Billy returned the general's stare, waiting for him to continue.

"Eventually, this land became part of the United States. It was the explicit objective of the Monroe Doctrine to achieve a great nation that stretched from the Atlantic to the Pacific. A nation free of influences from Europe."

"President James Monroe, I know. The Doctrine was largely written by John Quincy Adams. I'm a student of history."

Denson smiled. "Are you now? Well, what they don't write in those history books is that the Oregon Country was illegally acquired by the United States, and I can prove it. Since the coastal regions of Oregon and Washington, with their left-wing population centers, are sympathetic with the liberal federal government, I've decided to dedicate my effort and resources on liberating the inland portion of the former territory."

"Let me get this straight." Billy held up his hands. "You seriously think you can secede from the Union? You know that's been tried before. And it didn't work out so well."

"Times are different. This great swath of land from the Cascades to the Rocky Mountains is rural and conservative, not like the liberals populating Portland, Eugene, Seattle, and Olympia."

Billy was shaking his head. "That doesn't matter. The government will never go along."

"Like I said, I have proof of my claim. There was a great conspiracy that would make even our current politicians pale if they knew the truth."

"What kind of proof?" Billy squinted.

He loved early American history and had thought he knew it pretty well. But he'd never read anything of the sort that General Denson was claiming. Yet he also knew history wasn't stagnant. As previously lost documents were found, and as academicians with a fresh perspective examined personal correspondence and other historical records, it was not uncommon for the historical narrative to alter. But such changes were usually a nuance to the record. Was it possible that the northwest corner of the United States, the vast territory west of the Louisiana

Purchase, was acquired illegally, as Denson proclaimed? And if it was, what would the ramifications be today?

"The proof I have is not the subject of our meeting," Denson said, "nor the reason for my interest in your skills."

"Then what?" Billy said.

"There are certain...obstacles, for lack of a better term. Obstacles that need to be removed before our agenda may be advanced."

"What type of obstacles?"

"As you've no doubt surmised, the political landscape is challenging for a secession. Also, there are the courts which must certify our legal claim."

"If you ask me, sounds like you need a whole bunch of lobbyists and some damn good lawyers."

"I may be an old man, but don't take me for a fool. I've applied my money liberally to persuade key members of the House and Senate to support my cause. And as for the lawyers, well, I have the best legal minds working our case through the Tenth Circuit Court of Appeals, given that the lower court didn't seriously consider our arguments."

"I see."

"Do you? There are many in the judiciary—so-called activist judges—who see their role as not only to interpret the law, but to drive social agendas as well."

"I know the type." Billy recalled sitting in the courtroom when his father was sentenced.

He could still see the judge's face, how she seemed to smile when handing down the harshest sentence possible for a petty, victimless crime. Yes, she was exercising a political agenda—*her* agenda to be re-elected. And it cost the life of his father.

"Do you believe that, from time to time, the judiciary may need a...correction?" Denson said.

"Yeah, but what does this have to do with me?"

"Nothing. Not directly, anyway. We're just a couple of guys having a conversation. I'm only curious about where you stand on important issues."

"So now you know. The court, the police, the government—they took everything from me. Everything. How do you *think* I feel? Now that we've had our little chat, I'll be on my way."

"I do have a job for you, Billy. And it involves this new toy Captain Swanson mentioned."

Billy shifted his gaze back and forth between the two men sitting opposite him.

"Are you asking me to kill someone?"

Swanson cleared his throat. "I believe the correct term would be *assassinate*. And yes, that's the idea. Do you have a problem with that?"

With an expression as cold and hard as stone, Billy shook his head.

"No."

CHAPTER 7

THE SILVER RENTAL CAR DROVE EAST on Highway 20, headed for Burns, a small city in eastern Oregon.

"Just drive at the speed limit," McMullen said. "Don't attract any attention. Your gun is pressed into Governor Bingham's side. Understand?"

Jim glared at McMullen in the rearview mirror. "Yes." Then he returned his gaze to the road.

"What do you want with me?" Bingham said.

"You're my leverage. As long as Commander Nicolaou does as he's told, you'll be fine."

There was little traffic on the highway, and they passed only a few vehicles, mostly trucks traveling in the opposite direction, west toward Bend. Never one to give up, Jim was working through scenarios in his mind. He still had his cell phone and a spare magazine for the Super Hawg—no doubt oversights on the part of McMullen. But a magazine full of ammo was close to worthless without a gun to fire it. Still, he kept it in mind. It had some weight to it, and if clenched in his fist, it would add some force to his punches if he got in a hand-to-hand fight.

The phone was his best hope at the moment. He knew the phone was easy to track, at least for the analysts who worked for him at SGIT, since they knew his number. Eventually, the police would get that information, and then they, too, would search his phone's location. So for now, keeping the phone was a priority.

After Jim had driven for fifteen minutes, McMullen said, "Turn off up there, at Millican."

"Why? The gas station's been closed for years. Nothing's open. It's a ghost town." Originally one of four waypoints between Bend and Burns, the service station, general store, and post office had provided valuable service at one time. But that was years ago, and now the abandoned buildings were falling prey to vandals.

"Just do it."

Jim braked and turned to the right, off the paved roadway.

"Go around behind the general store," McMullen said. "Then stop and turn off the engine."

While the dust was still swirling around the rental car, the program manager ordered Jim out of the car and instructed him to walk up to the back wall of the old building.

"Place your hands up high, against the wall, face forward like you're kissing it. You can leave the door open."

Jim did as instructed, trying to spot an opportunity to reach his phone. He wanted to activate an app that would turn on the microphone. The app was programmed to store the information in the cloud. Once the SGIT analysts began to investigate his disappearance, they would check for any data uploaded from his phone and find the voice recording.

Bingham watched in silence as Jim left the car, fear of what the nerdish program manager had in mind beginning to creep back into her thoughts.

With Jim in clear sight against the wall, McMullen said, "Now it's our turn. I'm going to get out first, and then you."

When the governor stood on the gravel, McMullen nudged her forward with the barrel of his pistol.

"Just walk."

In a trembling voice, she said, "Where are we going?"

"Not far."

Kathrine Bingham shuffled forward. Stretching out as far as she could see was a vast and desolate expanse of sage brush and scrub juniper trees. She wondered if a shallow grave was waiting for her somewhere out there, but then remembered McMullen's words—he needed her to force Commander Nicolaou to cooperate.

After they'd walked about twenty yards, McMullen told her to stop. Her pulse quickened and terror rose in her throat, threatening to erupt in a scream.

He reached under his sweater to his waist band and removed a small case, flipped the lid open with his thumb, and then removed a syringe. With his teeth, he pulled off the plastic cap covering the needle. Bingham slowly began to turn her head, wondering what the sounds were from behind.

"Keep your eyes forward." He positioned the needle at the side of her neck.

She felt the stick of the needle and gasped, but it was over in two seconds. She turned around, pressing a finger against the puncture.

"What did you do?" She collapsed to her side.

Jim was just edging his hand down toward his jacket.

"Commander, please come here."

He froze.

"The governor needs your assistance."

He ran to the prone figure. "You son-of-a-bitch. What did you do?"

He knelt and placed a finger against her carotid artery. Finding a pulse, he exhaled a sigh of relief.

"Satisfied? I just gave her a sedative. It should keep her under for eight to ten hours, long enough for us to reach our destination."

"Which is?"

The DARPA man smiled. "You'll know when we get there. Now carry her back to the car, and we'll be on our way."

In Burns, McMullen told Jim to stop and buy gas, then to go through a McDonald's drive-thru for food. They ate as the silver sedan continued east. Governor Bingham remained slumped in the back seat, her head resting against the door. McMullen sat next to her, always keeping the pistol in her side.

After passing through Ontario and entering Idaho, McMullen ordered the car north on Interstate 95. An hour later, they were entering Riggins, and Jim was told to gas-up again. He decided this stop offered an opportunity.

"Hey, I need to use the restroom," Jim said, after filling the tank and using a credit card to pay at the pump.

He knew his credit card activity would be flagged by SGIT as well as law enforcement, but his presence in Riggins was but a single point that would not indicate his location, only where he had been.

"Hold it."

"Sure, for maybe thirty minutes. After that, you'll be riding with the smell of my piss for as long as it takes to get wherever it is we're going."

After several moments of consideration, McMullen said, "Okay. Pull over there to the side and park. I'm going with you."

He figured the governor was still sedated and wouldn't be waking up anytime soon.

Jim locked the car and strode to the restroom around the back of the gas station while McMullen waited outside the door, gun ready but tucked under his bulky sweater.

As Jim raised the toilet seat, he noticed the outside street sounds were coming through the gap under the door with clarity. He calculated that he had a minute before arousing the suspicion of the DARPA man.

He activated the app, then thought about calling the police or SGIT, but decided the risk of being overheard through the door was too great. When he was finished, he flushed the toilet and ran the sink.

With his phone in a jacket pocket, Jim exited the restroom and found McMullen right before him.

"Let's go. We have some miles to cover."

Jim hesitated. "Aren't you going to use the toilet?"

"Nice try. If I have to pee, I'll use a cup."

They rounded the corner of the gas station, McMullen a step behind. Standing next to the rental car and tapping the window with his knuckles, a Riggins Police officer was peering through the window. He appeared to be speaking into the radio mic fastened to the shoulder of his uniform.

McMullen grabbed Jim's arm, yanking him to a standstill. The officer seemed to sense their approach, and he pivoted so he was facing the two strangers. His thumbs were looped in his duty belt.

"This your car?" he said.

Jim blurted out, "Yes it is, sir."

"Who's the woman in the back seat? She seems unresponsive."

McMullen said, "She's my wife. She's just sleeping, that's all."

"Listen," Jim said. "I think we could use your help."

"Shut up," McMullen said, his voice menacing but low so the officer wouldn't hear.

Jim felt the muzzle of the pistol pressed into his back.

The officer listened for something more, but the strangers

remained silent. Then the police radio came to life, the dispatcher's voice clearly heard by Jim and McMullen.

"Be advised. Silver Chevrolet Malibu, Oregon license 294 LSN, last seen leaving the scene of a 187, multiple victims. Approach with caution."

Time seemed to slow. The officer stared at Jim and McMullen and seemed to take some seconds to digest the warning his dispatcher had just shared. No doubt the police force in sleepy small-town Riggins was not accustomed to dealing with murder suspects.

By the time the officer decided to reach for his sidearm, it was too late. McMullen pushed Jim aside and leveled the .45 at the lawman. He pulled the trigger three times, sending all three two-hundred-thirty-grain bullets slamming into the policeman's chest. Although he was wearing soft body armor, each projectile struck his chest with a monstrous force, as if he'd been hit with a hammer. The soft tissue injury was substantial, knocking the wind from his lungs and causing his diaphragm to cramp. Two ribs were also cracked, adding to the pain.

He fell to the pavement and lost consciousness, his radio still squawking away warnings and requesting a status report.

As soon as the third shot had been fired, Jim pivoted and shifted the balance on his feet, preparing to lunge.

"Do it," McMullen said, "and I'll put a bullet in you, too. Now get in the car. And if you try that again, I'll kill you. Understand?"

They drove on in silence save for the brief instructions when Jim was required to turn onto another road. Eventually, they found themselves on a secondary road surrounded by evergreen forest. Jim only had a general idea of their location.

"Where are we?" he said, for the benefit of the voice recording.

"Just keep driving. I'll tell you when to stop."

The sky had turned from blue to gray as dusk set in, and Jim turned on the headlights. Passage on the gravel road was limited to thirty-five miles per hour, even less over sections of washboard. Once, as the suspension bounced and rattled over the rutted roadbed, Bingham stirred, but she never woke up.

In the remaining minutes of twilight, the sedan followed a gentle curve and arrived at a metal gate blocking further advance.

"Tap the horn," McMullen said.

Several seconds later, two men emerged from the trees. Both were armed with military-style rifles, which they held in the low ready position. One of the men approached the driver's window while the other kept some distance.

"This is private land. Best turn around and go back to the main road."

The backseat passenger leaned forward. "I'm Tim McMullen. General Denson is expecting me…and my guests."

"Got some ID?" the guard said, and McMullen produced his driver's license.

The guard scrutinized the document. "This license is from Virginia. You're a long way from home."

"The general is expecting me. Radio him if you have any questions. We'll wait." McMullen leaned back in the seat while the call was made.

After a minute, the gate was opened and the guard addressed Jim. "You know where you're going?"

"No. But I'm guessing he does." He indicated the back seat with his thumb. "By the way, nice rifle."

The SGIT analysts wouldn't miss the meaning.

The comment earned Jim a sneer.

"Just follow the road about four miles. You'll know when you reach the main camp."

The gravel road had been recently graded, allowing for a

faster pace, and Jim reached the camp in about ten minutes. In the headlights, he counted more than twenty RVs and pickups. Beyond the parked vehicles was a large Quonset hut. He estimated it was about twenty-feet high at the peak of the curved roof. An exterior lamp illuminated a door, but he didn't see any windows.

A half-dozen armed men advanced toward the car, and Jim eased to a stop.

"What now?" he said.

McMullen seemed to relax for the first time since they'd left Bend.

"We get out."

⊕

In the glow from the headlights, Jim counted six, and then ten armed men. But more seemed to materialize out of nothingness until they were surrounded by two dozen or more militiamen. They kept their distance, never affording him the opportunity to get within arm's reach where he could potentially disarm one. Some of the men peeked inside the car and noticed the sleeping woman, but no one spoke up.

The group parted as a man with a beard and ponytail stepped forward. In the light beams, Jim saw his hollow cheeks and sickly complexion.

In a deep voice, he said, "I'm General Stuart Denson." Then he cast his gaze across the visitors' faces before continuing. "You have the weapon, Mister McMullen?"

"Yes, sir." He stepped forward and extended the PEAP in a manner that reminded Jim of a pagan offering riches to a demigod.

Denson turned the weapon over, scrutinizing every detail. "In the morning, we will have a demonstration." He raised his eyes to Jim. "And who are you?"

Jim stiffened. "Commander James Nicolaou."

McMullen said, "He's the one. You know, for the plan."

The general contemplated the junior man's words, appreciating his cryptic statement, given the public company they held.

"Let me have his phone," Denson said.

"Uh…" McMullen parted his lips, but no words came out.

"Tell me you did search him."

The DARPA man lowered his head, unable to meet the general's eyes.

"Oh, for God's sake, you moron. You could have jeopardized this entire operation!"

"I'm sorry, sir. I have his gun." Holding onto the barrel, he extended the Super Hawg.

Denson grabbed the weapon, then aimed it at Jim.

He addressed the man to his left. "Murphy, search him."

Jim held his arms up, and Murphy found the spare magazine and cell phone. He handed both over.

"Did you call anyone during your travel here?" Denson said.

"If I had, you'd be talking to the FBI, not me."

"No way he could have made any calls," McMullen said. "I was with him the whole time."

"Is that so?" Denson held the phone over his shoulder, and someone from behind took it. "Take the phone to the lab and remove the SIM card. Have one of the techs check the call log."

"Yes, sir." The man trotted off to the large window-less building.

"Since it's likely your phone has been tracked, Commander, we're going to change the plan. Murphy, bind his hands and place him in your truck, one man on either side, with a gun at his head. Any attempt to escape, and put a bullet in his brain."

"Yes, sir," Murphy replied, and then with the help of two other men, Jim was taken aside.

"Who's that in the back seat of your car?" Denson said to McMullen.

"Oh, that's the governor of Oregon. She was at the demonstration. I didn't know about her in advance. But it seemed like she might prove valuable to the mission."

"An improvisation to the plan?"

"Yes, I suppose so."

"It's okay, Mister McMullen. You did a good job. We have the pulsed-energy carbine and a sitting governor." His coal-black gaze drifted to Jim, who was being shoved onto the back seat of an extended cab pickup. "Not to mention, the perfect patsy…"

CHAPTER 8

WESTERN IDAHO
MAY 9

THE PORTE-COCHÈRE WAS INDIRECTLY ILLUMINATED in a warm glow cast by upturned flood lamps reflecting off the aged wood ceiling. Jim was persuaded to peacefully exit the back seat of the truck, no less than two guns pointed at him at any time.

From the granite landing before the oversized timber entrance door, he watched as Governor Bingham was manhandled out of a second vehicle. She was still too unsteady to stand without the help of two men, but at least she was coming around. Although she didn't utter a word, her face conveyed confusion as she took in the lodge first, and then the many armed militiamen surrounding her.

The double timber doors swung back silently on well-oiled hinges. The entrance was large enough that the two guards on Jim did not have to shuffle their positions as they escorted their prisoner inside, followed not far by the governor.

They entered into a spacious great room. The walls were

hewn timbers, cracked with age and patinaed to a mellow shade of honey. Persian rugs in bright shades of red, blue, and green covered patches of wood-plank flooring. A massive river-stone fireplace was directly ahead on the wall opposite the grand entrance, a fire crackling.

A sofa and four armchairs, all upholstered in distressed leather the color of ground coffee, were located around the room, creating both intimate and open conversation areas.

A blond muscular man stood before the fireplace. His shirt sleeves were rolled up to his shoulder, arms crossed over his barrel chest, exaggerating the size of his biceps. No doubt intended to intimidate. Colorful tattoos adorned his arms. The image of a bloody skull with a dagger in an eye socket was inked on his right forearm.

"Place the woman on the sofa," the man said.

Jim stared hard into the blond man's eyes behind circular eyeglasses, noticing the scar across his cheek and the hard edge to his jaw. He read him like the front page of *The New York Times*. Athletic build, hair cut high and tight, commanding presence. Definitely former military. Possibly special forces, but not likely. Those men were dedicated to their country and principled, two characteristics definitely not possessed by the blond man.

No, Jim pegged him for nothing more than a mercenary, motivated by a paycheck. On past missions, he'd met a few mercs in backwater dives and fleabag hotels more comfortable with renting rooms by the hour rather than by the night. Dangerous men when not drunk, and often unpredictable. But definitely second-string warriors on their best days, not even junior varsity on an average day.

"Who are you?" Jim said.

"Name's Walker."

Jim cast his gaze about the room. "Why are we here?

Wherever *here* is."

"You are inquisitive, aren't you? Part of your training, no doubt. McMullen tells me you lead a special outfit called the Strategic Global Intervention Team. Quite the mouthful. He say's you're like a special forces unit combined with military intelligence."

Jim nodded.

"Have a seat." Walker pointed to a chair positioned in front of the stone hearth.

"No, thanks. I'd rather stand."

"I said have seat." A rifle barrel was jabbed into Jim's back.

The blond man remained standing, allowing the radiant warmth from the flames to soak into his backside. He just stood there, looking down at Jim, before finally taking the opposite leather chair. He kept both feet planted on the floor, gripping the arms of the chair, ready to spring forward at the slightest hint of danger.

He said, to the closest guard, "Remove his bindings."

With the metal handcuffs removed, Jim flexed his wrists. He was relaxed, in contrast to Walker, with his hands folded on his lap and legs crossed at the ankles. He gave his best I'm-bored expression, and a lopsided frown.

"Okay, Mister Walker. You've got me. Now what?"

"That's up to General Denson."

"Sure, *General* Denson. Obviously you guys fancy yourself to be some kind of military unit, right?"

Walker returned a blank stare.

Jim snorted a mirthless laugh. "You guys are nothing but a bunch of wanna-be's. Amateurs who wouldn't last three seconds in a real firefight."

"You have a big mouth for a desk jockey."

"Desk jockey? Is that what you think I am?" Jim's lips spread in a genuine smile. "Why don't you tell your buddies to put the guns away, and you and I can go at it. Let's see if you've got what it takes to put this desk jockey down."

By outward appearances, he was still relaxed, but his mind was preparing to defend and then attack. He had no doubt he could best the merc in hand-to-hand if the big man was foolish enough to be goaded into a fight.

Walker seemed to be mulling over the offer as Jim was mentally stepping through his moves. Overconfident, the big man would almost certainly lead with a sharp right jab. Jim would deflect the blow and step inside his opponent's swing before countering with an upward open-hand strike to his jaw. Taking advantage of the stunning blow, he would spin his opponent and wrap an arm around his neck, holding him close.

Contrary to Hollywood films, the human body is a poor shield against bullets, especially when fired from a rifle. Still, holding Walker before him would give the guards pause for fear of shooting their teammate, as well as their prisoner.

Jim was still thinking through the many variables in the next stage of the fight when he sensed a new presence in the room.

Walker raised his gaze, looking beyond Commander Nicolaou.

"Another time." He stood to face General Denson.

"I see the governor is coming around," Denson said, his deep voice filling the room.

Bingham was sitting upright, but remained silent, no doubt still trying to make sense of her surroundings.

"I apologize for the manner in which you were..."

"Abducted?" Bingham said. "You might as well drop the pretense of civility. There's no polite way to apologize for kidnapping."

Denson raised an eyebrow. "Touché." He walked to the fireplace, displacing Walker to the side.

"Who are you and what do you want?" Bingham said.

"My name is Stuart Denson. General Stuart Denson. As for what I want…well, for now, your cooperation is sufficient."

"If you were smart, you'd release me now. I promise you I'll put in a good word—"

"I have no intention of releasing you or the commander."

"Law enforcement won't let this go," Jim said. "You can't expect to win. The FBI, state police, and sheriff will have you out-gunned. Hell, I wouldn't be surprised if they call up the National Guard. Your make-believe soldiers will be pissing their pants."

"If you're expecting another Waco or Ruby Ridge, don't. As long as I have Governor Bingham, all the police can do is bluster."

"You can only play that card once. If you kill the governor, there's nothing preventing the law from taking you down with extreme prejudice."

"They can send all the men they want. They'll never get close enough to take a shot. As soon as they show their faces, they'll be picked off. One by one."

Realization dawned on Jim, deflating his air of confidence. With the energy weapon McMullen had stolen from EJ Enterprises, one sharpshooter could defeat a hundred combat soldiers. If it performed as Peter had claimed, the laser pulse would pierce tires, making it impossible to approach in cars or SUVs. Armored military vehicles—tanks and personnel carriers—would be required in an all-out assault to level the lodge, blasting the heavy log and stone walls to splinters and likely killing everyone inside.

Jim knew that such a military action on American soil would never be authorized. Leaving only two possible outcomes—either law enforcement would retreat, allowing Denson and his inner cabal to escape and regroup, or there would be a protracted siege. The latter option was unlikely to last more than a few weeks, as law enforcement could not afford to maintain a strong presence indefinitely. As their numbers decreased, it would be easy for Denson's forces to find a weakness in the line and breakout.

As a master of military tactics, Jim understood it was the PEAP carbine that assured Denson's victory if and when the FBI located them. He knew his phone could be tracked, and that SGIT almost certainly had tracked it to the encampment. But that location was many kilometers from the lodge where he and the governor were presently held. By the time the tracking information was shared with the Bureau, the camp would have been dissolved, leaving only an empty building. He surmised Denson had already instructed his men to clean the sight of any evidence that he or the governor or his phone had ever been there, no matter how briefly.

Jim said, "It seems you've thought it all through."

"Thank you. I'll take that as a compliment."

"I'm not here to flatter you."

"No, you're not. But you do have a role in my plan."

"Speaking of which, you still haven't said why you kidnapped us. You have the energy weapon, and I imagine you plan to reverse engineer it and sell the design. Or maybe make life easy and just auction the prototype to the highest bidder. No doubt certain governments, as well as terrorist organizations, would enter into a bidding contest that nets you a tidy eight-figure payout."

The general paced slowly while contemplating how much to share.

He locked his gaze on Jim. "You think too small. This was never about money. Look around. I'm comfortable."

It's always about money...or power. "What do you hope to gain?"

Denson lowered his body into the leather chair opposite Jim, then crossed his legs.

"Would you be surprised to learn that my family settled this land generations ago? In fact, my roots in this vast acreage go back to the most famous expedition of our young nation's history."

Jim furrowed his brow. "The Lewis and Clark expedition."

The general slapped a hand on his knee, unfolded his legs, and leaned forward.

"Kudos! That's exactly right. The Corp of Discovery! The grand expedition to explore the lands west of the Mississippi. Did you also know that this mission was strongly opposed by powerful governments and many Indian tribes?"

"Yes…"

"It was the beginning of a foreign policy later known as the Monroe Doctrine. On two occasions, Spain sent her army to arrest Meriwether Lewis and William Clark, but good fortune smiled on the Americans, and Spain narrowly missed both opportunities."

"I appreciate the history lesson. But you'll have to forgive me. I fail to make the connection to our present circumstances."

"Nor do I," Bingham said. "You're nothing but a common criminal. You've committed serious crimes—kidnapping, accessory to murder, theft, and in all likelihood, acts of espionage. You'll never succeed."

"I imagine you are tired and hungry." Denson flashed a condescending smile at the governor, then motioned to one of the guards. "Show Miss Bingham to the guest bedroom and have the kitchen prepare a meal. Make sure she is comfortable."

At gunpoint, she was led from the great room to the second floor and a large, well-appointed bedroom with an en suite bath.

"You'll find toiletries in the bathroom." The guard closed

the door as he spoke.

Bingham checked, confirming that the door could not be opened from her side. She sighed and sat on the bed, wondering when this nightmare would end.

Denson continued after the governor left the room. "Did you know that Captain Meriwether Lewis died childless? I am the last direct descendent of his bloodline. My lineage traces back to his full sister, Jane. Being childless myself, when I die, so ends the bloodline."

"A tragedy, I'm sure." Jim rolled his eyes.

Denson gripped the arms of the chair and pulled himself upright. "It's been a long day, and I see I'm boring you. In the morning, I have something to show you. Call it a demonstration."

"Am I supposed to be impressed?"

"Oh, you will be. Now I must apologize, as I have another important visitor to meet." Then to Walker, he said, "Lock him in the basement."

CHAPTER 9

"AND EXACTLY WHY SHOULD I BELIEVE ANYTHING you've said?"

Amy Knowlton was not only the senior senator from Idaho, but also an extremely ambitious political animal. She was tall, athletic, and just shy of six feet, with cobalt blue eyes and dishwater blonde hair that flowed in shimmering waves to her shoulder blades. Now in her mid-fifties, she was still vain about her appearance, having had several nips and tucks to sculpt her shape to resemble *her* perception of the ideal woman. Except, that is, her nose. It hooked downward, like a raptor's beak. She abhorred her profile image. Soon, she would have the plastic surgeons correct that blight.

Denson opened his hands, an expression that he was not hiding anything. He sat behind the desk in his office. The senator was occupying a club chair opposite him, her legs crossed at the ankles.

"I've been very forthcoming, Senator."

"So you say. But what proof can you offer?"

"You mean, in addition to the diaries of my famous ancestor?"

She chortled. "As interesting and valuable as those journals may be to historians, all I see are vague references to early nineteenth-century political intrigue. Fascinating, I'm sure, but it doesn't really ring my bell."

"I see." Denson stood and walked to a bookcase on one wall of his study. "Then perhaps you'd like to see the Lost Treaty?"

Knowlton's eye's widened. "You have a copy?"

"But of course. How else could I know what I've shared." He released a latch and swung open the section of shelving, revealing a vault door.

After entering the combination and opening the door, he gestured for the senator to follow him into the small room. Directly before them was a bank of steel drawers, each with a lock. Denson inserted a key and opened the top drawer. Upon pulling it open, Senator Amy Knowlton looked upon an aged document with flowing handwriting in faded ink.

"This document," Denson said, as if lecturing to a classroom of students, "was composed in both Spanish and Cyrillic."

"It's the Lost Treaty!" Knowlton said.

"Exactly as I told you."

She leaned in for a closer inspection, then removed a pair of reading glasses from the inside pocket of her blazer. As she was reading, her lips moved, silently forming the words.

"I assume you're reading the Spanish text and not the Cyrillic?"

She looked up at Denson, annoyed with the interruption. "Yes. I studied Spanish throughout my education. I don't speak or read Russian."

Denson stood to the side, watching. He knew the hook was set, and now all he had to do was reel her in.

After ten minutes, the senator removed her reading glasses and looked at Denson.

"If this document is authentic, then you have an irrefutable argument."

"It's authentic, trust me."

"Trust you? Why?"

He grinned, as if cajoling a child. "I'm not wrong."

"What exactly do you need me to do?"

"I want your word that when you become president, you will recognize the claim of my movement that the former Oregon Country—well, not that costal portion west of the Cascades, that population would just be troublesome—should secede from the Union."

"When I become president? What do you mean by that?"

"Let's just say that when certain events happen, the path will be clear for you to assume the job of commander-in-chief."

She stared back at Denson, the enormity of his implied multidimensional message sinking in.

"I'm intrigued by your proposal. But it suffers from two fundamental flaws. I'm surprised you haven't recognized them."

"Flaws? My plan is perfect."

"First, you fail to comprehend the difficulty in secession from the Union. What you're suggesting has never been done. To carve out a section of the continental United States that has been part of the Union for more than a hundred fifty years…I mean, it's not a simple task. This is an entirely untested theory. In fact, I don't even think the theory has been invented yet. It will require action from Congress…you know that. Not to mention, the courts."

"Really? And what is the second so-called flaw?"

"I'm not the president, nor do I have plans to run for the office."

He smiled broadly, presenting an unattractive view of his stained teeth. "Very soon, the Tenth Circuit Court will issue a ruling that any treaties between the young United States and either Spain or Russia that were not tri-party agreements are invalid on the grounds of the pre-existing contract between

Spain and Russia, as evidenced by the Lost Treaty."

"And you've provided the Lost Treaty to the court?"

"A certified copy, of course. The original document is far too valuable to release from my control."

"Seems I read about your lawsuit in the *Idaho Statesman*. If I remember correctly, they characterized your legal theory as a crackpot notion that didn't merit the time of the court."

"Political propaganda. Don't believe everything you read in the papers or hear on the evening news."

"What makes you so confident the judges will rule in your favor?"

"Let's just say I've made plans to ensure the right judge gets on the case."

"But the case is already before the panel. And you can't select the judges you want, anyway."

"True. But if a judge is unable to continue deliberations, then a substitute will be appointed. In my case, I've already made arrangements to ensure a sympathetic judge is appointed."

"Did I miss something? According to the story in the *Statesman*, briefs have already been filed, and oral arguments will soon be made to the three-judge panel. You can't just take one of the judges off the panel and replace him with another."

"No, I can't. But things happen. Accidents, illness—it's a precarious and dangerous world we live in."

Knowlton narrowed her eyes. "You don't say."

Denson held her stare.

"And what about me not being president?"

"You're not grasping the big picture."

"And exactly what is the big picture?"

Denson waved a hand dismissively. "Simply that there have been forty-five presidents, and eight of those men acquired that position by being vice president when their boss died in office."

"Like I said, I'm not vice president. I'm not even Speaker of the House."

Denson drew a deep breath. He'd thought the senator was more in tune with his machination. She professed to support state's rights, and even claimed that the Cascadia Independence Movement was a legitimate organization under which individuals lobbied for greater personal freedoms. After all the information and innuendos he'd shared, how could she still be ignorant of his plan? And yet being more specific would leave him vulnerable to betrayal. She had to be fully committed, with no wiggle room to lay the blame at his feet and escape retribution. This was essential, not only for self-preservation, but also so he had leverage over her in case she tried to renege on the deal.

A deal they had yet to strike.

"No," he said. "But you are president of the Senate. Or more correctly, president pro tem."

"You can't seriously be suggesting that my position in the Senate, fourth in line of presidential succession, is a reasonable pathway to the office. It's never happened, outside of fiction, anyway. I mean, the odds that the president, vice president, and Speaker will all die on the same day, plus or minus...I mean, the odds of that happening are astronomical."

"You're right. But it's not impossible. It just takes a little..." He placed a finger to his lips and cast his gaze toward the ceiling. "...finessing."

Senator Amy Knowlton crossed her arms. Now there was no doubt in her mind as to exactly what game General Stuart Denson was playing. It was a dangerous game, to say the least. But the prospect of capturing the presidency, and being the first woman to do so, proved a powerful enticement.

She said, "It's not sufficient to remove the obstacles. It has to be done in a way that draws no attention to you and me. If there is even the slightest hint otherwise, the plan fails and we go to prison for the rest of our lives."

"Or face execution."

She turned her gaze to the yellowed document again, absorbing the historical significance of not only of the Lost Treaty, but also of what they were about to do.

Without averting her gaze, she said, "No one has ever been executed in the U.S. for treason."

"True. But then again, no one has ever accomplished what we're about to do."

CHAPTER 10

IT HAD BEEN A LONG DAY, mentally and emotionally draining. Having no appetite, Peter skipped dinner and opted for a tumbler with two fingers of Buffalo Trace Bourbon to take the edge off his nerves.

The evening temperature had already dropped under a clear, star-filled sky. He set a crackling fire on the hearthstone, the radiant heat warding off the chill. Diesel had settled in front of Peter's leather club chair, stretching his muscular body to take full advantage of the warmth cast by the flames.

He was lost in thought, a swirling whirlpool of regret and guilt threatening to draw him ever deeper into despair. Over and over, his mind replayed the day's events, second-guessing his actions. What if he'd removed the power pack before handing the weapon to McMullen? What if the governor had not been present? What if the State Police Dignitary Protection Unit had provided several bodyguards rather than only one? What if he'd hired an armed detail to provide security during the demonstration?

His mind was spinning in circles—endless hypothetical scenarios and impossible questions. None of it mattered, because the events could not be replayed. Time could not be reversed. There was no do-over, no mulligan.

He felt his head throb, and he walked into the kitchen and popped several ibuprofen tablets. As he returned the bottle to the cabinet, there was a knock at the front door.

Expecting it was either the Bend Police, or the state police, or the FBI, he opened the door with a sour expression. But it wasn't anyone from law enforcement.

"Oh, my gosh." Kate placed her hand over her mouth. "What happened to your face?"

"Long story."

"I heard on the news. About the—"

Peter wrapped his arms around her and drew her into his breast. For several moments, neither spoke.

Then Peter said, "Come inside. It's cold out here, and I have a fire burning."

Diesel bounded to Kate, his tail wagging. She leaned over and rubbed his large head and ears.

"How's my boy?" She then she sat in one of the overstuffed chairs before the fireplace.

Peter hung her jacket on a hook in the entry hall. "Would you like coffee or tea? Something stronger, maybe?"

Kate noticed the tumbler on the table next to the other chair. "Looks like you're already hitting the alcohol. Nothing for me. I'm fine."

Peter entered the great room and used the poker to jab at the half-burned logs in the fireplace, causing an eruption of orange sparks to rise up the flue, carried by the hot gases. The flames grew taller.

He sat in the chair and turned his gaze to Kate. Her brunette hair just touched her shoulders, curling under at the tips. Her cheeks and the tip of her nose were tinged with pink from being in the cold.

"Funny how it seems a tragedy is always needed to bring us together," Peter said.

He'd met Kate following the murder of her roommate. They'd hit it off well, finding comfort in each other through sharing their personal grief. For Peter, it was the death of his wife. For Kate, the loss of a close friend. Over time, that feeling of comfort grew into a deeper emotional bonding. But like a Greek tragedy, events beyond their control, or even their ability to predict, always seemed to conspire against them.

Peter had reasoned that it was time to move on. He'd mourned Maggie's passing for years. It was long enough. In Kate he saw a beautiful spirit—a caring and compassionate woman who shared a love for the outdoors, just as he did.

Kate only aspired for a normal life—whatever that was—and she thought Peter could be her lifelong companion. But however she attempted to define *normal,* it did not include Peter disappearing for days, sometimes weeks, without calling. Or returning home with knife or gunshot wounds. He'd always offered explanations—as much as he could, anyway, without violating government secrecy. She had come to understand that the man she was falling in love with felt a compulsion to help those in need. Admirable as it was, she viewed it as a curse. More than once, she'd said, *"Why does it always have to be you who saves the world?"*

That simple vexing question proved unanswerable. It became a wedge, always driven deeper, unrelentingly separating the two lonely souls.

She reached over and grasped his hand. The warmth of her touch, her soft skin, was electrifying, and Peter felt a surge of... what? Hope? Passion?

Although he didn't live a solitary life, ever since his children had become adults and moved on to live their own lives, he didn't have any deep relationships. Sure, he had many colleagues and friends, some close, but he'd always worked to keep them just outside his emotional inner sanctum.

Work became the focus of his life. A distraction, something to mask the loneliness he felt when his mind was not occupied. There was no one he could confide in, to share the little accomplishments and the big ones, as well as the setbacks. No one to share dreams with, to work together with through life's challenges. No one to build a future with. He was on a raft in the middle of an ocean.

And then he'd met Kate.

The warmth of her touch was a tonic, a drug coursing through his veins and healing the pain he'd grown numb to. His feelings of affection swelled, and he had to tell her how he felt.

He tried to speak, had the words formed in his head, but they wouldn't escape his throat. He searched her eyes for understanding.

"I...I don't know." He answered the question he knew to be on her mind, because it always was.

She just hadn't voiced it yet.

She withdrew her hand. "Don't know what?"

His mouth moved, but no words came out. He held her gaze until she turned away.

"I was worried about you," she said. "They said on the news that two people were murdered and the governor was kidnapped."

"I'm okay."

The passion had quelled, once again locked away behind a facade of strength, of indifference. He faced the fire, wishing he could open up to Kate. But no matter how hard he tried, he couldn't.

She sat still for a couple minutes. Diesel was asleep and snoring, occasionally a front paw would twitch as he reacted to his dreams. Finally, she looked at Peter, frustrated by his stubbornness.

"Is that all you have to say?"

He shrugged. "Jim is missing. I think he was kidnapped along with Governor Bingham, but the police seem to think he's an accomplice. They believe he killed one of the men."

"I'm sorry." She was wringing her hands and staring at the crackling fire, the wedge moving ever deeper.

She wondered if it was too late.

Her gaze remained on the dancing flames. "I suppose this means you're going away again."

He looked at her, his eyes narrow slits.

"I mean, to find Jim and the governor."

He nodded slowly. "Yes."

"You know, you don't have to. The police will find them. That's their job."

"What if they're too late? What if they kill Jim instead of bringing him in alive? I could never live with myself if I don't try."

"Yeah, I knew you would say that."

"I'm sorry. I can't change who I am."

She faced Peter, her chestnut eyes moist. "And where does that leave us?"

"Kate, I…I can't turn my back on my friends. You can't ask me to do that."

A solitary tear traced a line down her cheek. "You're a good man, Peter Savage." She drew in a deep breath. "I know I can't change who you are. But can't you make room for me, too?"

He rose from his chair and moved in front of Kate. Dropped to his knees and held her hands.

"I want to so much," he said. "I just don't know how. You

make me feel…alive. I thought I'd never feel that way again."

"You can't keep pushing me aside."

"I'm sorry. I'm just trying to protect you."

She pushed his hands aside. "Protect me? From what?"

"Come on, Kate. We've been over this before. I don't want to fight."

"Yes, we've had this argument before. And it has never been resolved. If you go away on these trips to help your friends, and come back stabbed and shot, you shouldn't be doing it. Let the police handle it if it's dangerous!"

"I've met some very bad people. I don't want them to hurt you to get back at me."

"And what about you? What about your safety?"

His mind flashed back to the first time he'd shot and killed a man. It was on a remote Aleutian Island, and terrorists were holding his father and a research group hostage. Peter had escaped and then shot to death two gunmen in a span of seconds. Since then, he'd been forced to kill others to protect his friends and family. He still saw those faces in the dead of night.

"You have no idea what I've done," he said. "What I've been forced to do. I don't want you to see that, ever."

She dismissed the explanation with a shake of her head. "I'm not a child. Remember, I'm the one who found Emma's body lying in the kitchen, an ugly red hole in her head." More tears streaked her face, and she snuffed her nose. "I know the world is dangerous and that there are bad people out there."

"I'm sorry. I didn't me to upset you."

"See, you just did it again."

"What? I don't understand."

"Don't you get it? You can't always protect me."

"If anything happened to you, I couldn't live with myself."

"But you can't always be there. Just like you couldn't when Maggie—I'm sorry. I had no right to say—"

Peter held up a hand. "It's okay."

He rose and grabbed the poker, working the fire again. Only this time the pokes and jabs had more force behind them.

"Life is so precarious." He was still gazing at the flames. "It seems like we balance on a razor's edge, everything moving along just fine, until it isn't."

"If you really believe that, then you owe it to yourself to live your life every day."

He turned and faced Kate, at a loss for words. She was right, he knew that. Many times he'd seen how quickly his life was thrown into turmoil by unexpected events. It could happen any time, and would certainly occur again.

He nodded. "But what if I can't be there for you?"

"Then we will at least have shared all that we can."

Another nod.

Kate stood within reach of Peter, maintaining separation. "I should go now. I didn't mean to keep you. I'm sure you're exhausted. Go to bed and get some rest. Then do what you need to do."

"And then what? Is there any chance for us?"

Kate gave a sad smile. "That's up to you."

CHAPTER 11

MAY 10

PETER WAS SITTING AT HIS OFFICE DESK, laptop open, and still on his first cup of coffee. It had been a fitful night, marked by deep sleep broken with periods of restlessness. The conversation he'd had with Kate still weighed heavy on his mind. A knock on the doorframe interrupted his thoughts.

Nancy said, "It's Detective Colson. She says she wants to ask you a few questions."

He sighed and closed out his email. "She always does," he grumbled.

"Should I ask her to wait?"

"No, it's fine. I'll talk to her now."

A few minutes later, Detective Ruth Colson was sitting in the chair at Peter's desk.

"Thank you, Mister Savage." She couldn't help but notice the bruises under both eyes and the bandage on the bridge of his nose. "How are you feeling?"

"Like someone rammed a six-pound chunk of aluminum into my face."

"I'm sorry. I don't think this will take long."

"I really don't know what else I can share, Detective. I already told you everything I know."

She flipped open her notepad. "We received the ballistics report last night. Given that Governor Bingham was kidnapped, the state police are putting every available resource into this investigation, and they've prioritized the lab work."

Peter sipped from his coffee, waiting for Colson to get to the point. He'd interacted with her several times before, and by now he could anticipate her pattern of communication, which seemed to be overly dramatic and drawn-out. He preferred more direct dialog. At moments like this, she reminded him of a female version of the fictional Detective Columbo, sans trench coat and lacking Peter Falk's raspy voice and cigar. If the circumstances weren't dire, he might even find her mannerisms humorous.

After several moments of silence, Peter prodded the detective along.

"And?" he said, with raised eyebrows.

"The slug that killed Major Hardwick was fired from a forty-five auto pistol. The bullet expanded rapidly and passed through his chest. It was recovered, lodged beneath the foam lining and against the cement block wall. It was a hollow point, most likely two-thirty grain. No cannelure in the bullet jacket, indicating it was not loaded for a revolver."

"A lot of forty-five ACP guns out there."

"We can narrow the search somewhat. The pattern of rifling on the bullet is consistent with barrels used by Para USA."

"I'd be surprised if they make their own barrels. Most boutique gun manufacturers buy the best components in their price range and then hire competent smiths to assemble the weapons."

"I wouldn't know, but I'll take your word for it."

Peter stared blankly at Colson and swirled his coffee.

"We know the gun wasn't carried by the state police officer, his nine-millimeter Smith and Wesson was still in his hand. He'd just cleared his holster when he was shot, what we assume was multiple times. Were any of the other three men armed?"

"I don't know. I didn't ask."

"Don't you have metal detectors for screening visitors?"

"We make high-tech weapons. The only visitors we get are from the Department of Defense, and they are scheduled in advance."

"Well, maybe you should rethink your policy."

Peter frowned. He didn't enjoy the implication that he was in some way responsible for the murders. His guilt didn't need any encouragement.

"I have a better idea. I'll just require all my employees to open carry. That way, if this ever happens again, the bad guy will be gunned down before he leaves the building. Would make your job easier, wouldn't it."

"Relax, Mister Savage. We're just having a conversation here."

He eased back in his chair, knowing more was coming.

Colson glanced again at her notes. "Hardwick and McMullen flew in earlier in the morning, right?"

"Yes. That's what they said. They stayed the previous night in San Francisco, then took the morning flight to Redmond. I think they rented a car at the airport, then drove to Bend."

"But not Commander Nicolaou. He didn't fly in, is that right?"

"What difference does it make?"

"Please answer the question."

Peter knew he was being manipulated, but couldn't see where Colson was trying to take the questioning.

"He landed at Bend Airport."

"Not a commercial flight?"

"No. He usually flies on a military aircraft."

"Very convenient, wouldn't you agree? No schedule to meet, no security…"

"Detective, I really don't know—"

"Would you like to know what I think? Hardwick and McMullen were not armed because they would never get their weapons through airport security, and they didn't have time or reason once they landed to go gun shopping. So that leaves James Nicolaou. He flew on a private aircraft. No problems bringing his side arm. Am I right?"

Peter furrowed his brow. "I wouldn't know."

"I called the Strategic Global Intervention Team in Sacramento. That's the organization that Commander Nicolaou is in charge of, right?"

Peter nodded.

"I inquired as to the commander's preferred choice of sidearm." She paused—more unnecessary drama. "Know what they told me?"

"I can guess. I'm sure it wasn't too flattering."

The detective flashed a fake smile. "Once I explained that we had two murders and a kidnapped governor, they became more cooperative. They said that the commander favors carrying a forty-five Super Hawg. Care to guess who makes that gun?"

"I don't need to guess. I know it's made by Para USA."

Colson nodded. "That's right. I find that very interesting, don't you?"

Peter pushed back from his desk, stood, and paced. He'd walked right into Colson's trap. He should have just stayed quiet. But what good would that have accomplished? He didn't tell her anything she didn't already know.

"You got it all wrong." He looked down at her. "Jim would never murder someone in cold blood."

Colson reached into her jacket pocket for her phone. "Let

me show you something. It's some of the video footage we recovered from your security camera."

The screen flashed to life, and she slid the phone across the desktop. Peter leaned over the video, recognizing the figures that were walking calmly out of his business and toward a car parked in front of EJ Enterprises. Jim was in the lead, followed by Governor Bingham, with McMullen close by her side. He held the PEAP carbine in one hand. They all entered the car, Jim taking the driver's seat, and the other two in the back. Then the car drove away and disappeared from the field of view.

"So? That doesn't prove anything."

"Mister Savage, we both know what that video shows. Commander Nicolaou was not under duress. Why didn't he call for help, or run away?"

No reply.

"In fact, Todd Steed said he approached Commander Nicolaou as the trio was exiting the building, and…" she looked at her notepad, reading from the page, "…Nicolaou said 'Stand down. Now is not the time.' That doesn't sound like a plea for help."

Peter rolled his eyes. "What could he do? McMullen obviously had a weapon aimed at the governor."

"A normal person would say call the police, or try to escape. Nicolaou did neither."

"Whatever. I'm telling you he's not a murderer. It's just not something he could do."

"Really?" Colson leaned forward over the desk. "Well, then, maybe you can tell me why two men matching the descriptions of the commander and Mister McMullen, and driving a silver Chevy Malibu with Oregon plates two-nine-four LSN, shot a small-town police officer in western Idaho yesterday?"

CHAPTER 12

LACKING ANY APPETITE, Peter worked through lunch, although he found it hard to concentrate. And he wasn't the only one. Most of his employees were engaged in chatter about the previous day's events. Rather than risk having mistakes occur while people's minds were on other topics, Peter sent everyone home for the remainder of the day.

He took the steps to his upstairs loft, unable to shake the images of Jim strolling to the car with McMullen and the governor. Inside the great room, Peter walked to the French doors opening onto the west-facing deck, leaving the door open behind him. The sun was bright, and the temperature already comfortable. He sat in a cushioned chair and propped his boots on the railing. Off in the distance, the snow-capped Three Sisters, along with Broken Top and Mt. Bachelor, were crisp images against the blue sky.

His mind drifted to happier times, more than two decades ago, when he and Maggie would visit those mountains and the cold, blue lakes nestled in between the peaks. It was up there, at Todd Lake, that he and Maggie had chosen the names for their two children. Years later, it was also in that wilderness that Peter had taught his young son, Ethan, to hunt. Joanna, too, although she didn't take to it like Ethan had.

Those were simpler days, filled with joy and the promise that life was overflowing with hope. Those days were gone. They died with Maggie. He wondered if he could recapture some of that joy and promise with Kate. Why couldn't he just tell her how he felt?

Diesel nudged his squat nose against Peter's leg, drawing him back to the present. He reached down and rubbed the dog's blocky head.

"Hey there, buddy."

Peter's mind returned to the conversation with Colson, and the video images. He figured that McMullen had a gun—certainly Jim's gun—pressed into Governor Bingham's side, which is why they were so close when walking to the car. Knowing that, Jim would have no choice but to appear cooperative and follow McMullen's orders.

And then there was the shooting of the Idaho police officer. How strong was the evidence? Or was it circumstantial? Regardless, he knew that taken as a whole, the evidence was incriminating.

His thoughts were interrupted by the ringing of his phone. The caller ID was blocked, which meant only one thing.

"Lieutenant Lacey, I presume."

"Yes, Mister Savage. How did you know? This number should be blocked."

"It is. That's how I knew."

Petite and attractive, with a fair Irish complexion and natural red hair, Ellen Lacey could have had her pick of eligible bachelors. But she'd learned to despise the dating ritual of small talk laced with suggestive innuendos, preferring the cerebral challenge of her work at SGIT. Widely regarded by her peers as brilliant, she headed a team comprised of some of the most capable intelligence analysts to be found anywhere—all handpicked for their loyalty, dedication, and brain power.

"We need to talk," she said. "The situation with Commander Nicolaou is deteriorating very quickly, and I'm going to have to brief my Director, Colonel Pierson, within the hour. Both the Bend Police and Oregon State Police have been in communication with me. The FBI is also involved and has been trying to reach me. So far, I've been able to dodge their calls."

"The FBI? Why?"

"Kidnapping of a governor. Anyway, I wanted to let you know that they think the commander is part of this."

"I know. The police shared that theory with me this morning."

"I'm mostly in the dark on this. I only know what I was able to piece together from the questions the police asked me. But it seems you were there. Tell me what happened."

Peter proceeded to retell the events up to the point at which McMullen slammed the PEAP carbine into his faced and knocked him out.

"When I came to, both Hardwick and the bodyguard were dead. McMullen, Jim, and the governor were gone."

"They were both shot?"

"From what I saw, no doubt the major was shot in the chest. The police believe Jim shot him. But I don't think the same weapon killed the bodyguard."

"Why not?"

"He was shot at the base of his neck. But the entrance hole wasn't small like from a bullet. The wound was large and ragged."

"If not a gun, then what killed him?"

Peter hesitated. "The pulsed-energy carbine that I was demonstrating just before all this happened. After McMullen cracked me in the face with it, I'd wager he turned it on the bodyguard. According to Detective Colson, the trooper was drawing his service weapon when he was killed."

"And that's why you had the people from DARPA, Commander Nicolaou, and the governor at EJ Enterprises? To demonstrate this new energy weapon?"

"Yes. And to brief Hardwick, McMullen, and Jim on its capabilities. The development was funded by DARPA, and McMullen was the program manager. I gave him frequent reports, and he read in Hardwick. I expected they would continue the program and that SGIT would be involved in field trials."

Peter shared additional information, including the contract number so Lieutenant Lacey would be able to pull up the internal DARPA files.

After a short pause, during which Peter assumed Lacey was completing her notes, she said, "Did the police share anything that might indicate what the motive was?"

"No, nothing. I assumed McMullen wanted to steal the prototype carbine. To what end, I don't have any clue."

"It seems the only eyewitnesses to the murders are the three missing people."

"That's right. We were in the live-fire lab—that's what we call the shooting range. It's close to soundproof, and lacking windows, for obvious reasons."

"I understand. You mentioned Detective Colson. She contacted me yesterday. Did she show you the security camera footage?"

"Yes. And the ballistics report."

"Without the gun that fired the bullet, there can't be a match. No proof. It's possible that McMullen figured out some way to get a gun."

"Possible? Sure. But we both know it would have been next to impossible to smuggle a weapon onto a commercial flight."

"Then he acquired one once he landed at Redmond Airport and prior to arriving at your shop."

"There was hardly enough time. According to what Hardwick shared with me at the beginning of our meeting, they landed, got the rental car, stopped for breakfast on the way to Bend, and then came directly to EJ Enterprises. Without stops, the drive from the airport is about thirty minutes. Add on an hour for breakfast, and it adds up. They arrived about ninety minutes after their scheduled landing time."

"Even if it was the commander's pistol that killed Major Hardwick, it doesn't mean he pulled the trigger."

"Of course he didn't pull the trigger. I've known Jim most of my life, and there's no way he'd have had any role in this. He's being framed. But why?"

"That's a good question."

"There's more. The detective also shared with me that there was a shooting in Idaho. A local police officer was shot at a gas station. She said the suspects are Jim and McMullen, based on eyewitness descriptions, and they were driving the same Chevy Malibu that McMullen, Jim, and the governor drove from EJ Enterprises."

Lacey sighed. "So it goes from bad to worse. Law enforcement will have little choice but to view Commander Nicolaou as a cop killer."

"We need to find Jim before the police do. What can I do to help?"

A pause before Lacey said, "Help? I don't think you understand. SGIT has been ordered to stand down."

With the phone to his ear, Peter stood and entered the great room, resuming his pacing, a subconscious behavioral trait when he was involved in a deep phone conversation.

"No, I don't understand. The analysts at SGIT could be instrumental in solving this. And you can track his phone, right?"

"We're too close. Commander Nicolaou is one of ours. Besides, the military is not allowed to be involved in domestic criminal investigations."

"There has to be something you can do. Any information you can share will help."

"I can't do that. Do you understand what you're asking for? SGIT is not a private detective agency. I could lose my job—and get arrested."

"We have to find Jim before the police do. At best, they're convinced he's an accomplice. At worst, a cop killer."

When Lacey spoke again, her voice was low. "I can access McMullen's personnel files. Maybe there's something about his political associations. He would have gone through a background check prior to working at DARPA. And I'll dig into the project file, too. Let me see what I learn, and then I'll call you back."

CHAPTER 13

FOLLOWING THE MEETING the previous day, near the confluence of the Salmon River and the Snake River, Captain Swanson drove into the early evening, to the small town of Hailey, less than ten miles south of Sun Valley. Riding shotgun was Finn Jensen, a veteran of two deployments in Iraq. In the back seat were Bode Ayers and Dwayne Danvers. Danvers hated his given name, thought it made him sound like a sissy, so he insisted on going only by his family name.

In the back of the old extended-cab, four-by-four pickup were two duffel bags and two rectangular hard-sided cases, like a gun case, only larger. A tarp, lashed down with rope, kept everything out of sight of passing motorists.

Swanson had handpicked the team, comprising two rookies and two senior members of the militia. Both he and Jensen were trusted members of the movement. Swanson was one of the first men to join General Denson's militia following a dishonorable discharge from the Marine Corps. He saw things differently from his commanding officer, and believed he was justified in pistol-whipping an Iraqi civilian who he suspected was involved in planting several roadside IEDs. One of those bombs blew the legs off his closest friend. The Iraqi civilian died from head trauma, and it was later learned that he was just an innocent teenager who stopped beside the road to relieve himself near the location where one of the IEDs was planted. The unlucky kid had no idea the bomb was there.

Jensen had followed a different path, but ended up at the same destination. He found it difficult to adjust to civilian life after his discharge from the Army. Life in the military had been simple for him. He was surrounded by fellow infantrymen that he mostly liked, and a few he even considered to be as close as brothers. As a corporal, decisions were made for him. There was a routine to daily life in the military that he found lacking in the civilian world.

Without structure being applied to his day-to-day activities, he was lost. His frustrations frequently erupted in violence, earning him several run-ins with the law. Holding down a job was difficult, and he seldom stayed with one employer for more than six months.

Eventually, after drifting around Idaho for more than a year, he found work on the Denson Ranch, doing manual labor under the supervision of the ranch foreman. One afternoon, he met Stuart Denson. That meeting had been fortuitous. The general saw potential in Jensen.

The two newcomers, Danvers and Bode, also were veterans. They both seemed idealistic—angry at what they believed was a classist government ,whereby only the wealthy and well-connected occupied seats in Congress. At the slightest provocation, they would cite a laundry list of items as proof that the government was not *of the people, by the people, for the people.* That list included taxation which favored the wealthy, laws to restrict ownership of guns, healthcare and retirement packages for congressmen and senators that grossly exceeded what blue-collar workers would receive, and the overreach of the federal government limiting state's rights.

Swanson picked Danvers and Bode mostly because he saw they had fire in their bellies. They were passionate and filled with conviction. They believed they were engaged in a righteous fight, a crusade.

And every crusade needed martyrs.

⊕

Allyson Schultz and her husband, Tony, had just completed a ten-day guided fly-fishing trip into the Sawtooth Mountains. The weather had cooperated, with no rain and only three days of partial overcast. Their guide had taken them along the north fork of the Big Wood River and into some of the most beautiful backcountry they'd ever seen. And that was quite the statement since they had taken many fishing trips into remote regions of the Rocky Mountains, even into Canada.

One day, Allyson and Tony planned to spend a month fishing Alaska, hopping around the wilderness in a chartered bush plane. But for now, that was a far-off dream. Her workload as a judge on the Tenth Circuit Court of Appeals kept her extremely busy.

Tony was a commercial architect, working for a large firm in Denver. He'd been with the company long enough to accrue two months of vacation each year. But it was more time than Allyson could afford to be away from her cases, so it wasn't unusual for Tony to take a week off and fish some of the high lakes with his buddies. Once, he and two good friends drove to the Oregon coast for three days of chartered saltwater fishing.

Making this trip together was the high point of the year for the couple. After their only daughter had graduated from college and moved away to Seattle, Tony and Allyson spent more time turning to each other for companionship, something they thought had been lost through the trials and tribulations that come with years of marriage, two careers, and raising a child.

After giving their orders to the waiter, Allyson reach across the table and held Tony's hand. She was more in love with her husband now than when they'd married, and believed Tony felt the same way toward her. She wondered if that was odd, or simply the normal evolution of relationships. Either way, the reason didn't matter.

They were seated at the Sawtooth Brewery Public House, looking forward to their last night in Ketchum before flying to Seattle in the morning for a short visit with their daughter. Not a heavy drinker, Allyson was enjoying a local IPA, while Tony preferred to sample the porter. For a while, they were content just to hold hands and gaze into each other's eyes. The moment was broken when their dishes were served.

They smiled and giggled like children while retelling of their exploits wrestling fish of various sizes, none longer than fourteen inches, along the Big Wood River. Although they didn't break any records, Allyson knew the memories would last a lifetime.

They finished their plates, and each enjoyed a second pint before Tony paid the bill. The night was still young, and it wasn't cold yet, so they decided to walk back to the Limelight Hotel where they'd booked into a suite with a fireplace.

"How come we don't do this more often?" Allyson looped her arm through Tony's.

He raised a hand in mock surrender. "It's not me. I'll take vacation anytime to be with you." He leaned over and kissed her on the lips.

She smiled. "Yeah, I know. It's just that these cases…they just never end."

"And they never will. That's the beauty of being an appellate judge. You have job security."

Allyson frowned, then stuck her tongue out at her husband. "You make it sound logical."

"Because it is. You can retire anytime you want. We don't need the income."

"The thought has occurred to me more than once. But then I get a really interesting case. Like this one before the court now. I've read the briefs, and we'll receive oral arguments in two weeks. The case is fascinating."

"Don't suppose you can tell me about it?"

"No, I really can't. But it deals with the claim that the northwest portion of the United States was acquired illegally through treaties with both Russia and England."

Tony raised his eyebrows. "Intriguing. Can you share anything more?"

"I can't talk about aspects of the case that aren't in the public record yet. But I can share that the crux of the argument is that Russia never had legal authority to enter into its treaty with the United States."

"That's a new one. Never heard such a proposition before."

"Neither had I. However, the argument does follow well-established contract law. If you ask me, I think the petitioner—it's a sketchy antigovernment group—is not especially credible."

"Can't wait to read about it in the newspaper."

"If it makes the news. It's pretty far from mainstream politics, so I doubt there'll be much interest in covering the ruling."

The couple finished their walk in silence, content to be in each other's company. Once back at their suite, Tony lit the kindling and soon had a roaring fire, the flickering light bathing the room in a romantic glow. He opened a bottle of Cabernet Sauvignon, poured two glasses, and then sat next to Allyson, feet propped on the oversized ottoman. They savored the wine, gazing at the dancing flames, and relaxed into the plush leather sofa.

She rested her head against Tony's shoulder, lost in the moment. When she spoke, her voice was soft but filled with conviction.

"When I was younger, all I wanted was to achieve the goals I'd set for myself. Successful career, big house, fancy car…a good marriage." She met Tony's gaze. "Raising a family. But now that I've accomplished those goals, it seems so foolish and short-sighted."

"Why's that?" Tony said, his brow pinched.

"Because I sacrificed too much time on my career. Time that can never be replaced. Time I wish I had spent with you instead of with my work."

"It's not like you to second-guess your decisions. There's nothing wrong with the choices you made." Then he squeezed her hand. "The choices we made."

"Maybe. But that doesn't mean we can't make other choices."

"I don't understand."

"Oh, can't you see? I'm agreeing with you."

Tony leaned forward and refilled their glasses. "I'm totally lost now."

"I'm saying that I agree with you. We don't need both incomes anymore. And I realize now that the time I spend engrossed in my work is time we can't share together. And I want to have more time with you, to make memories like we have from this trip. The court will function just fine without me."

"Not sure I'd agree with that—"

"You know I'm right. President Taylor won't have any difficulties coming up with another appointment."

Tony's eyes twinkled. "You're serious? You want to do this?"

Allyson smiled and nodded.

"Okay. A toast." He raised his glass. "To us."

The passage of time seemed to slow as they sat side by side, content with each other's company, watching the fire burn down. When only a few glowing embers remained, Tony stood, offered his hand to Allyson, and led her to the bed.

⊕

The rich aroma of brewed coffee titillated Allyson's senses, nudging her from a deep slumber. She opened her eyes to Tony sitting beside her on the bed and holding a steaming cup inches from her nose.

"There's pastries and fruit on the table if you're hungry," he said.

She rubbed the sleep from her eyes and sat upright, pulling the sheet with her.

"Is it any wonder I love you so much?" she said.

"Ditto." He leaned forward and kissed her on the lips.

After showering and dressing, Tony placed their luggage in the trunk of an Uber for the short drive to Friedman Memorial Airport in Hailey. Since it was a small airport, the process of checking in and clearing security was much faster than at Denver International.

With a half-hour before boarding would begin, they found two seats together. Allyson resisted the urge to look at her email—there would be plenty of time for that later in Seattle. For now, she was content to replay the memories of the previous evening, bringing a smile to her face.

She didn't pay much attention to the throng of passengers milling about the boarding area. It was the usual mix of order and chaos she'd become accustom to at airports. In particular, she didn't notice the man with short-cropped hair, cowboy boots, jeans, and a hooded sweatshirt across the room. His frequent stares went unobserved. And she didn't see him carry on a brief conversation on his phone. But if she had, she would have probably concluded it was nothing out of the ordinary.

And she would have been dead wrong.

CHAPTER 14

SACRAMENTO, CALIFORNIA
MAY 10

WITH THE CRISIS WORSENING by the hour, Lieutenant Ellen Lacey settled in for a long night at The Office, the nickname for the SGIT headquarters, located at the McClellan Business Park in Sacramento.

Sitting at her desk, her face illuminated by the blue screen of her monitor, her concentration was disturbed by the ringing of her phone. The stern voice came through the phone loud and clear, like the speaker was shouting, but Lacey knew he wasn't. It was just Colonel Pierson's normal method of communicating.

She'd been expecting his call, and glanced at the time—almost 9:00 p.m., meaning it was approaching midnight at Pierson's office at the Defense Intelligence Agency.

"What the hell is going on? I've just had my ass chewed by Senator Murkowski from Oregon. Both the FBI and the Oregon State Police are demanding the personnel file and cell number for Commander Nicolaou."

Having recognized the need for a streamlined quick-reaction military unit that combined brains and brawn, Colonel Pierson had worked tirelessly to found SGIT. Although technically a department of the DIA, the organization was small, with a flat org chart, that mostly functioned independently of its behemoth brother. Heading the organization was Commander James Nicolaou, personally recruited from the SEALs by Pierson. Second-in-command was Ellen Lacey. By design, she was also leading the team of analysts. Together, Lacey and Nicolaou were a formidable pair, and SGIT's long list of missions would remain classified for decades. Their successes, also veiled in deep secrecy, had helped to avoid global war and ensure the safety of Americans.

Lacey cleared her throat. "Sir, yesterday there was an incident at EJ Enterprises involving the commander and—"

"Incident! Is that what you call two murders and the kidnapping of a governor? Not to mention the theft of a classified weapon system?"

"DARPA was funding the development. Commander Nicolaou's presence at the meeting had been requested. DARPA expected the program to move into the next phase involving field trials. Given the classified nature of the project, they wanted SGIT to conduct the trials. Why McMullen stole the prototype and killed two people is unknown."

"According to the Bureau, they think Nicolaou shot Major Hardwick, possibly the governor's bodyguard as well."

"No, sir. We don't believe that's true."

"*We* don't believe? Or you?"

"There's no way the commander would have done this." Lacey's voice rose in pitch. "There has to be another explanation. All the facts aren't in yet."

"I know that." He paused. "Now tell me what I don't know."

She spent the next ten minutes reading Pierson into her discussion with Peter. Pierson listened without interruption, and when she was finished, he said, "You're going to have to give them what they've requested."

"But sir—"

"No buts, Lieutenant. That's a direct order. I just didn't say *when* you will provide the files. I'll buy you some time, saying I have to get approval from higher up the chain of command. I can stall, but it won't be long. Twenty-four hours, tops. When the official request comes to you again, you will comply. Is that understood?"

"Yes, sir."

"Look, Lieutenant, I know this is bullshit. You don't have to convince me that Jim is innocent."

"Yes, sir. It's just that…well…if we could help with the investigation, I know we can solve this faster than if we just sit on the sidelines."

"We cannot officially participate in any way, or otherwise interfere with this investigation. It is a civilian matter. Am I clear?"

"Perfectly."

Colonel Pierson sighed. "Good. Now, hypothetically," he whispered, "if it were me in temporary command of SGIT, I'd do everything I could to find and return my teammate." He paused, giving Lacey a moment to weigh his words. "But if you were to hypothetically help and screw up, there would be nothing I could do to protect you. If you were lucky, you'd only be court-marshaled and drummed out of the service with a dishonorable discharge. More likely, you would be charged with aiding a fugitive. That's a felony."

The number one rule of SGIT operators and analysts was never leave a team member behind.

Lacey cleared her throat a second time as she prepared to speak, but was cut off.

"Just hang up. We never had this conversation."

CHAPTER 15

HAILEY, IDAHO
MAY 11

LESS THAN FIVE HUNDRED FEET FROM THE END OF THE RUNWAY, the four men waited amongst the trees. Between their location and the airstrip was green pasture, a ranch house, and a barn a half-mile to the south. They'd driven their pickup off Marine Drive, an infrequently used loop road, and parked it in the trees and bushes. After hauling the two green-painted aluminum cases from the back, they tossed a camouflage tarp over the truck to hide it from any passersby.

Swanson glanced at his watch. "Should hear from the watcher any moment now—*if* she's on the flight."

Bode and Danvers sat beneath an oak tree, surveying the landscape in silence.

"Seems like a lot of trouble." Jensen kept his gaze on the runway.

Their view of the terminal building was blocked by hangars and maintenance sheds.

"This judge must really be important," Jensen said.

"She's using her position on the Tenth Circuit Court to carry out left-wing agendas," Swanson replied.

"What's new? A lot of judges do that. We can't take 'em all out."

"You ask a lot of questions. You just need to pull the trigger when you got a solid lock."

Jensen checked the time and then returned his gaze to the runway, preferring to bear his admonishment in silence.

The phone vibrated in Swanson's hand. "Yeah?"

"It's a go," the voice said.

"Is the flight still on schedule?"

"Yes, no delays."

"Good. Call back when you see her board the plane." Swanson ended the call and pocketed his phone. "Get ready. It's almost showtime."

Jensen popped the clasps on the container and pulled the lid open.

He emitted a low whistle. "Jackpot. Never thought I'd see one of these again. You can't just walk into Guns-R-Us and buy one. How did you come by it?"

"Don't know. Wasn't my responsibility. I heard we bought a couple from some retired general in Pakistan. How he came across them, who knows."

Jensen removed the launch tube from the padded case and completed a quick inspection. The tube was five-feet long and had a boxy addition to the front that housed the electronics and sighting system.

"From the markings," Jensen said, "this is an earlier version, maybe from the Soviet-Afghan War or the Angolan Civil War. Uncle Sam had no issues then providing Stingers to our allies. Should be fine, though. It's the BCU that goes bad after a few years of storage."

"Not a problem," Swanson replied. "There are three battery

coolant units in the case. All are from a recent production lot."

"We'll know right away if they're good or not."

"You worry too much. Just get the missile loaded and everything ready."

Bode and Danvers were the second fire team. Although neither had any experience from their military service with operating the Stinger weapon system, Swanson had made sure they received plenty of instruction prior to this mission. Problem was, that instruction never included a live firing because they only had the two missiles.

The process of loading and firing the FIM-92 Stinger missile was easy, and the rookies had memorized the steps. Bode was assigned to aim and fire the missile, with Danvers providing assurance to Bode of the proper operational steps, and to assist with locating the target since Bode's attention would be glued to the target acquisition screen on the missile launcher.

The trick, if there was one, was that the dual-color infrared/ ultraviolet seeker head had to be cooled to function. This was accomplished with a charge of liquid argon, delivered from the BCU. At the same time, it provided electrical power to turn on the target acquisition circuitry. But the BCU would only operate the launcher for about forty-five seconds, resulting in a short window of time to acquire the target and launch the missile. So Swanson had drilled into Bode and Danvers the importance of waiting until the last moment to insert the BCU. If they inserted the cartridge too soon, they'd run out of power and the missile wouldn't launch.

Swanson's phone vibrated—the call he was expecting.

"Is she on the plane?"

The watcher replied, "Saw her board with my own eyes."

"Good. Just sit tight and follow the plan."

The watcher had a ticket to Denver on a flight that was scheduled to depart in another hour. But his flight would never leave. Soon, Friedman Memorial Airport would be a disaster area.

In the distance, the throaty whine of turboprop engines became clear. The flight to Seattle was a Bombardier Q400 aircraft. The two PW150A engines hung below the overhead wing.

Jensen reached for the squat-cylinder shaped BCU and made ready to insert it into the grip.

"Wait," Swanson said. "The plane's taxiing now. We'll hear the change in tone when the engines run up and the pilot changes the pitch on the props. That'll signal the beginning of the takeoff roll. Bode, you fire as soon as Jensen does. Understand?"

"Copy that."

With the launcher tube loaded and resting on his shoulder, Jensen adopted a comfortable and stable stance, making sure he was clear of the trees. The range of the missile, over five miles, gave him ample time to get a solid lock on the hot engine exhaust before firing. The aircraft was most vulnerable immediately after taking to the air, when it was at low altitude and still well-below cruising speed.

Jensen visualized the commercial aircraft accelerating down the black tarmac, then the nose rotating upward. As the plane climbed, it would clear the end of the runway, presenting its hot exhaust to the seeker head. This is when he would fire.

The still air reverberated with a thunderous sound as the huge Pratt & Whitney engines drove the pair of six-bladed props at maximum speed, slicing through the air and pushing the aircraft forward.

Swanson spoke calmly, with his hand on Jensen's back. "Steady...steady..."

Just then, the white glint of fuselage and wing appeared, moving fast down the runway.

"Now," Swanson said.

Jensen slammed the BCU home. The launcher came to life, and two seconds later he had a thermal lock on the hot starboard engine nacelle. But he held his fire, moving the launch tube to match the foreword progress of the Bombardier Q400. Just as he'd visualized, the nose lifted, then the body of the plane. It clawed into the sky, rising ever faster from the tarmac, clearing the end. It was a few hundred feet above the pasture when he had a clear sight of the hot engine exhaust. By now, the aircraft was a quarter-mile away.

He pressed the trigger. The sleek missile jumped out of the launch tube, arcing skyward. Then the solid rocket motor ignited, and the weapon shot forward, accelerating to Mach 2. A second later, the warhead—high explosive packed within a pyrophoric titanium cylinder—detonated against the engine cowling at the junction with the wing. The unspent rocket fuel added to the destructive effect, further ripping apart the aerodynamic aluminum shell.

The explosive force ruptured the tanks and dispersed the volatile aviation fuel, generating an aerosol mixture with the streaming air. Ignited by the solid rocket propellant, the fuel-air mixture detonated in a secondary, and more powerful, explosion.

Upon hearing the command from Swanson, Bode slapped his palm against the BCU, but nothing happened. He slapped it again, harder, and this time it seated. His electronics powered up, but he had lost precious seconds. Jensen had just launched his missile. Bode hurried to point the tube toward the airplane, saw a large thermal image on the screen, and fired. The missile leaped from the launch tube, screaming for the Q400. Danvers watched, excitement building...but the Stinger raced over the aircraft. Without a thermal lock, it had simply traveled far beyond the intended target, exploding on impact in the forest.

But the damage from the solo missile strike was massive. A huge hole was ripped through the starboard wing of the Bombardier, extending from the middle to the trailing edge. Yellow flames erupted from the maw like a scorching blowtorch, trailing away to black sooty smoke. The conflagration, fed by abundant fuel and whipped to a fury by the hurricane-force wind streaming over the wing, was already melting away the ravaged edges of the airfoil.

The starboard engine was a shattered hulk of metal, dead weight that only added drag, which, combined with the unsymmetrical thrust of the remaining port engine, caused the aircraft to yaw.

Inside the cockpit, the flight crew fought to regain control. The pilot applied maximum rudder to correct for the sharp turn to the right. With the flaps still extended, he hoped to be able to complete a turn back to Friedman Memorial Airport, now several miles behind his aircraft. The copilot was radioing their emergency while also shutting down electrical power to the starboard engine. He stole a quick glance out the window toward the rear, and his eyes widened in horror at the sight of the inferno engulfing the wing.

The passenger cabin was chaos—screams gave way to sobs, and unheard over the din were the prayers voiced by many. Tony and Allyson were seated near the front of the cabin and had not seen the explosion nor the streaming flames. But they'd felt the plane rock from the blast, heard the wrenching of metal, felt the aircraft stutter, pitch to the right, and drop. Their eyes were locked together, faces racked with terror. Allyson gripped Tony's arms, pulling him close. As tears streamed down her cheeks, she leaned her head to his chest, closed her eyes, and recalled the beautiful memories of last night.

The decent of the aircraft slowed, and then it stayed in level flight. As the pilot gained a measure of control, he focused on completing the turn and lining up with the runway, now only three miles away. At dangerously low altitude, he'd only get one pass to land the aircraft. He instructed the copilot to inform the cabin crew to prepare for a rapid evacuation as soon as the plane came to a complete stop. With the fire raging from the starboard wing, it would spread quickly to the cabin. Smoke would soon be the deadliest threat.

A *bang!* rang through the plane, and it dipped to the right. The pilot and copilot fought to right the Bombardier, but the dip rapidly degraded into a spiral, and the nose dropped at an ever-increasing angle.

What the flight crew couldn't see was that the ravaged wing, weakened to the point of failure by explosion and fire, had folded inboard of the engine before breaking free. With most of the right wing gone, the aircraft dipped and spiraled downward.

The Bombardier bound for Seattle cratered into the grass-covered ground just short of the runway.

Jensen and Bode each placed their launchers back into the crates and latched the lids. The team hurried to the truck, carrying the cases, slid them into the back and lashed the tarp over the cargo once again. The camo tarp that had concealed the truck was ripped down and hurriedly stuffed behind the seat. They had no time to waste—the white smoke plumes from the two missiles was lingering in the still air, like two accusing fingers pointing directly to the launch location.

Swanson turned the key and the engine roared to life. He shifted into drive and stomped on the peddle, sending a rooster tail of gravel behind the truck. After cranking the wheel to the left, he was back on Marine Drive and accelerating. In the rearview mirror, the image of black smoke rising from the burning fuselage was becoming smaller and smaller.

CHAPTER 16

A COUPLE HOURS BEFORE SUNRISE, Peter awoke with a start to the sound of his phone ringing. He reached out to the nightstand and swiped the green button.

"Yeah, it's Peter."

"Mister Savage, its Lieutenant Lacey. I know it's early, but I have important information to share."

"Sure. Just give me a minute. I want to get a pen and paper." Peter threw back the covers and descended the spiral staircase to the main floor, then proceeded to his study. "Okay, Lieutenant. Go ahead."

"I accessed Tim McMullen's file from DARPA. The man had a stellar record at INL."

"Sorry, INL?"

"Idaho National Laboratory. It's located in Idaho Falls. His specialty was high-powered lasers for initiating fusion in deuterium pellets. Anyway, apparently he also had a life outside of work, because he listed a couple clubs he was a member of while in college"

"Which university?"

"UC Berkeley and graduate studies at Stanford. Anyway, what's really interesting is that after he moved to Idaho, he began to associate with a few right-wing groups. None on a regular basis that we can tell, until he came across the Cascadia Independence Movement."

"How did you get all this? Doesn't sound like the type of information someone would put on a job application."

"Standard background search by the FBI. He was required to have security clearance to work at DARPA and at INL. I presume the FBI got this information from interviewing his friends and associates."

"This all sounds interesting. But let me disclose right now that I haven't had one cup of coffee yet, so you'll have to break this down to the basics for me to follow."

"Sure. The Cascadia Independence Movement, or CIM, is considered by the FBI to be a group of interest."

"Meaning?"

"Nothing definitive. Just that the group has some of the earmarks of becoming radicalized. My sources tell me that the FBI has tried, unsuccessfully, to infiltrate their ranks, so not a lot is known. But I'll come back to this."

"Okay. Do you have any leads on Jim's location?"

"We do…and so do the police."

"Talk to me." Peter leaned forward at his desk, a shot of adrenaline surging through his veins.

"For some reason, they didn't remove his cell phone. I can't say why. Maybe this McMullen character is just a hack at kidnappings. Anyway, we traced his location. It's not far from you, the extreme western edge of Idaho, near the corners of Oregon and Washington. I'll text the coordinates to you."

"Can't you just give me a city and street address?"

"His location is in the wilderness, near the Snake River.

There aren't any paved roads within ten miles of his location. It's going to be difficult searching for him."

"With coordinates loaded into a GPS, I can find him."

"There's more. Somehow Commander Nicolaou also managed to turn on the microphone during the travel from Bend to his current location. The voice recording went to the cloud, and my team has been analyzing the data. We believe, based on the recorded conversation, that he is being held at a campsite by an organized and well-armed group."

"Good to know. What about the police? You said they also know Jim's location."

"The general location, at least. I have a good source within the FBI. He shared that two days ago, security cameras at a gas station and at a McDonald's in Burns showed Commander Nicolaou and a silver sedan that matches the description of the car he drove away with McMullen and Governor Bingham. Later the same day, he appeared, along with McMullen, on a security camera at a gas station in Riggins, Idaho. The commander used his credit card to pay for the fuel. Riggins is where the police officer was shot, and not too far from the location where we believe the commander is being held."

"And probably Governor Bingham, too."

Lacey sighed. "If she's still alive."

"Can't you or the police also track her phone?"

"It was left inside her purse at EJ Enterprises. Look, Mister Savage, we don't even know if she's alive. Some of the video images show a third figure slumped in the rear seat of the car."

Peter felt ripples of despair wash over him. "Have the police tracked Jim's phone?"

"No, not yet. They've been pressuring me to provide his number. But I've refused until I receive written permission from higher up. The phone numbers and personal information of SGIT employees are classified information."

"How much time do we have?"

"Maybe four hours...five, tops, if we're lucky."

"That's not enough time." Frustration crept into Peter's voice. "It'll take eight hours just to drive to the general coordinates, then God knows how long to search the area."

"I can help shorten that. I have the jet on standby. It could land at Bend within an hour. From there, the pilot will ferry you to Idaho County Airport in Grangeville. That's about thirty miles, as the crow flies, from the phone coordinates. I'll make sure a rental car is waiting for you."

"Better make it a four-wheel-drive truck or SUV."

"Understood. Is there anything else I can provide?"

Peter paused for a moment to run through the list of items he'd need.

"Weapons would be great," he said, "but I'd imagine that's problematic."

"I'm sorry, sir."

"Okay, I'll provide my own. How about a state-of-the-art GPS unit and sat phone so we can stay in touch? Cell reception may not be reliable. And your best body armor. I'll need two vests, plus one set of knee pads and elbow pads. Better toss in a helmet, too."

"Can do on all of the above. Why two vests?"

"One for me, and one for Diesel."

"I can try to get a canine vest from the sheriff."

"Don't bother. The protection's not as good as what the military has."

Lieutenant Lacey had second-hand knowledge that Diesel had accompanied Peter into several conflicts. The red pit bull was reported to be loyal to his master, and the SGIT operators spoke with awe of the dog's ferocity when confronted by a threat. She'd never met Diesel, but felt she knew the canine by his reputation.

On more than one occasion she'd heard the story of how Peter and Diesel had become companions. The pit bull had begun its life in the most horrible fashion—as a bait dog. Rescued from a dog-fighting ring, the six-month old puppy was turned over to the Humane Society more dead than alive, the scars on its neck and muzzle still fetid and septic.

A staff member at the Humane Society in Bend had introduced Peter to the puppy amid the near constant barking inside the shelter. The ravaged dog approached with its head lowered, ears back, and tail between its trembling legs. When the pup raised its head and their gazes met, Peter instantly connected and vowed to nurture the pit bull back to health. In that moment, their unbreakable bond was forged.

"I get it," Lacey said. "I'll call you if there's any new information."

"Roger that. I better go. I've got work to do to get ready."

"Mister Savage, just one more thing."

"Yes?"

"I'll stall as long as I can. But you have to find the commander before law enforcement does. We don't have much time. Once they get this information, they'll storm the location in force."

Peter had always known Lieutenant Lacey to be calm and rational—one who solved problems through logical analysis and reason without getting flustered. Now, the gravity of her plea weighed on him. It had always been Jim and the operators at SGIT who had rescued Peter from death. With the tables turned, there would be no help, no cavalry riding in to save the day.

Perhaps it was the tone of his voice, or maybe stress pheromones, or even the unusual early morning phone call. Whatever the reason, Diesel was at Peter's feet, looking expectantly at his master and companion. Peter ended the call, then reached down and rubbed the blocky head, speaking softly.

"We got a job to do, buddy. Just you and me."

Diesel cocked his head as if trying to understand.

"We have to get this right the first time. And we can't count on any help."

Peter quickly dressed in his camouflage hunting clothing, adding rain gear and both medium-weight and heavy jackets to an oversized rucksack. He provisioned like he was going on an overnight hunt, but skipped the sleeping bag and foam pad.

Next, he returned to the great room and approached the bookcase. He pulled a horizontal latch underneath a low shelf in one panel, unlocking a secret doorway. He swung the panel open and entered his safe room. Except for the vintage weapons displayed on wall mounts, it could almost pass for a modest armory. He skimmed over the replica flintlock and percussion rifles, muskets, and pistols hanging from brass hooks. In another era, these weapons were state-of-the-art and represented formidable firepower. But those days were gone.

In four strides, Peter was at the large double-doored gun vault. He spun the combination lock and opened the heavy steel doors. Arranged in two rows was his collection of long guns— bolt action and semiautomatic rifles and shotguns. Mounted to the inside of each door were his revolvers and pistols in various calibers. Stacked on shelving that occupied the central portion of the safe from bottom to top was a generous stockpile of ammunition.

Peter's taste in firearms had evolved over the recent years as a result of his interactions with the SGIT operators, as well as one former Mossad assassin who'd saved his life more than once. She was an enigma, a paradox. Peter doubted he'd ever cross paths with her again, but still she'd passed along some valuable tips—like the stopping power of a semiauto twelve-gauge tactical shotgun, and the versatility of a combat tomahawk.

Mindful of the passing minutes, he selected his .340 Weatherby with a Leupold scope, a Benelli M4 shotgun, and a Kimber long-slide .45 ACP. He secured the long guns in a hard-side gun case, holstered the pistol and placed it in a second case with room for his edged weapons—a forged steel combat tomahawk and a Cold Steel Frontier Bowie knife. As an afterthought, he grabbed the Bond Arms derringer from a hook at the top of the door. The tiny double-barrel handgun, chambered to use the same ammunition as the Kimber, would be his backup, to be used only as a last resort if everything went to hell.

Next, he loaded the pockets of the backpack with as much ammunition as they would hold, and slipped a bandolier holding fifty-six twelve-gauge shells, a mix of 00 buckshot and slugs, over his shoulder.

The last items he grabbed were a spotting scope and laser range-finding binoculars, which he nestled between the clothing in the pack.

In the kitchen, he stuffed bottles of water into the pack, along with a large Ziplock bag of dog kibble, and others with some shelled nuts, dried fruit, and hard salami. If they had to stay out overnight, he and Diesel wouldn't be eating luxuriously, but they would have food.

Satisfied he was as prepared as possible given the short notice, he loaded everything into his H3 Hummer, then clipped a leash to Diesel's collar and drove to Bend Airport, five miles northeast of the city.

He arrived at the airfield just as the C37A was touching down. Because it was a military version of the Gulfstream V executive jet, SGIT used the plane frequently to shuttle personnel around the country.

As the aircraft taxied to a stop, Peter walked Diesel through the administration building. At the stairs to the plane, he was met by the pilot.

"Name's Oslund. Nice to meet you, sir."

Peter noticed the double blue bars stitched onto the shoulder of his flight duty uniform.

"Thank you, Captain."

"Lieutenant Lacey said you'd have some gear." He pointed to the gun case in Peter's hand. "Is that it?"

Peter handed over the case and the bandolier, then hoisted Diesel into the cabin.

"I'll be right back," he said. "Just another small case and rucksack."

Several minutes later, he returned with the remainder of his gear, strapped into a seat, and the business jet took to the air. As the copilot was ascending to cruising altitude, the pilot returned with a handheld GPS unit and a satellite phone. Both devices were about the same size and shape as a cell phone, but each had a stubby antenna to receive satellite signals.

"Their fairly intuitive to use." Then he gave Peter a short tutorial. "Any questions?"

Peter repeated the key steps to activate and operate each device, and received a nod from the pilot.

"The lieutenant also instructed us to deliver body armor, pads, and helmet. They're in a duffel bag at the rear of the cabin. The vests are level IIIA, which means they'll protect against most pistol ammunition. There are also some hard armor plates. The plates are inserted into the pocket on the front and back of the vest, and they're good against standard rifle cartridges, including seven-point-six-two-millimeter. But don't think you're Iron Man by wearing this. If you get shot, it will hurt like hell."

Oslund's words brought home the real danger that Peter

and Diesel would be facing.

Peter nodded. "Tell Lieutenant Lacey I said thanks."

"Just find the commander and bring him home safe, and we'll all be in your debt. I've heard..." The pilot started to turn.

Peter reached out and grasped his arm. "You heard what?"

Oslund hesitated. "I overheard the lieutenant talking to Mona Stephens. She's another analyst."

"Yes, I know her. Go on."

"Well, the Oregon State Police and the FBI are really pissed off, to say the least, that she's not sharing the commander's phone number so they can trace his phone. I guess you could say they view him as guilty until proven innocent. It sounds like they're ready to shoot him on sight."

"They can't do that. I'm telling you, he didn't do any of those crimes."

"Law enforcement is especially angry that one of their own was killed. They think SGIT is trying to cover for the commander and protect him. It's a toxic brew. Listen, I've known Commander Nicolaou for the last five years. I piloted the mission that flew him and the team over to the South China Sea. Just find him before the police do."

Peter released Oslund's arm, and the pilot returned to the cockpit. Peter stared out the window without focusing on anything. His mind drifted to past events he'd wanted to forget but knew he never could. The faces of men and women he'd killed seemed to pass in a macabre parade before his mind's eye.

The first time he'd pulled the trigger and took a life, it seemed surreal, like it was a dream rather than reality. It mattered little that he was forced to do so to save the lives of his father and a group of students. Later, it was to protect his daughter and son.

But no matter the reason, no matter how he justified his actions, he knew the truth—he was a killer of men.

Thirty minutes later, with Peter still mired in self-reflection, they landed at Idaho County Airport.

⊕

Captain Oslund and the copilot carried the gear while Peter walked Diesel to the rental vehicle. Thankfully, it was a Jeep Gladiator, a four-door vehicle with a cargo bed behind the cab. It reminded Peter of his Hummer.

With the hard cases, rucksack, and duffel bag in the cargo bed, Diesel hopped in and Peter followed. As usual, the red pit bull rode shotgun.

The handheld GPS unit rested on the center console, and Peter charted what appeared to be the most direct route to the coordinates supplied by Lacey. He hoped and prayed that Jim's phone was still on his person and had not been discarded in the brush. Still, it was the only solid lead he had, and it was imperative that he reached Jim before law enforcement did.

After traveling southwest on US-95, he found his way along secondary roads to Boles Road. At the end of Boles Road, he would have to go cross country, as far as possible in the Jeep, and then on foot.

Too quickly, the minutes had turned to hours. Although the sun was still low on the eastern horizon, he knew he was running against the clock. He had no idea exactly how long Lacey could stall, or how long it would take the FBI to prepare a team—probably multiple teams—to move on the suspected location where they'd find the fugitives and Governor Bingham. He was racing against opponents he couldn't see. For all he knew, they could already be at the coordinates, or right on his heels.

It didn't help to worry about the many possible scenarios he had no control over. All he could do was move as directly and expeditiously as possible, to where he hoped he'd find his friend.

When the road ended, he was confronted by rocky terrain

and thick brush. He was able to navigate a path for a few hundred yards, avoiding large rocks that could take out the oil pan, and thick brush and trees that were impassible. But eventually, the Jeep could go no farther.

He took one of the ballistic vests and modified it to fit around the canine's chest by cutting two slots for his front legs. Using the dog leash made from an eight-foot length of nylon webbing, Peter secured the armor so it covered Diesel's chest and back from his neck to his tail. Then he donned the other vest and snugged the hook-and-loop tabs.

He had just opened the gun cases when the sat phone rang.

"Peter, it's Lacey. I have bad news. The order finally came down from Colonel Pierson to surrender Commander Nicolaou's phone number. I just got off the phone with the FBI."

"How long do I have?"

"Maybe an hour. They're probably tracking his phone now. They'll have the location within ten minutes. Meanwhile, they'll be mobilizing a strike team."

"Okay. I'm going in on foot now. Looks like only four or five miles cross country, according to the GPS coordinates. The terrain is rugged. It'll be slow going. I'll leave the phone on vibrate. Call if you have any updates."

With the sat phone in his pocket, he hefted the rucksack over his shoulders and then slung the long arms. His holstered pistol, knife, and tomahawk were all attached to his belt. He shoved extra magazines for the Kimber, plus two boxes of rifle ammunition, into cargo pockets in his fatigues. Diesel had already completed a cursory scouting, never wandering more than fifty feet from the truck.

With everything in place, he said, "Come on, Diesel. We have a governor to rescue and a friend to save."

CHAPTER 17

WITHOUT ANY HEAT, the stone walls and concrete floor of the basement served to keep the space cool all night. Jim had slept fitfully on a fabric cot with a thin blanket.

Still, this was like a luxury hotel room compared to many places he'd had to spend the night. On more than one occasion, during classified missions in Iran and Iraq, he'd awaken in the cold desert darkness to a female camel spider, half the size of a dinner plate, planted on his face. Or worse, a fattail scorpion searching for a way inside the neck of his shirt. As ugly as the camel spider was, its bite was relatively harmless. But the fattail scorpion was a different story. He knew that a sting from the scorpion could prove fatal, and had always insisted that at least two doses of antivenom be distributed among his team.

The first slivers of daylight were penetrating the dual hopper windows high on the south wall. The window latches worked, and they could be opened, but steel bars covered the outside—whether to keep bears from breaking the glass and entering, or to keep human prisoners inside, Jim had no idea. Not that it made any difference. The windows offered no avenue of egress.

Jim sat on the cot. While he was still contemplating escape, the door at the top of the stairs opened and two guards descended, one carrying a tray with a modest meal of toast, black coffee, and two fried eggs. He was unarmed and set the tray on the floor ten feet away from the cot. The second guard had his rifle pointed at Jim from a safe distance.

A plastic spoon was provided for the eggs, otherwise there were no utensils, and the plate was paper, as was the coffee cup. No potential to fabricate a shard of ceramic into a shiv. The spoon held potential, however slim.

"Eat up," one of the guards said. "In twenty minutes, we'll be back. General Denson has prepared a demonstration for you."

"I can hardly wait," Jim said.

When the guards were at the top of the stairs, he attacked the plate. He hadn't realized how hungry he was, but the aroma of food stimulated his appetite.

He had lost count of how many times he'd awakened during the night, his mind refusing to shut down while working the riddle presented by Denson. *What could he be talking about? What does any of this have to do with the Lewis and Clark expedition?*

Right on time, the two guards, both armed now, appeared on the wooden stairway.

"Put the plate, cup, and spoon on the cot where we can see them."

Jim followed the order.

"Okay, come on."

Both guards slowly backed up the stairs while maintaining at least ten feet of separation from their hostage.

On the main floor of the lodge, the guards separated and

then herded Jim toward a pair of French doors. They were open, inviting the occupants outside onto a large patio behind the grand and rustic home. The patio was large, easily the size of a tennis court, and paved with red clay bricks in a herringbone pattern. A table to seat eight occupied the center of the space. Two seating areas of wicker chairs and settees, lushly padded with bright green cushions, were on opposite sides of the dining table. A scattering of umbrellas in bright primary colors were strategically distributed to provide a mix of shade and sun throughout the day.

Stuart Denson was wearing camouflage fatigues and a black long-sleeve shirt. Around his waist was a web belt and holster holding a SIG Sauer P226 pistol. He was talking to a man Jim had not seen before. The man was big, easily topping six feet, and muscular. He was wearing a tight-fitting long-sleeve T-shirt that did little to hide his bulging biceps and pectorals. His short and trimmed beard was a perfect match to his black curly hair.

Beyond the brick patio, Jim saw an expanse of flat and treeless terrain that stretched for a mile. More than that in some directions. Bunch grass eked out an existence in the thin and parched soil, somehow managing to store enough moisture following snow melt in the spring, and from the occasional showers in summer, to remain green throughout the short growing season.

"Ah, Commander Nicolaou." Denson turned his attention to Jim. "Let me introduce you to Billy Reed."

Jim strode across the separation and stood before the general and his bearded associate. No one offered a hand in greeting. Reed was holding the PEAP carbine, and a dozen feet to the side was an M107 semiautomatic .50 caliber sniper rifle supported on a bipod. A large scope was fixed atop the receiver.

Denson continued. "Mr. Reed is an accomplished shooter. I've witnessed his skill with a rifle firsthand."

"Good for you," Jim said.

"Oh, I see. A bit grumpy this morning, are we?"

"Look, Mister Denson." Jim refused to refer to him by rank. He reserved that honor for actual servicemen and servicewomen.

"I didn't ask to be here, and I don't like you. We're not friends. We're not pals. You're nothing to me other than just another scumbag that needs to be put down. So cut the shit."

Jim was surprised to see the tiniest hint of a smile creep across Reed's face. In contrast, Denson scowled and his features flushed, unaccustomed to being told-off in front of his soldiers.

After several moments, Denson regained his composure. "Fine. Mr. Reed, how far is it to the target?"

"The melon?" Billy replied.

Denson nodded.

"Right at twenty-six hundred yards, plus or minus."

"Commander," Denson said. "Perhaps you'd like to take out some of your aggression by shooting the watermelon target?"

"I'm not interested in your games."

"Fair enough. Then I'll offer you a deal. I'll give you two shots to hit the target. If you succeed, I'll release the governor."

"You'll free Governor Bingham?"

"That's my offer. Do you accept?"

"And you'll grant my freedom as well?"

Denson shook his head. "I'm afraid I can't do that. You see, the governor was never part of my plan. Consider her excess baggage. You, on the other hand, are necessary to my plan. So do we have a deal?"

Jim eyed the heavy weapon system. The rifle weighed about thirty pounds, and it was long and ungainly in close combat. The guards on the patio, all armed with AR-style rifles fitted with standard thirty-round magazines, would have the overwhelming advantage if Jim tried to turn the M107 on his captors. He discarded the nascent plan as too unlikely to succeed.

"How can I trust you?" he said to Denson.

Denson shrugged. "What do you have to lose? There are two rounds in the magazine. The rifle is zeroed at three hundred yards. You hit the melon, and Governor Bingham goes free."

"That's nearly a mile and a half away."

"True. A difficult shot. But there is no wind, and I've been told you are an accomplished warrior. I'd imagine you are well-versed in all matters related to guns and shooting."

"And if I miss?"

"Having doubts, are we? If you miss, then nothing changes. The governor remains my prisoner."

Jim nodded.

Denson clasped his hands. "Excellent! Oh, and just a reminder, my guards have been ordered to shoot you if you try to turn that weapon anywhere other than downrange. Although not preferred, I can carry my plan forward even if you are dead."

"Yeah." Jim slid down to a prone position behind the big rifle, drawing the stock in tight against his cheek, and snugging the butt stock against his shoulder.

He peered through the scope, taking several seconds to find the watermelon propped end up on a stump. But that wasn't all he saw.

"What the hell?" he said. "You've got a man down there! Looks like McMullen."

Denson was already laughing. "Indeed."

"Sick bastard. Find someone else to do your killing."

"Oh, relax, would you? I didn't ask you to shoot Mister McMullen, although he has it coming. Just stay on task and shoot the watermelon. That's the deal."

Jim looked again through the scope and estimated at least ten yards separated McMullen from the target. The DARPA program manager appeared to be tethered to another stump, limiting his freedom of movement. Although it went against Jim's better judgement—these were not ideal circumstances— he knew he could avoid collateral damage to McMullen. Whether or not he could hit the watermelon at nearly one and a half miles was another question. Given enough rounds, he could make corrections for point of impact and eventually nail the target. But he had two shots. *If* the rifle was sighted in, he expected to hit close on the first shot. That left only one more bullet to adjust his aim and hopefully hit the target.

Still looking through the optics, Jim watched the clump grass across the expansive meadow. It didn't move, and he didn't feel even a light breeze. He adjusted the scope to account for the distance, placed the crosshairs on the melon, and took several deep breaths. As his pulse slowed, he steadily applied more pressure to the trigger.

He was familiar with the M107, having trained with it, and having employed it on several missions. Even with the muzzle break, it would kick with authority and probably bruise his shoulder. He pulled the butt stock tighter.

And then, *boom!*

The muzzle jumped ever so slightly, and Jim was peering back through the scope again before the bullet completed the journey downrange to the target. Another second, and he saw the cloud of dust kick up just before the stump, but right in line with the target. He had aimed too low.

After adjusting his point of aim higher by two feet, he repeated the process, drawing deep breaths to slow his respiration and pulse. Mentally blocking out all other thoughts. The only sensory input coming from the image in the scope and the sensation of pressure on his trigger finger.

Boom!

Hoping to see a cloud of pink mist through the scope, Jim

was disappointed. No visual clue indicated where the bullet had struck. It hadn't fallen short like the first shot, so it had passed to one side or the other of the melon and continued on some distance into the trees. Another second of study, and he confirmed that McMullen was unharmed, although he appeared frantic.

The slide locked open as the last cartridge case was ejected from the receiver, followed by a waft of gun smoke. The scent of burned cordite hung in the air like a uniquely male fragrance. The magazine was empty, eliminating any idea he had of turning on his captors.

Denson had been watching the display of marksmanship through a pair of high-magnification binoculars.

"Good try, Commander. I commend your marksmanship. However, you failed to hit the target."

Jim rolled to the side. "With a cold bore and only two rounds, that's an impossible shot to make."

"On that point, we agree. The challenge, as I'm sure you know, is gravity. Wind, also. But mostly that mysterious force of attraction between objects bearing mass. Thirty-two feet per second."

"The acceleration due to Earth's gravity," Jim said, matter-of-factly.

"Precisely. Over such a great distance, as we have employed in this demonstration, the bullet actually travels in an arc. Not unlike a baseball thrown from the outfield to the infield. That arc makes hitting a faraway target very difficult—as you have just proven—unless, of course, one uses a computer to calculate the ballistic trajectory. Even then, distance and elevation change must be known precisely. If those calculations are done, there is still the capricious influence of air currents."

"Thanks for the lecture, but there's nothing new in what you've shared. This is part of basic marksmanship instruction."

"Of course it is. But now we have a solution to this problem."

"The PEAP carbine." Jim turned his attention to Reed.

"Exactly. When Mister McMullen shared with me the plan to develop this weapon system, I was astonished. No... unbelieving. In my mind, I never thought it possible that this type of weapon could be real. I mean, it's like a blaster from *Star Wars*! Come on, that can't be real."

Jim drew a breath and raised his eyebrows. "Never say never."

"So true." Denson's excitement was like a child on Christmas morning who'd just discovered a brand-new shiny bicycle under the tree. "Imagine, a small arm that fires an energy pulse. That pulse has no mass, so it is unaffected by gravity or the vagaries of wind. The pulse travels at the speed of light, and it is lethal. That the PEAP carbine will be the dominate weapon on the battlefield for the next century at least, even in urban conflicts, is a given."

"What you have stolen is a laboratory prototype. Years of real-world testing under all conditions must still be completed. The design still needs to be ruggedized. What you have is a barely finished science project. It proves technical feasibility, but not practicality."

"My goals are not the same as yours. Technical feasibility is sufficient for my needs...for now. Please have a seat at the table. You'll find a spotting scope there."

"And just what am I supposed to observe?" Jim had a sickening feeling he already knew the answer to his question.

There could only be one reason why the PEAP carbine was present.

CHAPTER 18

"MR. REED," THE GENERAL SAID. He completed his request with a finger pointed toward of the watermelon. The guards were still vigilant, suppressing any ideas Jim had of trying to escape.

Over the past half-hour since Jim had arrived on the patio, the sun had begun to warm the ground, creating air currents that translated into sporadic mild breezes. The swirling air would have complicated his shooting, but he knew it would not affect the trajectory of the energy pulse.

Billy Reed had adopted a prone firing position for stability, with the PEAP carbine supported on a conventional bipod. Through the sixty-power magnification of the scope, the green striped fruit filled his field of vision.

Jim also had a clear view of the target. He nudged the spotting scope and observed Tim McMullen still shackled to the stump. The detailed magnification showed a terrified expression on the DARPA man. He tugged on his bindings, only to have the handcuffs chaff his wrists.

General Denson waited several more moments to ensure his prisoner was looking at the target.

Then he said, "When you are ready, Mister Reed."

No sooner had the words been spoken when the melon burst into a blossoming pink mist. Green rind was scattered in a twenty-foot radius around the stump. Seven seconds later, a muted *whump* reached the men on the patio. It was barely discernable, and if there had been any conversation or background chatter, it could have been easily missed.

"Very impressive, Mister Reed," Denson said. "Now the second target."

"No!" Jim lunged toward Denson.

One of the guard's rifles barked, the bullet gouging a hole in a brick just inches before Jim's right foot.

He drew to a stop and squared his shoulders. "You can't murder him in cold blood."

"Strong words for a man who has done more than his share of killing. Yes, I'm familiar with your record—at least, the parts that are not redacted."

"I'm a soldier. I've fought for my country, killing terrorists to save lives. I don't kill unarmed civilians."

The general drew his lips into a cruel smirk. "I'm sure you've rationalized your actions, and I really couldn't care less. For the present experiment, call it a sacrifice for the betterment of science. I need to know how effective the energy pulse is on human targets. It's one thing to shoot fruit, but another matter entirely to shoot a man. It's my understanding, from notes shared by Mister McMullen, based on conversations with engineers at EJ Enterprises, that the laser pulse dissipates due to scattering of the radiation from dust and other particles in the air. But to be effective, and shall I say, useful, this weapon has to be able to kill at a great distance. Lethality still has not been proven."

"So what? What is your point? To take a life just to say you've done so?"

"Oh, no, commander. I need to know with absolute certainty that not only can a trained sniper hit the target more than a mile away, but that the shot is assured to kill. One shot, one kill."

Jim shook his head. "You're deranged."

Even though he had witnessed McMullen murder two people at EJ Enterprises, he was sickened by this wanton disregard for life. It wasn't justice—that could only be administered through the courts.

"Whenever you are ready, Mister Reed."

"You don't have to do it," Jim said.

Billy hesitated, and Denson said, "Mister Reed. Please carry on."

Jim looked upon Billy Reed. He was motionless, focused on the object in his scope. His breathing was slow and regular as he gently applied more pressure to the trigger. And then a soft *click*.

At that instant, Jim knew McMullen was dead. Confirmation was received seven seconds later with the arrival of the *whump*, just like had followed the destruction of the melon, only this time he knew it was the man's skull that was destroyed. He couldn't bring himself to look through the spotting scope at what was certainly a macabre scene.

Reed, on the other hand, had confirmed the kill even before the sound arrived. For his part, Denson had observed the demise of the DARPA project manager through a pair of powerful binoculars, the instant the energy pulse had pierced the man's cranium and superheated his brain in milliseconds, resulting in a steam explosion that fractured his skull and expelled the fragments in a ghastly display of carnage.

"Bravo, Mister Reed." The general was giddy with excitement. To Jim, he said, "Looks like the PEAP carbine is one step closer to being a proven, effective combat weapon."

"You sick bastard. You tethered that man in place like an animal to be slaughtered."

"Come now, Commander. Admit it, you were just as curious as I was. Now we both know—it works!"

Filled with disgust, Jim shook his head. "When the opportunity presents itself, I *will* kill you."

General Denson's eyes hardened, his lips drawn flat. "Behave yourself. Else you become the next target."

Billy Reed was standing. He had turned off the power switch on the PEAP and handed it back to the general.

"Shoots right where the crosshairs are laid," he said, with clinical precision. "With no recoil, a follow on second or third shot shouldn't be a problem. But seeing the damage delivered by a head shot, I can't see anyway a target would survive. In my opinion, a one-shot kill is guaranteed."

"Very good. Thank you, Mister Reed. Continue your training, but be ready to move out on a moment's notice. Soon we will enter the final phase."

CHAPTER 19

THEY'D COVERED ONLY A COUPLE HUNDRED YARDS when a sharp boom reverberated off the mountains, followed quickly by a second boom. It was a distant gunshot, no doubt, and it seemed to originate from where Peter and Diesel were headed.

As if the reports portended the assault by law enforcement, which he knew was coming, he checked the GPS again and picked up his step.

"Come on, Diesel."

The handheld unit indicated Peter's present position with a red circle. Then it designated what the unit's small but powerful microprocessor interpreted to be the fastest route to the final coordinates, this indicated by a dashed line overlaid on a topographical map. Peter could separate his thumb and index finger to scroll in or pinch them to scroll out. Of course, the stored map had little information about vegetation, and he hoped he wouldn't encounter any dense stands of young evergreens. If he did, and passing was too slow, he'd have to detour until he could find a passable route, forcing the GPS unit to recalculate the path.

Diesel had no trouble staying by the side of his master, but after an hour his tongue was hanging low and he was panting, no doubt due in large part to the effect of the ballistic vest in trapping his body heat. Peter stopped next to a long-ago fallen tree and poured some water in a collapsible dish for Diesel to lap up. Peter swigged down the remainder of the bottle's contents and checked the GPS unit for the tenth time.

After two more minutes, he threw the empty bottle into the brush, retrieved Diesel's now-empty water dish, folding it and stuffing it into a cargo packet, and then moved forward along the charted route.

⊕

The three Idaho County Sheriff SUVs barreled along the gravel road toward the main gate, guided by a Bureau of Land management employee responsible for patrolling these roads. It was her job to report the condition of these unimproved roads, and to open or close gates, limiting passage when the snow accumulation was deemed too deep for safe transit.

She was familiar with a spur road that connected to a private drive. She'd never traveled it because it was always blocked by a locked gate. A sign on the gate, prominently displayed, proclaimed this to be private land, and that visitors were not welcome.

Being somewhat familiar with the area, the FBI Special Weapons and Tactics Team out of Boise enlisted the BLM employee right away. Based on her recommendation, they gambled that the spur road, which was not on any maps, was a driveway to the location where Commander Nicolaou's phone was last detected.

Two days had already passed by since the murders in Bend and the Oregon governor's kidnapping. Without wasting more time, the SWAT team had helicoptered from Boise to a farm on Boles Road, where they rendezvoused with Idaho County

Sheriff deputies and commandeered three of their vehicles.

The SWAT agents were dressed in olive drab BDUs, wearing helmets of the same color. The nine men, loaded three to each vehicle, carried a mix of weaponry, including MP5/10 submachine guns chambered for 10mm pistol ammunition; Remington 870 twelve-gauge riot guns; SIG Sauer 10mm pistols; and two Remington Model 700 sniper rifles. Given that two men had been murdered—one an Oregon State Police officer—and the Oregon governor had been kidnapped, they weren't taking any chances.

Riding in the front passenger seat of the lead SUV, the BLM employee said, "Just ahead, around the bend."

The driver slowed, forcing the trailing vehicles to do the same. As he rounded the curve, the driver saw the locked gate.

"Is that it?"

"Yes."

He slowed further, covering another two hundred yards before coming to a stop. He keyed his handheld radio and addressed the rest of the team.

"She says this is the gate." Pause. "I'm going to have a look, see how sturdy the lock is. Keep your vehicles back until I signal it's clear."

"Roger," came the reply over the radio. Followed by, "Be careful, Marco."

He eased the SUV to within twenty yards of the gate, then shifted into park, leaving the engine idling.

"Chad, you come with me. Tanner, stay by the vehicle."

Chad was holding his MP5/10 with the barrel pointed down as he examined the drop-off to the side of the spur road. It was steep, like a backhoe had cut a trench in both directions.

"Looks like the landowner was serious about keeping people out," he said. "No way we're going around the gate in anything short of a tracked vehicle. How's the gate look?"

Marco was on one knee, bending over at the waist and looking up inside a large-diameter metal pipe that served as a shield to the padlock latching the gate closed.

"Get the cutting torch," he said.

Chad jogged back to the vehicle, opened the rear hatch and retrieved the oxyacetylene torch set. The two steel bottles of compressed gas were latched into a cradle with a carrying handle, the torch and connecting hoses looped around the bottles. He set the cradle next to the gate latch, put on a pair of welding goggles, and used a flint sparker to ignite the torch. It took only a couple seconds to adjust the flame to a short blue cone. At the tip of the cone, the temperature reached more than six thousand degrees, hot enough to melt steel.

"Cut off the upright just below the lock." Marco pointed to the steel post that the gate was latched to.

It was a section of four-inch pipe, probably anchored in several hundred pounds of concrete.

As the steel pipe heated to the point of melting under the oxyacetylene flame, Chad pressed a lever on the torch that admitted a jet of pure oxygen into the flame, the excess oxygen burning the superheated steel and sending a cascade of yellow sparks away from the torch, into the center of the pipe. He methodically worked around the pipe, the loud hiss of the gas jet marking his progress.

Marco avoided looking at the flame, knowing the brilliant light would ruin his vision. Instead, he looked beyond the gate as far as he could, down the private drive. His MP5/10 was leveled, the weight supported by the sling hanging from his right shoulder. Tanner remained vigilant with his riot gun beside the sheriff vehicle.

A clang of steel and the cessation of the hiss from the torch indicated the pipe had been cut off. Chad closed the gas valves on the bottles and then pushed the gate open. It swung to the opposite side of the driveway.

From fifty yards away, militiamen looked out from concealment, watching the SWAT team approach the gate and then cut it open. As the team leader signaled for the vehicles to advance, the militia opened up with large-caliber rifles, and ARs firing 5.56 NATO rounds.

Marco's SUV, still at the front of the line, absorbed the majority of the bullets. Dozens of rounds pierced the windshield, killing the BLM employee in the first two seconds of engagement.

Tanner dropped behind the vehicle. Marco rolled off the gravel surface into the ditch just as a volley of bullets slammed into the two gas cylinders. The oxygen tank was punctured at the same time two rounds pierced the acetylene tank. The gases mixed, with the concussion from the bullet impacts, setting off the volatile acetylene. The ear-splitting explosion was accompanied by an enormous fireball, killing Chad instantly. His limp body was propelled two dozen feet away, landing before the idling SUV.

The concussive blast mostly passed over Marco, who was at the bottom of the ditch when the detonation occurred. Still, the back of his shirt was singed.

Between the fusillade of bullets and shrapnel from the exploding gas cylinders, the front of Marco's SUV was ruined. A large chunk of metal had punched a fist-sized hole through the radiator, yellow-green antifreeze pouring onto the gravel roadbed. And then, with a tortuous screech of metal on metal, the engine ground to a stop. The sheriff SUV was not going anywhere under its own power.

The next SUV in line accelerated forward, attempting to drive through the line of fire. It made it only as far as the gate before a hail of gunfire killed the driver. The vehicle coasted to the side of the drive and came to a stop when it smashed into a tree. The two SWAT agents ejected and scrambled for cover.

Tanner popped up from behind the vehicle and pumped off a full magazine of buckshot. Then he dropped to reload just as another volley of bullets ripped through the remains of the sheriff vehicle until not a shard of glass remained intact.

CHAPTER 20

THE SHARP CRACK OF GUNFIRE and the deep boom of an explosion cut through the still air. Unlike the previous two distant rifle reports Peter had heard over an hour ago, these shots were close, and to the left of his intended course.

The nuances of sound suggested that different weapons were involved in whatever was going on. Given the rapidity of the shots, it had to mean that many shooters were going at it at the same time. Sure, it was possible it was a group event at a target range. But given the remoteness of their location, he thought that unlikely.

He had a bad feeling about this. It was too much of a coincidence that the FBI was expected to be moving in on the GPS coordinates where Jim's phone was last pinged.

Convinced this was a gunfight, not recreational shooters, Peter was already in motion as he consulted the GPS unit. The topographic map indicated mostly level terrain toward the gunfire. He picked up his pace to a jog, not knowing how much ground he'd have to cover, but suspecting it was less than a mile given the intensity of the reports.

Five minutes later, he approached a small rise, an

outcropping of weathered stone only ten-feet high, with a cap of decayed bark and pine needles that served as soil. Wherever cracks in the stone ledge were wide enough, trees had taken root, many growing to a foot in diameter. Moss and clumps of bunch grass spotted the ground.

The sharp crack of rifle fire, and deeper booms of shotguns, had reached a feverish pitch, assaulting his ears.

"Diesel, stay."

The red pit bull lowered to his haunches in an alert sit. Leaving his backpack behind to reduce his profile, Peter slid the rifle from his shoulder and edged to the top of the rise.

At first, he couldn't see anything other than more evergreens. The ground sloped away gently, so he crawled farther forward until he could follow the terrain downward to a dirt road consisting of parallel tracks worn free of vegetation by vehicles traversing back and forth.

The road wasn't far away—a hundred yards, maybe a bit farther. Between the trees and scrub brush, his field of view was limited to a few narrow corridors. But off to the left, he could see portions of three sheriff vehicles, and all appeared to be shot up. Several men dressed in green BDUs and wearing Army-style helmets stood out against the gravel road and were clustered around the SUVs.

To his front were other men dressed differently. They wore a mix of camouflage hunting clothing and digital-pattern military fatigues. Brandishing semiauto rifles, they were obviously shooting at the SUVs and who Peter assumed were sheriff deputies.

He drew his eye up to the scope on his Weatherby, and dialed up the magnification. The men before him, scattered through the trees, were definitely civilians. There was no conformity in their wardrobe that he expected for law enforcement. Then he swiveled the rifle to the left. He had to scope several men before he saw the subdued black letters FBI on the chest of one of the uniforms. Why the FBI was using sheriff vehicles was a question that would remain unanswered for the moment.

As he watched through the magnified optics, he saw one of the FBI agents near the rear vehicle go down with a gunshot to the leg. Other agents were kneeling beside the SUVs, returning fire as best they could. But the civilians were shooting and moving, spreading out in what appeared to be an effort to flank the pinned-down agents.

Peter knew he had to turn the tide of battle for the FBI men, or they'd be wiped out. Had they radioed for backup? If so, how long until help arrived? He couldn't afford to be apprehended by the agents, or worse. He had to get to the GPS coordinates and rescue Jim before law enforcement took him into custody.

It was the Devil's dilemma, but he made his choice.

He crawled a yard to his right and adjusted the rifle so the forestock was resting on a rocky knob protruding six inches from the dank soil. Motion of men moving toward him drew his attention, and he placed the crosshairs on the nearest. The figure couldn't have been more than eighty yards away, and he had just fired a large number of rounds at the FBI agents before reloading and sprinting from his position of concealment.

Peter eased his fingertip against the trigger, applying ever more pressure, until...*boom!*

The Weatherby barked, jerking the stock into Peter's shoulder, and sending the 225-grain bonded hunting bullet downrange at nearly three thousand feet per second. Less than a heartbeat later, the bullet rocketed through the chest of the gunman, blowing a fist-sized hole in his back. Designed to kill large game quickly, the bullet expanded in the man's chest, dumping energy into his heart, lungs, and aorta. His forward momentum carried him another step before plowing him face first into the dirt.

Without dwelling on the shot, Peter cycled the bolt and acquired another target. It was the same modus operandi. The shooter had fired upon the law enforcement agents before abandoning his position in search of a new spot farther to their side. The man had just settled into a crouch next to a large tree, exposed to the Weatherby.

Boom! Another militiaman down.

Peter had one shot left in the magazine. He ejected the spent cartridge and rammed home his last round before he'd have to reload. He spotted his target. The man was swiveling his head, no doubt trying to make sense of the booming report coming from the side of his position. Peter didn't give him any more time to figure it out.

That was three bad guys down and out. Whether they were dead, dying, or merely wounded made no difference—they were out of the fight. Now Peter had to move. He couldn't keep shooting from the same position for fear of the militia spotting him and then overrunning his location once he stopped to reload. He couldn't put up the volume of fire necessary to keep the gunmen at a distance. Whatever their numbers, it was a lot of guns. Right now they were focused on the FBI they had trapped. He would use their distraction to his advantage.

He slid back behind the lip of the ledge, taking care not to make any sudden movements that might attract attention. After loading three more rounds in the rifle magazine, plus one in the chamber, he put the safety on and placed the sling over his shoulder.

With his backpack in place and the riot gun gripped, he followed the ledge to the right, hoping it would take him to the rear of the militia line. After covering the length of two football fields, the height of the stone ledge diminished and then abruptly disappeared, buried beneath a field of boulders and gnarled pine trees no more than six inches in diameter.

The sounds of battle continued and were definitely to his left. Surmising he was well behind the strung-out line of militiamen, man and canine broke cover and darted forward, dodging the boulders and scrub trees. His aim was a large root ball from a giant pine tree. Judging by the weathering of the tree roots and what he could see of the trunk, the tree had fallen decades ago. The bark had long since flaked away from the trunk, and the branches had decayed and broken off.

What was left behind was perfect for Peter's needs. He took a running jump and landed within the depression left by the root ball. The hole was three-feet deep and ten-feet across. Diesel ran down the sloped side, then looked at his master expectantly.

Forward of their position, the battled raged, giving no indication the intensity was letting up. He placed the shotgun with the butt dug in the loose soil and the barrel wedged against a large root, the bare wood now gray but still solid.

Shouldering the rifle again, Peter placed his eye behind the scope and searched out targets. It wasn't long before he spotted a camo-clothed militiaman with his back against a large tree, ramming home a fresh magazine in his AR rifle. The man then pivoted to the side, bracing the stock against the tree, and squeezed off round after round.

From his prone position on the side of the depression, Peter placed the scope crosshairs on the gunman's back and fired. He cycled the bolt, running home a new round, and then walked the scope back and forth. Each time he found a target, it was the same drill. Aim, steady, squeeze…*boom!* And each time, one of the gunmen went down.

His bolt-action Weatherby was zeroed with point-of-aim shooting out to three hundred yards. And he practiced frequently at that distance, working up his own handloaded ammunition that was optimized for accuracy. At the relatively close distances he encountered now, the shots were fast.

After the fourth militiaman dropped, Peter prepared to reload. From the corner of his field of vision, he saw a man point in his direction. The man yelled something unintelligible to Peter's ringing ears. Then two more men joined the first, and all three raised their ARs and charged Peter, firing while running.

If their rifles had been capable of full-auto firing, they would have stood a chance of hitting Peter. As it was, the volley of fire was poorly aimed, with bullets digging up plumes of dirt around the lip of the hole, and occasionally chipping chunks of wood from the root ball. Every now and then, Peter heard a sonic whistle as a round whizzed by his head.

The trio was covering ground quickly, and once they reached the fallen tree, they'd make short work of Peter. His hunting rifle was no longer the weapon of choice. After leaving it lay, he wrapped a hand around the Benelli M4 shotgun. It was loaded with 00 buckshot—five rounds in the tube magazine and one in the chamber, ready to fire. The load of nine .33-caliber lead balls was a real manstopper, especially at close range.

He pulled the Benelli in tight and sighted through the tritium ghost ring sights. The gunmen still charged, three in a line, side by side, spraying lead at Peter. But so far, only coming close.

Long ago, Peter had discovered that trouble had a way of finding him. And when it did, it got ugly in a hurry. It was in those times that he learned the best defense was a strong, unyielding offense. And so it was that now he had the willpower to ignore the incoming rounds and focus on aiming and squeezing the trigger. At fifty yards out, the Benelli bucked and a load of buckshot hit the man on the left of the line. The lead pellets had spread into a large pattern, and only a few connected with his legs, but it was enough to spill him onto his face. Screams of agony escaped his lips, merging with the sharp crack of gunshots and the smell of burned gunpowder, enhancing the hellish atmosphere.

Too late, the other two militiamen seemed to rethink their strategy of charging into a twelve-gauge shotgun. The autoloading Benelli had already chambered another round even before Peter recovered from the recoil. He adjusted the sights and squeezed. The cluster of shot just missed the gunman, but Peter quickly leveled the barrel and fired again, this time connecting. The buckshot ripped open the man's belly from his groin to his ribcage.

The third and last gunman dropped to the ground and rolled behind a boulder. He peeked around the edge and squeezed off a couple quick shots at Peter. Without the jostle of running, his aim improved remarkably, and Peter had to pull farther back behind the ancient root ball.

He fired the M4 three more times until the magazine was empty. After the last shot, he saw no movement and hoped he had either hit the militiaman or convinced him to quit the assault. He pulled shotshells one by one from the bandolero draped across his chest. Preferring to stay with 00 buckshot for this close quarters work, he shoved shells into the M4 magazine.

With the magazine only half-loaded, Diesel emitted a guttural growl. From experience, Peter knew this to be a warning. He stopped his work and looked up. Another militiaman was bobbing and weaving as he charged the fallen tree. Peter released the slide, sending a load of shot into the chamber, sighted the shotgun, and fired just as the man darted behind a large tree. The cluster of lead balls blasted bark off the tree.

The other gunman rose from behind the boulder and fired again at Peter, forcing him back again behind the protection of the fallen trunk. Although he was safe from bullets, he couldn't see the advance of the two militiamen.

The rounds kept coming in, one after the other, a relentless volley of lead. Peter stuck his head and shotgun around the root ball and fired at the closest of the men, but missed. He ducked back behind the solid wood and shoved another two shells into the magazine. When he peeked around the trunk again, only one man was in sight, and he was close.

The rushing gunman squeezed off round after round. Peter fired the M4 from his hip, hoping for a lucky shot, knowing that even close might be good enough.

The gap closed to less than thirty yards, and Peter knew he was cheating the odds. He was down to his last round when a bullet from the AR rifle tore through his left shoulder. It was a grazing wound, but still hurt like hell. The Benelli sagged before Peter was able to raise the muzzle and fire the last round.

The load of buckshot had hardly spread before blasting into the man's chest, halting his forward momentum. The rifle flew from his grasp and his head whipped back on his shoulders before slumping forward. Then he dropped to his knees, and finally onto his face.

Peter had barely exhaled a sigh of relief when Diesel renewed his snarls. Only now, he was facing toward the rear, away from the charging gunman.

The dog erupted from the depression. Once he landed on level ground, he launched, propelling all seventy pounds of muscle and bone at the intruder who'd attempted to circle the fallen tree.

Diesel collided with the belly of the gunman, knocking him backwards. The man landed hard, the pit bull on top. Teeth flashed white in the sun as they slashed through air. Four canines pierced the first thing within reach, which happened to be the man's arm. As blood flowed over his tongue, further fueling his basic instincts, Diesel whipped his blocky head from

Diesel, but the canine held his ground.

"Anything in that chest magazine pouch?" Peter said.

It was a black nylon affair with pockets for three high-capacity rifle magazines.

"No," the gunman replied. "Emptied the last mag when your dog attacked me."

"Any other magazines or ammo on you? Any other weapons?"

"No, just the rifle."

"No pistol?"

The gunman shook his head.

"Knife?"

"Just this folding blade." The man reached to his belt, and Diesel bared his teeth, taking a step forward and snarling.

"Diesel! Sit."

The militiaman held the folding knife up with two fingers and a thumb. He raised his other arm in surrender.

"Throw me the knife." Peter caught it and pocketed it while keeping his pistol aimed. "How many of your friends are out there?"

"I don't know. Maybe five or six. The cops killed a few, and you killed several more."

Peter nodded over his shoulder toward the primitive road and away from the gun battle.

"Where does the road go?"

"It follows an old dry creek bed for a couple miles."

"Then what?"

"General Denson has a shooting range. It's where we gather to do most of our training."

"That's it? Just a shooting range?"

"There's a storeroom and shop there, too."

"Who's General Denson?"

"He founded the militia. The Cascadia Independence Movement."

"Is that so? And just what is the purpose of this militia?"

"To free the Northwest from the United States. You know, as an independent country. According to General Denson, under Presidents Jefferson, Madison, and Monroe, the government illegally seized the Northwest. It was called the Oregon Country at the time."

"And you believe that crap?"

The man shrugged. "He says he has proof. Some sort of secret document or something."

Distant shouts drew Peter's attention. They seemed to be calling a name. Sounded like *Andy*.

"Is that you?" Peter said. "Andy?"

"Yeah, that's me. When my friends get here, you're a dead man. Your dog, too."

"I don't think so." Peter grabbed the man's AR by the barrel and swung it against the tree trunk once, then twice.

The optical sight shattered on impact. Then he heaved the rifle into the forest.

"Here's what's gonna happen. You're gonna walk that way, toward your friends. If you're smart, you'll get that arm stitched. Diesel and I are walking the other direction."

"What for?"

Peter considered if he should ask this guy if Jim and the governor had been brought there, or somewhere else. It would save a lot of time if he knew exactly where to go. But he already had the GPS coordinates of Jim's phone, and the gunman could share false information to steer Peter in the wrong direction. In the end, he decided not to let on to what he was after.

"Doesn't matter," he said. "Maybe I just want to borrow your range and check the zero on my rifle."

"Whatever. You're as good as dead. You can't hide. This is all General Denson's land. He can do whatever he wants."

"So that would make him...what? King of the Hundred Acre Woods?"

"Sure, laugh all you want. Maybe you'll find a bullet to the head funny, too."

"You got off lucky, Andy. Don't count on it a second time. Now go before I change my mind."

Holding his bandaged arm, Andy jogged away and was soon out of sight. Peter hoisted the pack and both long guns, then trotted off with Diesel. His left shoulder stung, but the pain was manageable. Through the ragged tear in his shirt, he saw the blood had mostly coagulated around the wound. But with every movement some seeped out, creating rivulets down his arm that he could feel but not see beneath the shirt sleeve. Later, when he had time, he'd take a large adhesive bandage from the kit in his backpack and slap it over the laceration.

They stayed on the dirt path, making good time, for about five minutes. When he figured that Andy had probably connected with the remaining militiamen and told them that the man who had attacked him was headed to the range, Peter left the road for the cover of the forest. He'd recalled from the GPS display the dry creek that Andy had mentioned. It looped in graceful arcs, eventually reaching an opening indicated on the map. He knew he could take a shortcut through the forest and cut the two-mile trek on the road down to under a half-mile. But before he disappeared into the tree line, he had a task to do.

He removed a trail camera from an outer pocket on his backpack. Selecting one of the trees alongside the road, he fastened the camera to the trunk such that it was pointed back toward where he'd just come from.

Then he switched the camera on, and with Diesel by his side, evaporated into the shadows.

CHAPTER 21

IN ALL HIS YEARS SERVING IN SWAT, Marco had never experienced such intense gunfire. Every time he stole a glance around the sheriff SUV, a hail of bullets forced him back.

Three militiamen broke free of the forest and took up firing positions in the ditch alongside the gravel road. They'd moved into a flanking position to the left of his column of SUVs, driving him to the rear of the vehicle next to Tanner.

"This isn't good." Tanner fired off three rounds of buckshot through the empty spaces left by the shattered windows.

The flanking militia gunmen fired a volley into the lead SUV, which had gone off the gravel road, into a tree. With one agent dead in the driver's seat, the remaining two agents had ejected themselves to continue the fight from outside the truck. They found themselves on the left side of the vehicle, the wrong side, and were exposed. They spun to the side and returned fire, joined by Marco and Tanner. But the militia had good cover within the drainage ditch.

One of the agents was killed with a round to his head. The other took a rifle bullet in the thigh. He slumped to the side, removing weight from the injured leg, but continued to fire his

MP5/10 until the magazine was empty. Above the din of battle, Marco heard his groans while he reloaded.

"Jones, you okay?" Marco called.

"I'm hit." Jones popped off more rounds at the gunmen in the ditch.

Most of the bullets cratered into the dirt a couple feet in front of the shooters. Several went over their heads and kicked up dust from the gravel roadbed.

"Hold tight, Jones," Marco called. "I'm coming for you."

Tanner grabbed Marco's arm. "Wait! You can't go out there. You'll be totally exposed."

"Jones has no cover." Marco tugged his arm back and prepared to dart around the SUV.

"Wait! I'll go. You're the leader of this team. Besides, those assholes are too far way for anything but a lucky hit with buckshot. You cover me." Tanner laid the Remington 870 shotgun down and then sprinted toward the wounded agent.

Marco kneeled at the rear bumper and fired a murderous barrage from his submachine gun. He ran the magazine empty and reloaded.

Tanner reached Jones and grabbed him by his load harness and dragged him back toward the relative safety of the other vehicles. He was about ten feet from the SUV when he took a bullet through his left arm, shattering the humerus. He lost his grip and staggered before regaining his balance. Then he turned and continue tugging Jones, gripping the load harness with only one hand.

He made it another three steps when a round slammed into his hip, piercing the bone and ripping through his small intestines before exiting his lower back. He collapsed as if his legs had been pulled out. Writhing in pain, he still had a hold on the load harness. He tried to crawl the last two feet, but was unable to make any progress.

Marco kept firing, unaware of the injuries Tanner had suffered. He paused just long enough to glance to his right, expecting to see Tanner coming around the backside of the SUV. But no one was there.

"Tanner!" he called.

Tanner groaned and struggled to get his words out. "I'm... I'm hit."

Marco fired as he back-peddled. When he reached the side of the sheriff vehicle, he saw Tanner and Jones, their blood mingling in a large pool that was soaking into the dusty gravel.

"Rodgers!" Marco called to the agents at the last vehicle. "Rodgers! I need some help! Agents down!"

Marco sprinted to Tanner, who was the closest. He grabbed his load harness and tugged him to the safety of the vehicle. Rodgers appeared alongside and provided suppressive fire while Marco returned to drag Jones back. He knelt beside the front tire, now flat like the other three, and checked for a pulse.

"Shit!"

"What is it?" Rodgers said.

"Jones is dead. Bled out from the leg wound. Probably the femoral artery." Marco focused on Tanner, who's breathing was rapid and shallow, his face pasty. "You're gonna be all right."

But Marco and Rodgers knew better. If backup didn't arrive soon so they could airlift Tanner to a hospital, he wouldn't make it. Shock was already taking hold, and he was losing a lot of blood.

"Any update on our backup?" Marco said.

The radio in his vehicle had been shot up in the first minute of engagement, but the last vehicle, the one Rodgers had been in, had managed to get out a call.

"They were still fueling the chopper. Once airborne, flight time is fifty-five minutes."

Marco dug into his first aid kit and placed antiseptic powder and sterile gauze over the arm wound. As he did, Tanner grimaced in pain as bone fragments sawed against tissue, and then he passed out.

The bullet wound to the hip was a bigger problem. The entry wound was only seeping a small amount of blood, and Marco couldn't see an exit wound. He chanced rolling Tanner onto his side so he could examine his back.

"Shit!" he said again. "Bullet came out the back. He's bleeding pretty bad out the exit wound."

He placed antiseptic powder on a wad of gauze pads and then pressed it against the wound. It soaked up blood fast, and before he could secure it in place with a wrap, the gauze was already soaked through.

"We've gotta get him stable."

Rodgers had continued firing at the gunmen in the ditch. If he couldn't kill them, at least he could keep them in place. Behind and to his left, the other two SWAT agents were still locked in battle, with the militia dispersed among the trees, although their numbers had seemed to thin.

He heard an agonizing scream and knew one of the agents had been hit. There was no longer the staccato of submachine gun fire from the last vehicle, only the deep boom of the twelve-gauge shotgun. And then it, too, fell silent.

"Just us, boss," Rodgers said, although he suspected Marco also understood their dire situation.

"How's your ammo?" Marco said.

"Last mag. How about you?"

"Same. None on Jones. We need to fall back to the last SUV. You go first. I'll cover you."

Rodgers dashed across the opening between the vehicles. He was halfway there when a rifle bullet penetrated his shoulder, smashed through the upper part of his chest, and then severed his spine. Marco heard his body crash to the ground.

Fueled by rage, Marco squeezed of the last of the 10mm ammo and then retrieved the riot gun. He picked the ammo from Tanner's chest rig, stuffing shells into the magazine until it was full. He placed the remainder of the ammo on Tanner's chest. He couldn't see it moving up and down anymore, and checked for a pulse. Dead.

Marco huddled low behind the engine block and front wheel. And waited.

The gunshots ended, and the ringing in his ears subsided, if only a little. He decided to lay prone and look under the SUV for approaching militia. At least he'd get the drop on anyone coming in, and at close range, the buckshot would be devastating.

Good. Just what these bastards deserve.

A minute ticked by. Then two. Finally, he saw a pair of dusty boots coming down the gravel road from the gate. He waited, expecting to see more, but it was just one pair. When the gunman was twenty yards away, Marco jumped to his feet, aimed the Remington, and pulled the trigger. A cluster of buckshot grazed the man's shoulder, causing him to let his rifle slump. Marco corrected his aim and fired again, this time hitting center of mass. The militiaman toppled backwards.

That was the last thing Marco saw. The shot came from behind him. A single bullet to the back of his head.

CHAPTER 22

ACCORDING TO PETER'S GPS, the coordinates for Jim's cell phone were only a couple hundred yards ahead, and bushwhacking through the forest had been easy going. He had been able to stay at a constant elevation, following the natural contours of the land. And the undergrowth—small evergreens, manzanita, rabbit brush, and other small bushes—had been thin. This also afforded good visibility.

Jogging, he'd covered a lot of ground since leaving the dirt road. He had a limited window of opportunity to find Jim, and it was likely that Andy and his pals would be gunning for him. There was also a better-than-even chance that armed militiamen would be at the building. Hopefully not in large numbers.

His phone vibrated, and without breaking his stride, he checked the screen. A collection of four still photos from the trail camera appeared in a two-by-two grid. The camera was programmed to shoot four images when motion was detected—in this case, the pursuing gunmen. Without slowing, Peter studied the pictures and counted six militiamen. Andy was among them, identifiable by the gauze bandage wrapping his arm.

That didn't take long.

If they stayed on the road—and why wouldn't they?—they'd make good time to the shop.

Peter picked up his pace and soon saw a break in the trees. Ahead was a large clearing. And directly in front was a large white Quonset hut. The shop.

After dropping to a squat and resting his good shoulder against a tree trunk, Peter scanned the windowless building for signs of activity. But he only saw one man standing near an entry door about thirty yards away. The man seemed to be deep in thought, smoking a cigarette and pacing, a rifle slung over his shoulder.

He seemed to follow a routine—five steps, then turn, and five steps back. All the while, he kept his head tilted down, drawing regularly on his smoke, and occasionally flicking the ash to the ground.

"Diesel, stay," Peter ordered, then he grasped the Benelli and waited until the guard had just turned his back.

In five steps, the guard would turn again. Peter rose and moved forward in long, silent strides. When he was two paces away, the guard pivoted. At first he didn't see Peter, and he took a step forward.

"Stop," Peter said. "Slide the rifle off your shoulder, then raise your hands."

Looking into the large bore of the twelve-gauge, the guard's eyes widened in surprise. He dropped his cigarette and then the gun. He raised his arms and placed his hands on his head.

"Anyone inside?"

"Yeah, a couple technicians."

"Anyone else? Any prisoners?"

The man pinched his brows. Then realization dawned on him.

"Oh, you mean the military guy and the governor. No, not here."

"Don't lie to me." Peter shoved the barrel of the shotgun closer to the man's face. "I know they're here. I've tracked Commander Nicolaou's phone to this location."

The guard bent backwards, trying to create a larger buffer between his face and the scatter gun.

"No," he shook his head. "They *were* here last night, but General Denson moved them."

"Then why does Commander Nicolaou's phone ping to this spot? You're lying!"

"No. No. General Denson had the phone delivered to the lab."

"Where's the lab?"

Peter felt he'd already spent too much time questioning this man. He didn't have much time before the militia arrived.

"Inside." The guard motioned with a nod of his head. "We call it the lab, but it's really an electronics shop."

"Open the door. Hurry!"

With the muzzle of the M4 pressed against his back, the guard led Peter inside. The interior was brightly lit by overhead lights. A storeroom was to the left, the front of the room open. Floor-to-ceiling shelves lined the three walls. The shelves were loaded with transparent plastic storage containers. Inside many of the containers were packaged foods—protein bars, nuts, dried fruit, and MREs. Other containers held radios, a wide variety of batteries, and even bottled water.

In the middle of the floor were two wood pallets, each stacked with olive-green metal boxes in several different sizes. The smaller containers Peter recognized as ammo boxes for 5.56mm NATO rifle ammunition. He didn't recognize the other boxes, but he made a mental note of the stenciled lettering on the side of one of the largest cases—8-CARTRIDGE, 60MM, HE, M720A1.

Peter was led farther into the building, to a hallway that extended to the left. Several doors were on both sides of the hall, with a side window beside each door. It reminded Peter of classrooms at a school.

The guard stopped at an open door and knocked on the doorframe. "Hey, Darrell."

"What is it? I'm busy." The technician kept his head down on his work.

"My business is more important," Peter said.

Darrell looked up through thick lenses. His jaw dropped and he raised his hands, leaning back in his chair.

"Who else is here?"

"Jack." His voice trembled. "Just Jack."

"And where is Jack?"

"In the breakroom. Said he was going to fix something to eat."

Peter shoved the guard forward next to Darrell. "Where is it? The phone taken from Commander Nicolaou?"

"There." Darrell pointed toward the work surface. "I was ordered to remove the SIM card and download the data."

Peter cast a glance to the bench. A black phone lay there to the right of a computer monitor. Several screwdrivers and small pliers were scattered about, along with electrical wire. Different types of industrial tape and several plastic organizer boxes filled with crimp-on wire connectors lay off to the side. Nearby, in a plastic tray, was a gold-colored nano SIM card.

"That phone?" he said.

"Yes," the technician replied.

Suspecting a trick, Peter asked, "Where's your phone?"

"In my pocket." the technician lowered his hand to his fatigues.

"Slowly. At this distance, I can't miss."

Darrell produced a silver iPhone from his pocket,

displaying it for his captor to inspect.

"Fine," Peter said. "Toss it on the table." Holding the shotgun in one hand, he sidestepped to the workbench and retrieved Jim's phone and SIM card and pocketed both.

"You," Peter said to the guard. "Use that roll of duct tape to secure Darrell's hands behind the back of the chair. Then bind his ankles, too."

"Aw, come on man. I've answered all your questions. I'm not going to cause any problems."

"That's right, because you'll be bound in place on that chair. Now if you don't shut up, you'll have a gag stuffed in your mouth, too."

The technician lowered his head while his limbs were wrapped in heavy tape.

With the guard leading the way, Peter retraced the way he'd entered. As he pushed open the exit door, the guard seized upon his opportunity. He feared having to explain to General Denson that he'd been surprised by the intruder and disarmed. If he could regain the upper hand, then his dereliction of duty would never be known—he'd be the hero who captured this guy, whoever he was.

With his hand on the door, the guard spun his body outside and then raised his leg, planting a powerful kick against the door. It snapped closed, catching the barrel of the Benelli between the door and the jamb, almost yanking the gun from Peter's grasp.

The guard pivoted. His rifle was only a handful of steps away. He completed two strides, then dove the remaining distance, landing hard on his belly. A grunt was forced from his open mouth, along with the air in his lungs.

Peter threw his weight into the door, his shoulder absorbing the impact. Blood flowed anew from the raw gash where the bullet had cleaved the skin.

The door flew open and clanged as it slammed into the exterior wall. The guard had both hands on his rifle, and swiftly rolled onto his back, weapon aimed.

Peter had expected this, mentally chastising his decision not to toss the guard's rifle farther from the entrance.

He had the shotgun aimed at the guard. The two froze, neither trying to provoke the other man to shoot.

"Looks like we have a standoff." The guard pulled his body up to a sitting position. "Drop the riot gun. You can't win."

"I don't think so," Peter said.

From behind the guard, a bestial growl emanated. It started slow and soft, but quickly grew into a menacing snarl. He swore he could feel hot, damp breath on his neck. He hazarded a glance over his shoulder. Less than an arm's length away Diesel stood, motionless as a statue. Only moments earlier, he'd silently crept up from behind. And now he was a coiled spring, ready to release his preternatural strength and dagger-like teeth in a vicious fight to the death.

Peter released a lopsided grin. "Seems I've got you surrounded. Better just release the gun and raise your hands. Slowly, so my dog doesn't consider you a threat."

As if to punctuate Peter's command, Diesel exhaled a growl that sounded like a rumbling volcano ready to blow.

"Okay. Just call him off. I'm putting the gun down." The guard raised his hands and locked the fingers together on his head, but he could still feel Diesel's hot breath. "I did what you said. Call him off!"

Peter stepped forward and grabbed the rifle. With a press of his finger, he ejected the magazine. Then he did what he should have done before, and heaved the rifle as far as he could. Next, he did the same with the magazine, but in the opposite direction. By the time the militiaman recovered and reloaded his weapon, Peter and Diesel would be out of sight in the forest.

A bullet passed Peter's head, issuing a sonic crack. He ducked and focused toward the primitive road. Two riflemen were standing in the open. One had his weapon shouldered, and the other was looking through a pair of binoculars. A volley of bullets peppered the wall of the building, and Peter reasoned that more gunmen would be coming soon.

"Diesel, come!"

With the red pit bull at his side, he once again disappeared into the timber.

CHAPTER 23

PETER AND DIESEL CHARGED EVER DEEPER into the woods, angling away from the road and the Quonset hut. In the distance, men were shouting, rallying the militia force to surround the intruder.

A voice carried through the timber. "He's over there!"

A moment later, two gunshots split the air.

Another shouted, "Cut him off!"

More gunfire followed. Whether the bullets were close, or missed by a large margin, Peter didn't know. He just kept running, hellbent on covering as much ground as fast as humanly possible, seeking better cover from his pursuers.

A copse of young pine trees came into view. It was appealing cover, and Peter angled toward the dense greenery. Diesel's pace was not affected by the closely spaced trees, none more than twelve-feet tall. But Peter had to slow as he was forced to pick through the evergreens. Few of the trunks were flexible enough to bend to the side for passage. And more than once, he felt the sting of a needle-covered branch lashing across his face as he dashed deeper into the thicket.

A tactical error. But the realization came too late.

"He's in there! We've got him trapped!"

Peter stopped and looked around. A couple of the voices sounded close, but most were more distant. He crouched and strained to see through the closely spaced trees, but failed to spot any of the militiamen. Diesel remained at his side, the pit bull's body tense, his gaze darting from point to point, trying to locate the threats.

Then a flash of movement, and Diesel was locked onto the approaching gunman like a heat seeking missile on the afterburner of a jet engine.

"Easy, boy," Peter whispered.

He tried to raise the Benelli, only to have it hang up on the multitude of branches intruding his space. He reversed directions, lowering the shotgun and unholstering his .45 pistol, the long slide providing an extra inch between the front and rear sight for improved accuracy.

As he labored to find a clear field of vison through the young trees, Peter caught a glimpse of motion. The image was fleeting, but real. He raised the pistol in a two-hand grip. A few seconds later, a camouflaged gunman crossed an opening before vanishing behind another tree.

Peter lowered his body and crawled forward. Not only did he minimize his profile, but the long guns slung across his back more easily cleared the branches of the small trees. Diesel imitated his master by lowering his head, a straight line from the ridge of his skull, across his back, to the base of his lowered tail.

"I can't see him," a near voice called out.

"Are you sure he's in there?" replied another.

Heavy footsteps and the rustling of pine needles against clothing drew Peter's attention. He turned his gaze to the side, the source of the noise, and picked up the ambulation of a militiaman probing the perimeter of the copse of evergreens. His head was weaving from side to side as he attempted to peer ever deeper into the thicket, occasionally using the muzzle of his weapon to move tree branches aside for a better view.

The gunman must have assumed the intruder was standing, because his eyes never diverted to the forest floor.

After a tense thirty seconds, the gunman moved on, and Peter exhaled the breath he'd been holding. Slithering forward, he resumed his advance to the edge of the grove. Once there, he planned to wait for the militia to move onward, and then he'd dash in the opposite direction to distance himself from the gunmen.

He thought about the FBI agents. Had any survived? Were they successful in sending out a radio call for backup? How long would it take for backup to arrive? He wanted to believe that help was on the way…that it would arrive at any moment to arrest the militia searching the forest for him. But reason squelched that belief, replacing his hope with a bleak certainty—there would be no help.

No one was coming to his rescue, for the simple truth that no one knew he was there.

No one, that is, except those hunting him.

At the edge of the thicket, half-buried in decaying pine needles and duff, he counted sixteen militia men amble by. And yet voices, some faint, suggested there were more out there. And they weren't giving up the search.

Finally seeing a break with no gunmen in sight, Peter decided it was time to scoot in the opposite direction for a new hide. The terrain sloped uphill, and near the crest about fifty yards away was a rock outcropping. At some time in the past, a tree had fallen and broken in half over the rock. It would provide decent protection from rifle fire, and maybe a clear avenue of escape on the far side of the log.

He looked to his canine companion only to discover a pair of amber eyes staring back at him. Although Peter used verbal commands, mostly he *sensed* a degree of communication with Diesel that went beyond spoken language or hand signals. He didn't believe that the canine could actually read his mind, yet somehow the pit bull seemed to understand Peter's thoughts. Maybe it was his body language, the way he held himself—was he relaxed or tense? Maybe there was a scent, some collection of pheromones, that his body excreted in response to joy or stress or danger or fear. Whatever it was, Peter had no doubt that Diesel understood, that they communicated.

He nodded, acknowledgement for the exchange of information, as much as a signal to be ready. Then he lifted himself to a kneeling position, being slow and deliberate to avoid any jerky or sudden movement that would surely give away his position if anyone was watching.

After repositioning both the shotgun and rifle strapped across his back, and holstering the Kimber pistol, he darted forward. Sprinting, with Diesel keeping pace just to his right, he was halfway across the open ground when he heard a shout.

"There he is!"

Then a rifle barked once, twice. Two bullets gouged out detritus only a yard before him.

Still, he kept running. Even faster now, encouraged by the supersonic projectiles seeking him out.

He didn't slow as he came to the three-foot-diameter log. He adjusted his stride, planted a foot just before the fallen timber, and launched over the top.

Crack!

Peter was still midair when the bullet slammed into his back. The added momentum of the bullet was like a hammer blow, pushing his torso forward, bending him over at the waist. He crumpled to the ground, face down.

Diesel easily cleared the hurdle and circled Peter, searching for injuries, blood. Not finding any, he settled for licking Peter's ear and the side of his face.

Slowly, Peter rose to his knees and unlimbered the long guns. His back ached like nothing he'd ever felt before. Still, it didn't feel like the gunshot wound he'd received through his arm some time ago, long-since heeled. The sharp stabbing pain, the ferocious burning sensation, was lacking.

And then he remembered…the body armor.

He wasn't wearing common soft armor. Suitable for protection from most handgun rounds, soft armor was easily defeated by rifle rounds. The armor Lieutenant Lacey had provided included composite ceramic and steel plates. And it was one of these plates that had intercepted the bullet meant to take his life.

"Oh, man, that hurts," Peter mumbled, recalling Captain Oslund's warning.

Diesel took a step back and dropped to his haunches, seemingly hanging on Peter's words.

Returning his focus to his immediate environment and challenge, he scrambled closer to the log and peered over the top. His courage was rewarded with another shot that burrowed deep into the solid pine log. In that brief interlude, he spotted three gunmen moving on his position.

"This way! We found him!" a voice cried out.

The pathway to egress that he hoped was on the far side of the fallen tree was disheartening. Four-feet-tall Manzanita bushes covered the forest in a dense underlayer. He would have to push through, the hard and stiff manzanita wood impeding his progress with every step. He wouldn't even be able to move at a walking pace, and the impenetrable limbs would make crawling at ground-level impossible.

If he entered the patch, he'd be picked off easily. That was the bad news.

The good news was that he was unlikely to be attacked from the rear. The militia certainly had the numbers to flank his position. And they could overwhelm him with a frontal charge. But that would be costly, as he had excellent weapons, plenty of ammo, and a strong defensive position.

But merely defending the expected attack did not bring him any closer to locating Jim. He didn't travel all this way to fight this crazed group of armed civilians. No. His mission was to find Jim and bring him home. The governor, too, if she was being held in the same location.

In due time, law enforcement would deal with the militia and Tim McMullen. Probably sooner rather than later, given the assault on the FBI raiding party, and the casualties the Bureau had taken.

More shouted commands, and Peter ventured to peek over the log. The militia was assembling, their numbers had more than doubled since his last quick glance.

These guys are multiplying like rabbits.

Obviously, the militia was connected to Jim's kidnapping. Of that, there was no doubt. But where were they holding him? Peter could not be certain his friend was even alive, but he refused to dwell on that thought.

He continued to work the problem. There had to be more buildings, places for the militia leaders and members to meet, eat, sleep. Maybe a barn that was converted to a barracks? Or a house? And what about vehicles and machinery like tractors for maintaining the roads and snow removal. There had to be a maintenance shed and garage. But where?

More rifles barked, and more bullets slammed into the log. Time was running out.

A satellite image of the area would be really handy, but all he had was the topographic display on the GPS unit. With almost no useful intelligence gained from his brief conversations with the electronics technician and the guard, Peter decided on the only remaining course of action.

CHAPTER 24

A VOLLEY OF RIFLE FIRE POUNDED THE LOG and zinged over Peter's head. Any moment, he expected a charge over the open ground. Or maybe the attacking force would split in two and storm from both flanks. Regardless, he knew the end was rapidly approaching.

His mind conjured up memories from decades past, when he and his best friend were still in high school in Sacramento. The innocence of youth as they cranked up the radio while cruising J Street in Jim's 1964 Chevy—his mom's car, actually. His infectious laugh at some unremarkable thing the DJ said. And then Jim was older, a warrior saving Peter's life and that of his father at a remote hunting cabin in the Aleutian Islands.

Time always seems to be infinite, until it's running out.

He retrieved the satellite phone and dialed the number that would connect with Lieutenant Ellen Lacey.

"Lacey," she said.

"It's real bad. I've recovered Jim's phone, but he's not with it. I don't know where they're holding him."

"Where are you?"

"Within a mile of the location pinged by his phone. This

seems to be a private ranch used by a bunch of lunatics who like to play soldier."

"I'll notify the FBI. They can have a—"

Peter cut her off, time was running out. "The FBI already sent an assault team here, and the militia chewed them up."

Lacey paused for a heartbeat. "Okay. What do you need?"

"How about a miracle?"

"Sorry, I can't requisition a miracle."

"Just stay by the phone. Soon I'm going to learn Jim's location."

"What? But how?"

"I'm going to surrender to these assholes."

"Mister Savage, no! You can't do that. They might just kill you rather than take you prisoner."

"I'm open to ideas. But you better speak fast. My position is about to be overrun."

He closed his eyes, and he was in the Sudan, under a blistering sun, low on ammo, and about to be overrun by Janjaweed militia. His son, Ethan, was by his side. When all seemed lost, Jim appeared out of nowhere, leading a squad of SGIT soldiers. Once again, Peter had walked away from certain death.

"But..."

"Look, if they take me prisoner, I'm gambling they'll hold me at the same place where they have Jim and the governor."

"That's nothing more than a guess!"

"Call it what you want. He's always been there for me, for my family. He's saved my life more than once. I can't leave him."

Lacey gave in, knowing she couldn't change Peter's mind. "Assuming you're right, how will you reach me? They'll search you and take the sat phone *and* your cell phone."

"No, they won't."

"No? But—"

"Gotta go. Just stay by the phone."

Peter disconnected the call and then summoned Diesel closer. As the pit bull stood at attention, he shoved the sat phone deep under the body armor wrapped around the dog's chest, the phone resting snug between the loins along Diesel's back and the black vest. Then he removed the palm-sized derringer from his pocket and slipped it into a pouch on the underside of Diesel's chest.

He cradled the canine's blocky head. "Go…hide…follow me."

He released his friend, and Diesel took two steps back, then halted.

Peter pointed to the forest away from the assaulting militia. "Go! Hide. Follow me."

He reared on his hind legs, turned, and ran for the undergrowth. The last image Peter saw was the red haunches dissolving in the dark shadows and heavy foliage.

Peter crawled on hands and knees to lay his Weatherby rifle and Benelli shotgun on the ground more than ten feet away. As an afterthought, he also deposited the Kimber there. Then he raised his hands high above the log.

"Don't shoot!" he called out. "I surrender."

"Hold your fire, men," he heard a voice say. "We've got more than a dozen rifles aimed at you. Stand up real slow. If any of my men suspect your pulling a fast one, they'll shoot you sure as shit stinks. Do you understand?"

"I understand." Peter continued to hold his hands up as he rose to a knee and then to his feet.

When he turned, he saw a line of militia. All were shouldering ARs or AKs. And every one of them was aimed right at his heart.

"Easy now," he said. "My guns are over there." He tipped his head to the left. "Behind the log."

"Clint, check it out," the leader said. "And search him for any blades he might be carrying."

As Clint jogged toward the log, the remaining rifles all stayed locked on Peter. He expected no less.

"It's just like he said." Clint held up first the rifle and then the shotgun before leaning both against the log, in view of the militia men. He leaned over and grabbed the Kimber. "That's a nice pistol, mister. Think I'll keep this for myself." He tucked the long slide .45 underneath his belt. "Carefully now, remove the backpack and vest. And don't try anything stupid, or you'll be dead."

With a shrug, the backpack slid to the ground. Next, he tugged at the hook-and-loop straps at each side of his vest, and the armor came free, dropping around his feet. Then he laced his fingers on top his head.

"Turn around."

Without lowering his hands, Peter turned his back to Clint, who exhaled a piercing whistle.

"Is that an axe?"

"It's called a tomahawk."

"You some kind of mountain man or something? Slide it out of your belt and toss it to the side. The knife, too. Gently. Or I'll put five bullets through your chest before you hit the ground."

Peter used one hand to slide the tomahawk from his belt, and then the Bowie knife from its sheath. He tossed both over the log, out of reach and where the line of riflemen could see.

"Bring him here," the leader said.

With his AR still aimed at Peter, Clint said, "You heard Jacob."

Peter lowered his hands and eased over the log, taking precautions to not appear threatening. With his hands raised again, he marched forward to meet Jacob.

Three men broke free from the line closest to the confiscated weapons.

One grabbed the Weatherby. "This will make a fine elk rifle."

The other two had their hands on the Benelli M4.

"It's mine!" one said.

They tugged on the shotgun and argued like toddlers.

Jacob looked over Peter's shoulder. "That's enough!" he shouted.

Both men stopped arguing, but neither relinquished grip on the Italian riot gun.

"Gather up his weapons, including the knife and axe."

Peter squared his shoulders and locked eyes with Jacob. "The FBI will be back in force."

"We kicked their asses before. We can do it again."

"You can't win. No matter how many agents you murder, there will be more."

Jacob furrowed his brow. Was it concern or concentration?

"Got a phone?" Jacob said.

Peter reached into a cargo pocket and handed over the phone.

Jacob tossed it to a nearby militiaman. "Run it over to the electronics shop. We wouldn't want anyone tracking us to the house." To Peter, he said, "Come on. We're going for a short ride."

At gunpoint, Peter was marched out of the timber, then forced into the back seat of an SUV, sandwiched between Clint and another gunman. Clint had the Kimber .45 pointed across his lap. If he pulled the trigger, a two-hundred-thirty-grain hollow point would crater into Peter's gut, wrecking his stomach and intestines, not to mention his day.

The SUV circled the electronics shop and joined the primitive road. It bounced over the bumpy trail, traveling in the opposite direction from the main road and the gate. Peter craned his neck to look out the side windows. He hoped Diesel would be able to keep up.

About ten minutes passed during which no one said a word. Clint had never taken his eyes off Peter, and the handgun never strayed from his midsection.

The last two hundred yards of road was smooth and paved. The SUV brakes screeched as the vehicle came to a stop under the porte-cochère of the stately home. Clint stepped out first and then gave his prisoner plenty of room to exit the vehicle while the second militiaman followed Clint's example.

As Peter stood on the cobblestone driveway, the massive front door opened and a lanky man stood in the opening.

"Parker, we have a guest," Jacob said. "Please let General Denson know."

With Clint trailing, Peter was led into the foyer. The floor was covered in large irregular-shaped slabs of polished granite. The hewn log walls with ivory chinking, river-stone fireplace, and antique plank flooring were all characteristics of an early nineteenth century frontier homestead. Peter assumed the home's owner had a strong bond to American history.

"Have a seat." Jacob pointed to a leather chair near the fireplace.

Two of the guards stood behind Peter, their rifles in the low ready position, while Clint and Jacob anchored either end of a leather sofa positioned at a right angle to Peter's chair. Clint allowed the .45 to rest on his lap, his finger just outside the trigger guard.

They didn't wait long before a tall man with eyes like obsidian marbles, a gray beard, and hair pulled back in a ponytail, entered the room. Parker was two steps behind, carrying Peter's backpack, combat tomahawk, and both long guns. The Bowie knife was absent, no doubt appropriated by one of the militiamen. He stood the rifle and shotgun against the stone fireplace and laid the axe on the mantel. He dropped the pack to the floor.

Clint and Jacob rose to attention. The bearded man motioned with his hand, signaling his men to be seated.

The man stood next to the fireplace with one hand resting on the smooth stone, and the other on his hip, appraising Peter. His impenetrable eyes and inscrutable countenance gave little away. After noticing the bloodied rip in the shirt sleeve at Peter's left shoulder, he faced Clint.

"Get a clean bandage on this man's wound. I don't want his blood on my furniture and rugs."

Clint stood and left the room in silence.

"I'm Stuart Denson. Although, everyone here refers to me as General Denson."

Peter tipped his head in acknowledgement.

"What is your name?"

"Peter Savage."

"And what is your business here on my land?"

Peter cracked a lopsided grin. "Looking for a friend. I'm sure you know who I'm talking about."

"Why do you think that?"

"Because his cell phone was in your electronics shop. Look, you can pretend to be ignorant, but this will go faster if you just cut to the chase."

The general smiled and folded his arms across his chest. "And just what is it that I'm supposed to know?"

"You mean to say that McMullen didn't tell you who I am?"

With an expression of amusement, Denson shook his head.

"I own EJ Enterprises."

Denson's eyes brightened with understanding. He sensed an opportunity, another sign that destiny was on his side. It would not be easy, and he would have to be persuasive.

"I was there when McMullen stole the PEAP carbine and murdered two men. Video surveillance shows McMullen leading Jim Nicolaou and the Oregon governor into his car, then driving off."

"I see." Denson's gaze never wavered. "So you have a personal interest?"

"*Very* personal."

"Hmm." Denson paced in front of the stone hearth, his chin lowered to his chest.

Clint returned with a large gauze bandage and a roll of adhesive tape. He enlarged the tear in the shirt sleeve and did a decent job of dressing Peter's wound, which was only a superficial laceration. Painful, but not immobilizing.

Finally, Denson said, "Parker. Please bring out a glass of bourbon for my guest. One for me, too."

Peter glanced over his shoulder. The two gunmen were still there.

"Is this how you treat all your guests? Or am I just special?"

"Please accept my apologies. We are too close to completing our mission to take any unnecessary chances."

Parker silently entered with a tray holding two six-ounce tumblers, each with a generous amount of deep amber liquid. Denson placed a hand around each, offering one to Peter, who declined with a curt shake of his head.

"Suit yourself." Denson placed one of the tumblers on an antique tool chest that served as a coffee table, then consumed the contents of his glass in one gulp. "In my family, it's customary to discuss business over whiskey—usually bourbon, in keeping with my historical roots in the South."

"Where is Commander Nicolaou and Governor Bingham?"

"They're both safe and unharmed."

"Where?"

Denson considered the question for a moment. "Here. In this house."

Peter felt a measure of relief. At least he was no longer in search mode. Now it was time to switch to rescue mode.

The general continued. "I'm descended from Captain Meriwether Lewis. No doubt you've heard the name?"

"I have. His accomplishments leading the Corp of Discovery have left a lasting impact on the Pacific Northwest."

"Indeed. And does the name Nova Albion mean anything to you?"

After a moment of thought, Peter said, "No. Should it?"

"I suppose that depends on whether or not you are a student of the early history of this continent. You see, in the middle part of the sixteenth century, Spain and England were locked in a cold war. Francis Drake was busy plundering Spanish treasure for the benefit of Queen Elizabeth. In 1579, Drake's ship, the *Golden Hind*, landed at what is now northern California and southern Oregon. He claimed the Northwest for England, naming it Nova Albion. Nova means new, and Albion is an archaic name for the island of Great Britain."

Peter shifted in his chair, crossing his ankles, and presented a look of boredom. He had zero interest in a history lesson, and only wanted to find Jim's exact location, and the governor. Exactly how he would escape with them would be the next problem to solve.

One step at a time. "Fascinating, I'm sure."

"Oh, it is. Nova Albion was later renamed Oregon Country. In 1848, it was officially recognized as the Oregon Territory, part of the ever-expanding U.S., under the Monroe Doctrine. Except that the annexation of the Northwest by the United States was illegal."

"And I thought I'd heard all the conspiracy theories."

"Not just a theory. In fact, I sued the U.S. Government, demanding the independence of the land that was formerly the Oregon Territory—large portions of Wyoming and Montana, and all of Idaho, Washington, and Oregon. Essentially, from the Continental Divide west to the Pacific Ocean, and north of the California and Nevada borders. Well, not all of this land—I'm willing to concede that the Willamette Valley and Western Washington may remain part of the Union."

"Very generous."

"I'll ignore your sarcasm. But yes, it is generous—also practical. I have no use for those liberal population centers. And the military bases in Washington are best left to the U.S. I have no use for them, either."

"I find it extremely unlikely that any court will find your claims to be valid, and reverse more than one hundred fifty years of history. I can't think of any legal precedent for what you are trying to achieve."

Denson shrugged. "The case has been presented to the Tenth Circuit Court of Appeals, and I'm expecting a favorable decision soon. In part, based on a lost journal of Meriwether Lewis from the final months of his life before he was murdered."

"Let's suppose, just for the moment, that the Tenth Circuit agrees with you. Do you think President Taylor and Congress are just going to let the Northwest go?"

"Not directly, no." A sly grin spread across Denson's face. "But political winds can change very quickly. Even…suddenly."

Peter placed a finger against his chin. "Let me guess. You really aspired to be a professor of early American history, but had to settle for running this group of toy soldiers, using a make-believe title."

The creases in General Denson's forehead deepened, and his lips pinched in a tight line.

"You'd be wise not to antagonize me. I can be a very magnanimous friend, or a ruthless adversary."

Peter rolled his eyes. "Yeah, sure. I've heard it all before."

CHAPTER 25

GENERAL DENSON SETTLED BACK in the plush leather chair opposite Peter. He placed both hands on the arm rests and slid his legs forward, outstretched, until his head was cradled in the leather backrest. When he finally spoke, his voice was calm, his tone measured.

"What legacy do you expect to leave when your life is over?"

The question caught Peter unprepared, and he stared back, his mouth agape at a loss for words.

"It's a valid question—surely one you've thought about. I can see you're not an ordinary man. What you did, coming here to rescue your friend, goes far beyond what almost any other person would do. You are loyal, courageous, intelligent. And you're not easily intimidated, either. All attributes I highly prize."

"Am I supposed to say thank you?"

Denson smiled, then rubbed his hands back and forth on the armrests. He drew in a deep breath, then exhaled and pulled himself upright in the chair.

"I have a proposition for you. Come join me and—"

"And what?

"We are on the eve of changing history. A new nation is about to emerge, born from the forges of liberty and justice— values that have seemingly been eroded by Congress and the president. This is your chance to have future generations speak your name in the same breath with George Washington, Thomas Paine, Samuel Adams, and Thomas Jefferson."

Peter made a show of looking over his shoulder. "I can think more clearly without fear that one of your guards might brush his finger a bit too hard against the trigger and put a bullet in my back."

With a wiggle of General Denson's fingers, the two militiamen behind Peter lowered their rifles.

"How do you propose to found a new country?" Peter said.

"The United States is fractured like never before. Both the Republicans and Democrats are seeing their parties torn in two by new voices demanding radical change. The separation between the haves and have-nots is enlarging. Racism. Civil unrest. Pandemics. Even global climate change is pitting urbanites against those who earn their living from working the land—farmers, ranchers, and loggers. Congress is locked in stagnation, unable to move any meaningful legislation forward. Meanwhile, the federal courts are no longer content with interpreting the law, choosing instead to apply their own political agenda and bias in cases of constitutionality and federal governance."

"Tell me something I don't know. But what does any of this have to do with me or your grand plan to give birth to a nation?"

"As I have already explained, the Cascadia Independence Movement—I like to call it CIM—has a nice ring, doesn't it? Anyway, we have already filed suit against the government, and our claim is presently before the Tenth Circuit. As of this morning, tragic events have, sadly, caused the loss of one of the judges hearing the case. I'm told she was unlikely to rule in our favor, and—"

"What did you do to her?" Peter started to rise, but a strong hand on his shoulder shoved him back down into the chair.

"Oh, my. I didn't say I did anything to the judge. But the news this morning is reporting that a commercial aircraft she and her husband are believed to have crashed shortly after takeoff from the airport in Hailey, Idaho. Reports are that there were no survivors. A terrible tragedy, really."

Peter's eyes widened. "You expect me to believe that was just an accident?"

Denson waved a hand dismissively. "It doesn't matter what you choose to believe. I was only going to say that we believe a more sympathetic judge will take her place. As I insinuated before, I am confident the court will rule in our favor. That will provide the legal precedence for separating the Northwest from the Union. We will call our new country Nova Albion, in honor of Sir Francis Drake."

As the depth of Denson's homicidal madness was sinking in, Peter decided the best thing to do was play along. In any case, he doubted that further antagonizing the general would be in his best interest, certainly not when the rifles brandished by his guards could be raised at a moment's notice.

"Seems like you have it all figured out. Still, you haven't said what evidence you have that will sway the court to side with your claim."

"The possibility that I'm right has titillated your interest?" Denson tented his fingers.

Through squinted eyes, he studied Peter for a moment. What he saw was rapt curiosity.

He turned his head enough to make eye contact with Jacob. "Please get the journal. You'll find it on my desk in the study."

Jacob departed the great room and returned in short order

with a bound book. The cover and binding were worn and in varied shades of brown, from tan to dark coffee. He offered the book to Denson with both hands, suggesting its importance.

Denson laid a solemn hand on the cover. "This is the personal journal of my fourth great-grand uncle, Meriwether Lewis. The last words he wrote are in this book."

"Given the historical importance of that document, shouldn't it be in a museum?"

"It's a family heirloom. Why would I surrender it to a museum?"

Peter rolled his eyes.

"Anyway, this is a firsthand account of the final months of Meriwether's life. He was governor of the Upper Louisiana Territory at the time. His servant, John Pernier, recovered this journal, along with what was left of his possessions after he was murdered at a lodging house and tavern called Grinder's Stand—more commonly known as an inn—on the morning of October eleventh, 1809."

"You make it sound like he was robbed."

"He was. He'd borrowed a considerable sum from Major Gilbert Russell at Fort Pickering to cover his expenses to travel to Washington D.C. That money was never found in his possessions. Some important papers were missing as well."

"Papers? Like what?"

"Correspondence with Thomas Jefferson. And some pages from this journal had been removed, torn out."

Peter shifted in his chair, pulling himself upright. "I'm no expert on Meriwether Lewis, but I did watch a documentary about his death. They said the consensus at the time was that he committed suicide. And he had a history of depression. Didn't the innkeeper's wife say Lewis was acting strangely on the night of October tenth?"

"Many people wanted Meriwether dead. Some argue

that General James Wilkinson, who preceded Meriwether as governor of the Upper Louisiana Territory, ordered his assassination. However, only speculation is offered for motive, vague suggestions that Meriwether was about to reveal secrets of nefarious dealings by Wilkinson, or some such thing. Robert Grinder, the owner of the inn, was absent on October tenth and eleventh. Perhaps he arrived and found his wife, Priscilla, with Meriwether, and in a fit of rage, killed him. Doubtful. Besides, there isn't a shred of testimony or other evidence to support such wild accusations. Although it is interesting that Robert came upon a considerable sum of money shortly after the death of Meriwether. And then there's Major Neelly. He was the U.S. Agent to the Chickasaw Nation. He and his servant joined Meriwether at Fort Pickering at what is now Memphis, although at the time it was called Chickasaw Bluffs. Neelly was known to be deeply in debt. Sometime during the night of October ninth, two of the pack horses wandered off and Neelly volunteered to round them up. He instructed Meriwether to continue on with the two servants and to stay at the first house he came upon occupied by white people. Late in the afternoon of October tenth, Meriwether arrived at Grinder's Inn. He was given a room, food, and drink. That night, he was shot twice. He died sometime during the morning of October eleventh. Neelly showed up shortly thereafter, and according to Priscilla Grinder, he did not appear very surprised by Meriwether's death."

Peter searched his memory for relevant details from the documentary he'd watched, but all he could recall was how odd it sounded that a man would shoot himself both in the gut and in the head in an attempt to commit suicide.

He said, "How is it that Lewis could inflict two gunshots upon his torso and head, and not die quickly?"

"The answer to that question is as elusive today as it was

more than two hundred years ago. According to Neelly, Meriwether had shot himself in the head and in the side of his abdomen. He reported that Patricia Grinder claimed the two gunshots came close together in the early morning hours, and yet Meriwether didn't perish until many hours later, well after dawn. Later, in 1811, a longtime friend of Meriwether, a naturalist named Alexander Wilson, traveled to Grinder's Inn and interviewed Patricia Grinder. She reportedly said that the gunshot wound to Meriwether's head had blown off part of his skull, exposing his brain. She also told Wilson that she'd seen, through the cracks in the log wall, the gravely injured man wandering around the compound in search of water. The night of October tenth was nearly moonless, so how Missus Grinder could see a man wandering around in the dead of night is unknown. Also, is seems unlikely that, suffering from two gunshots, including one to the head, he would in any way have had the strength to walk around, or the coherency to search for water."

Peter spread his hands. "I agree that it seems unlikely Lewis attempted to kill himself. Still, I doubt this mystery can ever be solved, given the passing of two centuries since his death."

"My family has petitioned the Tennessee State Park Service to allow his body to be exhumed for proper analysis, but so far our reasonable requests have been refused."

"I can't help you, and I still don't see what any of this has to do with me."

Denson smiled, his hand still resting reverently on the journal. "Would you care for that bourbon now, Mister Savage?"

The general raised an eyebrow toward his guest, but Peter declined with a shake of his head. As much as he wanted several shots of whiskey, he needed to remain sharp.

The general picked up the tumbler from the coffee table and sipped the contents.

"What I want from you is your creative genius. You see, when we split away from the United States as a free and independent nation, we will have to fend for ourselves. It is much better to do so from a position of strength, wouldn't you agree?"

"You want me to supply you with small arms?" Peter chuckled. "I've got to believe you have all the weapons you need. Well, not artillery and aircraft, but you have enough rifles and ammunition to take over a third-world country. I glimpsed your stockpile in that Quonset hut of yours, and I saw your men murder those FBI agents."

"Yes, we are well armed. But you can offer something no other military force in the world has."

Peter bobbed his head. "I see. You want me to give you the blueprints for the PEAP carbine. Why don't you just copy the prototype you stole? You don't need me."

Denson placed the journal on the coffee table and stood, pacing in front of the hearth.

"True, we can copy your new weapon. But there is always a chance that my engineers will make a mistake or two when attempting to reproduce your prototype. And then there is the question of testing it and improvements. Something, I dare say, my engineers and technicians are unlikely to succeed at. Besides, I have more immediate plans for your weapon."

Peter narrowed his eyes, the furrows between his eyebrows growing more pronounced.

"Let's say—for the sake of argument—I agree. What do I get in return for my fealty?"

Denson stopped his pacing and locked eyes with Peter. His lips, peeking through the opening in his beard, drew back in a smile, although the mirth did not extend higher on his face.

He said, "What everyone wants—unimaginable wealth and power."

Peter was almost enjoying himself, and if it had not been for the matter of finding Jim and the kidnapped governor, he would have prolonged the discussion, playing Stuart Denson for the shear amusement factor. Still, there was something missing, something the general had not shared yet, and he believed it might be the key to unlocking the motive for the crimes that had transpired.

He said, "Your offer is intriguing, and I have a very active imagination. I doubt you can pay that much money."

"There's one way to find out."

"Why should I believe your word? You've shared nothing but a retelling of known history, none of which is going to sway the Tenth Circuit Court to rule in your favor. Not to mention, convincing Congress to go along with the court's decision."

Denson considered the statement. He realized that in this mental game of poker, his guest had just gone all-in and called his hand. He took down the remainder of his bourbon in one shot.

"Very well." He sat in the chair, picked up the last journal of Meriwether Lewis, and opened to a page marked with a strip of green ribbon. "What I am about to share has never been spoken outside the walls of this dwelling. It is a tale of conquest. Of riches gained and riches lost. A tale of greed and power. Men have died to keep this information secret. Are you prepared?"

Peter drew in a breath and exhaled. Finally, he hoped to learn what Denson and the CIM were really aiming to achieve.

"I am."

CHAPTER 26

DURING HIS YOUTH, Stuart Denson was often regaled with stories of the frontier that inevitably included tales of his fourth great-grand uncle, Meriwether Lewis. Being an only child growing up on the family ranch in western Idaho meant he spent hours and hours exploring the forest and observing nature. He often imagined he was a pioneer, pushing into the largely uncharted Northwest, sometimes a member of the Corps of Discovery, sometimes a lone trapper.

He was homeschooled until such age as he could be enrolled in a military school in Boise. There, he completed his studies, graduating near the top of his class. After finishing his education at Virginia Military Institute, having majored in history and minored in rhetoric & writing, he turned down a commission in the military, preferring to return to his family ranch in Idaho.

Thanks to generational wealth acquired through ranching and leasing grazing rights on their vast estate, young Stuart Denson was not compelled to find employment. So rather than putting his education to use, he learned from his father how to manage the land and the several dozen head of cattle. Fifteen years later, in his early thirties, he'd look back on that time as his indoctrination into conservative ideology.

Two months following his thirty-eighth birthday, his father became gravely ill from influenza.

For three days, his father's sickness worsened, with fluid collecting in his lungs, causing fits of raspy coughs. On the morning of the fourth day, the elder Denson called his son to his bedside. Burning up with fever, and barely able to get a half-dozen words out between prolonged bouts of coughing, he squeezed his son's hand. Stuart noticed how weak his grip was.

In a hoarse voice, his father said, "In my dresser, top drawer, there's an old book." He labored for a full two minutes in an uncontrollable cough before he was able to continue. "It is the key to decode—"

The croup overcame him again. When it subsided, it seemed to have weakened the old man even more.

"The journal. In my gun safe."

"I don't understand," the younger man said.

"You will," his father whispered. "It is our heritage."

As Stuart gazed upon the frail features of his father, a lump lodged in his throat. The man who had always been full of vigor and fortitude, now was as frail as a newborn. The cycle had come full circle.

"Please send your mother in."

Stuart left his father's room to relay the message to his mother. That was the last time he spoke to the old man. He passed, holding the hand of his wife of sixty years.

Five days later, Stuart's mother died from a massive heart attack when she was toweling off after her morning shower.

Alone for the first time in his life, he buried his parents on the family property at the edge of a meadow bordering a seasonal creek. He sat there next to the heaped earth, in silence, for the remainder of the day. About three hours after sunset, he walked back to the log house. Overwhelmed with grief, he plopped into a chair, closed his eyes, and wept uncontrollably.

He awoke to bright rays of light beaming in through the large picture windows. Surprisingly, he felt rested. Although the sorrow was still there, it had subsided. Recalling his father's words, he went upstairs to the bedroom. Upon entering, he stopped and looked upon the bed his father had died in. He shook the memory, strode to the dresser and opened the top drawer. Socks, boxers, and bandanas were folded and stacked, filling the compartment to the top. One by one, he removed the articles of clothing, images of his father flashing through his brain, a kaleidoscope of memories—most happy, some sad. He felt ghoulish searching through his father's personal effects.

He scraped his fingers scrapped against the bottom of the drawer, but there was only varnished plywood. Even after removing all the clothing, there was nothing—no book, no papers.

He stared at the blank plywood for a minute. The words were soft but distinct. Maybe his mother had removed the book. If so, where would she have placed it?

No. He dismissed the thought. The instructions were clear, and his father would have also informed his mother of his final directive. She would never disobey him.

Stuart removed the drawer from the dresser and turned it over on the bed. Nothing. Then he turned it right-side up again. It appeared that the bottom was just a bit higher than the blanket the drawer was resting on—*A false bottom.*

Flipping the drawer over again revealed a set of metal nails securing the thin veneer to the drawer frame—easily overlooked. He made a fist and smashed it into the brittle wood. With a crack, it gave way. Stuart pulled away the pieces of veneer, exposing a cavity only an inch deep. There lay the book. It was the size of half-sheet of paper, with a cardboard cover and stitched binding. The edges of the lined sheets were yellowed and brittle. He thumbed through, page by page. On each sheet, written in pencil by his father's hand, was the key to a cipher.

Then he remembered…the gun safe. There was something in it—a journal. He ran down the stairs, nearly slipping on the treads. In the mudroom near the rear door was an antique steel safe. Standing five-feet tall and resting on four large cast iron wheels, it had two side-by-side doors. He'd memorized the combination by the time he was seven, and a quick spin of the dial—left-right-left-right—was followed by a crank of the brass handle and a tug. First the right door, and then the left door pivoted open on greased hinges.

A noteworthy collection of rifles and shotguns in a wide range of calibers from small to large, and periods from late nineteenth century to contemporary, were stood upright with the barrels cradled in felt-covered slots that ran along both side walls and the back. His father's revolvers and semiauto pistols were wrapped in padded leather cases and stacked to one side. In the center of the safe were three metal file-storage boxes stacked one atop the other.

Some of his mother's jewelry, nestled in velvet-lined polished wood cases were in one of the metal boxes, while others held tax filings, social security cards, his parents' marriage license, bills of sale and receipts, and other important documents. He emptied all three metal boxes, searching for a journal, or something resembling what he thought a journal would look like.

After only a few minutes, he found a leather-bound book. It was about an inch thick and large, maybe ten-by-twelve inches. A leather cord was wrapped twice around the book and tied in a bow knot at the center of the cover. He drew it close and smelled the age—a musky odor combined with earthen mildew scents.

Gently he pulled both ends of the leather cord and opened the cover. At first he couldn't believe what he was looking at. Written on the first page, in faded ink and graceful script, were the words *Personal Journal of Meriwether Lewis.*

He slumped to the floor of the mud room, his back against the wall, and turned page after page. Each was filled with the same script, handwritten in ink that had long since lost its black shade. Although the letters were familiar, the words didn't make sense.—*Encryption.*

For the rest of the day and into the night, Stuart sat at the dining table and began the laborious process of decoding the journal with the key from his father's dresser drawer. The first entry in the journal was dated February 20, 1809. The last entry was dated October 10th of the same year.

The task of decoding the personal records of Meriwether Lewis became an obsession that occupied most of Denson's waking hours for the next month. When completed, he'd transcribed the daily observations and thoughts of the famous explorer, as recorded over the final months of his life.

CHAPTER 27

STUART DENSON CLEARED HIS THROAT. "To fully understand the secret I am about to share, you must understand that the first few decades of the nineteenth century were filled with intrigue as colonial powers vied with each other and the fledgling United States for a piece of the North American continent. You are familiar with the Monroe Doctrine?"

"I am," Peter said.

"Good. Then you know that the purpose of this cornerstone of American foreign policy was to block European nations from having a toehold in North America. Although the Doctrine was formally established in 1823, two decades earlier the same principles dominated the ambitions of President Thomas Jefferson. This is why he pounced on the opportunity to purchase the Louisiana Territory from France, and then quickly organized and funded an expedition to map the major water ways all the way to the Pacific Ocean. This, of course, was the Corps of Discovery, or, as more commonly termed, the Lewis and Clark Expedition." He moved the green ribbon from the open page of the journal, then ran his finger halfway down the paper until he found the line he was looking for. "The revelation begins here. The date is May twenty-fifth, 1809. But one can't make sense of the words written on the page—it has to be deciphered. I've memorized this passage, but in fairness to your search for truth, I'd prefer you read the wording after it was decoded." Denson stood and looked expectantly at Peter. "If you will follow me to my study, I will allow you to read the translated document."

With Denson in the lead, Peter followed, along with his entourage of guards. A pair of glazed doors separated the study from the great room. A simple oak desk stood in the middle of the room, surrounded by bookcases packed so full of books, magazines, and papers that the shelves sagged under the weight. Denson opened a desk drawer and removed a large bound book with a green cover, twice the size of the original Meriwether Lewis journal. He placed it on the desktop and opened it. After finding the page he sought, he backed away from the desk, and with a motion of his hand, invited Peter to step forward so he could read the pages.

"These pages don't appear to be very old," Peter said.

"Correct. This is the transcription of the original journal. I completed this work about twenty years ago. Take a look."

Peter leaned closer. "I see lines of text that seem to make sense, separated by lines that are gibberish."

"Exactly. I copied the historic journal line by line, keeping the pagination the same so that it would be easy to cross reference the two books. Beneath each coded line of script is the actual message. Had it not been for the cipher key that my father created and passed down to me, I may have never been able to complete this work."

"How did your father know what the key was for breaking the code?"

"He was always good at puzzles, and especially enjoyed crossword puzzles. But his skills were not unique, and others have also broken the code used by Lewis and Clark."

Peter sat in the desk chair and began to read the section aloud:

> May 25, 1809—I fear that agents sympathetic to the policies of James Monroe are plotting to secure my papers, including the journals of our Corps of Discovery expedition to the great Pacific Ocean. Not the least of which is the Lost Treaty between the Viceroyalty of New Spain and the Emperor of all the Russias. As a reasonable precaution, I shall take to carrying two pistols, loaded with fresh powder and ball, on my person at all times.

His voice trailed off as he finished the passage, and he raised his gaze to Denson's. "What is this Lost Treaty?"

"I asked myself the same question when I first translated that page. Obviously it was important at this stage of Meriwether's life, since he capitalizes the term. But it is not mentioned again until July fourth. Please continue. Although one could spend days, weeks, studying this historical record, we do not have that luxury. The most important entries are bookmarked."

Peter flipped forward through the pages until he found the entry for July fourth:

> July 4, 1809—It is appropriate on this day marking the anniversary of our independence from the tyranny of King George and the British Parliament, that I vow to deliver the Lost Treaty to His Excellency Thomas Jefferson, for he has the wisdom and honor to ensure this issue, which is of paramount importance, will be handled correctly and expediently. Today I sealed the Treaty in a parfleche using beeswax to secure the cover. Under

the misguided influence of James Monroe, I fear our young nation is about to embark on a perilous course of action from which there may be no return. I am deeply indebted to my friend, the Big White, Chief of the Mandan Village Mitutanka, for entrusting me to bring the Lost Treaty to Monticello and to Washington so the truth can be learned by all.

"Why Jefferson?" Peter said. "I mean, didn't Madison succeed Jefferson, being sworn in as the fourth president in March 1809?"

"Yes, you are correct. But Madison had fought a difficult campaign against Monroe. Perhaps Meriwether believed Jefferson would be in a stronger position to lobby Congress. Perhaps Meriwether simply trusted Jefferson more than he did Madison."

Peter drew back the side of his mouth. "Maybe." He paused, still staring at the printing on the open pages. "You said Jefferson might have been in a better position to lobby Congress. To what end?"

"Exactly! Please continue to the next bookmark:"

August 30, 1809—It is not with paranoia that I say Monroe's agents are closing in on me. In the morning I will depart for Fort Pickering with my servant. From there, we will travel down the Mississippi River to Fort Adams, where I will meet my good friend Amos Stoddard before continuing onward. The Lost Treaty cannot fall into the hands of those foul devils, lest all be lost.

Peter looked up into Denson's black eyes, each a bottomless well into the man's soul. "Is there any evidence that men were trying to rob or kill Lewis?"

"Of course. The Spanish dispatched forces on three separate occasions between 1804 and 1806, to halt the advance of the Corps of Discovery and arrest Meriwether Lewis and William Clark. As we know, all of those attempts failed, and the expedition was successfully completed. This is an important point to remember. As to agents of James Monroe pursuing Meriwether? No, there is no direct evidence that implicates the future president on this charge. However, there can be no doubt as to what Meriwether believed to be true."

Peter advanced to the next and final bookmark:

> October 10, 1809—I am consumed with a growing dread for what is to come. The loss of our stock last night was not a quirk of luck so much as it was a manifestation of the dastardly plot. I dare say it was foolish of me to so readily accept the offer of Major Neelly to accompany me to Nashville, for there can be no mistake that he is in lot with Monroe's wretched bidders.
>
> I am greatly indebted to Mrs. Grinder for granting permission to stay at her husband's inn, but am concerned that Mr. Grinder is far from home. I am alone, save for my servant and that of Major Neelly, and Mrs. Grinder.
>
> It will be a nearly moonless night, having just had the new moon the previous night. The house is sturdily constructed of aged chestnut logs, and if the devils chose to attack in pitch darkness, this is as good a defensive position as any, and much superior to any I would find on the road. I have instructed my servant to bring a flask of powder to my room, and my rifle. Being a veteran of military campaigns,

as well as experiencing numerous skirmishes with the Natives, for whom I mostly hold no grudge, I am ready to fight and do not fear death.

If I should fall to the gun or the dirk, the knowledge of the Lost Treaty cannot be allowed to pass with me. To this end, I have placed the parfleche holding this most important document, with the personal effects of my servant, who is a trustworthy and free man. The Big White, known by his Mandan name of Sheheke-shote, chief of the Mitutanka Village, came upon the Lost Treaty in the summer of 1806. The Mandan people are generally welcoming, and our experience with these people was always friendly. During the return of the Corps of Discovery, we rested at Mitutanka village for several days in August, barely a month after the Big White was visited by diplomatic parties from the Viceroyalty of New Spain and the Empire of Russia. There, they signed a secret treaty pledging the mutual defense of their claims to Upper Louisiana all the way to the Pacific Ocean. The next day, Lakota warriors descended upon the Russian emissaries. Their fate, as well as that of the Spanish delegation, remains a mystery. However, the horse belonging to Ivan Kuskov, Commerce Counselor of the Russian-American Company, walked into Mitutanka village some days later. Inside a leather case tied to the back of the saddle was a copy of the Treaty. The Big White told his people this was an omen, a gift in return for their generosity to strangers.

Peter pushed back the chair and rested his palms on the edge of the desk.

After a moment of reflection he said, "I don't get it. Even if this Lost Treaty is real, and it is a pledge between Spain and Russia to come to the defense of the other if there was an attack on their colonial claims in North America, what does that have to do with your claim to split off the Northwest from the United States?"

Denson moved to a bookcase along a side wall in the study. He placed his fingers under the edge of a shelf, and with a sharp pull to the side, displaced a hidden locking pin. The center section of shelves, from the floor to the ceiling, pivoted open silently to reveal a steel vault door. To the side of the door, where a knob would be expected, was a brass wheel with three spokes. The tumbler was centered, and he entered the combination with practiced efficiency, then spun the brass wheel and opened the heavy door.

He walked through, followed by Peter and two guards, entering a modest-sized room. Covering the lower portion of the largest wall were wide stainless-steel drawers, each with a keyed lock. Denson removed a set of keys from his pocket and opened the top drawer. It was two-feet deep and served as a table when pulled to its full extent.

He removed a pair of white knitted gloves from the drawer and pulled them over his large hands. A single aged document lay in full view. It was written in Spanish and Cyrillic script, which Peter assumed was Russian. The paper appeared thick and stiff, yellowed with dark brown ink.

"Over time," Denson said, "the ink has faded from black. The parchment is still in excellent condition, thanks in part to conditions it is kept in. This room is climate-controlled, and of course, exposure of the Lost Treaty to light is very limited."

"This is the Lost Treaty referred to by Lewis?" Peter said.

Denson pointed to the bottom of the document. "You see the signatures? Nemesio de Salcedo, Commandant General of the Provincias Internas, signed on behalf of Spain. And the other signature is that of Ivan Kuskov—"

"Commerce Counselor of the Russian-American Company."

"Correct. Kuskov was the senior assistant to Aleksandr Baranov, Chief of Administration of the Russian-American Company. Between 1808 and 1812, Kuskov led five exploratory expeditions to the Pacific Coast of North America. I've hired many expert linguists to translate the document—each just having a small piece of it so no one person would know the complete contents of the treaty."

"And what did you learn?"

"This document is more than a mutual defense pact. It is a binding obligation that neither Spain nor Russia will concede their colonial claims without the consent of the other party. You see, at the beginning of the nineteenth century, Europe was in turmoil. The Napoleonic Wars were coming to an end, Latin America was rising against Spain and Portugal, tensions were growing between the United States and England over trade, in part because Jefferson refused to allow the Monroe-Pinkney Treaty to go before the Senate for ratification. In North America, the Louisiana Purchase was made. Russia had only a tenuous hold on the Pacific Northwest, constantly being challenged by the British. And New Spain was being eroded. In secret, Russia and Spain entered into negotiations to ensure that neither Britain nor the U.S. would whittle away at their claims. They quickly negotiated the treaty, signing it in the summer of 1806. But in a historic stroke of bad luck, both diplomatic parties were set upon by hostile Native Americans, who were the original inhabitants of all of North America. Understandably, they were not at all happy by the encroachment of white settlers, regardless which country they were from."

Peter kept his gaze on the document. "I assume both parties

had a signed copy of the treaty to return to their respective governments. But I've never heard of such arrangement between Spain and Russia."

"Exactly. Whereas I have one copy, the other was apparently lost—maybe when the delegations were decimated and scattered by the attacking Indians. We may never know. However, that the ruling governments of Spain and Russia never learned of the success their diplomats had achieved became a windfall for James Monroe by opening the door, following the War of 1812, for the United States and England to conspire to negotiate treaties with each of Spain and Russia, independently of the other. For Spain, it was the Transcontinental Treaty, signed in 1819. And for Russia, the Russo-American Treaty of 1824. These treaties led to the annexation of the entire Northwest, at that time called the Oregon Country, into the United States, thereby realizing a unified nation from shore to shore, just as Monroe had envisioned. Of course, California and the Southwest came along a few years later, giving shape to the continental United States as we now know it."

Peter felt a growing sense of dread as he came to fully comprehend the enormity of this revelation.

In a tight voice, the words scraping past the knot in his throat, he said, "And here you have proof that the Russo-American Treaty and the Transcontinental Treaty were unlawful."

"Irrefutable. The kind of proof that will cause history books to be rewritten, and will change the boundaries of the United States."

Peter met Denson's gaze. "Wait a minute. For the sake of argument, let's say you're right—"

"I am right. Of that there is no doubt."

"And the court accepts your argument. Then wouldn't it follow that the land claim would revert to Spain and Russia?"

Denson smiled. "Very good. You are indeed a clever man. However, what you have failed to grasp is that the government will never allow the former colonial powers to have a foothold on the North American continent."

"I don't get it. Why are you trying so hard to have a legal ruling that the U.S. doesn't have a legitimate claim to the Northwest if you also believe the government will never give up the territory. What's the point?"

"You have misconstrued my statement. When faced with either relinquishing the territory to Spain and Russia, or agreeing to allow the Northwest to become the new nation of Nova Albion, a friendly ally of the United States, I think the choice will be obvious."

Peter's steel-gray eyes shed any indication of curiosity, replaced with an inescapable coldness.

"You're crazy if you think the government will ever agree to your proposal. Historical rights are often clouded by vague, incorrect, and competing claims."

Denson raised a finger. "But I will have the consensus of the Tenth Circuit Court. And that of the president and the president's cabinet."

Peter scoffed. "President Taylor will never support your arguments."

With a sardonic grin, the general said, "Like I said before, the political winds can change quickly. And with them, so can those in power." He extended his hand to Peter, but the gesture was refused.

"I'm not going to work with you or help you. My loyalty is to my country, not to some crazy lunatic with delusions of grandeur."

CHAPTER 28

"LOCK OUR GUEST UP IN THE BASEMENT," General Denson said. "And get the men prepared to leave within the hour. The FBI will return, and we must be gone before they do. I've wasted too much time on this fool. I won't sacrifice our schedule, is that clear?"

"Crystal clear." Jacob grabbed Peter by the arm and pulled him from the study.

Flanked by the guards, this time with rifles aimed at Peter despite his prior protests, they marched to a locked door— ordinary in appearance, by any measure. Jacob produced a key and unlocked the passage. Then with Peter in the lead, they descended the staircase.

The room was large but spartan, comprising a gray concrete floor, stone walls, and hopper windows high on one wall. A single bulb hung from the center of the ceiling, providing meager illumination. The space was cool, like a cavern.

As Peter took in the room, he saw the figure sitting on a cot. The figure was in the shadows and had escaped Peter's notice upon first survey. But now he recognized the man as Commander James Nicolaou.

"Boy am I glad to see you." Jim strode across the basement floor to greet his friend.

"Don't make yourself too comfortable," Jacob said. "Neither of you will be here long."

Then Jacob and the guards ascended the stairs, leaving the sound of the deadbolt locking to echo off the hard surfaces.

Jim rose from the cot and grasped Peter by the shoulders, causing a wince of pain from his bullet graze.

Seeing the distressed appearance on his friend's face, Jim said, "Are you okay?"

"Yeah. Just a minor cut on my shoulder. It'll be fine."

"Looks like McMullen clocked you pretty good," Jim said, referring to the scabbed-over scrap on Peter's nose.

The bruising, especially under his eyes, had mostly faded over the past two days.

"Yeah, he did."

Jim took a half-step back. "What are you doing here?"

"I came to rescue you. Figured it was time to repay my debt. By my accounting, my ledger is pretty lopsided in your favor."

Jim frowned. "It doesn't look like your plan is working very well. Unless you have something in mind that I'm not aware of."

Peter smiled. "That, I do."

"Care to enlighten me?"

"I've got backup. Once night falls, we call for help."

"Really? Get a phone and call for backup. Just like that."

"Well, yeah. Why not?"

"You have a phone? Because I don't."

"No, they took mine, along with the rest of my gear and weapons. But don't worry. I've got this figured out." Then, changing subjects, Peter said, "I had a quick walk through a portion of that Quonset hut they call the shop, or the electronics lab. It's where they had your phone."

Understanding suddenly registered with Jim. "Lieutenant

Lacey tracked my phone and fed the coordinates to you."

"Exactly. Anyway, these militia guys all seem to be well armed with rifles. That's serious enough. But they have some other military hardware as well. I saw a number of olive-green crates. One was labeled 8-CARTRIDGE, 60MM, HE, M720A1. I made a point of memorizing it. I assume that means something to you?"

Jim let out a low whistle. "Bad news. Those crates are holding sixty-millimeter mortar rounds. High explosive. Can do a lot of damage against lightly armored vehicles, and devastating against personnel. If they have the rounds, they must also have the mortars. Which means Denson has artillery he can deploy against any law enforcement who storms this compound."

"And that's not all. Denson shared with me that he plans to split off the Northwest from the rest of the nation. He's pursuing a legal challenge, and he might have assassinated a judge from the Tenth Circuit, the court hearing his lawsuit, to influence the decision. He claims to have a lost treaty that proves that Russia and Spain could not have lawfully ceded their colonial claims to the U.S., leading to the formation of the Oregon Territory."

"Never saw *that* coming."

"I believe Denson has assembled this militia to achieve his goals by armed conflict, if necessary."

Jim started to pace. "Denson was definitely after the laser weapon, the PEAP carbine. But why? There has to be a good reason. He took a tremendous risk in having two men murdered, plus kidnapping the governor. But what can one weapon do if he's facing an overwhelming number of law enforcement officers, not to mention the national guard?"

Peter shook his head. "I don't have an answer for you."

The sound of the deadbolt clanking open interrupted their conversation. Heavy footsteps accompanied two guards down the stairs.

One of the men pointed at Jim. "Come along. Time to go."

"Go where?"

"I guess you'll find out when you get there," the other guard said, and both men laughed.

Peter followed Jim to the base of the stairs, but was blocked from further advance with a rifle barrel jabbed into his sternum.

Jim held out a hand toward his friend. "Not now."

Peter stood solemnly as Jim trudged up the stairs with the guards close, but not too close, behind.

After the door was closed and locked again, muffled voices filtered down to the basement, but the conversation was unintelligible. Several minutes later, the dialog ended and Peter heard a car engine fire up. He rushed to the hopper windows, which were opened slightly. Standing on his tiptoes and stretching his neck, he saw Jim ushered into one of two black Suburbans. Denson was in the front passenger seat. Other men were loading large duffle bags into the back of each vehicle, straining under the weight of each nylon satchel.

Loaded down with men and gear, both vehicles drove away.

Why is it important to take Jim?

Peter explored every square-foot of the basement. A small table next to the cot Jim had been sitting on held a paper plate with a half-eaten peanut butter sandwich. The bread was soft, suggesting it was fresh. Two bottles of water, one opened and mostly consumed, were also on the table.

Continuing his search, he found nothing that might be fashioned into a makeshift weapon. He had to give Denson credit—the guy was thorough.

Peter assumed he was being held captive in case there was any problem with the PEAP carbine. Somewhat confident that his life was not imminently at risk, he lay down on the cot, folded his hands under his head, and closed his eyes. He would not sleep deeply, still acutely tuned in to any sound that could remotely be associated with a threat. Nevertheless, even a small amount of rest was welcome.

⊕

Something in Peter's subconscious stirred him from a light sleep. The sunlight had vanished, and now only gray filtered light seeped in through the hopper windows. He checked his watch—almost 8:30 p.m. The sun was setting, and darkness would envelop the forest and the log house.

Soon it would be time to act.

With the hopper windows opened to their fullest, he could hear sounds from outside the log house with ease, and he hadn't heard any vehicles come or go since the two SUVs had driven off late in the afternoon. Occasionally he'd heard the squeaking of floorboards overhead, and muffled voices now and then. How many guards were left in the house? How many were nearby in case of trouble?

Imponderable.

As he lay on the cot engrossed in his thoughts, the door at the top of the stairs opened. A giant of a man soon appeared carrying two bottles of water and a paper plate holding a peanut butter sandwich. His bald head was supported by a short, thick neck, and his barrel chest and large biceps strained to break free of his tight-fitting T-shirt. A Beretta Model 92 pistol was holstered on his hip.

After ordering Peter to lay face-down on the concrete floor, he set the food and drink on the table, gathered up the previous remains, and turned to leave.

"How long until I can leave?" Peter said.

The man stopped and looked back over his shoulder. "That's up to General Denson."

Then he climbed the stairs and locked the heavy deadbolt.

Peter ate half the sandwich and consumed the contents of one of the bottles.

CHAPTER 29

May 12

SEVERAL HOURS LATER, Peter's internal alarm clock woke him from a restless sleep. He checked his watch—just before 3:00 a.m. Without making a sound, he moved the cot underneath the hopper windows. The opening was large enough for him to stick his arm through.

After extinguishing the solitary electric bulb, he squatted on the cot with his head just below the open windows, listening for any sounds of guards nearby. All he heard was an occasional bark and howl of coyotes in the distance.

Reasoning that General Denson departed the house with a contingent of his men, plus Jim, to execute some part of his plan—whatever his plan was—he was counting on security being lax. So far, that appeared to be the case.

He stood again and peered out the window. By now, his eyes had adjusted to the darkness. After another several minutes, and failing to see any guards, he let out a shrill whistle. It was short, hopefully short enough to avoid attention.

A dark shape arrived just outside the open window. Peter extended his hand through the exterior bars and was greeted with a warm, wet tongue.

"Good boy, Diesel." He ran his fingers along the soft fur on the side of the canine's face, then retracted his arm.

He broke the seal on the bottle of water and then worked the bottle and his free hand back out the window. As he poured the cool liquid in his hand, Diesel lapped up the entire contents. Next, Peter offered the half-eaten peanut butter sandwich, and it was snatched from his fingers and consumed in three ravenous gulps.

With only the illumination of a half-moon high in the night sky, he could see the wagging red tail. He used both hands to pet the pit bull's neck, and worked his way to the vest still wrapped securely in place.

"Good boy," he said again, his words soothing to his best friend.

Then he slipped his fingers under the vest and removed the sat phone, and then the Bond Arms derringer.

With a final pat to the head, he said. "Go, hide."

Diesel trotted off into the darkness, his hunger and thirst satiated for the moment.

His luck had held, and no guards investigated the brief exchange.

Timing was crucial, with little margin for error. He turned the light on and squinted until his eyes adjusted. The sat phone powered up normally and appeared to be in good condition, so Peter turned it off to save battery life, and stashed it under his pillow. Then he checked the derringer, ensuring a shiny brass .45 ACP case shown in the breach of each of the two barrels, before stuffing the tiny gun into a hip pocket.

Time to wait again.

Unable to sleep any more, his thoughts drifted until they ultimately landed on the events at EJ Enterprises when this entire mess started. If only he'd removed the battery pack from the PEAP carbine, rendering it harmless, before handing it over to McMullen. What he'd done, handing a loaded weapon to another person, violated one of the fundamental tenants of firearms safety. *Always ensure the gun is unloaded before giving it to another person.* That is the rule. And he'd broken it, triggering two murders, two kidnappings, and a cascade of events with, as yet, unknown consequences.

He'd been far too trusting, recklessly so. Although he'd been working with Tim McMullen for months, they'd never met prior to that fateful project review and demonstration at his company. Sure, McMullen had been pleasant enough and always professional during their phone calls and email exchanges. But Peter didn't know the man. At best, he could characterize McMullen as a professional acquaintance. Only now, too late, had he understood that McMullen was taking advantage of his trust, all the while plotting his criminal strategies.

A contingent of armed security would have halted the execution of the plan just as it started. Especially with the governor present, he should have insisted on an adequate number of state troopers in the dignitary protection unit. At least three men. They could have been positioned around the governor during the demonstration, increasing the response-time window so at least one of them could draw on McMullen.

And if the state police refused to provide the necessary number of men in the governor's protection detail, then he could have hired a security team. He should have done that.

The minutes slowly ticked by, and then the hours. Between pacing and resting on the cot, he passed the time with his mind oscillating between remorse and optimism. But even his optimism was moderated by not knowing where Jim had been taken. He'd come so close to rescuing his friend...or had he? Although he'd been confined to the same basement room with Jim, would they have been able to escape? That thought just led to more despair.

At last, the blackness at the hopper windows turned to gray, and then to bright daylight. Morning had broken. And now he had to clear his mind and focus on getting away with the governor. Hopefully, Lieutenant Lacey would have an idea how to find Jim.

Another thirty minutes passed, the only sounds from outside were those of birds and squirrels making their morning rounds in search of food. The rumbling in his stomach reminded him how little he'd eaten over the past twenty-four hours.

The sound of metal sliding against metal as the deadbolt was opened was followed by the hulk descending the stairs. As before, he carried a sandwich on a paper plate, and two bottles of water. Peter looked at the sandwich from a dozen feet away and noticed the smear of brown butter between two slices of bleached-white bread.

"Peanut butter again? Doesn't anyone in your kitchen have even a little imagination?"

The giant man sneered at him. "What were you expecting? Steak and eggs?"

"Yes. With coffee and orange juice."

The guard bellowed a laugh. "That's pretty good. I'll be sure to tell the chef."

"You can also let him know that I intend to file a complaint with the manager."

"Knock yourself out," the guard said, between chortles.

He turned and took one step toward the stairs.

Peter said, "That's far enough. Put your hands up."

The giant turned back to Peter, his eyes sparkling with amusement. The levity drained away when he saw the tiny gun with the big bore held by his prisoner. He considered his options. In two strides, he could be on Peter. But the gun gave him reason for pause—a miss would be next to impossible at this close distance.

"Tell you what," the guard said. "Drop that pea shooter, and I won't pound your face into the concrete floor."

"Nah, I don't think so." Peter stood with his weight on his left leg, his body turned slightly to the side. "But let me counter your offer with mine. Drop your pistol on the cot, nice and slow, and I won't have to put a forty-five hollow-point though the middle of your chest."

The guard roared in laughter again, then lowered his head and sprang forward, a blur of motion. He was surprisingly fast for a big man.

Peter pushed off with his leg and pirouetted just as the mountain of muscle brushed past. Then he adjusted his aim and squeezed the trigger.

A brilliant flash of incandescent gasses escaping the muzzle coincided with an ear-splitting report and a violent kick that yanked Peter's hand backwards, bending it at the wrist. Even before the barrels came horizontal again, Peter cocked the hammer. He leveled the derringer at the guard, who was staggering on his feet. The bullet had penetrated the side of his chest and was lodged in a lung.

Wheezing, and with frothy blood working out between his lips, the guard turned, preparing for another charge. His rage-filled glare drilled into Peter with burning malevolence. Given the opportunity, Peter knew the man would relish killing him.

"Last warning," Peter said.

The giant opened his arms and charged a second time, only much slower. Peter fired the second and final bullet. It thudded into his chest, destroying his heart and stopping against the man's spine. He dropped with a hollow thump, and his head cracked against the slab floor.

After returning the derringer to his hip pocket, Peter

grabbed the guard's Beretta and the sat phone, then ascended the stairs two at a time. He inched the door open, expecting to find guards rushing to the sound of gunshots. But the room was empty.

Leading with the pistol, he crossed the great room and then climbed the staircase. On the second floor was a short hallway with a door at each end. The door to the left was open, but the one to the right was closed and locked with a surface bolt. He dashed for the door, threw open the bolt, and barged in.

Governor Bingham was standing in the farthest corner of the room, her eyes moist and filled with dread.

"It's okay governor. I'm not going to hurt you."

She recognized him from a few days ago as the owner of EJ Enterprises, and she relaxed.

"I thought you were one of those men, here to kill me."

"No. We're leaving."

"But…how?"

"Never mind. I don't have time to explain. We have to go— now."

Peter held out a hand, and she stepped forward.

In the hallway at the top of the staircase, Peter waited several heartbeats to be sure no one was coming.

"I don't understand where all the guards are," he said.

"The big guy—he told me his name is Mike—said it was just him and the red-haired man."

"Parker. I met him yesterday. You and Mike friends?"

"He seems nice enough. He brought my meals. We talked a little."

"Okay. Let's hope he didn't tell you lies."

They descended the steps and Peter went to the fireplace. There, he retrieved his gear—body armor, backpack, tomahawk, rifle, and shotgun. He checked the long guns. Both were still loaded. The bandolero with his spare shotshell rounds was missing, but there was still a box of rifle ammo in his pack.

The governor was standing near the center of the room, watching for guards while Peter slipped into the vest.

"Watch out!" she screamed, as Parker entered and leveled a pistol at Peter.

The shot rang out and the round hit Peter in the chest, causing him to exhale a grunt and twist his body. He pointed the Beretta at his adversary and fired three shots in rapid succession. The first two missed, but the third clipped Parker in the thigh.

The militia man dropped to one knee and tried to reacquire Peter in his sights. But Peter had slipped behind the leather sofa. He rolled onto his side and looked under the couch. He had a clear view of Parker from the waist down, and he fired again, sending a 9mm bullet into the man's groin. With an agonizing scream, he fell to his side. Peter fired a final shot into his chest.

He rose from behind the sofa and approached the downed man. With a finger against his ceratoid artery, he confirmed the man was dead.

"What size shoes do you wear?" Peter said to Bingham.

"What?"

He stripped off the lightweight hikers and tossed them to her. "Take 'em. Might be better than your dress shoes."

She glanced down at her polished black shoes with one-inch heels. "I don't want to wear his boots. He might have some sort of foot fungus or something."

Peter shoved the handle of the tomahawk through his belt.

"Look, foot fungus should be the least of your worries under the present circumstances. Personally, I'm more concerned with ingesting an overabundance of lead, if you understand my meaning."

She nodded, still holding the boots away from her body.

"It would really be helpful if our priorities were even just a little bit aligned. Okay?"

She nodded again.

With mounting concern that the gunfight would draw a bevy of well-armed militiamen to the house, Peter grabbed Governor Bingham's hand.

"We have to go." He yanked her arm to follow him to the front door.

All the vehicles that had been parked under the porte-cochère the previous day were gone.

Won't be leaving by car.

Peter whistled, casting his gaze back and forth. He whistled again, and this time Diesel broke cover and ran to him.

Governor Bingham recoiled.

"Don't worry. He won't hurt you."

She appeared to relax.

"This is Diesel. He's my buddy."

She pointed at him, still standing behind Peter. "He's wearing body armor, just like you."

"That's right. I don't want him to get hurt."

"You mean to tell me you brought your dog here on purpose? Knowing he might get shot?"

"I trust him. He's my backup. Besides, it's not like I had a long list of names to choose from."

"Why didn't you just let the police handle this? They should have been here already—stormed this place and arrested everyone."

"They were here yesterday. FBI. And Denson's militia killed them all."

Bingham placed a hand over her mouth, stifling a cry.

"Now listen to me. I'm all you have. Well, me and Diesel. And if you don't start listening, and stop asking questions, we won't make it out of here."

CHAPTER 30

PETER POWERED UP THE SAT PHONE. "Lieutenant. I have the governor. We're safe at the moment, but we need help to get out of here. Can you track the location of this satellite phone?"

Lacey sighed in relief. "Affirmative. Keep the phone powered on, and I can trace the signal. Are you still in western Idaho?"

"Yes, only a couple miles away from the location you tracked Jim's phone to."

"Is the commander with you?"

The pause that followed her question was answer enough.

"Do you know where he is?" she pressed.

"No. He was taken yesterday by about a dozen militia members, including their leader. A guy named Stuart Denson. He fancies calling himself *general*."

"Taken where?"

"I don't know! I saw Jim get into one of two black Suburbans with Denson and other militiamen. They drove away from my present location, along with a bunch of gear."

"What type of gear?"

"I don't know. It was all packaged in large duffle bags.

Judging by the way the men handled the bags, they must have been heavy. Weapons, I assume."

"Okay. Will you be safe at your location until I can get a backup team there and an evac bird for the governor?"

Peter looked down at Diesel, who was sitting at his feet, turning his head side to side. Always on guard and searching for danger.

"Yes. We can hold out here for a while. We're at a log house. I believe it's owned by Denson. And he said he owns this land. It's a huge tract. And..."

"Yes?" Lacey said.

"And he claims to be a descendant of Captain Meriwether Lewis."

"Is that important?"

Peter's mind was now spinning in a new direction. He chastised himself for wasting hours last night wallowing in self-pity instead of working the problem.

"It may be," he replied.

Another pause.

"Denson has this crazy belief that the United States illegally negotiated treaties with Spain and Russia to acquire the Pacific Northwest during the early part of the nineteenth century. He even showed me documents, including a lost journal of Captain Lewis, to support his conclusion."

"Even so, other than historical significance, what does that have to do with kidnapping the commander and Governor Bingham, and stealing the PEAP carbine?"

"He said he intends to split the Northwest out of the U.S. by a legal secession that would be recognized by Congress and the president. He said he even has a case pending before the Tenth Circuit Court of Appeals."

"My God!" Lacey said. "It's all over the news. A judge hearing this case, and her husband, were onboard a commercial plane flying out of Hailey, Idaho, yesterday morning. The plane crashed during takeoff. There were no survivors. The investigation has just begun, but classified preliminary forensics reports circulating the intelligence community indicate the aircraft was shot down with a missile. Most likely a shoulder-fired Stinger. That's why the DIA, NSA, CIA, Homeland Security, and others became involved."

"That bastard. That's what he meant."

"What?"

"Yesterday, Denson told me about the accident, and he knew the judge was killed. He must have been involved. How could he know that so soon after the plane crashed?"

"This still doesn't get us closer to locating Commander Nicolaou."

"I suggest you get your team of analysts working on it. I need to get the governor inside this log house and set up a defensive position in case more militia try to show up."

"Understood. Keep the phone powered on. I'll trace the signal and get help coming."

With the sat phone in a cargo pocket, he led Governor Bingham from the porte-cochère, back inside.

"Why are we going back inside the house? We should leave before more men arrive, or before General Denson comes back."

"Just relax. Help is coming. We can mount a stronger defense here than if we are running through the forest. Besides, I don't think you're the type to go running around the woods. Are you?"

"No. Born and raised a city girl." She still held the boots away from her body. "If we're gonna stay here until help arrives, then I don't need these." She tossed the hiking shoes toward the fireplace.

Peter did a quick walk through the entire house and then

returned to the great room.

"I'll set up a sniper hide in the kitchen. The window looks out over the driveway—it's the only approach likely to be taken by cars or trucks."

"How do you know that?"

"Because the drive circles under the porte-cochère. It doesn't go anywhere else."

Unconvinced, Bingham pushed harder. "What if they have all-terrain vehicles, and come out of the forest?"

"ATVs are loud. We'll hear them from a half-mile away."

Peter moved for the kitchen and placed his rifle on the center island. One end of the island was about five feet from a large window. Then he hefted the tomahawk in one hand and smashed the glass, leaving an opening where the glazing had been mounted. He used his range-finder binoculars to determine the distance to key landmarks along the drive—a tree with a distinctive bend to its trunk, a boulder beside the gravel road, a gray, bark-less stump, the end of a split-rail fence. He memorized these distances.

He was nearly prepared.

"Have you ever fired a gun?" he said.

Standing just inside the kitchen, her arms clutched across her chest, Bingham nodded. "Yes, many years ago. I was dating a lobbyist for the NRA. He took me to an indoor range a couple times."

"How'd that go?"

"I'm left-wing. He was right-wing. It didn't last."

"I meant the shooting. Do you remember what you learned?"

"Yes, but I don't like guns."

He handed her the shotgun, and she took it with both hands.

"You don't have to like them. You just have to be ready to use this one."

With trepidation, she said, "Okay."

He showed her how to hold the Benelli snug against her hip, barrel level.

"This is the safety." He pointed to a button with a red ring just behind the trigger guard. "It's on now because you can't see the red. Push it again, and now the red shows. This means the safety is off and the shotgun is ready to fire. Do you have that?"

"Yes. Red for danger, meaning the safety is off."

"Good. The safety is off now, so keep your finger away from the trigger and don't point the barrel at me. If anyone comes through the front door, you shout at them in your meanest, most authoritative voice to drop to their knees and raise their hands. If they don't, if they keep coming for you, point the barrel at them and squeeze the trigger."

"I...I don't think I can kill anyone." She extended the Benelli, offering it back.

"Listen to me." He placed both hands on her shoulders, staring into her eyes, which showed genuine fear. "If you don't, they will kill you first, and then me. These people aren't playing around. Whatever they're up to, they have already committed murder and kidnapping. I truly hope you don't have to pull that trigger. But you must be ready to do so. I can't watch the front and back at the same time."

She nodded and drew the shotgun against her waist. "Okay."

Diesel sauntered to her side and leaned against her calf.

"I think he likes you."

She forced a smile, but it faded almost immediately. "I'm supposed to meet with President Taylor tonight. He'd invited me and the governors of Washington and Idaho to discuss issues important to the Northwest. On the agenda is gun control. Kinda ironic, don't you think?"

"Why do you say that?"

"Well, let me see..." She raised the muzzle of the shotgun.

"You know that a gun is simply a tool for a specific job. Nothing more, nothing less. How that tool is used is up to the person holding the weapon."

"Listen, I've heard every argument in the book, so don't patronize me. I'm hardly in the mood."

"Suit yourself. I was just answering your question. Besides, it could be worse."

"And what is that supposed to mean?"

"Well, you could be holding an assault rifle and not a shotgun. Your constituency should cut you some slack for that."

She scrunched the side of her mouth and raised an eyebrow. "You're not making me feel better. If anything, this experience has made me even more determined to get guns out of the hands of civilians. Only our police and military should have these types of weapons."

"Tell you what. If you can disarm the criminal gangs and extremist militia groups first, I'll be number one in line to surrender my guns. But for now, can we just focus on surviving the next few hours? And to do that, I need you to be ready to use that scatter gun."

Diesel lowered his haunches and sat next to the governor.

Peter pointed at the dining table. "Take a chair and make yourself comfortable. Diesel has taken to you, and he will protect you."

"He's just a dog."

"Wrong. He's my buddy. And he's saved my life more than once."

She sagged into an oak dining chair. She looked much older than her years. Exhaustion was taking a toll, as was the emotional turmoil and anxiety.

"I just want this nightmare to end."

"Soon. We don't have to wait long. A helicopter is coming for us. And I suspect a second one loaded with FBI agents is going to storm this property and arrest or shoot every member of the militia."

"Why didn't they come already?"

"Because they didn't know our location."

"How do they know where we are now?"

Peter produced the satellite phone. "Because I have this. I hid it on Diesel before they took me prisoner. They can track the location of this phone, same as with a cell phone."

He climbed upon the island counter and lay flat, assuming a prone shooting position and wincing as the wound on his shoulder was flexed. The granite surface was cold and hard, so he folded a few kitchen towels to place under his elbows. After sighting through the scope to determine the appropriate amount of elevation for the barrel, he placed his day pack on the counter and laid the forestock across the makeshift rest. After a few adjustments of the contents to reduce the height of the pack, he did one final check. He had a good sight picture down the drive, all the way to the curve, where it continued into the forest and out of sight.

The final act of preparation was to remove a box of shells from an outside pocket of the pack. He dumped the contents on the granite surface. Twenty rifles cartridges, plus the three in the Weatherby.

Wasn't much if the militia came at him in force.

CHAPTER 31

LIEUTENANT LACEY SUMMONED her best analyst, Mona Stephens, to her office. A petite blond with a mind every bit as sharp as her boss's, Stephens had exhibited tenacity and brilliant insight that was pivotal in solving several previous challenging cases. And like her boss, Stephens was married to the job, preferring the challenges of her career over the challenges of a relationship.

She took a seat in front of Lacey's desk, and knew by the look on the lieutenant's face that this was something more than routine business. Perhaps some news about Commander Nicolaou. Although she and the other members of SGIT—analysts and operators—were aware of the basic information surrounding the kidnapping of their commander, the lack of details led to rampant speculation. For professionals used to dealing in facts, this only served to amplify their frustration.

Lacey was tapping a pencil against her desktop. "We know the location of Governor Bingham. I need for you to contact the Oregon State Police and request they send a helicopter to evacuate her and one other person, Peter Savage."

"Not the commander?"

"No. He was there, but he was moved less than twenty-four hours ago. We don't have a lead on his location."

Stephens nodded, deciding not to pursue that line of questioning. More information would be shared when the lieutenant was ready.

"You said Mister Savage is involved? Didn't he also play a role in solving those mysterious missile launches in the South China Sea?"

"You have a good memory. Yes. He's been involved in many SGIT missions. Enough, in fact, that Colonel Pierson views him as an honorary member of the team." She handed Stephens a slip of paper with longitude and latitude coordinates. "I tracked his sat phone. He says he has the governor in a log cabin. It's a large house, more like a lodge the way he described it. She and the commander were being held by a militia group. The same one McMullen was supporting. He says there's an open field surrounding the cabin, so landing a helicopter shouldn't be a problem. At least for now, no one's shooting, but caution the state police to be prepared for resistance. The militia wiped out an FBI assault team trying to gain access to the property yesterday. Last night, the Feds tried to send in another team, but they encountered booby traps along a narrow access road that winds through forested land. They put a freeze on that operation until daylight. But they're almost ten miles away from the coordinates that I have."

"I'll get right on it." Stephens rose to leave, but Lacey stopped her.

"I'll hold off notifying the FBI until you speak with the state police. The Feds will go in hot, looking to avenge the loss of their team. Would be good if we can get both agencies to coordinate. Less likely that innocents will get shot. But to be on the safe side, I'd like the state police helicopter to get Mister Savage and the governor out first."

Stephens strode to the door, then turned to face her boss. "We'll find the commander."

⊕

Thirty-five minutes later, Stephens was again in Lieutenant Lacey's office. She was joined by a more junior member of the analyst team, David Sanchez. Although Sanchez matched the brainpower of Stephens, in almost every other way he was her polar opposite. His happy-go-lucky personality often gave the impression that he put more energy into providing comic relief than he did into the serious side of being an intelligence analyst. He also made frequent appearances at the most popular singles bars within a thirty-minute driving radius of The Office.

Nonetheless, under the leadership of Ellen Lacey, Sanchez had blossomed into a valued asset of her team.

Lacey leaned back in her chair and looked across her desk at her handpicked analysts. For several moments, she moved her gaze back and forth, gauging the emotional readiness of each. As expected, she saw only professionalism and commitment to the job.

Just as the silence was reaching the point of being awkward, she said, "I've called you here for an assignment of the highest level of importance."

Her statement was answered with two clipped nods.

"By now, I expect the Oregon State Police have dispatched a helicopter to exfiltrate their governor and Peter Savage from a private ranch in Western Idaho. I also expect the FBI is scrambling to get a SWAT team in the air and headed for the same location. The mission of the FBI will be to quash the CIM militia."

"Excuse me," Sanchez said. "CIM?"

"Cascadia Independence Movement. Just hold your questions on that. I'll come back to them shortly." Lacey leaned forward, placing her hands on her desk. "The coordinates for the location of the governor match the location of the sat phone in the possession of Mister Savage. Within the past hour, he provided limited intel on the location and possible OPFOR. It's not much, but it's all we have."

Sanchez said, "The opposing force is the militia, right?"

"Correct. They are a capable force and have bloodied the nose of the FBI. However, we do not know their numbers and location at this time. Mister Savage has the governor in a log house, where he has taken a defensive position while waiting for the evac chopper to arrive."

Stephens said, "The state police had a helicopter and team on standby, awaiting this news. They didn't waste any time getting airborne."

"Good," Lacey replied. "Although my contact at the FBI assured me the SWAT team would be fully briefed, I'm concerned about blue-on-blue casualties if they arrive at the scene at the same time. With a little luck, the governor and Mister Savage will be extracted prior to the Feds arriving."

Sanchez said, "What do you need us to do, boss."

Lacey returned a scowl to the junior analyst. She didn't care for his casual disregard for proper military protocol.

"What I need is everything you can dig up on the Cascadia Independence Movement and it's leader. A man by the name of Stuart Denson, although he prefers to go by General Denson."

"Is he ex-military?" Stephens said.

"That's what you're going to find out. I want to know who he is, where he's from, and what he does. His parents, grandparents, aunts, uncles, siblings. Is he married, or does he have a girlfriend? Any kids? Who are his friends and confidants? His entire life story. All of it. Is he religious? Political leanings, social circles, who he donates money to or receives money from. Everything. Nothing is too insignificant."

"We're on it, boss."

Lacy snapped her gaze to Sanchez. "It's *lieutenant* to you, mister."

"Yes ma'am. I mean, lieutenant."

"Do you have any other leads?" Stephens said.

Over the next five minutes, Lacey shared the key aspects of her conversation with Peter.

"Check with our sister agencies and get what you can on that regional aircraft that crashed at Hailey, Idaho."

"Yes ma'am," Stephens said. "Is there anything else?"

"Just this—this investigation is not officially sanctioned. You discuss this with no one. Am I clear? You report only to me. If anyone asks what you are doing, tell them it's background research on a potential domestic terrorist organization. Nothing more. If necessary, send them to me."

Sanchez and Stephens stood and strode to the door.

Lacey said, "Oh, and one more thing."

They both turned.

"I want a preliminary report in two hours."

CHAPTER 32

THE TWO BLACK SUBURBANS were as out-of-place in the low-rent neighborhood as a miniskirt in church. Still, Stuart Denson doubted any of the neighbors would be reaching out to the Boise police. And even if they did, so what? No crime with owning two nice SUVs.

They'd arrived at the safe house shortly after dark the previous day. One of the men made a trip to the grocery store and then cooked a meal consisting of bratwurst, fried potatoes, and salad.

Jim was confined to one of the bedrooms, the window having been previously boarded over with a sheet of plywood screwed to the exterior wall. A plate of food was placed on the floor, along with a bottle of water. The door was solid and locked from the outside. Even if he could bust his way out, there were at least a half-dozen guns ready to bring his great escape to an early and unsuccessful end.

The general had been clear—he preferred to have Jim

alive, but if he caused too much trouble, killing him was not a problem. The big man named Walker seemed especially happy with that prospect, and even eager to make it happen.

Well into the night, he heard the distinctive sounds of gun bolts being cycled back and forth in the receiver, and the *click, click, click* of rounds being inserted into magazines.

Cleaning and readying weapons.

When the task was completed, Walker and another six militiamen left in one of the SUVs. They drove to an abandoned warehouse on West Franklin Road a few miles west of the state capitol. They parked the Suburban there and piled into the back of a twenty-foot U-Haul rental truck. Their duffle bags loaded with weapons and ammunition were added to a cargo already in the truck—five motorcycles and several olive-drab cases, the lids latched.

The driver of the rental truck met Walker at the door. "Everything you asked for is already loaded."

Walker counted the cases.

Satisfied with the tally, he said, "Good job, Mick. Is the gas tank full?"

Mick nodded. "Should be able to make it to Central Oregon without stopping. But if there's any doubt, I can find a gas station in Burns or Prineville and top it up."

"Make sure you do. We can't afford to run out of gas out there on the BLM dirt roads."

⊕

Sometime after sunrise, the smell of bacon aroused Jim from a light sleep. After all the other men had eaten their fill, he was escorted at gun point from the room and given a plate of eggs, two slices of toast—no butter—and burnt black coffee to wash it down.

"Where's the bacon?" Jim said.

"It's all gone," Jacob said. "Be glad you're getting anything.

The boys weren't too hungry this morning."

"Where is everyone?"

"Never mind. Just eat. We'll be leaving soon. Clint and Ben are going to keep an eye on you, just in case you get any ideas."

While Jim ate, Denson left the main room—a combination of living room and dining room—and entered the garage. Jim had noticed upon arrival the previous night that the house no longer had a garage door. Jacob and Billy Reed followed him out. Once the door was closed, Jim couldn't hear anything they were discussing.

Sometime in the past, the former single-car garage had been converted into a bedroom, which Denson used as his private retreat. A single bed was placed lengthwise against one of the long walls, and a desk against the other. A cheap printer was supported on a two-drawer file cabinet, and a laptop was open on the desk. A handful of printed images, aerial views of Boise taken from Google Maps, were scattered across the desk.

With a yellow marking pen, Denson circled the State Capitol on the map. The majestic southwest-facing building was located on two city blocks and surrounded by lawn and trees. The buff-colored sandstone structure was adorned with an ornate dome similar in appearance, but smaller than the U.S. Capitol building. A broad stone staircase climbed from street level to the first floor, with the main entrance marked by four Doric columns three-stories high.

With the tip of the pen, Denson stabbed at the staircase.

"Here," he kept his gaze down, "between the two center columns, the vice president and Speaker of the House are scheduled for a short speech and photo op this afternoon at 1:15 p.m."

"Right after lunch," Jacob said.

"That's right. The veep is here to campaign on behalf of Congresswoman Maybridge. Even though she's won the Second

District for the past twenty-seven years, she's got a tough battle in front of her. They're scheduled to have a high-roller lunch at Trillium Restaurant in the Grove Hotel, and then drive northeast up Capitol Boulevard to the capitol. I imagine they'll climb the steps, side by side. Then at the top, they'll face the crowd, each offering a short feel-good speech, and then depart into the capitol for additional meetings with party elite."

Billy had been studying the map. He was confident in his ability to carry out the mission, but he still didn't know the details of the plan.

He said, "They'll be sitting ducks on the landing atop the staircase."

"Exactly my thought," Denson replied.

"How will you get close enough?" Jacob said, as ignorant about the plan as Billy. "What about the Secret Service?"

Denson nodded. "Very true. There will be an audience, of course, in the square and park in front of the capitol. Everyone will have to go through a metal detector. And with help from the local police, they'll sweep all the buildings within four blocks that could possibly hide a sniper or bomber. The air space will be closed, and they'll have anti-drone defenses in place as well. No vehicles will be allowed within the same four-block cordon, so no car bombs."

Billy leaned closer, studying an enlarged aerial view. The capitol was in the upper right corner of the page. He ran his finger along a straight line to the lower left corner.

"Here," he said. "What is this building?"

"You have good instincts," Denson said.

"Not instinct. Training."

The general shuffled through a short pile of papers, found the one he wanted and laid it atop the stack for Jacob and Billy to see. It was a photograph of a Spanish-style building with a tall clock tower.

Denson said, "This is the Boise Depot. It used to be the Union Pacific train station. Now it's used for social events like weddings and bar mitzvahs."

Jacob raised his eyebrows. "You expecting us to crash a wedding?"

"Not at all. You see, I have booked the great hall for a family gathering this afternoon. We will arrive at noon and begin decorating while the staff places tables and chairs for seventy-five guests—"

"Who will never show up," Billy said.

Jacob grinned. "I like it."

Billy said, "Do we have access to the clock tower?"

"All ninety-six feet of it. The line of fire is straight up Capitol Boulevard, to the steps where the veep and Speaker will be standing. Hard to imagine a better setup."

Billy used his fingers like a pair of dividers to measure the length of the scale on the photo, and then estimate the distance from the tower to the steps.

"Looks like about two thousand yards."

"Two thousand and fifty, to be precise," Denson said. "Should be an easy shot. Weather will remain sunny today, so no issues with rain or fog obscuring your vision or scattering the energy of the laser pulse."

"Laser what?" Jacob said.

Over the next fifteen minutes, General Denson read Jacob and Billy Reed fully into the plan, focusing on the logistics of getting their gear into the clock tower without raising suspicions. It was the first time Jacob had learned about the PEAP carbine—information Denson did not want known outside a small group. He insisted Jacob and Billy each recite a step-by-step walk-through of what they would be required to do.

"Good," Denson said. "Once the job is completed, remove

the battery from the PEAP carbine and replace it with the dead battery packed in the case. It has a yellow band of tape to make certain there is no confusion."

"Understood," Billy said. "And how do we get away?"

"We'll all walk out of the train depot, nice and casual, to the parking lot. From there, we drive to Ontario, just across the border in Oregon. A chartered helicopter is waiting for us at the municipal airport to ferry us back to my ranch."

"Is that smart?" Billy said. "Won't the Feds be waiting?"

"Why? That altercation yesterday at the gate to my property was miles from my house. There is no evidence to connect that to me, or any of you."

Jacob said, "What if the police lock everything down before we get away?"

"They'll waste a lot of time trying to figure out what happened. Initially, they'll focus on nearby buildings within a thousand yards of the capitol. By the time they expand their search radius to include the train depot, we'll be long gone."

CHAPTER 33

GOVERNOR BINGHAM SETTLED INTO HER OAK CHAIR. The straight back wasn't the most comfortable, but her mind was elsewhere. It seemed like weeks had passed since she'd visited EJ Enterprises and was kidnapped, although it had only been a few days. She noticed she was beginning to acquire an aroma, and she longed for a hot shower and clean clothes.

Eventually. But it would have to wait.

She didn't like the shotgun on her lap. It was unfamiliar, ugly, and evil. Led by a strong anti-gun sentiment among the population in the Willamette Valley and Portland Metro Area, she'd encouraged the Democratic majority in the state legislature to author bills restricting gun ownership. That she was brandishing a gun now in self-defense seemed otherworldly. Since she was accustomed to having a security detail twenty-four-seven, the notion of having to protect herself was equally foreign.

She turned her head toward Peter. He was still—a granite

statue laying on the granite countertop, legs spread, focused on the magnified image coming through the rifle scope.

Diesel stirred and whined, then lowered his head onto his paws and continued staring at the front door. As more time ticked by, the red pit bull began to lick his lips and swivel his head from the front door to the kitchen window—all signals of anxiety. Every now and then, he emitted a throaty rumble.

"Looks like company is coming," Peter said, without removing his eye from the scope.

The governor looked to Peter, silently pleading for directions. But he said nothing more. He just lay there on the island counter, motionless, aiming through the open window at some far-off threat.

"Two pickup trucks. I see men in the back of each."

"Maybe they're friendly."

"Don't think so. They all have rifles."

"Police or FBI?"

After another several moments to further scrutinize the objects, he said, "Nope. The trucks are not marked, and the men are not wearing law enforcement uniforms."

Her hopes were dashed. "Oh."

"Pay attention and be ready."

She swallowed, her mouth dry. Deep inside, she searched for courage. She'd never thought about defending herself. What would she do if a man appeared at the door, aiming to kill her?

Boom!

She jumped and nearly dropped the riot gun. Then another rifle shot, and another.

She gasped, fighting back mounting panic.

Peter was stuffing the large brass shells into the rifle magazine. Then he rammed the bolt home, aimed, and fired.

Steam was gushing from the radiator of the lead truck, but it didn't slow. Still nearly four hundred yards out, Peter aimed for the driver and squeezed the trigger with the tip of his index finger. The rifle barked and the stock smacked his shoulder. He reacquired the driver and fired a second bullet.

The truck veered to the right and slowed. Before it came to a stop, the men riding in the back jumped over the rear fenders and fanned out. Brandishing their weapons, they ran for the log house and were soon passed by the second truck.

Peter fired two more shots in quick succession, either disabling or killing the driver. The vehicle coasted to a stop, disgorging its load of militiamen, too.

With every shot, Governor Bingham jumped. Her ears rang, and she wondered if she could still hear anything. She stood and held the Benelli against her hip as Peter had shown her to do. She rested her finger against the trigger guard, mindful not to inadvertently pull the trigger and waste a round.

She felt a wave of heat and droplets of sweat form on her forehead and neck. Her body felt clammy.

"They're charging us!" Peter shouted, his ears ringing, too. "I count about ten men. Be ready!"

He was grabbing rifle cartridges from the granite counter, but each time he picked one up he scattered several others. Two rolled off onto the floor, out of reach. After four rounds were loaded, he centered the crosshairs on one of the closest men. He was running directly at Peter.

At about two-hundred-yard's distance, the shot was easy.

Boom!

The militiaman did a somersault as his momentum carried him forward. Peter didn't dwell on his condition. Instead, he picked another target, aligned the crosshairs, and squeezed the trigger. The man went down hard, and Peter moved on to another, and then another before having to reload.

The shots became harder as he aimed at militiamen running across his field of vision. He wasted three bullets because he had led too much or not enough. Finally he connected, sending a big man tumbling, his arms flailing like a rag doll.

While Peter was reloading, he shouted, "Get down! But keep that shotgun pointed at the front door."

He dropped his eye behind the scope again. Three targets. He aimed and fired, the four rounds going quickly. He thought he hit two militiamen. Surely there were more out there, but being removed by five feet from the window had some drawbacks, and the most significant was a limited field of view up close.

He groped his hand over the counter, but came back with only one rifle shell. He pressed it into the empty magazine when the sound of a heavy object slamming into the front door caught his attention. It was repeated, and this time accompanied by the crackling sound of splintering wood.

The front door was swinging on its hinges, and a militiaman barreled through the opening, stumbled, and fell to the floor. Right behind him, a second gunman entered while Peter was still shimmying off the island.

Peter rolled onto his feet just as the Benelli erupted, the deep boom distinguishable from the sharp rifle report. He faced the governor. She was struggling to recover from the recoil which had come close to stripping the weapon from her grip. The load of buckshot had missed, blasting away a portion of the doorframe. Although the shot had caused the gunman to duck, he quickly recovered.

To Peter's mind, everything slowed by a hundred-fold. His vision narrowed as if he were gazing through a tunnel with a tiny shaft of light at the end. And yet he clearly saw the gunman raising his rifle, and Bingham fighting to get the muzzle of the shotgun lowered. Too soon, she touched the trigger, sending another volley of buckshot into the wall above the swinging door, the deep report deafening in the confined space.

The gunman had his weapon almost level with Bingham. She now held the weapon with only one hand, the bucking shotgun almost lost from her grip. Peter did the calculus in the blink of an eye and knew with absolute certainty she would not get a third shot before high-velocity rifle bullets ripped through her chest.

He moved his arms sluggishly, trying to overcome inertia and swing the barrel of his Weatherby into position. At the same time, he slammed home the bolt and locked it down. The milliseconds ticked by, agonizingly slow. It was now a duel— Peter against the gunman. Who would get their rifle aimed and fire their shot first?

With one round chambered, and an empty magazine, Peter had to be true. He would not get a second chance. If he missed, the militiaman would kill them both.

Without any conscious order from his brain, his index moved inside the trigger guard. The muzzle was almost in position, just an inch more.

But it was too late. The gunman beat him, with his assault rifle pointed squarely at the governor's chest. With his finger on the trigger and his face a grimace, he squeezed.

But nothing happened. The air should have been split by the sharp report of the rifle shot, but there was nothing.

The gunman looked down at his weapon. The safety was on. With a flick of his thumb, he moved the lever to the fire position.

Boom!

The Weatherby jumped in Peter's hands, but the shot was true. At only fifteen yards distance, the heavy bullet blew a massive hole in the gunman's chest before traveling onward through the open doorway.

Peter exhaled a sigh of relief and allowed the heavy weapon to pull his arms down. But the fight wasn't over. The first militiaman had regained his feet, but his rifle was still pointed at the floor. Peter charged forward, shifting his grip from the stock to the hot barrel. He felt the sting of burns to his fingers and palms, but held fast.

The militiaman had the barrel of his weapon moving upwards when Peter swung the rifle like a club. The synthetic butt stock connected with the barrel of the AR, knocking it sideways with enough force that the gunman had trouble holding on.

Then Peter returned a backhand swing that slammed the stock into the militiaman's right hand and the receiver of his weapon. The blow was enough to make him release his grip.

Twisted off balance, Peter tried to recover. But the gunman rammed his fist into Peter's cheek. He stumbled back, and the gunman lashed out with a vicious kick. Peter turned just enough to avoid having the steel-toed boot connect with his groin.

Peter dropped the rifle and scrambled four steps back. He dropped his hand to his lower back and wrapped his fingers around the tomahawk. Yanked it up, free of his belt, and shifted his hold to the end of the handle.

By now, the gunman had regained his hold on his AR and was moving the muzzle in line with Peter. In practiced, graceful movement, Peter cocked his arm and then whipped it forward. Released the handle. The tomahawk tumbled through space, the razor-sharp blade and polished steel spike glinting flashes of light as it flew in a deadly arc. With a sickening thud, the spike drove deep into the gunman's torso, just below his sternum.

The steel tip penetrated the man's aorta, the largest blood vessel in the human body, causing massive blood loss. He wilted to his knees, too weak to hold onto his rifle. With wide eyes, he moved his mouth like a fish out of water. But no sound came out. He fell to his side amid a growing pool of red.

Peter retrieved his tomahawk and wiped the blood onto the dead man's trousers. Then he checked on the governor.

"Are you okay?" he said.

She was shaking and staring at the corpses. He approached her and gently removed the shotgun from her grasp, placing it on the table. Then he cupped her shoulders in his hands.

"Are you all right?"

"You killed them." Her voice was flat, devoid of the emotion that was racking her body and mind.

"Yes, I did."

Diesel growled and then began barking. Peter knew the growl to be a challenge to a threat the canine sensed, while the bark was a warning for Peter. He released Bingham just as the pit bull launched for the open door. He was at full speed in three strides, meeting a militiaman charging through the opening.

Diesel slammed into the gunman—seventy pounds of muscle, bone, and teeth crashing into the man's belly at thirty miles per hour. The man was doubled over by the impact and propelled backwards. The canine's momentum carried the gunman several feet, where he landed hard on his back, ivory fangs flashing in front of his face.

With the dog pinning his rifle to his chest, the gunman managed to snake his forearm under Diesel's neck. Using all his strength to keep the gnashing teeth away from his face, he used his free hand to punch the dog's ribs.

As soon as his dog charged for the threat coming at the front door, Peter had yanked the Benelli M4 from the dining table. With no time to shoulder the weapon and aim, he pointed it at the opening. Two more militiamen had just arrived. One was using his rifle butt to bash Diesel, trying to make him disengage. But with every blow, Diesel's frenzied state just amped higher. With his head thrashing, he managed to get his mouth wrapped around the man's wrist. He clamped down with bone-crushing strength, fracturing several of the small carpal bones and tearing the transverse carpal ligament as well as the median nerve. The man screamed in unbearable agony.

Peter fired the shotgun, sending nine lead balls into the shoulder of the militiaman who was beating Diesel. The impact spun the man away, his arm dangling by only a few strips of skin and muscle. He crashed into the doorframe and sank until he rested on his haunches.

The third man stood outside the opening and raised his rifle. But Peter was ready, and he fired again, striking the man in the chest, sending him sprawling backwards.

With no other militiamen in sight, Peter said, "Diesel! Enough!"

The pit bull ceased the frenetic gyrations of his head and released his prey. The man lay unconscious, bleeding profusely from his left wrist.

Peter advanced to the doorway, leading with the business end of the M4. Diesel stayed at his side while Peter moved onto the landing just outside the front door, kicking rifles away from the fallen militiamen. He searched left and then right, but saw no more combatants. Only once he was satisfied that there was no longer any immediate threat, Peter squatted next to the man he'd shot in the shoulder. The wound was ghastly since the buckshot was still in a tight cluster when it struck the man. There was a large pool of blood next to him. Peter reached forward and check for a pulse, but there was none.

Standing and facing Governor Bingham through the doorway, Peter said, "In the kitchen, get a clean towel and bring my pack. It's on the center island."

Still dazed, she merely nodded and then ambled into the adjoining room. A minute later, she emerged with the items he'd asked for.

Turning his attention to the man Diesel had mauled, he

dug through his backpack and removed the first aid kit. Finding two large square gauze pads, he ripped open the packaging and placed them on the most serious bleeding from wounds on the palm side of the wrist. Then he folded the kitchen towel lengthwise and wrapped it around the injury to hold the bandage in place, using tape to secure the towel.

He said, "That's going to hurt like hell when he wakes up, but he'll live. More than I can say for his friends."

Peter pulled a length of parachute cord from a pocket and wrapped it around the militiaman's wrists three times before tying it off in a tight knot.

"When he comes to, he'll spend at least an hour trying to undo that knot with his teeth. By then we should be long gone."

Governor Bingham was standing to the side, watching, her arms folded across her chest.

She said, "He was going to kill us."

Peter nodded. "That's right."

"But you helped him anyway."

"His fight is over."

Her face was deathly pale, and she swayed on her feet.

"Come on. Let's get you sitting before you fall over." With one hand carrying the shotgun, and the other on her arm, he led her to the leather sofa in front of the fireplace. He lowered himself into one of the chairs. It felt good to take the weight off his feet and be still.

For several moments, they both just sat there in silence while the color returned to her face.

Finally, Bingham said, "It wasn't hard for you to kill those men, was it?"

It was as much a question as it was an accusation.

"I did what had to be done."

"Of course. The ends always justify the means."

"You're delusional if you think we could've talked those

men out of killing us."

"You didn't even try. Just boom, boom, boom. Some of them didn't even fire a shot."

"Would you feel better if I'd let them kill you first?"

"Oh, get real. You're just as bad as they are. Men with guns. All you want to do is go shooting people."

"I've had just about enough from you, *Governor*. I did what had to be done because bad men will do bad things. Would you feel better if your security detail had been here to shoot them instead? The results would have been the same. Bad guys dead. Period."

"It's the job of law enforcement, not you or any private citizen."

"Except that I was here, and they weren't."

She snorted in disgust and looked away. Sitting at her feet, Diesel whimpered, then lowered his head onto his front paws.

"Look," Peter said. "I'm sorry I snapped at you. I was wrong to do so. This isn't easy."

She drew in a breath and looked at Peter. "My big mouth. It's a personality flaw, I suppose. I can't help saying what's on my mind."

"Not especially good for a politician, I'd think."

She chuckled grimly. "I manage to keep it in check. Most of the time." She paused. "I was out of line. I should be thanking you for saving my life."

"No worries." Peter forced a smile. "You're under a lot of stress."

"Still—"

"It's not easy, taking another's life."

Governor Bingham stared at Peter, waiting for his next words.

He averted his gaze to the floor. "Anyone who says otherwise is a liar. I'm sorry you had to be here to witness this."

"I think that is the most truthful admission I've ever heard. You've given me much to think about." She extended her hand, and Peter clasped it.

He checked his watch—just before 1:00 p.m.

"The helicopter should be here soon, I hope." He rose to his feet. "Diesel. Stay. Guard."

Then he shuffled into the kitchen, where he gathered up his weapons and belongings. He was ready to leave.

The sound came in through the busted-out window in the kitchen. A faint *whump, whump* of rotors beating the air. It grew progressively louder. He dashed for the front door and ran out into the grassy opening beside the driveway. The helicopter was hovering, and Peter waved his arms to draw the attention of the pilot. Slowly, the aircraft settled to a landing. The sleek fuselage was dark blue with a silver star—Oregon State Police.

The copilot slid open the door as Peter ran up, keeping his head ducked below the spinning rotors.

"Am I glad to see you!" he shouted over the whine of the engine.

"I'm Sergeant Torres. Where's the governor?" the copilot said.

"Inside with my dog. I'll get her."

A couple minutes later, Peter returned. After Governor Bingham climbed aboard, Peter tossed in his rifle, shotgun, and backpack. Then he lifted Diesel up before climbing onboard. Sergeant Torres made certain his passengers were strapped in, and he pointed to headsets hanging from a hook next to each seat. The headsets would allow the governor and Peter to converse with the cockpit crew. The pitch of the turbine engine increased. Slowly at first, and then rapidly, the helicopter gained altitude.

Looking over his shoulder, Torres addressed the governor. "We have a medical team on standby to take you to the hospital once we land in Salem."

"It's not necessary. I'm not hurt."

"Respectfully, ma'am, I think—"

"We're not going to Salem. I have a meeting with President Taylor this evening, and I'm not going to miss it."

"But—"

"I won't hear any objections. My mind is made up. The governors of Washington and Idaho are going to be there, and I'll be damned if I'm going to miss this opportunity." *Besides, just coming back from being kidnapped and all, I'll steal the spotlight, maybe even from President Taylor. This couldn't be better if scripted for Hollywood.* "Just fly directly to Redmond Airport. My meeting with the president is this evening at the Redmond Hotel. Book a room for me anywhere nearby so I can shower and brush my teeth. And order in a pant suit. I can't go to the meeting smelling like week-old gym clothes. My aide has my sizes. Something conservative and that goes well with black shoes. Maybe in navy or dark gray. She'll know. Is there's a Nordstrom or Macy's in Redmond?"

The copilot and pilot exchanged looks.

"I doubt it," Torres said, "but I'll radio ahead and do my best."

Diesel sat between his master's feet, his tongue hanging low as he panted. Peter removed the canine's vest to help him shed heat. It was also the first opportunity he had to check his companion for injuries. The beating he'd taken likely left bruising, but thankfully no broken ribs. Clearly the vest, although intended to protect against bullets, had also helped to deflect the energy from the physical blows.

Rubbing Diesel's head, Peter leaned back in the seat and closed his eyes. Although his body was resting, his mind was fully engaged. He was missing something—something important. Obviously, Denson had held the governor as leverage to make certain Jim cooperated. But why did they need Jim? And why was it necessary to move him to another location, but not Governor Bingham?

He knew that answering these questions was the key to solving the puzzle.

CHAPTER 34

STEPHENS AND SANCHEZ ARRIVED at Lieutenant Laccy's office on schedule. They sat before the lieutenant's desk, each cradling an iPad on their lap.

"Talk to me," Lacey said.

Sanchez scrolled through his notes. "Socially, this guy Stuart Denson is pretty boring. Never been married. No significant other or children, that I can find. Never been arrested. No service record. Never ran for office. He does pay his taxes, and on time."

"Where does his money come from?"

"That's a bit more interesting," Stephens said. "His family has owned a large tract of land in western Idaho for many generations. Income from leasing grazing rights is substantial. His father and preceding generations also raised cattle. Apparently, that business never took with Stuart because he's the first generation not to raise livestock."

"Bet daddy's rolling over in his grave," Sanchez said, earning a glare from Lacey.

"Anyway," Stephens continued, "that explains the income he reports on his tax return."

Lacey raised an eyebrow. "Meaning, there is other income that is not reported?"

"Yes, ma'am. As founder and self-proclaimed leader of the Cascadia Independence Movement, or CIM, Denson has received several large contributions from various right-wing groups and individuals."

"Such as?"

"The New Sons and Daughter of Liberty, Free Men Against Tyranny, and the King brothers."

"Who are they?"

"Alfred and Franklin King. Identical twins. Born in June of 1950, in Dearborn, Michigan. Their father, Melvin, worked as an accountant for Ford Motor Company."

"And their mother?"

"An alcoholic. She died before her thirtieth birthday. Melvin never remarried. The twins showed a remarkable ability to carry out complex mathematics in their head without having to write anything on paper. They went on to earn business degrees at the University of Michigan. They made their fortune trading commodities. And they've remained inseparable all these years. They share the same mansion, and neither Alfred nor Franklin ever married."

"Estimated net worth?"

"According to Forbes, just over $3.4 billion."

Lacey whistled. "That kind of money could wipe out hunger across the nation."

"The brothers appear to be on a giving campaign, donating millions to various charities, special interest groups, and politicians. On the later point, they are equal-opportunity donors, giving the maximum amounts allowed by law to both Republicans and Democrats. The only catch is they must support conservative causes important to the brothers."

"And how much have they donated to CIM?"

"As near as I can figure, at least $26 million over the last three years. Some of that money can be traced back to Alfred and Franklin, but most of it was passed through conservative special interest groups, including the two I mentioned."

Lacey leaned back in her chair, her gaze cast down at her desk, deep in thought.

One of the reasons she excelled at her job was that she was always thinking many steps ahead. Now was no different. She'd listened to everything her analysts had learned, digested it, formulated questions and answers. But there was more. Missing pieces that remained to be discovered.

"Ma'am?" Stephens said.

"Sorry." Lacey glanced to Sanchez and then Stephens. "Just thinking that a man can do a lot of things with that much money. And not all of them are good."

"Yes, ma'am."

Lacey nodded. "Were you able to confirm that Stuart Denson is, in fact, a descendant of Meriwether Lewis of Lewis and Clark fame?"

Sanchez said, "Affirmative, Lieutenant. Captain Meriwether Lewis never married and had no offspring. However, his sister, named Jane, did marry and have children. It is from this lineage that Stuart Denson is descended."

"Interesting. So the family blood does run through his veins. Anything else?"

"You mean about how the U.S. acquired the Oregon Territory?" Sanchez said.

"Of course. That does seem to be the crux of the argument as to why Denson and the CIM are arguing for the secession of a major part of the Pacific Northwest."

Sanchez nodded. "Well, the history is very interesting. At

the beginning of the nineteenth century, the west coast of North America was claimed by Spain, Russia, England, and France. When Thomas Jefferson commissioned the Corps of Discovery, under the command of Meriwether Lewis and William Clark, to explore the Louisiana Purchase, he ordered them to proceed all the way to the Pacific Ocean to strengthen claims by the young United States to that region. You see, James Monroe was already gaining influence for his strategic policy that the U.S. should govern from ocean to ocean. Anyway, although the Corps of Discovery was supposed to be a secret mission, Spain caught wind and tried, unsuccessfully, to intercept the band of explorers and arrest Lewis and Clark. The rest, as the saying goes, is history."

"Yes, Mister Sanchez, we all know this. Please enlighten me with something I don't know."

"Yes, ma'am." Sanchez straightened his back. "Okay. So fast forward several years. Spain is struggling with revolutions throughout Latin America, although they still have strong control over California and the Southwest. However, Spanish claims to the Pacific Northwest, weakened by the Nootka Conventions of the 1790s, were not terminated until the Adams-Onis Treaty of 1819. Meanwhile, the Russo-American Treaty of 1824 relinquished Russian claims to the coastal region south of parallel fifty-four degrees, forty minutes to the United States, although Great Britain also had competing claims with sound historical basis, to the same territory. This left the region from the Rocky Mountains, west to the ocean, and north of California, under joint administration by Great Britain and the U.S. It remained this way until the Oregon Treaty of 1846, establishing U.S. governance up to the forty-ninth parallel."

Stephens had been listening attentively, and said, "The history is fascinating. I had no idea how complicated that time was. It seems like there is plenty of material for a creative mind to come up with all kinds of wild conspiracy theories."

Lieutenant Lacey raised her eyebrows. "Maybe. But sometimes fact is stranger than fiction."

"With all due respect, ma'am," Stephens said, "historians have surely combed every relevant document. I can't imagine that somehow they simply missed a key treaty."

"You're probably right. But keep digging. There has to be something we're missing. Denson obviously had enough solid evidence to convince the Tenth Circuit Court to take on his claim and give it a hearing. Dig into the court records, see what you can find."

"Yes, ma'am."

The two analysts left, knowing the work was only going to get harder, and mentally prepared for a late night at The Office.

Alone with her thoughts, Ellen Lacey mulled over the facts. Denson had a small army under his command, and loads of money. But why? If his plan was to pursue secession based on historical facts and legal arguments, why did he need an army? And what was he spending all those millions on?

CHAPTER 35

IN THE GREAT HALL OF THE BOISE STATION, a radio was playing in the background as several militiamen masquerading as extended family members were inflating balloons with helium and placing paper decorations at each table. Since Denson did not hire extra staff to help with decorations, there were only two employees from the station to unlock the two entrance doors and ensure tables and chairs had been arranged as planned. Catering would arrive at 1:30 p.m. to greet the guests, who were expected to arrive an hour later, and serve a late lunch.

Of course, there wouldn't be any guests, because a national tragedy would preempt their arrival.

With a subcompact 9mm pistol pressing into his back, Jim climbed the stairs to the top floor of the bell tower. The square-shaped room was just below the outdoor observation deck which surrounded the bells. In keeping with the Spanish architecture, the floor of the room was tiled with one-foot-square brick-red Saltillo tiles, contrasting with the white painted walls. An arched window was centered on each of the four walls, glazed with stained leaded glass. Each window depicted a scene from early twentieth-century Idaho.

"Have a seat, Commander," Denson said.

He was wearing latex gloves, as was the other man in the room, Jacob.

Jim looked around. The room was devoid of furniture. There was only one old-style steam radiator against the wall to heat the space in the winter. Hinged from the ceiling ten feet above the floor was a simple ladder which could be pulled down by a rope to provide access to the observation deck and the bells.

"Over there." Denson motioned with the pistol to the far corner of the room. "You can sit on the floor."

"And if I'd rather not?" Jim said.

"It wasn't a suggestion."

Jim abided by the order. He would wait and take action when the timing was in his favor.

Clint entered the room, carrying a hard-sided plastic case just as the clock struck one bell. He was closely followed by Billy Reed.

"Jacob, stand outside the door and make certain no one climbs the stairs," Denson said.

"Yes, sir."

Clint opened the case. Inside was a small lecture bottle of nitrous oxide blended with pure oxygen. There was also a gas regulator, some tubing, and an inhalation mask. He assembled the apparatus, then opened the main valve on the lecture bottle to hear a hiss, indicating gas was flowing. Satisfied, he closed the valve.

"Should I start the party?" Clint said.

"No. If you start the flow of nitrous now, we'll all be affected. Handcuff him to that radiator. He won't go anywhere."

"Why do you need me, General?" Jim said.

With a squeeze, the cuffs ratcheted tight around one wrist, the other end clamped around a stout portion of the radiator.

"Watch, and you will see."

Billy opened another hard-sided case he'd been carrying. Inside, Jim recognized a spotting scope and the PEAP carbine. As Billy prepped the weapon, Jim's pulse quickened.

He also recognized a second item from the case. A telescoping bipod. Billy fixed it to the carbine with a single knurled thumbscrew. Obviously, Denson's machinist at his shop in the white Quonset hut had fashioned the accessory for this purpose.

Next, Billy used a glass cutter to remove an oval-shaped piece of glass from the window facing northeast. He then sat cross-legged five feet back from the window, rested the PEAP carbine on the bipod, and sighted through the scope. That, too, looked to Jim like a modification from the original weapon.

Denson was amused by Jim's studious observations. "So what do you think, Commander?"

"You've converted the PEAP carbine into a sniper's weapon."

"Indeed. It is the ideal application for this unique weapon system, don't you think? Look." He stood to the side of Billy, pointing out the features. "Bipod for stability. Forty-five power Leupold competition scope. In the hands of a competent marksman, a deadly combination."

"I'm sure you didn't go to all this trouble just to blast some melons."

Denson bellowed a laugh. "Oh, you are very astute, Commander. No, Mister Reed is not going to shoot melons. We have more interesting targets in mind."

"Such as?"

"You are very curious. Almost as curious as your friend, Peter Savage."

Jim raised his eyebrows.

"Yes, that's right. We had a long conversation. You see, I value his intellect, and I offered him a position in my organization."

"What organization is that?"

"The new nation of Nova Albion."

"You're delusional."

Denson cocked his head to the side, then began slowly pacing. "Your friend said the same thing."

"I'm not surprised Peter turned you down. He's loyal. To his friends and country. And he's smart enough to know you'll never succeed in splitting off part of the nation."

"That's where you're wrong. The United States is about to undergo a painful change of leadership that will bring new thinking on this topic."

Jim considered Denson's claims. Was he planning to assassinate President Taylor? Is that why they were here in the clock tower?

"Even if you kill the president, the vice president will carry on with the same policy. You won't change anything."

"Vice President Vince Nagashima. Yes, he is of the same mind as President Taylor. And I agree with your assessment. That is why my plan became complicated. You know, killing one man, even the president, isn't all that challenging if you set your mind to the task."

Jim looked upon Denson in amazement. The man really was insane.

General Denson continued while Billy peered through the scope in silence, ignoring the conversation.

"Three years in the making. That's how long it's taken to put all the pieces in place. And if it wasn't for this marvelous invention from the brilliant minds at EJ Enterprises, I dare say the plan would not succeed."

"You can't kill the president. You know it won't gain you anything."

Denson laughed again. "We are not here to kill President Taylor. In fact, the president is not even in the state. But he is close by, visiting a dear friend in Redmond. From his university days, they say."

Billy said, "General?"

Denson checked his watch. "It's almost time."

He dropped to one knee and looked through the spotting scope. In silence, Billy and the general watched through their high-magnification optics.

"Who's the target, General?" Jim said.

No reply.

Jim tugged at the steel manacle around his wrist, but it didn't give.

"Just take it easy." Clint watched their prisoner.

Another minute passed in silence, and then Denson said, "There, climbing the steps. You see them?"

"I got them," Billy replied.

The brief conversation wasn't lost on Jim.

Multiple targets. "What's the mission?"

Still no reply.

"Wait until they are at the top of the steps. They will probably shake hands and then turn and wave to the crowd. At that point, take them. Both of them."

Now Jim knew the number of targets, but still nothing more specific.

"What about the Secret Service agents?" Billy said.

"Only after you have taken the primary targets, eliminate as many agents as you can. That will cause fear and confusion and slow their response time. But when I slap your shoulder, stop immediately. Understood?"

"Crystal clear."

CHAPTER 36

TINY DROPLETS OF SWEAT FORMED on Jim's forehead, and his respiration increased. His pulse remained faster than normal. A familiar physiological response. His body was preparing to fight.

He squeezed the thumb against his little finger, trying to make his hand skinny so it would slide free of the handcuff, but it was no use. The more he tugged, the more the flesh swelled from constriction and irritation.

While he struggled, he heard the almost inaudible *click* of the PEAP carbine firing.

With the exception of movement of his index finger, Billy was like a stone statue. He held the buttstock tight against his shoulder although there was no recoil. His eye was fixed behind the scope, his breathing slow and regular. Perfected muscle tone honed over hundreds of hours of practice.

Then he fired again.

Denson still watched through the spotting scope. "Both primaries are down. Shoot at will."

Jim watched as Billy's gloved finger flexed against the trigger…again…and again…and again. He knew death was

being delivered at the speed of light, and he was powerless to stop the carnage.

"No! You can't just slaughter them!"

Clint whipped his pistol across Jim's cheek, drawing blood.

Jim's head rolled on his shoulders, on the verge of unconsciousness.

"Gas him," Denson said.

Clint placed the mask over Jim's mouth and nose, and opened the valve on the lecture bottle. As the nitrous oxide flowed into his lungs, his eyelids drooped and then stayed shut. But Clint allowed the gas to continue to flow, knowing that the effects were short-lived.

Finally, Denson slapped a meaty palm against Billy's shoulder. The sniper stopped shooting and carried the PEAP carbine to the unconscious form chained to the radiator. He manipulated Jim's hands on the grip, forestock, and tripod of the carbine. Then he repeated the process of placing Jim's fingerprints on the discharged battery pack with the yellow stripe of tape. This would ensure that Jim would be unable to use the weapon if he regained his senses before Denson's team had fled.

With these tasks done and the PEAP carbine back in place before the window, Billy packed up the spotting scope and good battery, and clasped the case closed.

Denson texted a short message—*Done*—and then completed a final sweep of the room to make sure nothing but the pulsed-energy weapon was left behind. He signaled for Clint to turn off the gas, removed the mask and handcuffs, and packed everything up.

With this stage of the mission accomplished, the trio joined Jacob and descended the stairs. In the great room, the decorations had been completed and the militiamen were milling about near the door.

In the distance, sirens blared. And then a breaking news report broadcasted over the radio.

⊕

Shoulder to shoulder, Vice President Vince Nagashima and Speaker Dorothy Maybridge strode up the granite steps to the Idaho Capitol. The fundraiser luncheon had been successful, with fifty high-rollers paying $5,000 a plate to listen to the vice president and speaker give their stump speeches.

Maybridge was polling well, and she had every reason to be buoyant as she climbed the steps. One of a small cadre of members of the House who was willing to reach across the aisle to build bipartisan support for new legislation, she was masterful at balancing what was best for her constituents in Idaho with what was best for the nation. And it was a formidable challenge. With a significant political divide between urban populations centers, like Boise, and rural areas, navigating to common ground was often elusive. But time and again she'd demonstrated she was up to the task.

At the top of the stairs, they strode to the podium and then turned to face the assembled throng in the square and park. The applause roared, and a chant erupted.

"May-bridge! May-bridge! May-bridge!"

The vice president stood before the microphone and gazed across the crowd. They had assembled to show their support for their congresswoman, but he was not above taking advantage of the opportunity to make a few plugs for the Taylor Administration.

A half-step behind and to his left stood the Speaker, waving to the crowd.

Nagashima collapsed to the stone landing, a red hole in his forehead. A gruesome popping sound, far too soft to be a gunshot, occurred simultaneously with his collapse. A second later, Maybridge collapsed likewise.

The Secret Service agents on and around the landing drew their weapons—pistols and MP5 submachine guns. In those first few seconds, they expected two sharp reports indicating a distant rifle shot, but that never happened.

The audience still didn't comprehend the magnitude of what they'd just witnessed. The chanting had ceased, replaced with unintelligible chatter.

Then, as the Secret Service agents started to fall, with bloody trauma to the chest or head, the people closest to the stone steps began to scream. Turning about-face, the people in the crowd fled, some being knocked to the ground and trampled.

Idaho State Troopers who'd been positioned farther away from the podium, with orders to keep the crowd from approaching too close, were the first to radio in.

⊕

Without any visible sense of urgency, Denson and his men walked to the parking lot in front of the depot. From there, they departed for the interstate and headed west.

By the time the police arrived to seal off the station, they had all disappeared.

CHAPTER 37

WITHIN MINUTES OF CLINT TURNING OFF the supply of nitrous oxide, Jim began to regain consciousness. His first sensation was throbbing pain in the side of his face. As the fog continued to lift, he opened his eyes and became aware of his surroundings. His mind registered confusion that no one was in the room. Where had Denson, Billy, and Clint gone?

The sirens were loud now as one after another, emergency vehicles sped down Capitol Boulevard. Jim was surprised that his wrist was no longer handcuffed to the radiator. He touched his cheek and felt damp, clotting blood. The recent events came back to him. He grabbed hold of the radiator for support as he stood, only to stumble and then regain his balance.

Groggily, he took in his surroundings. The PEAP carbine was positioned in front of the oval cutout in the glass window, exactly where Billy had positioned it. He looked through the scope. It was focused on the capitol steps almost one and a quarter miles away. Many bodies lay haphazardly across the steps and landing. They were all wearing suits, and he assumed they were the security detail. Next to the podium, emergency medical technicians were lifting two other bodies onto gurneys, and then covering them with white cloths. He knew from the yellow and green dress with a matching blazer that one of the victims was a woman.

Jim examined the carbine without touching it. He noticed the yellow marking on the battery pack. He didn't recall seeing that when Billy had unpacked the carbine. But the significance of the stripe escaped him.

He looked through the window, down to the parking lot just in time to see several men climb into a black SUV and drive away. He swore one of them was Billy and another was Denson, but the coloration of the stained glass made positive ID questionable.

He ran for the stairway and stumbled on rubbery legs, catching himself on the railing. He headed down the stairs, taking deliberate steps and keeping one hand on the railing.

On the ground floor, the great room had a festive appearance, with linen-covered tables grouped near the middle of the room. Each table was adorned with a cheerful centerpiece that included a large bouquet of colorful balloons.

Near one of the doors, two police officers were speaking with one of the staff members who'd allowed Denson's men to enter. Jim walked to the other door, trying to be inconspicuous.

Just as he reached the door, a voice called out, "Hey! That's him! That's one of the guys. He was up in the tower."

The two officers made eye contact with Jim. For a moment, they just stared at each other. Then Jim pushed the door open and sprinted for the parking lot.

One of the officers, a young man of about thirty, with a slim athletic frame, gave chase while the other radioed in and then ran for the squad car.

With the nitrous still working out of his body, Jim's coordination was on par with someone who'd had six beers too many. He struggled to get his feet placed securely, stumbling twice, but then regaining his balance. He reached the parking lot and bounced off the side of a Cadillac. The collision checked his momentum just enough that he was able to plant his right foot and complete a sharp turn toward the nearby garden.

The young cop had stamina, cutting the commander's corner and catching up with him on a lawn between two flower beds. With outstretched arms, he dove forward and snagged Jim's leg. His grasp was firm, but as Jim struggled, his hands slid down to Jim's ankle.

With a human anchor attached to his foot, Jim was unable to move both feet in time with his body, and he fell face-first onto the green turf. The police officer was also prone, but he refused to give up his hand hold.

Jim kicked violently, eventually causing the grip to slacken and then release. He scrambled to his feet at the same time as the officer, who reached for his service weapon.

Drawing on his expertise in hand-to-hand combat, Jim released a kick that sent the pistol flying. He followed up with a right cross that connected head-on with the officer's jaw, and then a left jab that bloodied the man's nose and dropped him to his knees. Taking advantage of the momentary lull in the fight, Jim picked up the semiauto pistol and pointed it at the policeman.

"Stay down," he said, between breaths. "I don't want to hurt you anymore."

Staring into the barrel of his service piece, eyes wide with fear, the officer said, "I've got a wife and daughter—"

"Take it easy. I'm not going to kill you."

"What do you want?"

"Toss the Taser over here. Easy. Spare mags, too. Then cuff your hands."

The young man complied.

Jim said, "How old is she?"

"My daughter? She just turned six months two days ago."

"Give her a hug when you go home tonight."

He nodded.

"Look, whatever you think I did, I didn't do it."

With blood covering his upper lip, the officer said, "Then why did you run and assault me?"

"Would you have listened to me?"

"I would have taken you in for questioning. That's standard procedure."

"I've been framed. The men that did this planned out every detail. They gassed me and left me with the murder weapon, so I'm betting you'll find my prints on it. But I didn't do it. I didn't kill anyone. I know you don't believe me, but I'm telling the truth."

"You'll only make it worse by running."

Jim shook his head. "No. Something tells me this is much more than it seems. I can't be of any help if I'm locked up."

The approaching sirens encouraged Jim to end the conversation. He jogged off, disappearing into the gardens.

CHAPTER 38

FOR THE DURATION OF THE FLIGHT, Peter had reclined in his seat, motionless, eyes closed, and by all appearances, asleep. Except for the fingers rhythmically kneading the folds of flesh covering Diesel's neck. As much as the massage assured and relaxed the red pit bull, it also eased Peter's tension.

Several times, Governor Bingham had glanced toward Peter, but she didn't want to disturb his rest. The torn shirt sleeve and bloody bandage on his shoulder, the scabs across the bridge of his nose, were constant reminders of the ordeal they'd just gone through. Not that she was likely to forget anytime soon.

How odd that he could be so violent, and yet so gentle. The bond between man and canine was obvious. Although she didn't have any pets—her always-on-the-go job and lifestyle was not conducive to having dependents, human or otherwise—she understood that Diesel's trust and loyalty had been earned, not commanded.

She concluded that Peter Savage, a man she barely knew, was an enigma. A rare quality, one she'd never seen before in any person, least of all in politics. In her cut-throat business, it was all about getting ahead, beating the opponent. And then once the office had been won—fairly or otherwise, it didn't really matter—the game became self-enrichment. She'd been at it so long, she didn't think men like Peter Savage existed outside of novels or fairy tales.

Once again, she regretted chastising him over his actions to protect her. She felt selfish and hypocritical. He'd risked everything to save her.

You're an idiot, Kathrine. When will you learn to control your temper and keep your mouth shut?

But that wasn't all she was thinking over. As she replayed the day's events in her mind, she felt a mounting anger for being forced to fire a gun at another person. It was an act that ran against her beliefs. Reluctantly, she had to admit that Peter was right. If they—he—hadn't defended them, they would both be dead.

Her ruminations were interrupted by Sergeant Torres as he spoke over the intercom.

"Excuse me, Governor. But we just received an urgent message."

"Yes?"

Although the exchange was also playing through Peter's headset, he didn't show any reaction.

"Approximately twenty minutes ago, the vice president and Speaker of the House were shot and killed on the steps of the Idaho Capitol building. Almost the entire Secret Service detail was also killed."

"Oh, my God."

"I strongly suggest we divert to Salem."

Governor Bingham didn't answer. After all she had been

through, and now this horrible news. It was a nightmare that wouldn't end.

"Governor? Ma'am?" Torres said, trying to gain her attention.

"Yes, Sergeant. I heard you."

"Ma'am, we are being advised to fly to Salem, where we have the resources to secure your safety either at your residence or at your office."

"No," she said with conviction. "We are going to Redmond. Even if I can't meet with the president, I can't be a no-show. Now, more than ever, I need to show strength. How long until we land. We must be getting close."

Torres did a quick check of the instrument panel. "Seven minutes. But the tower may refuse our clearance."

"Why would they do that? They know this is a state police helicopter and that I'm onboard, right?"

"Yes, ma'am. But it's not that simple. Air Force One is on the ground there while the president is in Redmond. With the assassination of the vice president and the Speaker, they're going to get the president on that aircraft and on his way back to Washington. Until Air Force One is in the air and has cleared the area, they won't allow other aircraft into the same airspace. It's standard procedure."

Peter sat upright and opened his eyes.

"That's it." He pulled his hand back from Diesel and twisted in his seat to face the governor. "It makes sense now."

"What makes sense?" she said.

"What Denson is after. His plot is to decapitate the government. Why didn't I see it sooner?" Peter slapped the palm of his hand against his forehead.

"What are you talking about? Denson is trying to decapitate the government?"

"Yes, exactly. Don't you see. Denson is a student of history.

And he wants a radical change in government. It's the only way he can hope to succeed in carving the Northwest out of the U.S. So he borrowed a page from history. Another time, when part of the nation declared their secession from the Union."

"The Civil War?"

"That's right. And what monumental event happened right after Lee surrendered?"

"Lincoln was assassinated. But what does that have to do with anything that Denson is up to?"

"Everything. Denson is smart, but he's not original. The plot hatched by John Wilkes Booth and his fellow conspirators was not to merely murder Lincoln, but also to overthrow the government and have a new leadership put in place, one that was more sympathetic to the defeated Confederate States. Everyone remembers that Booth shot Lincoln in the head while the president and First Lady were attending a play at Ford's Theater. But almost no one recalls that Lewis Powell forced his way into the home of Secretary of State William Seward and severely injured him, leaving him for dead. Or that George Azterodt was supposed to assassinate Vice President Andrew Johnson, but got cold feet and decided to get drunk at a bar instead. If the assassins had been more competent, the plan probably would have succeeded."

"And you think Denson is trying to do the same thing here?"

"I'm certain of it. He as much as admitted to me that his men shot down that commuter plane in Hailey yesterday. His goal was to assassinate Judge Schultz of the Tenth Circuit Court because he thought she was not sympathetic to his case."

"What case?" Bingham sounded exasperated. "I'm not following you."

"That doesn't matter. He killed the judge. And then he murdered the vice president and the Speaker. If he assassinates the president, who's next in line to take the office?"

"The president pro tem of the Senate."

"And who holds that position?"

"Amy Knowlton, I think. She's the senior senator from… Idaho. Oh, my God. He's going to assassinate the president."

"No, he's not. Because we're going to stop him."

"But how?"

"We know his plan now. We can be proactive instead of reactive."

She pinched her eyebrows, deepening the furrows at the bridge of her nose. "Who is this *we* you keep referring to? In case you missed something back there, I'm not cut out for this macho bullshit."

Peter smiled, grateful she'd listened and not just dismissed him as a crackpot. Maybe she was learning.

"You did fine. Most women—"

She glared at him, preempting what she expected to be a sexist comment.

Peter cleared his throat. "Most *people* would have frozen under those circumstances. You didn't."

"Still, don't count on it a second time."

"Fair enough."

She stared at him. "You can't defend the president all by yourself. Besides, he has a security detail."

"First, Denson knows the president's defensive team. Just like he did for the vice president and the Speaker. And he will have devised a plan to neutralize those defenses. And second, I won't be alone. I'll have Diesel backing me up. Right, buddy?" He looked down at his friend, and Diesel replied with a *ruff* and a wagging tail. "Plus, I'd wage your security detail will help in a pinch. Right, gentlemen?"

"Hoorah," Torres said. "If even half of what you say is true, we're in. Right, Gardner?" He backhanded the pilot on the shoulder.

"Ten-four, good buddy," Gardner replied with a southern drawl.

Torres said, "The sarge here doesn't say much, but he's a good man to have your back. Even if he is Air Force."

Peter rolled his eyes.

Governor Bingham said, "Sergeant Torres is a former Marine. And Sergeant Gardner is ex-Air Force."

Peter said, "Now that we have that cleared up, can we get back to business?"

"Mr. Savage, we are all business, all the time," Torres replied.

"Glad to hear it. Now can you land near the control tower?"

"Sergeant Gardner can put this bird down anywhere big enough for a bar-b-que and a keg of beer."

"I'll take that as a yes."

"Well, there is one problem," Torres said. "If the Secret Service is serious about keeping the airspace clear, they could fire a Stinger up our ass."

Peter had already considered that possibility. He hoped there was still enough confusion that they could get in quickly before the presidential detail had completely organized its defenses.

"You and Sergeant Gardner are going to have to sweet talk your way in. Make sure they know the governor is onboard. Tell them it's a medical emergency."

"Roger that."

CHAPTER 39

COMMANDER NICOLAOU HAD NOTHING but the clothes he was wearing. His wallet, money, and phone had all been taken by the militia. He'd put considerable distance between himself and the Boise Depot, but police cars seemed to be everywhere. He got off the major thoroughfares and onto a two-lane road that appeared to lead to a commercial district that was well-past its prime. Although he'd been to Boise a couple times, that was years ago, and he had no idea where he was.

What he did know was where he needed to go. He needed a phone. And without money, the best place to find one was on another person. So all he had to do was convince someone to let him borrow theirs.

A change of clothes was also advised since he was sure every cop in Boise had his description and was looking for him.

On the opposite side of the next block was a coin-op laundry. He crossed the street at the corner and wandered into the facility. It was empty other than a young woman folding a load of clothes. Her toddler was sitting on the floor, doodling a picture with a few crayons. She didn't even glance at him when he walked in.

He casually walked to the bank of dryers. One had just completed its cycle, but the owner had yet to return to claim the clothes. Through the glass window, he saw a patterned flannel shirt. He opened the door and exchanged his windbreaker for the shirt. It was large, but workable. He left the shirt tails untucked and buttoned it up, nearly covering his tan turtleneck.

As he left the laundry, he spotted a tavern just a few doors away. Probably a favored hangout while people were passing time waiting for their wash to finish. He walked into the bar like he owned the place and headed straight for the restroom. He pushed the door aside, and as expected, a patron wearing a Seattle Seahawks ball cap was reliving himself at the urinal. Jim waited for him to finish and wash his hands before making his move.

"Excuse me," Jim said.

The man looked up and saw Jim's reflection in the mirror.

"May I borrow your phone? I need to make a call."

"Piss off, buddy."

"Come on, man. Give me a break. Just one call. I'll keep it short."

"I'll make it real short. No."

Jim slammed him forward against the counter, and pushed his face down in the sink while pulling his arm behind his back and up, pulling the ligaments in his shoulder.

"I asked politely. Now I'll ask again. May I borrow your phone, or should I break your arm?"

"Yeah, sure. It's in my pocket."

Jim released his arm and snagged the phone from his hip. "What's the PIN?"

With his face still held in the sink, the guy said, "Two, three, four, two."

"Thank you." Jim unlocked the phone and dialed the memorized number.

After three rings, the other party picked up.

"Hello." The voice was feminine and familiar.

"Lieutenant, I don't have much time, so listen carefully."

"Commander, it's good to hear from you. Please continue."

He rattled off the events in the clock tower and his current situation as a wanted man.

Lacey said, "It was Vice President Nagashima and Speaker Maybridge who were assassinated, plus more than a half-dozen Secret Service agents."

"That explains why there are police cars all over the streets. They'll have the city locked down by nightfall, if not sooner."

"What can we do?"

"Don't worry about me. Have you heard anything from Peter? Is the governor safe?"

She briefed her commander on the sat phone conversation with Jim's best friend.

"That's all I know. He and the governor should be safely on the ground in Oregon, but he hasn't checked in."

Jim ended the call and gave the phone back. "See, I told you it wouldn't be long." He released the man and pulled his face from the sink.

"You didn't call long distance, did you?"

"Really? That's what worries you?" Jim snagged the hat from the man's head, causing him to flinch. "Think I'll take this. You know, for the trouble."

He left the man in the restroom, then exited the tavern in search of a quiet ally to hole up in.

⊕

The news quickly spread within the intelligence circle, military as well as civilian. With simultaneous assassinations of two top government officials, law enforcement across the nation was on high alert, and more information was needed. Was this a case of foreign terrorism? Domestic? Or just a random nut job trying to gain Internet fame? So far, SGIT wasn't tasked with a significant role, merely requested to pass along anything they thought might be of use.

Lacey considered the directive. *Anything that might be of use* was a vague phrase, giving her plenty of room to skirt the intent without disobeying the black-and-white request. She resisted sharing that she had been in communication with Commander Nicolaou. That would earn her a charge of accomplice after the fact. Besides, it was likely that law enforcement had already recovered the PEAP carbine and sealed off the clock tower.

The connection to Stuart Denson was significant, but how could she share that without giving up her conversation with the commander? She was pondering this when her cell phone rang. It was sitting on her desk, and the name of the caller was displayed.

She snatched it up. "Yes, Mister Savage."

"Lieutenant, I don't have much time. We're about to land at Roberts Field in Redmond. That's the commercial airport."

"Yes, I know it."

"I have Governor Bingham with me." He went on to brief her on his theory and plan.

"I don't think that's a good idea. If you're right, the governor will be in danger."

"They don't want to kill her, only the president."

"It's too risky. Don't do it."

"Lieutenant, listen to me. Denson has been ahead of us every step. The president's security detail won't be able to protect him. They don't know what to expect."

"And you do?"

"The PEAP carbine. They stole it because they plan to assassinate President Taylor from a distance that is outside the secure bubble they placed around him."

"The carbine is in Boise. Apparently it was the weapon used to kill the veep and the Speaker."

Peter paused. He didn't expect this twist, or understand what it meant.

Over the intercom, Torres said, "Two minutes out. The tower was refusing to give us permission to land, but I did what you said and told them we have Governor Bingham and are declaring a medical emergency. I think it worked."

Peter returned his attention to Lacey. "They will make an attempt on the president's life. And they will do it in a manner not expected."

"Forget it. Let the Secret Service handle it. I'll notify the FBI and request they have a team on standby, in case you're right. Get the governor to safety."

"I will. She has two state police officers flying this helicopter. They'll escort her into the control tower where they'll be safe."

"What about you?"

For almost a half-minute, Peter didn't answer. His mind was churning over facts, possibilities, and capabilities, until it all seemed to crystalize.

"Lieutenant, what is the protocol under the current situation?"

"You mean the security protocol? I don't know the details, but I imagine they would escort the president back to Air Force One so he could return to Washington or some other designated secure location."

Another pause.

"Mr. Savage? Are you there?"

"That's just what I expected. I don't have time to explain, but you have to believe me. Denson knows that's how the Secret Service will respond. He's set a trap, and the president is about to run right into it."

CHAPTER 40

DANVERS PARKED THE U-HAUL on a dirt road about two hundred fifty yards off the Prineville-Redmond Highway. He'd found a spot next to three juniper trees that would offer some seclusion from view by passing motorists on the two-lane road. Earlier that morning, he and Bode and Finn Jensen had departed from the safe house in Prineville. Walker had remained behind and would travel later with four other men to the Redmond airport.

General Denson had appointed Walker as commander of this mission while Denson led the operation in Boise. And Walker had made it clear that he didn't want any more screwups like they'd done when they were supposed to fire their Stinger missile *into* the airplane, not over it.

That's what happens when you don't have live-fire training.

After pocketing the keys and locking the cab, they unloaded the mortar and eight shells from the back of the truck, dispersing the load among each of the three backpacks.

The load was heavy and irregularly shaped, resulting in metal rubbing each man's back, but they didn't have far to go. About five miles is what Danvers thought.

"Couldn't you have driven in just another mile or two before stopping?" Bode said.

"You know the answer to that," Jensen said. "Walker was clear. Park near the road. If we were to drive to the fire position, or even close to it, the dust trail would alert the security patrols."

Although a six-foot-high cyclone fence surrounded the runways at Redmond Airport—mostly to prevent deer from wandering in front of moving aircraft—while the president was in town, security teams were patrolling the outer perimeter of the fence. These patrols were manned by sheriff deputies and Redmond Police officers who seemed happy to draw easy overtime pay for simply walking around the fence line. Naturally they were armed, and they were instructed to be vigilant for potential terrorists. But the most excitement any expected was to warn away off-road enthusiasts riding motocross bikes or ATVs, who wanted to drive up to the fence to get a better view of Air Force One parked nearly a mile north of the departure terminal.

Jensen was in the lead as they marched single file. It was late morning, and although the air temperature was cool, the sun beating down on them, combined with the load each carried, had them sweating within a half-hour.

They stopped in the shade of a juniper tree and drank plenty of water. Danvers tossed his empty bottle aside.

"You'll want to pick that up," Jensen said.

"Why's that?"

"Because your fingerprints and DNA are on it."

He picked up the empty and stuffed it into a cargo pocket. "Sorry, Mom."

Jensen ignored him.

Bode said, "You know, I've never seen a forest like this. I mean, it's not like Idaho or the Rocky Mountains. Or anywhere I've been in the Northwest. All they have are these scrubby juniper trees. You couldn't cut a four-foot board from these things. Can't imagine their good for much other than firewood."

"Gin," Jensen said.

"What?"

"Gin. They use the berries to flavor gin."

"Is that a fact?" Bode reached up and pulled several blue-green berries from a low-hanging branch.

They were hard, and smaller than blueberries. He put one between his teeth and squished it, then spit it out.

"God, that's awful." He continued to spit while Jensen and Danvers laughed.

"I didn't tell you to eat them," Jensen said.

"Whatever," Bode mumbled.

Jensen got them moving again, frequently checking the military-grade handheld GPS unit. Accurate to within less than a yard, it was essential for their task.

He raised his fist. They stopped. Jensen faced the other two and held his index finger to his lips. Ahead was a small rise, maybe twenty-feet tall. They crept around it, staying on level sandy soil. On the far side of the rise, Jensen dropped to a crouch and froze. Bode and Danvers follow suit. They all remained motionless for two minutes, until Jensen motioned them forward.

"What is it?" Bode whispered.

"Up there. Maybe a couple hundred yards, I thought I saw movement."

"Deer?" Danvers said.

"No, I don't think so."

They waited another thirty seconds, all probing for movement.

Finally, Bode said, "I don't see anything."

"I don't either," Jensen said. "Whatever it was, it's gone now."

He checked the GPS. The screen showed a line that indicated the fence surrounding the airport, and a dot which was their planned fire position.

He enlarged the map on the screen. "We're about seven hundred yards from the fence."

"There shouldn't be any security patrols out this far," Danvers said.

"Maybe it was just a hiker, or one of the cops leaving a dump," Bode said.

Jensen thought through the situation. "Doesn't matter. We have to move farther away, another seven hundred to eight hundred yards of separation, just in case. This is going to put us behind schedule. Let's go. But be careful of your footing. No noise."

⊕

At the Prineville safe house, Walker, Mick, and three other militiamen prepared by donning studio-quality makeup that included different types of facial hair and wigs. Since none were experienced in applying makeup, they avoided any powders or creams intended to alter their skin tone for fear that it would look amateurish and draw attention.

Walker applied a bushy black mustache and wig with long black hair. When he put on a hat and dark sunglasses, he could barely recognize himself in the mirror.

Since they took turns sharing a single bathroom, it took two hours for all the men to get ready.

Mick said, "I grew up with four sisters, in a small house. This is what it was like every morning."

Walker checked the time—11:33 a.m. "Gear up. We're an hour behind Boise. Time to go."

Each man had a large recreational backpack strapped to his

back. They straddled Kawasaki dirt bikes and road to Redmond Airport. The parking lot had a large number of cars, as usual, but they found plenty of empty slots at a far corner of the lot.

They split into two separate groups and entered the terminal through different entrances. Although each pack was bulging, their upright posture hinted that the loads were not as heavy as they appeared. Their clothing was casual—jeans, lightweight T-shirts, and hiking boots. Together with the backpacks, they all looked to be going on, or coming from, a fishing or hiking expedition.

They took seats at different locations throughout the small terminal building—two outside the gift shop, one at the north entrance, and two more at the south entrance. Each man kept his chin down, either scanning his phone or thumbing through a magazine, making it impossible for the security cameras to get a full facial image.

Walker glanced at his watch—12:15 p.m. He removed a bottle of water from a pocket on the outside of his pack and drew a deep swig, then leaned back in his chair and stretched his legs out. He tried not to stare at the time.

Relax. Just like you're on vacation.

"Everything okay?" Mick said.

"We'll know soon enough."

Several more minutes passed, and then his phone buzzed. He looked at the incoming text message. It read, *Done.*

"That's it," Walker said. "The message. We're committed now." He typed a text to the group of five. *Be ready. Everything proceeding on schedule.*

He visually checked his men. They were all reading the message on their phones.

All they could do now was to wait. The next step had to come from the airport staff. Once the news reached President Taylor's security detail, and the president himself, an order would be given to evacuate the president. At that time, TSA and the airport police would evacuate the terminal because of its proximity to the runway. They couldn't take the chance that one or a few crazies with rifles might be inside the terminal, just waiting for an opportunity to take pot shots at Air Force One.

Since the president was at the Redmond Hotel, he would be hurried into his armored limousine and whisked away to the airport—a five-minute drive away. The presidential limousine, or Cadillac One, was armored to be invulnerable to small arms. With run-flat tires, eight inches of armor surrounding the passenger compartment, and five-inch thick bulletproof windows, the car carried the unofficial moniker of The Beast. Once inside, President Taylor would be in what was essentially a rolling safe.

Cadillac One would drive to a little-used civilian aviation terminal, which had been closed since the arrival of the chief executive, rather than the commercial departure terminal. The civilian aviation terminal was at the north end of runway 11/29. The motorcade would then follow the taxiway to the crossing runway 05/23, and drive to the north end, where the modified 747 was parked far from any traffic.

Walker and his small band of men would take control of the commercial departure terminal about a mile to the south of Air Force One. They had reviewed the plan over and over, committing every detail to memory. It was easy to assassinate the president of the United States. But to get away with it—that was the challenge.

And shortly, their hard work and planning would be put to the test.

CHAPTER 41

A CONVOY OF EIGHTEEN-WHEELERS, six in all, were driving north on Highway 97, and approaching Redmond Airport. Each trailer was fully loaded, pushing each truck close to the maximum rating of forty tons. After staying within the speed limit and driving in the right-most lane to avoid attention, they slowed and took the Yew Avenue exit, to the right. The road wound northeast, heading toward the airport.

Vehicle access to the departure terminal was via a loop road with a north and south entrance. Each entrance was marked with a masonry wall bearing the words WELCOME TO ROBERTS FIELD. The convoy slowed, allowing three trucks to peel off at the south entrance. The lead tractor-trailer made a sharp left turn across the road, steering the cab into the masonry wall. It was constructed of concrete and lava rock. The truck cab ground to a halt, its nose pressed into the stone wall, and the fully loaded trailer stretched across the road, blocking all lanes.

The second followed, but it turned right. The cab plowed into a raised planting bed with spring flowers, bushes, and evergreen trees, before high centering and coming to a stop.

The third truck pulled in across the overlap between the first and second trucks, driving the tractor so that it carved into the side of the first trailer.

This log jam of eighteen-wheelers was repeated at the north entrance to the airport, sealing off vehicle access. In between the south and north entrances was the parking lot, surrounded by a sturdy metal fence erected on top of a concrete stem wall two-feet tall. Nothing less than a tracked vehicle was going to cut through the parking lot to approach the terminal entrance. And local law enforcement didn't have tracked vehicles.

Men carrying rifle cases disgorged from the cabs, three from each, and moved on the terminal building about four hundred yards away. On schedule, civilians began exiting the building from all three entrances. It was an orderly exodus, but the long faces indicated they were not happy at being told to leave.

Inside the terminal, as the last civilians left, TSA and airport police approached each of the three groups of men. A tall and lanky TSA agent stepped up to Walker, who had slid low in his chair, legs crossed, and arms dangling.

"Didn't you hear the announcement?" the TSA agent said. "You are ordered to leave the building."

Walker looked up at the man, smiled, then swung his arm up. In his hand, which had been hidden behind his back, was a 9mm Glock pistol. He fired two shots in quick succession—a double tap—and the TSA man was dead before he hit the floor.

At the sound of the two gunshots, the airport police officers that had approached the other two groups of men turned and saw their fellow officer hit the floor. They drew their weapons on Walker. But behind each of them, the militiamen also drew Glock pistols and shot both officers in the back multiple times.

The crack of gunfire drew a trio of TSA agents. As they converged on the scene, only one had his service weapon drawn. Walker took him down with two bullets to his torso. The other two TSA officers, who were slow to comprehend the severity of their situation, paid for their mistake with their lives.

Shocked into action, the remaining four TSA officers and one airport police officer hunkered down behind the X-ray machines, metal detector, and body scanner in the security screening area. As cover goes, the machines provided little protection from bullets.

Walker and his men fanned out and focused their aim on the cluster of targets. Never expecting to be in a shootout, the TSA agents and airport policeman were ill-trained and in a state of panic. Their aim was poor, and it cost them.

One by one, the disciplined shooting from the militiamen dwindled the security force—first to four, then to three, then two. The last stood in surrender, her hands raised. She was African American and wore the blue TSA uniform. She was slim and attractive, young. She'd only been on the job for three months. Blood stained her left shirt sleeve. Her face was wet from tears.

"Please. Please just let me go. I won't cause any—"

Walker put a bullet though her forehead.

"Damn," Mick said. "That was cold."

"Shut up. We've got work to do." Then to the rest of the team, "Shoot out all the cameras. Hurry!"

His team dispersed throughout the public spaces of the building, placing one or two pistol bullets into each and every security camera.

Outside, the scrum of eighteen militiamen heard the gunshots and darted into the building. Inside, they gathered around Walker and removed their weapons from the cases. Several brandished Mossberg 590A1 military shotguns, but most were armed with M4 carbines. Chambered in 5.56mm NATO and select fire, they were the real deal, paid for with U.S.

dollars, and purchased from the same Pakistani general that had sold Denson the Stingers and 60mm mortar.

Walker looked across the faces. He knew every one of them, their training, and their capabilities. He stopped his gaze on one man in particular. He was older by several years, but equally fit. As usual, his long hair, a mix of black with streaks of gray, was wild and unkept, just like his beard. He wore dark blue coveralls just like the ground crew that serviced the commercial aircraft. Four other men were dressed similarly.

"Swanson, my friend," Walker said, and the man stepped forward.

He pointed at Walker's face. "You kinda look like Frank Zappa, just not as handsome."

"Very funny."

Swanson counted the bodies. "That's all? I expected heavier resistance. Why do you need all of us?"

"Because in my experience, no plan, no matter how well-thought-out, survives the first several minutes of engagement. You, my friend," he pointed at Swanson, "are the contingency."

"Contingency?"

"That's right."

"Gotcha."

"Good. Any problems?" Walker pulled at the facial hair and removed his wig.

The other men in Walker's cadre were doing the same, happy to remove the itchy disguises.

"Nope," Swanson said. "Just like clockwork. We got those trucks packed in tight, and the trailers are loaded down with hoppers filled with dirt. It will take hours for them to get heavy tow trucks in place to pull that mess apart."

"You have the remote?"

Swanson smiled and produced a small black box with two buttons and an LED.

"Wouldn't leave home without it. Press this button," he pointed, "and the device is armed. The LED will flash red. Press the other button, and the LED will go solid red and the remote will send a signal activating all the gas valves on each truck."

"How many?"

"Two cylinders of compressed liquified chlorine on each truck. Twelve in total. Enough to gas a small city. The valves are set to slowly release the chlorine over about a half-hour."

"Good thinking. That will slow the operation of the wrecking trucks, and keep the emergency response teams tied up for hours as they try to rescue people trapped in the parking lot. Should give us a large window to complete the mission."

"I sure hope you have a good plan for getting out of here. Ain't no one going back the way we came in."

"Don't worry. I've got that covered. We'll be leaving out the back door."

"Good plan. But..."

"But what?"

"Well, with the poison gas and all, maybe President Taylor will just stay in Redmond. You know, at a police station or something, rather than chancing it and having his driver take him to Air Force One."

Walker shook his head. "Not gonna happen. That fancy jet is his security. Not much can touch him more than eight miles up. Besides, Air Force One is parked at the north end of the runway. It's about a mile from here, and the road access is even farther away. This barricade with the semi-trucks in front of the terminal provides a diversion. The secret service will think all the action is taking place here, and they have a clear shot at escape. All part of the plan."

Walker took a step back from the assembled group. "Okay, gentlemen, listen up. The president will be on his way to Air Force One. Our first priority is to set up a strong defense.

Mister Swanson, I want your six best riflemen outside the three entrances—two at each door. It will be difficult for the police to get here. You have impeded their access. But make no mistake, they will get here. So be vigilant. Remember, they will be wearing body armor, so aim for their legs. Shoot to incapacitate. Everyone else follow me to the departure hall."

Swanson selected his best long-distance shooters and led them outside. Each of the three entrances was covered with an overhanging section of roof supported by pillars to provide shelter from rain and snow. The pillars were structural concrete columns faced with lava stone.

Each rifleman took up a kneeling position next to a column. Not only would they have excellent protection from incoming bullets, but they also had the benefit of using the columns to help support their carbines for better aiming.

Satisfied with their positions, Swanson dashed back inside to the departure hall, a long corridor with windows along the entire east-facing wall. Just beyond the windows, three regional commuter jets were parked. They'd been grounded to clear the way for Air Force One to depart as soon as President Taylor was onboard. Under normal circumstances, departing passengers would board their aircraft through one of six doors exiting from the hallway.

Three airport tugs were located near the planes, and several more, along with baggage carts, were parked at the north end of the terminal, just beyond the parked aircraft.

Swanson strode up to Walker, who was standing away from the rest of the men.

"The front entrances are covered," Swanson said. "Each team has a radio. As soon as contact is made, they'll report in."

"And I'll release the chlorine."

"You know, you're a few years younger than me, but you're a hell of a tactician."

"Just say what's on your mind. I don't like it when you compliment me."

"Fair enough. I don't like this part of the plan. It doesn't seem right."

"It's necessary." Walker placed a hand on his friend's shoulder. "Someone has to take the blame. This only works if we remove all suspicion from the movement. You know that."

Swanson nodded.

"Good. Now go on. We can't see the north end of the runway and Air Force One from in here. I need eyes out there. As soon as you see the motorcade pull up, radio me. I'll wait two minutes and then order Jensen to fire."

"Got it."

As he strode by, Walker called after him. "And send the newbies to me."

Swanson and the four other men dressed in blue coveralls exited through two of the departure doors closest to the parked planes. They held their carbines close by their sides and discretely placed them on the seats of two tugs, then ambled around the aircraft as they imagined maintenance personal might do. Their acting didn't have to be stellar, just good enough to convince any Secret Service agents watching through spotting scopes from the north end of the runway, two thousand yards away, that everything was normal.

All of the men were covertly looking in every direction for any sign of impending threat. Each carried a radio and could communicate with Walker should something untoward be spotted.

Swanson used a pair of pocket-sized binoculars to survey Air Force One and the activity surrounding it. So far, no black limousine. The plane sat at the end of the runway. The lettering on the fuselage, spelling UNITED STATES OF AMERICA, and the large American flag on the tail, left no doubt as to who rode in this 747.

The control tower was also in the same direction as the president's plane, but only three hundred yards away. With the aid of the binoculars, Swanson noticed a helicopter with special markings parked near the base of the tower.

He moved closer to one of the men "There's a police helicopter over by the tower. See it?"

The man squinted as he looked over Swanson's shoulder. "Yeah."

"Go check it out. Take your carbine, but keep it out of sight. Find out if there are any cops in the tower."

⊕

Sirens, loud enough to hear inside the terminal, announced the approach of emergency vehicles.

Fifteen seconds later the radio squawked, and a tinny voice said, "We have red and blue lights just beyond the south blockade."

Walker raised a portable radio to his lips. "Just stay calm. Don't shoot until you have a good target. I'm releasing the gas. If the chlorine reaches you, fall back inside the glass doors."

He activated the remote. Although he couldn't see it, greenish clouds of vapor streamed from the cylinders on each truck, combining to make a noxious cloud that hung close to the ground, spreading slowly.

The first responders, two patrol units from the Redmond Police Department, were stopped by the trucks blocking the road, still four hundred yards from the terminal building. The officers left the protection of their SUVs for a closer look at the semitrucks when they heard the hissing before seeing the gas. Within seconds, the gas enveloped them. The chlorine burned their eyes, nose, throat, and lungs. Raised blisters on exposed skin.

Coughing and gagging for air, the officers stumbled back to their vehicles. One fell to the ground within arm's reach of the SUV. The other made it inside. Unable to see, he found the radio and keyed the mic.

"Officer down. Some kind of gas," was all he got out before succumbing to the toxic vapors.

CHAPTER 42

WALKER PROPPED OPEN THREE of the departure doors so he could better hear the sounds from outside. He relied on all his senses, not only sight, when engaged in battle. It was a discipline he'd learned in the Marine Corps, on deployment in Afghanistan, and the practice had saved his life on more than one occasion.

With the doors cracked, he could now hear what he'd been deprived of. The air was filled with the sound of sirens—some near and some far—overlaid one another, creating a cacophony. To this mix, a new tone emerged. The high-pitch roar of jet engines.

Air Force One was powering up.

Walker keyed his handheld radio. "Swanson. What do you see?"

"Nothing. No motorcade. But it must be close, because they're warming up the engines."

"Roger that."

"Tell Jensen to be ready. Once the boss is onboard, that plane ain't waitin' for no one."

"Will do. Out."

When Walker ended the radio call, it occurred to him that Jensen hadn't checked in. Although not mandatory, it was odd for him not to do so.

He changed channel and keyed the mic. "Jensen, copy?"

"Jensen here. I was just about to report. We've had a setback."

⊕

Like most traffic control towers, the one at Roberts Field was constructed of concrete, and left in the natural dreary gray color of cement. With a wide base, slim waste, and flared top surrounded with windows, air traffic controllers had an unobstructed view of the runways and taxi lanes. Presently, all eyes, including those of Governor Bingham, were on Air Force One.

The militiaman approached the police helicopter. His carbine was held behind his back with one hand, the other swinging at his side. From twenty-feet away, he could see that the pilot and copilot were not in the aircraft. He stopped, reasoning that they must be in the tower. Maybe having a cup of coffee and BS-ing with the traffic controllers, waiting for a great view of the president's plane as it took off.

He cautiously strode to the tower door constructed of steel with plates over the hinges and bolt for added security. With his weapon in the low ready position, he reached for the doorknob, but it wouldn't turn. He was considering his next move when he heard a rumbling growl.

He froze.

"Don't you know they keep the door locked?" Peter was standing several paces behind the man. "Keeps unwanted visitors from getting in."

Without turning, the man said, "Who are you?"

"Nobody, really. Just someone who happens to be in the wrong place at the wrong time. Or, in your case, maybe it's the right place at the right time."

"You a cop?"

"No. Saw you and your friends exit the terminal all at once. Seemed odd that five maintenance personnel would exit the passenger departure doors and inspect three aircraft at the same time. So I hopped in that helicopter you were checking out, hid behind the pilot's seat. You should have looked more closely. Lazy, if you ask me."

"You have a big mouth, but you're not very smart."

"Oh? What makes you say that?"

"Because if you're not a cop, no reason I shouldn't just kill you. And your dog." The man spun on his left foot, raising his weapon.

Boom!

The Benelli bucked in Peter's hands. The buckshot ripped a ghastly hole in the man's chest, destroying his heart, a major portion of his left lung, and severing his spine. His angular momentum carried him though a complete rotation, and he came to rest on his side.

Peter exhaled the breath he'd been holding. "Never said I wasn't armed."

The Benelli was now empty, so he slung it over his shoulder. Diesel followed him as he walked up to the body and confiscated the M4 carbine, plus all three spare magazines. Each held thirty rounds—one hundred twenty rounds total, assuming the mag in the carbine was full.

The steel tower door swung open, and Sergeant Gardner stood in the doorframe with his sidearm aimed at Peter. Without his flight helmet on, it was the first time Peter had a good look at him. His short hair was light brown, a couple shades darker than blond, and his eyes were chestnut brown. He sported a tight mustache, but no other facial hair.

As soon as he realized there was no threat, he lowered his

gun. "Heard the shot."

"Yeah, that was me. Why is it these guys always think they're fast on the trigger?"

"Good thing for you, he wasn't."

"Is the governor safe?"

Gardner nodded. "That stairway up to the top of the tower is a kill box, and Torres is damn good with a pistol. Anyone tries to enter the control room, and he'll stop them."

A half-dozen bullets skipped off the macadam near Peter, accompanied by the sharp report of rifle fire. Several more cratered into the concrete tower near Sergeant Gardner.

They both dashed around the side of the tower for temporary protection, Diesel right by his master. It would take a minute or two for militia men to flank them.

"Look," Gardner said, "we have a pretty good view from up there, and it's going to be rough going for any help to get in here. They have the loop road blocked with semitrucks and are releasing gas. Already killed two Redmond officers."

"I'm sorry."

Gardner lifted a hand. "The gas seems to be coming from the trucks. It's spreading and hugging the ground. The stuff's covering the parking lot, and we've got maybe a hundred civilians trapped there. The fire department has cut down sections of fence to allow people to escape. They're setting up a triage across the street in the business park."

"Is the gas colored?" Peter said.

"I can't tell through the tower windows. They're tinted. But some of the reports say it's greenish, with a noxious odor. It burns any tissue it comes in contact with."

"Chlorine." Peter inspected the M4, making sure he was comfortable with the operation of the safety and the select fire lever. "Terrible stuff. Good news is the fire department can knock it down with a spray of water."

"They already have hoses out, but they can't get close enough to the trucks to contain it."

"That means they'll have to come across the runways. That's a lot of flat, open ground. If the militia is as good as I fear they are, a lot of good men are going to get hurt."

"You're assuming they have more than a handful of men."

"They went to a lot of planning and expense to pull this off. Trust me, they'll have a small army of men here. We just haven't met them all yet."

A new volley of bullets reminded them they needed better cover.

Peter pointed to a pushback tug only twenty yards away, and they sprinted for it. The squat machine had a large engine behind the bench seat that the driver sat on, and it was used to move commercial aircraft. It sat low to the ground and had hard rubber tires, making it a good barrier to bullets.

"Diesel. Stay." Peter pointed at the state police sergeant. "Guard."

The pit bull tilted his head to the side in a questioning gesture.

"Guard."

The dog sat and licked his lips.

"What's that about?" Gardner said.

"I don't want him breaking cover and charging one of the riflemen."

Confident now that Diesel would stay put, he sighted the carbine around the end of the tug, using what passed for a bumper as a rest. He squeezed off three rounds and took down the militiamen that had been shooting at him. Another gunman ducked behind the landing gear of a Bombardier Regional Jet, and then resumed shooting. He placed several rounds onto the tug, but none came through.

"I need a rifle," Gardner said.

"Well, this one is mine. Won it fair and square. You have to do what I did and go out there and convince one of those militia fellas to give you one."

The volume of fire intensified as two more militiamen took positions next to the landing gear under the regional jet. Peter fired back occasionally, just enough to keep them from advancing.

Peter glanced at Gardner. "Why isn't Air Force One moving into takeoff position? It's just sitting there. Maybe the president isn't onboard yet?" He fired off a couple more shots, puncturing a pair of tires and causing the plane to settle nine inches.

"He's gotta be onboard. But they won't risk running the gauntlet of rifle fire. We have to suppress these guns before they'll take to the air."

CHAPTER 43

PRESIDENT JOSHUA TAYLOR was pulled out of Cadillac One by the Secret Service agent. Surrounded by five more agents, he dashed for the steps leading up to the open hatch of the 747. Men on the ground dressed in khaki slacks and wearing navy-blue windbreakers over polo shirts were armed with an assortment of military-grade arms, including full-auto MP5s, bullpup shotguns, and M4 carbines. They surrounded the giant plane, vigilant for danger.

Other men, armed with Stinger shoulder-fired missile systems, were stationed around Air Force One and ready to fire on a moment's notice should unauthorized aircraft approach. And given the circumstances, that meant *any* aircraft.

Once the president was in the air, his security detail, aircraft maintenance crew, Cadillac One, and other special motorcade vehicles would all be loaded into the C17 cargo plane parked nearby at the civilian aviation terminal.

Located at the front of the Boeing airplane, opposite the entrance door, was the presidential office, which is where Joshua Taylor presently sat at his desk. He'd already been briefed on the assassination of his vice president and the Speaker of the House.

That briefing didn't take long because few facts were known, and there were many more questions than answers. Now the chief of security, Senior Master Sergeant Landis, was reading the president in on the chaos unfolding at Roberts Field.

President Taylor was about to boil over. "You mean to tell me the airport is under siege? What the hell is going on?"

"That's an accurate statement, Mister President. As to who is behind this and what they want, we don't know yet."

Taylor sank lower in his chair. "So why aren't we airborne? What are we waiting for?"

"Sir, there's a gunfight underway on the tarmac near the terminal. One of the agents has a spotting scope on them. He said a couple men in blue coveralls, thought to be maintenance personnel, are shooting at a civilian and a man dressed in a flight suit. Colonel Norton is strapped in at the controls and ready to takeoff once the men with rifles are no longer shooting. He says one lucky bullet in the right place can bring this plane down."

"That doesn't make any sense. Why would maintenance personnel have guns?"

"No, Mister President, they would not. They must be terrorists dressed as airport staff. We do not know who they are shooting at, or why."

"Whoever they are, if the terrorists are trying to kill them, they must be good guys. Maybe air marshals or plain clothes officers?"

Landis shrugged.

⊕

Flying north at thirty-two thousand feet, the modified HC 130J Combat King IIB aircraft, tail number VZ22, was closing on Roberts Field at three hundred fifty knots. The one-of-a-kind aircraft was used exclusively by SGIT for field operations. However, the present operation was highly irregular since it was both unsanctioned and taking place on U.S. soil.

Following her phone conversation with Commander Nicolaou, only seventy minutes ago, Lacey made a snap decision. As acting director of SGIT, she deployed a five-man strike team to Boise. The Combat King was always fueled and equipped within general mission parameters, so it took less than ten minutes to get the transport in the air.

The five SGIT operators, all highly experienced, officially volunteered for the mission, thus saving Lacey the formality of issuing an order. If it went bad, it might help at Lacey's court martial.

While en route to Boise, the Lieutenant had a second call, this time with Peter. Based on that call, she ordered the plane to change course for Redmond, Oregon. If Peter was right, and she had come to believe he was, they would be flying into combat against a well-armed, well-trained, and determined domestic terrorist cell.

⊕

"What the hell are you talking about?" Walker was in no mood for riddles.

The gunfire just outside on the tarmac was another problem, but Swanson could take care of that, at least until he understood what Jensen was talking about.

"We almost bumped into a security team operating seven hundred yards outside the fence. We had to abandon the firing position in favor of one farther from the perimeter, and better concealed."

"So? I don't have time for this."

"So we are too far away to reach the target at the north end of the runway."

"You'd better not be joking, or I'll cut your tongue out and feed it to you for dinner."

"No joke, Mister Walker. The GPS places us at just about

four thousand yards from the target. Max range of the sixty mike mike HE shell is a little over thirty-eight hundred yards."

"Dammit. You really screwed up big time. Do you have any idea what Denson is going to do to you?"

Jensen swallowed hard before continuing. "Listen. It's not that bad. The mission's not over."

"The hell you say!"

"Please. Just give me a minute. Like I said, we are out of range of the north end of the runway. But we are only three thousand seven hundred thirty yards from the south end. That's the direction the plane will depart. So we target the south portion of the runway as the plane is in its takeoff roll. Even if we don't get a direct hit, shrapnel and debris is likely to shred the turbines, and if the landing gear hits a crater, it'll rip right off."

The radio band was silent for an uncomfortable several seconds, long enough that Jensen thought Walker may have signed off.

And then he spoke, more calmly than before. "Not bad. It just might work. But timing will be critical. If you fire too early, they'll abort the takeoff. Too late, and they'll be airborne, and our chance will be lost. And you know what that will mean for you and your team."

CHAPTER 44

FROM BEHIND THE TUG, Peter calmed his nerves and reminded himself of the principles of marksmanship. Several deep breaths, and then he slowly exhaled. Placed the tip of his finger against the trigger. Lined up his sights. Squeezed.

The shot drilled one of the gunmen kneeling behind the landing gear.

More bullets pinged off the tug and the tarmac, skipping past him. He adjusted his aim and repeated the process, striking the second gunman in the chest.

A fourth militiaman dashed for the front landing wheels and began shooting at Peter, while a fifth man skidded to a stop behind the push away tug parked in front of the commuter jet, and then disappeared from view.

Although the gunman was kneeling behind the landing-gear tire, half his body was still exposed. He was firing single shots in rapid succession, and the bullets were going all over the place, but none close to Peter.

Hunkered down, with his back against the tug, Sergeant Gardner watched as bullets skipped off the hard pavement.

"That guy can't shoot worth a damn. Surprised he hasn't

flipped the lever to full-auto and gone Rambo."

The staccato of fully automatic fire ripped the air.

Peter ducked even lower. "I think he heard you."

In a second, the magazine was emptied. And while the militiaman was attempting to replace it, Peter regained his shooting position. He took aim and squeezed off two shots. The first punctured the tire, and the second took the man down.

⊕

From behind the tug, Swanson's radio squawked.

"Yeah." He kept his head down behind the steel machine.

"Who the hell are you shooting at?" Walker said.

He could only see half the gun battle. Peter and Gardner were too far to the north, to Walker's left, for him to see through the plate glass windows.

"There's a police helicopter by the tower," Swanson replied. "I spotted it from out here and had one of the guys check it out. Must have been two cops in it—"

"You idiot! Air Force One won't take off with you guys out there shooting it up."

"We don't want them to take off! Jensen should be dropping mortar shells on them."

"Change of plans. He's out of range. He can only reach the south end of the runway."

Swanson exhaled his frustration. "Johnson and I will break off. Stop shooting. Then the plane can take off."

"They won't fall for that. They know there are two more shooters. I'm calling three of the men stationed out front to offset your losses."

"But what if the police storm the front entrances?"

"They won't. Besides, three men are enough to hold them. And if necessary, I'll shift reinforcements. Now, listen. Here's what I want you to do." Walker explained his plan.

When finished, he ordered the rest of the team to stay below the windows and out of sight.

⊕

The fifth gunman popped up from behind the tug, his hands raised. He wasn't holding a rifle.

"I surrender!" he shouted.

Gardner raised his head to see what was going on. "Looks like you got 'em on the run, Tex."

"Maybe." Peter didn't share his partner's confidence.

Based on his experience with the militia, they didn't give up easily.

"Do you see anyone else?" Peter said.

"No. You think it's a trap?"

"I'm pretty sure these guys are from the same militia that kidnapped the governor. I had a skirmish with them yesterday. They slaughtered an FBI SWAT team. If I'm right, and they are from the same militia, I can't see them giving up without a fight."

"Doesn't that gun battle you just had qualify as a fight?"

"Not for that guy raising his hands. He didn't fire a single round. And he's not wounded, that I can see."

"Be that as it may, my job is to arrest him. Would feel much better if you and your dog came along with me. You know, as backup."

Peter smiled. "Come on, Diesel. Let's help the man."

With Diesel between them, they marched toward the tug and the militiaman with his hands on his head. Peter kept his weapon aimed at the man, and Gardner had his pistol drawn. They didn't see anyone around the aircraft or near the terminal building, and no one shot at them. When they got close, they gave the tug a wide berth in case there were others hiding behind it, but there was only the one man.

With Peter's gun trained on him, Gardner ordered the man

forward. He complied, making no threatening moves, and then stopped two paces in front of the officer.

"Lie face down on the pavement, hands out to the side."

"Can I use my hands to get down?"

"Yes. Just don't be stupid. What's your name?"

"Swanson."

"That's it? Just Swanson?"

"Bill Swanson." His head was turned sideways, and his cheek pressed against the blacktop.

Peter had relaxed after failing to see any threat, and lowered his gun barrel, but still kept it pointed at Swanson.

"How are you going to restrain him?" He suspected that there was not a pair of handcuffs under the sergeant's flight suit.

"I'm wearing a paracord belt. It's braided from nylon parachute cord. Just have to cut off a length long enough to wrap several times around his wrists. Always thought it would come in handy someday. Never dreamed it would be like—"

Crack! Captain Gardner collapsed. Diesel bolted. Peter pivoted, raising his carbine and trying to acquire the shooter.

Crack! Peter was sure he felt the air stir from the bullet passing by his head.

The pit bull was close now. The gunman was standing in a maintenance doorway, and he shifted his aim, firing again and again. But the canine was moving too fast, and every bullet was striking the tarmac just behind him.

Swanson jumped to his feet and ran into the departure hall, through one of the doors Walker had left ajar.

Peter fired and kept firing until the militiaman fell.

"Diesel!"

His buddy turned and trotted back, satisfied the danger was no longer.

Sergeant Gardner was sitting with both legs out straight. The blood stain on the left leg of the flight suit told Peter what had happened.

"How bad is it?"

Gardner was cutting the cloth to expose the wound.

Through gritted teeth, he said, "Hurts like a son of a bitch. But it didn't hit any major artery."

Blood was oozing out, but not pumping.

"I think it missed the bone, too."

"Let me have your knife." Peter cut off the pant leg and made strips to wrap around the bullet wound.

It didn't take long, and soon the field dressing was secured in place. Then Peter helped him to his feet.

The smell of blood associated with Peter's friend made Diesel anxious. He was pacing in tight circles around them, constantly moving his head , searching for elements of danger.

"Let's get you seated on this tug. We'll drive to the control tower and get you comfortable."

"There's a first aid kit in the helicopter." Gardner winced as a new spasm of pain burned up his leg.

"Good, because my supplies are mostly used up." Peter smiled, hoping to cheer up the officer.

He turned the key left in the ignition, and the engine fired up. It was a short but bumpy ride to the tower, and Peter helped Gardner to the door. Torres was right there, opening the door and helping his partner inside while Peter ran to the helicopter and grabbed the medical supply kit.

He returned to find Diesel sitting next to the wounded sergeant.

"Looks like you have a new friend."

Gardner petted his head. "He's a good dog."

"You don't have to tell me that. Oh, by the way, here's Swanson's carbine. I'd say you earned it." Peter stood the weapon against the wall, and Torres set to work, properly dressing the wound with antiseptic and sterile bandages.

Diesel noticed it first and turned his head toward the north.

Then Peter heard it. The four General Electric engines were powering up.

He stepped outside the control tower and walked several paces until he had a clear view. As he watched, Air Force One crept forward, aligning with the center of the runway. The whine of the turbines grew even louder, and the Boeing 747 began accelerating.

⊕

Jensen was fixated on a small display centered on the radio remote control unit. He used both hands to operate the controller. It required skill, but he'd put in a lot of practice and had a good feel for maneuvering the quadcopter. He had the drone hovering five hundred feet above their firing position. It carried a small and ultralight weight video camera.

The camera was pointed at Air Force One, parked at the end of runway 05/23. He'd been watching it for the past twelve minutes and was wondering if the plane was going to takeoff.

What is the delay?

Finally, his patience was rewarded.

"Get those rounds ready," he said. "I think I see movement."

Seconds later, the increased roar of the engines reached his ears, confirming his suspicions.

"They're getting ready to takeoff."

Bode was on the sight, ready to make minute adjustments based on visual feedback from the video. Danvers was responsible for dropping the 60mm high-explosive rounds down the mortar tube. When the round struck the bottom of the tube, the firing pin would set off the propellant charge.

"Ready...ready...fire!"

CHAPTER 45

WITH COMMAND OF AIR FORCE ONE, Colonel Norton had the last word concerning everything related to his aircraft, it's flight schedule, and onboard activities. Theoretically, in these matters, he even had authority over the president, although that theory had never been tested.

Sitting three stories above the reinforced tarmac, Norton looked down the seven-thousand-feet of black ribbon, toward the airport terminal at the south end of the runway. Without a plane load of passengers and luggage, and only carrying half the fuel load, his 747 performed like a lean thoroughbred. With the brakes engaged and his left hand on the yoke, he advanced all four throttles stepwise, giving the engine thrust time to equalize.

He felt the four-hundred-thousand-pound machine bucking and pulling, straining to be released so it could sprint forward and take to the air. He completed one more scan of the instruments—all readouts looked normal. The gunfire had ceased. The Secret Service spotter had confirmed that the gunmen had been taken down. And a state police sergeant had reported through the control tower that all the terrorists had been killed, with the exception of one, who got away after being disarmed.

Norton made the command decision that now was their best opportunity to takeoff and enter the safety afforded by traveling at Mach 0.9, through the thin air, at forty-five thousand feet.

"Inform the cabin crew to take their seats and strap in," Norton said to his copilot, Colonel Sheri Ortega. "We're going to see just how fast this puppy can climb."

With the brakes released, the aircraft shot forward, pressing his body into the seatback. Ortega called out the speed. Norton never allowed his gaze to waver from the view out the cockpit window.

"Thirty knots…fifty knots…"

An explosion erupted on the edge of the runway and in front of the aircraft, blasting bits of paving and rubble into the air. The sharp boom even penetrated the insulated aluminum fuselage over the whine of the turbine engines. Norton pulled back on the throttles and applied the brakes to slow the big plane, and then nudged the yoke and the rudder to steer around the debris tossed up by the explosion in an effort to protect the engines.

"What the hell was that?" Ortega said. "Artillery?"

With a hundred-fifty-foot-wide runway, he had plenty of room to clear the crater. But the maneuver came at the expense of speed.

"Save it for later," Norton said. "Air speed? Call it out."

He advanced the throttles again, taking care to avoid imbalanced thrust, which could push the plane off the runway.

"Fifty knots," Ortega said. "Seventy…eighty-five…looks like we're gonna make it, sir."

⊕

Captain Oslund dropped the Combat King to ten thousand

feet and reduced his airspeed to two hundred knots for a flyover of Roberts Field. First Sergeant Mark Beaumont—call sign Bull, due to his large size and strength—was sharing the cockpit and wanted a quick visual before determining the drop zone for his team. Lieutenant Lacey had said to expect an armed domestic terrorist cell intent on killing President Taylor, and he knew she wasn't one to inflate the facts.

Even before the airfield was in sight, Oslund received a directive from the tower.

He relayed the message to Bull. "Tower is ordering us on a new vector. We are not allowed within five miles of the airport."

"Not surprising," Bull said. "Tell the tower we are a unit of the Strategic Global Intervention Team, and have been ordered to render necessary assistance. That should buy us a minute, maybe two, while they noodle it over."

"Roger that." Oslund relayed the message.

As the Combat King drew nearer, Oslund said, "The airport is directly ahead. As we pass, it will be on the left side. I'll bank into a sharp turn to give you a few more seconds viewing time. Take a good look. They're not going to be happy with us making a second pass."

Bull was craning his head forward, straining to make out details in the distance. He was pretty sure he saw flashing blue and red lights. Emergency vehicles—not a good sign.

The Combat King banked to the right.

Captain Oslund said, "We've been ordered to clear the airspace. Sorry, Sergeant. Sounds like Air Force One is ready to takeoff."

The nose of the aircraft moved progressively toward the east. Just before the airport was lost from view, Bull saw a flash of light where the runway was located, like a giant flashbulb. His years of combat experience told him what caused that type of brilliant strobe.

"You have to turn back," he said to Oslund.

"Once Air Force One has taken off, the tower will open the air space."

"You didn't see that?"

"See what?"

"Down there on the runway. There was an explosion."

Oslund didn't answer right away, preoccupied with a frantic message from the tower.

Finally, he said, "Air traffic control is reporting an artillery attack on the president's plane."

"Turn us back," Bull said.

The Combat King banked to the right. Oslund intended to bring the aircraft around and approach the airport again from the south. Halfway through the turn, the copilot was the first to spot it.

A white smoke trail arced up from the far end of the runway. And yet no alarms sounded in the cockpit.

"We got a heat seeker at three o'clock," the copilot said. "Looks like it has a lock."

"Flares and chaff." Oslund yanked the yoke to the left, turning away from the missile.

The copilot flipped switches that ejected the decoys. Although the chaff was designed to fool radar-guided weapons, Oslund wasn't taking any chances that the threat receivers might have failed to detect the characteristic radar emissions from a guided weapon.

Canisters of aluminum-foil ribbon popped open in the slipstream behind the Combat King to spoof homing radar. At the same time, a stream of flares ejected out both sides of the fuselage, burning white-hot, much hotter than the engine exhaust. But they didn't always trick the missile guidance system.

The other defensive strategy was to outrun the missile.

Oslund was certain it had to be a shoulder-fired weapon—short-range, but deadly, nonetheless.

Captain Oslund pushed the yoke forward and shoved the throttles to full power.

⊕

The real-time video feed from the drone showed where the first shell had hit. The three-man mortar team had gotten a lucky break that Air Force One slowed to avoid the first explosion. Now they had to fire as quickly as possible, causing the shells to follow a line down the runway.

"Two hundred yards left," Jensen said.

In frantic movements, Bode made the sight adjustment, and Danvers dropped the next round down the tube.

Whump! The high-explosive shell fired in an arcing trajectory.

Jensen shouted, "Two hundred left."

And like a choreographed dance, Bode adjusted, and Danvers dropped the round down the tube.

Whump!

Three shells were in the air before the first one hit, blasting another crater in the runway. All seven 60mm shells were fired within eighteen seconds.

CHAPTER 46

"EIGHTY-FIVE...LOOKS LIKE we're gonna make it, sir," Colonel Ortega said.

The aircraft continued to accelerate, pushed by the four GE turbofan engines, each pumping out sixty-three thousand pounds of thrust.

Then an explosion off to the left, just about even with the nose of the aircraft, and short of the runway. The blast sent a plume of dust into the air, but the wingtip whisked by it, leaving swirling air currents to stir the tan cloud.

"Come on, baby, come on," Norton said.

"One hundred knots."

The engines were screaming. Another explosion shook the fuselage violently.

Ortega checked the instruments. "All good. Must have hit just behind the wing. Engines reading normal."

"Come on..."

Halfway down the runway. Just a little more speed, and he'd pull back on the yoke.

Boom!

The blinding flash was right in front of the cockpit. The

nose was pelted with hundreds of pieces of rock and metal shrapnel. He felt a sudden bump, like a car hitting a pothole, but the aircraft was over it in a fraction of a second, although it cost him precious speed, losing five knots. The vibration he felt caused some concern, but he dismissed it as a shredded set of tires on the front landing gear.

Another blast, just off the left side, and this time right in front of the wing, followed by a *Bam!* Sounded like a giant hand had slapped the side of the fuselage. Debris was sucked into engines one and two. The rapidly spinning turbine blades shattered on contact with stone and steel. The centrifugal force of the spinning turbines launched sharp pieces of metal into the engine cowlings. Other pieces severed fuel and hydraulic lines.

"One and two shut down." Ortega studied the instrument panel. "Activating fire suppression."

Colonel Norton fought to maintain control as the sudden unsymmetrical thrust pushed his aircraft hard to the left. He had to act immediately, or the nose would plow into the soft earth.

He jammed the rudder to correct the yaw, and the nose moved, pointing back down the center of the runway.

Airspeed continued to climb, only more slowly.

Ortega called out, "One hundred knots...one hundred ten..."

An earsplitting *crack!* resounded through the cockpit, and a violent shutter racked the airframe. Norton and Ortega twisted in their seats, trying to get a full view of the wings.

It was on the left side, and Norton saw it easily. The last shell had blasted away the wing tip. Fuel was spewing from the severed aluminum appendage, and fire was now a serious danger. The loss in lift combined with the added aerodynamic drag caused the steering of the nose landing gear to feel heavy and sluggish.

Colonel Norton ran the math in his mind. The conclusion was clear. They weren't going to get off the ground.

He slammed the throttles back to idle and jammed the brakes. He and Ortega were thrown forward, their bodies restrained by the shoulder harnesses and lap belts. The end of the runway loomed ever closer in the cockpit window. The brakes squealed in protests, but Norton held them tight.

Ortega activated the handset and flipped the PA switch. "Brace for impact! Brace for impact!"

Air Force One was still moving at fifty knots when the front landing gear left the pavement for packed gravel. The rubber tires shredded and flew off, leaving just the metal rims, which gouged a trough. Then the gravel gave way to sandy dirt. Bogged down, the landing gear snapped off. The nose of the 747 dropped, digging a trench a quarter the length of the plane, before finally coming to rest.

Colonel Ortega was on the radio. "Mayday! Mayday! Angel is down. Repeat, Angel is down. Under attack by ground forces. Angel is no longer viable."

"Stay on the radio." Norton unstrapped and met Master Sergeant Landis at the door.

"What's the status of the aircraft?" Landis said.

He'd seen the explosions through the cabin windows, heard the engines self-destruct, and seen the tip of the left wing blasted away.

Norton shook his head. "You have to get Eagle into Cadillac One, ASAP. The left wing is leaking fuel, and the brakes are probably red hot. If the tires haven't caught fire yet, they soon will. Everyone has to evacuate."

⊕

Walker was crouched low, conversing with Swanson in the departure hallway. The rest of the team was also staying low and peering over the knee-high window ledge. At the end of the runway was an incredible sight. Air Force One, perhaps the most potent symbol of Western power, sat with its nose buried in the dirt off the end of the runway.

As they watched, several of the main landing gear tires burst into flames, heated to ignition by the red-hot brake discs. As the fires grew, one by one the tires burst with a *bang!*, like a series of small explosions. A light breeze, blowing from the terminal across the runway, carried the thick black smoke, engulfing the left side of the aircraft in acrid vapors. Fuel was still pouring out the severed left wing, spreading in a pool that would soon reach the burning tires.

"Not quite what I planned," Walker said. "But a damn good outcome, anyway."

"What do you want us to do?" Swanson said.

"They have no choice but to evacuate everyone onboard. Get your team ready. Everyone will be coming out the side facing us. That means the security detail will be concentrated between us and the plane."

Swanson hurried down the length of the departure corridor, sharing the directive.

"The security detail will be wearing body armor," he said. "Conserve your ammo and aim for the legs."

The militiamen were grouped at each of six doors opening onto the tarmac. Each man checked his weapon, and checked it again. The memorized activity occupied their attention, denying fear a place to take root.

Another half-minute passed and Walker heard engines racing, still distant, but getting closer.

"Now!" he shouted down the hallway.

The militiamen scurried out the doors, spreading and seeking whatever cover was nearby.

⊕

Colonel Norton spoke over the PA system. "With smoke

engulfing the left side of the plane, and a significant fuel leak, we cannot exit through the main cabin door. Crew members, open all three right-side emergency exits. Right-side exits only! Standby to evacuate."

Senior Master Sergeant Landis watched as the forward hatch was opened and the evacuation chute was inflated. He knew other crew members were simultaneously opening the overwing exit and the aft hatch. If this had been a normal commercial flight, passengers would have already been filing out, and the entire aircraft evacuated in less than ninety seconds. But this wasn't an ordinary flight. Whoever had shelled the runway could also have gunmen surrounding Air Force One.

President Taylor was standing only ten feet from Landis, but out of view through the open hatch.

"Sergeant Landis, I think we should go."

"One minute, sir. The security team is almost here."

The black smoke was obscuring the view out the left side of the plane. Colonel Norton had his face pressed against a window, monitoring the spread of pooling aviation fuel. Soon it would be close enough to the burning tires to ignite.

He called to Landis, "We need to get a move on, Sergeant."

Although he tried to hide it, the anxiety in his voice was noticed by those nearby, including the president.

Taylor said to Landis, "Just so you know, if it comes to choosing between dying of smoke inhalation or being shot, the later sounds like a better option."

"My job, sir, is to make certain you never have to make that choice."

Taylor smiled grimly. "I like your attitude, Sergeant. I'm sure the First Lady would approve, too."

Cadillac One was racing for the aircraft, surrounded by four black SUVs carrying the security detail. They didn't start to slow until even with the tail. Then brakes squealed as they came to a stop.

All hell broke loose.

⊕

"Fire!" Walker said.

The nineteen militiamen opened up with buckshot and rifle rounds in a murderous barrage. They fired from a long skirmish line that had one end anchored at the parked regional jets at the terminal, and the opposite end seventy yards south of the terminal. But they weren't shooting at anyone. The Secret Service detail was still in the vehicles, and the president, his staff, and air crew were still onboard.

The onslaught of lead and jacketed bullets ripped into the inflated evacuation slides, and in a handful of seconds, all that was left were three large yellow flaps of rubberized fabric. The flaccid material, hanging down from the open hatches, was caught by the breeze and pushed under the fuselage. The burning tires of the main landing gear set flame to the overwing chute, and a quick-thinking crew member tore the fabric free. It fluttered to the ground, along with their hopes of escape.

Secret Service agents disgorged from the SUVs and returned fire. A trained response, intended to provide cover long enough to get the president into the safety of the armored limousine.

Half the militiamen hunkered down behind tugs and reinforced concrete highway barriers that lined the tarmac from the terminal building south, separating the employee parking lot from the active taxiway. The others fired back. It wasn't an intense volume of fire like they'd unleased to shred the evacuation slides—it didn't have to be. With the security detail pinned down behind the vehicles, a stalemate was a win for Walker and his team. Soon the jet fuel would catch fire, and Air Force One would become a funeral pyre.

The drone of a propeller-driven aircraft cut through the sound of gunfire. Walker looked to the sky, searching for the plane. He'd considered that the Air National Guard might be called for support. But with bases at Portland and Klamath Falls, each more than a hundred miles from Roberts Field, the flight time alone would be at least fifteen minutes. Plus time to organize a response, and he didn't think it possible that any backup would arrive in less than thirty minutes from the first call for help.

He finally located the aircraft. It was on course for Roberts Field and it was low, probably only a few thousand feet. It was too large to be a civilian aviation plane, and his instincts warned him that something was not right about this. But as he considered the possibilities, one of the Secret Service agents aimed a second Stinger at the approaching aircraft.

Seconds later, he fired.

CHAPTER 47

FROM FOUR MILES OUT, Captain Oslund saw the white smoke trail. He banked hard right, and his copilot dispensed flares. Having been shot at already, Oslund was approaching the airport with the engines at full throttle, and ready to make a run if needed.

And it was.

The Combat King outdistanced the heat-seeking missile, but there wasn't a lot of room to spare.

Oslund got on the radio and addressed the tower. "This is victor-zulu-two-two. We are an authorized military flight responding to mayday. Repeat, we are friendlies. Please tell whichever jackass is firing those Stingers to cease fire immediately. Over."

"Uh, victor-zulu-two-two. This is tower control. Listen, I don't know how you guys happened to be in the area, but it's the wild west down here. Air Force One is off the runway, and terrorists are shooting at it. I think the president must still be inside."

"Roger that. Before we had to turn away from the missile,

I thought I saw black smoke coming from Angel. Can you confirm?"

"Yes, the tires are on fire. The left wing exploded during the takeoff roll. I think it was hit by a shell of some kind. It's gotta be leaking fuel. I don't know why the whole plane hasn't gone up in one big fireball."

"Roger that. Can you get a message to the security detail to cease fire and allow us to approach?"

"Negative. Negative. Can't you radio them? I mean, you guys must use the same frequencies?"

The copilot had been broadcasting since the first missile launch, hoping to get through. But he hadn't, and Oslund concluded the security detail was communicating using short-range, frequency-hopping encrypted radios. There was virtually no chance VZ22 would make contact.

Oslund was on the radio again. "Tower, relay message through Angel to cease fire. Repeat, cease fire."

The copilot was already attempting to communicate the same message to Angel, but had no response yet.

"Victor-zulu-two-two, roger that," the tower replied.

s

Bull was in the cargo bay of the Combat King, briefing his team. They'd all suited up and geared up. The intercom buzzed, and Bull picked up the handset. He listened to Oslund, asked two brief questions, then hung up.

"Okay! Everyone listen up! There's been a change of plans. Angel has been hit. It is off the runway and on fire. Tangos have the security team pinned down, and evacuation is not possible. No one gets off that aircraft until the threat is neutralized. Priority one is to secure Eagle. After that, get as many to safety as we can."

While he spoke, the Combat King was climbing rapidly and circling the airfield, just outside a five-mile radius.

Bull paused, allowing several moments for the gravity of his message to sink in. He'd trained with this team, worked with this team, bled with this team. He considered these men to be the best group of operators of any elite military team anywhere in the world. All were recruited from different branches of the military. Bull himself came from the Marine Corps. It was a family tradition that he had embraced upon turning eighteen to get off the streets of Oakland, California. In addition to being the team leader, he was also the medic.

He moved his gaze from team member to team member. He knew their resumes by memory. Staff Sergeant Ryan Moore, who went by the nom de guerre of Ghost. Despite the size of the former SEAL—weighing two hundred pounds and topping six feet—he moved with effortless grace, a skill he'd honed to perfection after years of hunting the remote evergreen forests of Northeastern Oregon and Western Idaho.

Standing next to Ghost was another former SEAL, call sign Magnum, aka Percival Dexter, or Percy, as his friends called him. Magnum had joined the navy right out of high school to see the world, believing it would be far more attractive and inviting than his South-Central Los Angeles neighborhood.

Then there was Sergeant Jesper Mortensen. He was considered the most skilled member of the team at long-range sniping. He favored the .50 caliber M107 semiautomatic rifle, and held the official record for longest and second-longest confirmed kill—a record still classified. Jesper, call sign Homer, was also a lady-killer with a ruggedly handsome appearance, hair that was just a shade lighter than coal-black, and cobalt-blue eyes.

Finally, Bull's piercing stare settled on Jerry Balvanz. With a head of curly snow-white hair, it was no surprise his teammates called him Iceberg. Like Homer, he was recruited from the Army, Delta Force. Jerry was tall and lanky, yet lightning fast and strong. Prior to enlisting, he'd played college basketball for two seasons, and still loved to shoot hoops in his down time.

"Shoulder-fired heat seekers are preventing this aircraft from coming in low," Bull said. "Therefore, we will drop from twenty-five thousand feet and pop chutes at a thousand feet."

He received a mixture of whistles and eye rolls.

Iceberg said, "There's no margin for error. If the main chute doesn't deploy, there won't be time for the backup."

"That's right. So leave the backup here. No point in dealing with the bulk and weight. We're going in hot. As soon has your boots touch earth, shed the parachute and ready your weapon. Time is of the essence. That should be obvious."

"Landing coordinates?" Homer said.

"Gather around." Bull produced a tablet displaying a high-resolution satellite image of the terminal and south end of the main runway, then placed a stylus on the screen and drew a tight red circle. "You and Iceberg will land here at the south end of the employee parking lot. Expect close-in fighting, so I want you packing MP5s, and max out on mags. The rest of us will land here," he drew another circle, "aft and just east of Angel. We will snipe from across the runway and try to draw fire from the terrorists."

"Radio frequencies the Secret Service is using?" Ghost said.

Bull pursed his lips. "We don't have that information."

"What?" Iceberg said. "How are we supposed to let the security team know we're friendlies?"

"That's the rub," Bull said. "We don't have direct communication with them. Attempts are being made to relay the message through Angel, but they're understandably edgy, and probably don't believe we are who we say we are."

"Let me get this straight." Iceberg narrowed his eyes. "They've tried twice to blow us out of the air, and now we're going to crash their party and hope they don't shoot us?"

Bull locked gazes with Iceberg. "You volunteered for this mission. You can stand down any time you feel it's too dangerous."

Homer slapped Iceberg on the shoulder. "Come on, man, it's your chance to meet the president."

"I didn't vote for him."

"So? He's still the president."

"Whatever." Iceberg took one last look at the satellite image. "I've got nothing planned for tonight, anyway."

⊕

Peter drove the tug up to the entrance door to the control tower. Four baggage carts, all filled with luggage, were hitched to the back of the tug. Diesel was sitting on the seat next to him, and Torres and Gardner looked at him in amazement.

"What are you doing!" Torres shouted, to be heard over the raging gunfight.

"I'm not standing around anymore."

They had a good view of the stricken 747 and the besieged presidential security team. The black SUVs were not armored like Cadillac One, but they did have belts of Kevlar in the body panels, and bullet resistant windows to deliver a degree of protection to the occupants. And they rolled on run-flat tires. But they still had a vulnerability, an Achilles heel—the engine compartment.

The militiamen seized on this and shot out the radiators. The idling engines on all four vehicles soon overheated and seized. Even from four hundred yards away, Peter could see the white clouds of boiling antifreeze issuing from the motionless SUVs.

He said, "The plane's on fire, the evacuation slides are shredded, and the Secret Service is outgunned. Look for yourself. Their vehicles are disabled."

"And you're gonna help." Torres scoffed.

"Damn right I am."

"Wait, I'm going, too." Gardner pushed himself upright and grabbed the rifle.

Then he hobbled to the last baggage cart and pushed some of the suitcases aside to make room.

"All right," Torres said. "I'm coming."

"Shouldn't you stay and guard the governor?" Peter said.

"I think—"

"I can take care of myself, Sergeant," Governor Kathrine Bingham said, as she descended the stairs. "Your services are needed out there." With a nod, she indicated Air Force One.

"Respectfully, ma'am," Peter said, "you should have protection."

"With the president out there, the terrorists are not going to bother with a governor. But if it makes you feel better…" she held out her hand, "Sergeant, give me your pistol."

Peter raised an eyebrow at Bingham.

"Don't say a word, Mister Savage."

Torres made sure a round was chambered, then handed the Smith & Wesson M&P to her.

"All you have to do is aim and squeeze the trigger." Then he dashed to the string of baggage carts.

Gardner handed his sidearm to Torres, and then his copilot hopped on as Peter drove off.

CHAPTER 48

THE MILITIAMEN HAD ALREADY KILLED two of the Secret Service agents with head shots, including the agent who'd fired the missiles at the approaching aircraft. A third had been wounded with buckshot in his legs. And a fourth was likewise wounded when he tried to pull his teammate to safety. The security detail was now down to four able shooters.

For their part, the Secret Service had also drawn blood, taking out one militiaman who was foolish enough to use a carbon dioxide fire extinguisher as cover. The device appeared substantial, consisting of two red-painted steel cylinders about four-feet tall, mounted on a hand cart. But a single 40mm grenade blasted apart the cylinders and the man behind them. Three other militiamen were wounded and out of the fight. Even so, the presidential security detail was grossly outnumbered and outgunned.

Onboard Air Force One, Sergeant Landis had unlocked a wall safe and removed four pistols, arming himself and three of his security team. They took up shooting positions from the open hatches. Two were shot within seconds, and Landis pulled the third man back.

The belly of the 747 was blackened with soot from the fires as the rubber tires continued to burn fiercely. Walker sensed that the pool of aviation fuel would soon reach the fire. He eagerly anticipated the wall of yellow flames that would race outward, tracing back to the source of the spill. He imagined how the intense heat would bath the underside of the wing, forcing fuel out faster. It would not take long for the flames and superheated air to melt the aluminum skin. Insulation in the wall of the fuselage would pyrolyze and release hydrogen cyanide, carbon monoxide, and other toxic gases.

"Any time now," he muttered.

Whoosh!

⊕

Peter floored the accelerator on the tug, and it jerked the string of baggage carts forward. But instead of driving for Air Force One, he did a U-turn and aimed the tug for a connector that joined the taxiway with the runway.

"Where are you going?" Torres shouted from the second baggage cart.

"We have to get onto the runway. Then we can approach from the far side of the aircraft. If we stay on the taxiway, I'll have to drive right past the gunmen."

The tug's engine was roaring, and the four baggage carts whipped left and right, just on the edge of stability. He reached the runway, and without slowing, cranked the steering wheel and turned right. Diesel shifted and caught his balance. Peter extended his arm and placed a hand on the canine's chest.

And then there was a yellow fireball under the left side of the plane, followed a second later by the deep base reverberation of the igniting fuel vapors.

He pressed his foot harder against the peddle, but it was already flat against the floor. As he closed the distance, he could hear screams coming from the open hatches. Amidst the gunfire, he saw two bodies fall out of the aircraft.

They're shooting people in the openings.

Radiated heat from the inferno bathed the backs of the Secret Service agents, but they still held their ground and fought on. Another went down, his throat gushing blood.

The tug and baggage carts barreled forward along the edge of the runway, skirting under the tail. Just as Torres thought Peter was mad and going to drive into the fire, he veered to the right, using his hand to stabilize Diesel, who seemed happy riding in this noisy, open-air contraption.

Peter was aiming for Cadillac One, which was parked where the base of the emergency slide had been positioned. Two of the Secret Service agents spun around at the sound of the tug and baggage carts.

They aimed their guns at the tug, and Peter shouted, "Don't shoot! Friendlies!"

Perhaps it was the absurdity of a civilian driving a tug with a dog riding shotgun next to him. Or perhaps they just couldn't accept yet another threat. Or perhaps the exhaustion slowed their reflexes. Whatever the reason, they hesitated long enough for Peter to stop and raise his hands.

"I'm on your side!" He rolled out of the tug.

Gardner and Torres bailed from the piles of suitcases, adding their guns to the diminished ranks of the security detail from the shelter of Cadillac One.

One of the agents resumed firing on the militiamen, while the second ran over to Peter. The baggage carts were parked in a line, under the forward hatch. The drop from the hatch to the top of the carts was about ten feet. Manageable.

Peter yelled, "You've got to have the president jump down onto the roof of the cart. Then he can roll off, and you can get him into the car."

"He won't have any cover!" the agent said.

The heat from the conflagration was like a blast furnace, and the pool of burning fuel was quickly growing larger.

"He has a chance if he jumps. If he stays onboard, he dies!"

The agent nodded, then spoke into his radio. "Tell Eagle he has to jump. There's a baggage cart just below the opening. The drop is not too far. He has to do it."

Inside the airplane, Landis listened to the radio message. "Affirmative."

⊕

The five men were falling at terminal velocity, in a loose formation. Gradually, Homer and Iceberg separated from the group. At a thousand feet, they all pulled their ripcords—an upward jerk, and then a gentle landing, followed by a roll. The fire was raging under the 747, and they knew they had to act swiftly before everyone onboard was dead.

Bull, Ghost, and Homer all drew fire from the militia as soon as their canopies filled with air. But by then, they were close to the ground. Each was armed with the M107 .50 caliber rifle. With high-magnification scopes, each operator went to a prone shooting position and lined up their sights. They were only five hundred yards from the terminal building.

"Call 'em," Bull said, over the squad radio net.

It was a standard practice to avoid two or more snipers aiming for the same target and wasting ammunition as well as opportunity to kill more bad guys.

With precision bred from hundreds of hours of practice, each man sought targets through their scopes, making minor adjustments for distance and air movement.

"Right-most tug." Homer fired.

Because they had no intel on what force they would be going up against, Bull had them carrying magazines loaded with explosive armor-piercing rounds, called a Raufoss round.

Homer's shot entered the tug and exploded halfway

through, blowing hundreds of pieces of metal shrapnel into the body of the shooter.

"Bearded guy, far left, behind concrete barrier." Ghost fired, and the effect was the same, blasting a fist-sized hole through the concrete and into the chest of the militiaman.

With Bull, Ghost, and Homer keeping up the pace, calling out targets and neutralizing them, Homer and Iceberg dropped into the employee parking lot behind the militia.

Caught in a crossfire, Walker's team was running out of time.

⊕

The beautifully decorated cabin of Air Force One was rapidly filling with thick, noxious smoke. To escape the poisonous vapors, everyone was hugging the floor. With each passing second, the smoke got thicker and moved lower. Soon it would reach the floor, turning the plane into an executioner's gas chamber.

The timely arrival of the SGIT operators drew enough fire from the militia that some of the president's staff began jumping from the rear hatch, injuring ankles and knees. Others rolled out the overwing exit and then jumped down to the ground before hobbling past the rear of the huge plane for the open land on the far side of the runway. Several were shot in the back as they fled.

Walker and Swanson realized what was happening, and the risk that President Taylor might sneak out with the others—maybe by masquerading as one of the crew.

Walker waved an arm and shouted over the gunfire. "Forget about the security detail! Shoot the people in the openings!"

Swanson echoed the message down the line of militiamen.

Even with the din of battle, Peter also heard the order, faint but discernable.

Must be the leader.

He spotted him near the terminal building, using the main landing gear of one of the commuter jets for cover. A big man with blond hair, eyeglasses, and tattoos on his arms.

Peter said to the Secret Service agent, "Get the president down! Hurry!"

"We can't! Their shooting everyone in the open hatches!"

Peter opened the coupling, releasing the baggage carts. Then he hopped behind the wheel of the tug. Diesel was on the floor now, anxious and alternating between panting and licking his lips.

"You have to get him out!"

"What are you going to do?"

"I'm giving you a distraction. Get him out before he suffocates."

Peter stomped on the peddle and the tug shot forward, even faster than before without the four loaded carts in tow. He steered right for the commuter jet where Walker was crouched.

After only twenty yards, bullets began hitting the vehicle. It was a stout machine, designed for hard use. But he doubted it was bulletproof. He kept barreling for Walker.

Peter had slid low in the seat, just barely seeing over the hood of the machine. He heard the ping of bullets pounding the steel utility vehicle, and yet it kept moving. Somehow the engine was still churning out power.

Another fifty yards closer, and the gunfire was more intense. He saw Walker rise and take aim at the tug and fire, again and again. He saw the muzzle flashes clearly, heard the bullets striking the machine. But the sound was different now, like the metal was being pierced.

Another fifty yards, and still the engine was running, but it had developed a grinding noise. The tug slowed, but still advanced fast. He could clearly see Walker's face now. One eye squinted behind John Lennon glasses, while the other sighted along the length of the carbine. He was squeezing off shot after shot after shot. Diesel was laying on all fours to keep his balance, searching for the source of danger. But he couldn't see it from the floor of the tug.

Closer still. Peter was almost there. He lowered his body even further, aiming to use the tug's engine as a shield. Only his eyes and forehead were above the hood now. Bullets were sailing over his head, cratering into the engine, and some were even skipping off the hood. He could clearly see the cleft chin and scar across the blond man's cheek.

Boom! Boom! Boom!

And then Peter fell to his side. Diesel whimpered and licked his face, nudging his still hand with his nose. As he lay motionless on the seat, blood trickled from his head.

⊕

Recognizing the slackening volume of fire from the dwindling number of militiamen, and the distraction provided by the apparent suicidal charge of the tug toward the blond-haired shooter, the agent shouted into the radio mic.

"Now! Evacuate Eagle, now!"

Landis didn't hesitate as he, too, saw the chance amid the rapidly closing window of opportunity. The top half of the cabin was filled with thick, choking smoke, and the temperature had risen to an uncomfortable level as the fire spread beneath the aircraft. The overwing door would have been engulfed already were it not for the breeze pushing the flames under the fuselage to the left side of the plane.

The Senior Master Sergeant was just inside the open forward hatch, his body serving as a shield for President Taylor. They were both squatting, sucking in fresh air entering through the opening.

"Sir, do exactly as I say. There is no time for discussion."

The leader of the free world nodded. For the first time in

his life, he was afraid of dying.

"Take a deep breath, close your eyes, and stand up. We're getting you out."

Grasping the president in a vice-like bear hug, Landis backed to the opening and fell backwards, dragging Joshua Taylor with him. The sudden and unexpected free fall terrified Taylor. But as fast as it began, it ended with a thud that knocked the wind from him.

Together, the Secret Service agent and Sergeant Torres pulled President Taylor off Landis, helped him to his feet and into the back seat of Cadillac One. The agent jumped behind the wheel, but Taylor stopped him.

"Get Landis in here. Your wounded men, too."

Bearing the brunt of the fall, Landis suffer several cracked and broken ribs, and torn ligaments in his left shoulder. As he rolled off the cart, he was laboring to breathe.

"Sir, my priority—"

"It's an order!" the president shouted.

Gardner was laying prone behind the big limousine, taking aimed shots to provide some cover while the wounded men were helped into the back seat. It was a snug fit, but they did fit. Then Torres slammed the rear door and slapped a hand on the roof. The driver floored the accelerator and the car sped forward, clear of the disabled SUVs, and then completed a high-speed, tire-squealing U-turn before heading back for the north end of the runway and safety.

CHAPTER 49

ICEBERG AND HOMER ADVANCED between cars in the employee parking lot. When they reached the last row of vehicles closest to the tarmac, the line of militiamen came into view. Their backs were to the SGIT operators, and they were firing over the top of the concrete highway barriers. Chunks were blasted in some of the concrete forms, telltale evidence of being hit with a Raufoss round.

The only defense the gunmen had against the devastating explosive rounds was to pop up, fire, and then change position. The tactic was working, but at the expense of reducing their volume of fire and allowing more people to jump from the burning aircraft.

Iceberg and Homer communicated with hand signs since the closest terrorists were only ten yards away. A final nod of confirmation, then Homer raised one finger, followed by two. When he had three fingers up, they both pivoted from behind their cover and opened up with their submachine guns.

A ubiquitous and highly favored weapon of law enforcement and elite military teams, the MP5 was exceptionally reliable and deadly at close distance. Each operator fired aimed single shots, two per tango, and then moved to the next.

They worked along the line and had slain many militiamen within the first five seconds of engagement without any opposition.

But that soon changed.

$\oplus$

The fire advanced, and now flames were licking up to the open overwing hatch. With only two functional exits, and seconds left with breathable air, Colonel Norton activated the PA system.

"Eagle is out and safely away. Everyone is to evacuate immediately. Forward and aft exits only."

Those who hadn't already braved the bullets to jump from the open hatches scooted to the nearest exit. Fire entering the overwing exit was melting the plastic covering over the inside of the fuselage. It was fire retardant, but decomposed under the heat to add toxic vapors to the dense smoke that had nearly filled the cabin.

On hands and knees, people scurried for the openings and then rose to their feet and jumped. Although the gunfire had died down over the last two minutes, it hadn't ceased. The cabin steward for the president stood at the forward opening and was shot dead, the body falling to the pavement. Two galley chefs were next. The first one was shot in the shoulder, but the second made it out without a scratch—though she broke her ankle after tumbling off the top of the baggage cart.

With each passing second, there was less and less gunfire aimed at the emergency exits. The irony being that those who waited longest, risking suffocation, had an easier go running the gauntlet of gunfire.

The survivors on the tarmac helped those in greatest need. Most of the injuries were sprained or broken ankles. There were several gunshot wounds, too. All the evacuees scrambled away from the 747 and terminal building.

Inside the cabin, only the pilot and copilot remained.

"It's your turn," Norton said to Colonel Ortega. "Remember to flex your knees to absorb the shock. It's not that far down to the baggage cart. Then roll off to the side and get as far away as fast as you can."

"I'll go after you, sir."

"That was an order, Colonel. Now get out while you can. I'm going to check that no one is left behind. I'll be going out the aft hatch."

"Make it snappy, sir."

"I have no intention of being stuck in here." He turned and crawled toward the rear, calling along the way and shining a pen light.

Ortega jumped out, landed and rolled. She was on the ground and helping the flight engineer, who had sprained his ankle. They scrambled forward of the aircraft, skirting the pool of burning fuel to gather a hundred yards beyond the edge of the runway, in the dirt and bunch grass. The ground sloped away from the runway to drain rainwater, and they amassed in the depression with other survivors.

She looked across the faces. "Did anyone see the captain? Anyone?"

No reply.

She focused on the rear of the 747, expecting to see a figure drop from the hatch near the tail. But no one came out. And then, while she watched with anticipation, the rear of the aircraft burst into flames.

Furnace-like heat from the initial inferno had weakened a center fuel tank to the point of failure. A thousand pounds of jet fuel spewed onto the gravel and pavement, igniting. The conflagration swallowed the aft portion of the fuselage.

Ortega gasped and placed a hand to her mouth, stifling a cry. She blinked, and tears ran down her cheek.

⊕

Peter didn't hear the roaring engine and screeching tires of Cadillac One as it swept President Taylor to safety. He didn't have the satisfaction of knowing that Denson's assassination attempt had failed. He didn't feel his heart ache, knowing the number of innocent lives that had been lost when Air Force One was turned into a death trap.

As his still body lay on the seat of the baggage tug, the machine continued its advance toward Walker, but much slower now without pressure on the gas pedal. Walker bellowed a banshee scream, emptying the remainder of the rounds in his rifle magazine into the engine of the tug. With a final gasp, the engine ground to a halt only feet from the front landing gear of the regional jet.

Out of ammunition, Walker dropped the rifle and stormed to the side of the tug. In blind rage, he reached for Peter, intending to expend his fury, regardless whether the man was alive or dead.

He reached for Peter's throat, but his hand never made it.

Diesel erupted from the floor with bestial ferocity, driven by a singular purpose, born of instinct and loyalty to protect the only pack member he'd ever known. He crunched his jaws down on Walker's forearm just above his wrist, ripping muscles and tendons and bruising the bones.

He screamed and tried to withdraw his arm, but the large dog pulled and thrashed his head, exacerbating the wounds. The harder he pulled, the more violent the response from the pit bull.

Walker leaned in and started pummeling the canine's head. Diesel still wouldn't release. He absorbed blow after blow, but kept his jaws clenched tight. Not until Walker punched one of the dog's eyes did the bite slack. Then he rammed his fist into the eye again, and with a yelp, Diesel let go. As walker withdrew his arm, Diesel shook his head, trying to recover from the pain. His right eye was completely closed, and the eyelid was lacerated and bleeding.

Walker's right arm was on fire and bleeding profusely from numerous punctures and torn blood vessels, adding fuel to his frenzy.

"Son of a bitch! I'm gonna kill you, dog." He retreated several steps to where he had dropped his rifle.

Although he had no more bullets for it, it could still serve as a club.

Once the threat backed away, Diesel turned his attention to Peter and licked the blood from his face. The lack of movement seemed to confuse the canine, and he tipped his head to the side, trying to understand. He placed a front paw against Peter's chest and pushed.

Still no response.

Then Diesel lowered his nose and pressed it against his master's lips. He held that position for several seconds. Then he lay his big, blocky head across Peter's chest and whimpered.

CHAPTER 50

ONCE THE MILITIAMEN REALIZED Iceberg and Homer were behind them, they abandoned their positions and sought cover in the employee parking lot. The SGIT operators moved from car to car in a cat-and-mouse game, trying to get the drop on the gunmen, who were playing the same deadly game.

Two rows away, Homer glimpsed a wild-eyed man with shaggy salt-and-pepper hair and matching beard, issuing orders to several militiamen. Homer fired at him but missed, driving him to take cover behind a truck.

"We have to stop them before they flank us," he said to Iceberg.

"What do you think I'm trying to do?"

"Try harder." Homer winked.

Iceberg squeezed off three shots at a fleeting shadow.

"Got an idea," Homer said.

"Yeah, I'm listening."

"Did you bring any grenades?"

"Really? Have you ever known me to *not* load up with grenades?"

Homer smiled and fired two shots. He thought he might

have winged one of the gunmen, but he wasn't certain. Regardless, he was still in the fight.

"Thought so," he said. "See that blue Chevy truck a little to the right and two rows in front of us?"

Iceberg stole a glance around the fender of his cover, and then nodded.

"Can you lob a grenade into the bed of that truck?"

Now it was Iceberg's turn to smile. "Just give me some cover."

With his weapon hanging from his shoulder, he removed the safety and popped the pin on a grenade, then stood and let it fly. His sudden appearance drew gunfire from the blue truck and the neighboring car.

Two seconds later, the detonation shredded the truck, rupturing the fuel tank and starting a fire. Two more militiamen down, including the wild-eyed leader.

Homer repositioned himself to the left and lowered his face to the blacktop. He saw three pairs of boots moving farther from the flaming debris, and then stop. They were still in the same row. He readied a grenade and then threw it intentionally short. The steel orb hit the pavement and then slid forward another twenty feet. It came to rest under the vehicle the militiamen had just repositioned to.

Another explosion accompanied by a fireball, and three more gunmen dead.

The sixth and last militiaman raised his hands and tossed down his weapon.

⊕

With his mangled arm cradled against his chest, Walker gripped the rifle barrel with his other hand.

"I'm gonna kill you, dog, just like I killed your asshole owner. He got off lucky with a bullet to the head. But I'm gonna beat you to until every bone in your body is broken."

Walker's approach drew a renewed round of growls from Diesel. He bared his teeth and intensified the snarl, then progressed to air snaps.

"You stupid dog. He's dead. You should run away while you still can." Walker raised the rifle and then swung it down, the butt stock hitting Diesel's rear haunches.

He yelped and snapped at the rifle, but Walker drew it back, laughing at the helpless dog.

The pit bull refused to surrender his position as he stood over his master's prone body.

The dark void in Peter's mind flashed to color, filled with images of the scrawny pit bull puppy, cowering in a corner of his holding pen, tail tucked between his legs, and head lowered in submission. His red fur was matted with dirt, and his nose and ears showed festering wounds. With nowhere to retreat, he trembled. The innocent amber eyes, wide with fear, refused to meet his own. To prove he wasn't a threat, he lay on the cold concrete floor and waited until the terrified little dog that had only known pain his entire short life, pressed its small damp nose to his lips.

With a jolt of adrenaline, Peter's eyes snapped open. His head throbbed, and sharp sounds seemed to drive daggers into his brain. Like a punch-drunk fighter, he was slowly gaining awareness of his surroundings. The last thing he remembered was staring into the scarred face of the blond man trying to shoot him.

He was facing the dashboard of the tug, laying on his side. Something heavy weighed him down. He moved his fingers. The weight was warm and furry—Diesel.

Then his mind registered snarls and a yelp. He turned his head and saw the rifle coming down. He raised his arm, and a new explosion of pain fired up his limb.

"Son of a bitch!" Walker said. "I thought I killed you."

Peter pushed Diesel to the floor and struggled to sit upright. He was almost there when the rifle came down, this time aimed at his head.

He raised his left arm again, once more taking the blow on his forearm. The pain was sharp and burning, like red-hot knives were being plunged into his muscle and bone.

"I guess I'll just have to finish the job and then kill your ugly mutt."

Peter managed to get himself upright, but he wouldn't be able to take a third strike on the same arm. Walker's eyes were wide, and spittle was at the corners of his mouth. He was mad with rage.

Peter pulled the tomahawk from under his belt at his back. One-handed, Walker raised the rifle and swung it down again. But this time, the steel tomahawk was shoved up to block the blow. As Walker drew the club back, Peter seized the opening and stood next to the tug, the movement sending icepicks of pain into his skull. He wobbled, and his vision blurred.

As if sensing danger, Walker stepped backwards. He assessed his enemy. The pain in his arm, combined with the humiliation of failing his mission, drove him to attack when he should have retreated. With a piercing scream, he rushed forward, driving down the rifle-club, aiming for Peter's head.

Again the tomahawk intercepted the blow before the rifle completed its downward arc. Only this time, after stopping the blow, Peter drove the blade downward, cutting across Walker's abdomen.

Surprise gave way to shock, and then excruciating pain as his bowels spilled onto the blacktop. The rifle slipped from his grasp, and he teetered on his feet.

As the color drained from his face, his knees buckled, and he collapsed into his own waste.

CHAPTER 51

ICEBERG AND HOMER FLEXICUFFED their prisoner to an EMPLOYEE PARKING ONLY sign, and then made their sweep of the front of the terminal. The chlorine gas had dissipated, leaving only a faint residual odor reminiscent of bleach.

They encountered the lone guard at the south entrance and eliminated him with a hand grenade. After entering the terminal, it took little time to clear the building. They shot the guard at the main entrance from behind, as he was expecting an assault from the front. The third and final guard at the north entrance fired a half-dozen rounds before rethinking his predicament and choosing surrender over death. He was handcuffed to the door handle.

They finished their sweep of the baggage collection area and then the departure lounge.

"All clear," Homer radioed to Bull.

"Roger that," Bull replied. "Homer and Ghost are going in for a body count, but I think we got 'em all. A crazy-ass civilian killed the last one—a big blond SOB."

From the departure hallway, they saw the carnage of dead militiamen. And then, as a lone beacon of life, they saw a man standing motionless. His head and face were bloodied, and he favored his left arm. In his right hand was a tomahawk. He was looking down. At his feet was a mutilated corpse with blond hair. From the way he stood, they could tell he was exhausted and...sad.

Something about him was familiar, although in his present state he was unrecognizable.

Iceberg call to him from five yards away. "Hey, mister? You okay?"

He and Homer approached with caution, as their training dictated.

Peter looked up with vacant eyes that seemed to see through them. "Diesel. He needs a vet."

"Mr. Savage? It's me, Homer."

The SGIT operator would never forget helping to secure the rescue of Peter and Diesel from the mountains of Central Oregon.

Hearing the name jogged Peter's memory and helped him focus.

"He's hurt. He needs a vet." Peter swayed, stumbled, and then regained his balance.

The tomahawk slipped from his fingers, clattering on the ground. Iceberg and Homer rushed forward, caught Peter and lowered him to a sitting position with his back resting against the tug.

Inside, Diesel lay on the floorboard, panting. Homer reached to pet the dog, but upon touching his head, Diesel yelped. His right eye was swollen shut.

"No telling what injuries he has," Homer activated the squad net. "Bull, we have two injured, both civilian. Recommend immediate medivac."

"Roger that. Call it in."

Bull was with the evacuees. Fortunately, the flight doctor

and two nurses had made it out and set up a triage. The most serious injuries—six with bullet wounds—required immediate surgery.

Homer changed radio frequencies to communicate with the Combat King circling overhead.

"Victor-zulu-two-two, copy?"

"Copy. This is victor-zulu-two-two," Oslund said.

Homer requested the medivac.

"Say again? Did you request one canine trauma evac?"

"That's affirmative. One civilian, name Peter Savage, and his dog, Diesel. They've both taken a beating. Looks like Savage took a grazing bullet wound to the head, plus trauma on his left arm. Possible broken bone. The dog—I don't know what to tell you. One eye is lacerated and swollen closed. Probable internal injuries. Likely broken bones. I think he's going into shock."

"Say again? What's the name of the civilian?"

"Peter Savage. Know him?"

"Yeah, we met when he was going in to find Commander Nicolaou. Met his dog, too. I'll see what I can do, but the medivac choppers are already committed. Several victims of gunshot wounds from the crew of Air Force One. Might be half an hour before they can get Mister Savage to the hospital."

Homer ended the call. "Help is on the way. It'll be here soon."

Peter nodded, but he saw through the lie. Slowly regaining his wits, he struggled to his feet and positioned himself in the tug next to Diesel. He knew the nonstop panting was a sign of extreme pain.

"It's okay, buddy. We'll get you taken care of. Just hang in there."

He swiveled his head, looking for any mode of transportation he could use to get Diesel to an emergency veterinary clinic. The only option was the state police helicopter.

And then he saw Sergeant Torres running across the taxiway.

"Sergeant," Peter called. "I need to borrow your helicopter."

With each word, pain erupted in his head, along with a wave of nausea.

He attempted to scoop up Diesel, but his left arm refused to cooperate.

"I got him," Homer said.

Minutes later, with Torres at the controls, the police helicopter departed low and fast.

EPILOGUE

THE CRACKLE AND RUMBLE of thunder accompanying spring showers renewed unwanted memories of recent events. He was home now, and he felt comfort in the familiar surroundings. But also melancholy, for these walls were inextricably related to memories of Maggie, from years ago, and more recently of Kate. Relationships that, for different reasons, the Fates seemed to have doomed.

The emergency room doctor who had treated him two days ago had commented, dryly, that were it not for his thick skull the bullet would have killed him. Peter thought it more likely that the round had ricocheted off the hood of the tug, thereby losing much of its energy before grazing his head. After ten stiches to close the gash, he now wore a white bandage on his forehead.

His left arm had favored better, if only marginally. Another collection of sutures to the shoulder laceration, plus a soft cast to immobilize his arm while his cracked ulna healed.

"Keep that on for three weeks. Then we'll take another X-ray," the doctor had said.

Diesel was also recovering. The laceration on his left eyelid had been treated with antibiotic salve and was scabbed over. No stiches were required to close the gash. The swelling had gone down, but still had a ways to go. Although the veterinary doctor believed his eyesight was not permanently damaged, it was too early to be certain. His entire body had been bruised by the beating, but no bones were broken. He was being given carprofen and tramadol twice daily to reduce the inflammation and pain. Since the pills were wrapped in sliced lunch meat, Diesel exhibited no objections to taking his medicine.

Another clap of thunder, this time close, caused Diesel to raise his head and whine. Peter sat on the floor next to the pit bull, and Diesel climbed onto his lap, curled into a ball, but still didn't get his entire body off the floor. He closed his eyes as Peter ran his fingers gently along the side of his face and nose. They both just sat there, lost in time and each other's companionship.

Peter was startled by the knock on the door.

"Who is it?"

"Detective Colson. I'd like to have a word with you."

"Go away. No one's home."

She knocked again, more persistently.

Peter extracted himself and made sure Diesel was comfortable. Then he opened the door.

Colson sported a forest-green hoody sweatshirt with yellow lettering that read GO DUCKS! As usual, she was wearing a scowl.

"You're a one-man wrecking crew."

"Well, hello, detective. Nice to see you, too. By the way, I'm doing fine. Thanks for asking."

She stared back. "May I come it?"

He stood aside and motioned forward. As she entered, Diesel raised his head and growled.

"Your dog still doesn't like me."

"He's not the only one." Peter sighed. "Coffee?"

"No, thanks. I won't keep you. Just wanted to give you an update. It's against department policy, but the captain said okay, given the rather unusual circumstances."

"Thank you."

"The FBI is running the investigation, so we don't know everything. But they have shared that it's a militia group out of western Idaho that's behind the assassination plots and the theft of your property, plus the two murders at your company, and the kidnapping of Governor Bingham. Commander Nicolaou is no longer a suspect."

Peter nodded. "Good to know."

She stood in silence, appraising Peter.

"Anything else?" he said.

"No."

"You could've shared that over the phone."

Her lips curled into a smirk. "True, but I wanted to make sure you're okay."

"Thank you. But don't expect a hug."

After the detective left, he poured a cup of coffee and sat in the leather chair nearest to Diesel. With the information that Jim was no longer a wanted man, he decided it was time to call Lacey. Hopefully she would have more to share.

They exchanged greetings, and then Peter opened with the news shared by Colson.

"Yes. In fact, the commander is on his way back to SGIT as we speak. After the rescue of President Taylor, Bull and Ghost flew to Boise. Once they made contact with Commander Nicolaou, they were able to discretely transport him to Mountain Home Air Force Base, where they boarded the Combat King for the flight home. Colonel Pierson made certain the base commander understood he was to cooperate and not ask questions."

Peter thanked her for the information. "You may not be able to answer my next question, but is there anything else from the FBI you can share with me?"

"Just a minute." She closed her door and then returned to her desk. "You mean about Denson and the militia?"

"Yes."

"He must have truly believed they were going to succeed with the assassination plots, and overthrow the executive branch. Unbelievably, he and several co-conspirators returned to his ranch after the assassinations in Boise. That only makes sense if he thought there was zero chance the plot would fail, and the militia would become prime suspects. Anyway, agents were waiting and took them all into custody. With the information you shared with me, I was able to guide the FBI to the secret vault in Denson's study. Apparently it took a little work to get past the combination lock, but they managed. Once inside, they found the missing journal from Meriwether Lewis. They also found the Lost Treaty. Only, there's a rub."

"Go on," Peter said.

"The treaty was rushed to the National Archives. They received it twenty-four hours ago. First thing they did was run a series of nondestructive tests to ascertain its authenticity. I just received a copy of their report this morning. The document's a fake."

"What?"

"That's right. The giveaway was the ink. They used an electron microscope and X-rays—"

"Yes, I'm familiar with the technique. Go on. What were the results?"

"If the treaty was genuine, it would have been written using ink made from iron and tannic acid. The ink on this document contains organic pigments derived from coal. It's old, but not two hundred years old. The archivists date it to about 1890 to 1910."

Peter was stunned. Everything that had happened, the elaborate planning, the dozens of innocent people who were murdered…it was all based on a forged document, a lie.

"Hello? Mister Savage, can you hear me?"

"Yes. I'm still here."

"Well, that's all there is for now. The investigation will probably go on for months as they dig deeper in the Cascadia Independence Movement. Only two militiamen were captured at Redmond Airport—nearly all were killed. And the three-man mortar team was apprehended by sheriff K9 units that were assigned to patrol the perimeter. They're all being cooperative."

"But how did they figure to get away with the attack on Air Force One?"

"Oh, yes. Another interesting twist. Several of those gunmen were active members of the Idaho National Guard. It seems the idea was to pin the blame on a military uprising. A coup, if you like. The FBI believes that those guard members were never supposed to leave. The rest of the militiamen were to escape in two vehicles that an employee was bribed to leave in the parking lot, with keys above the visors. The weapons that were used all appear to be U.S. military, sold to Pakistan. And that's why framing Commander Nicolaou for the theft of the PEAP carbine and the assassination of the vice president and the Speaker was important."

"They came very close to succeeding," Peter said. "Just like John Wilkes Booth. And if they had, the coup would have been blamed on rogue members of the military."

"Once the plot failed, Denson began singing like a bird. He threw Senator Knowlton under the bus in exchange for the Feds promise to take the death penalty off the table."

⊕

Later that evening, Peter called Kate. He couldn't put it off any longer. Predictably, she wasn't happy when she answered the phone.

"I knew you were back."

"I'm sorry I didn't call sooner. I just—"

"Save it. So how are you this time? Shot, stabbed, banged up? Lose any limbs?"

It was starting already. He'd hoped they could at least make it an hour before the fighting began.

"I just wanted to cook dinner for you. How does steak sound?"

He figured he wasn't much to look at under the best of circumstances. But now, with the bandage on his forehead and his nose bearing the scab from where McMullen hit him with the carbine days ago, he didn't want to be seen in public.

She didn't reply.

"Kate? Please? I'd like to see you."

Another pause, and then, "Okay."

Over the next half-hour, Peter worked in the kitchen— salad with diced avocado and bell pepper, potatoes drizzled with olive oil and rosemary, and thick steaks seasoned with salt and pepper. With the food prepped, wrapped, and stored in the refrigerator, he opened a bottle of merlot he'd been saving for a special occasion—2014 vintage from San Juan Cellars. It took considerable effort with only the one hand, but he managed.

Diesel was standing with his tail wagging moments before she opened the door, somehow knowing who was coming.

Kate gasped upon seeing his swollen eye. "What happened?"

Peter stepped out of the kitchen, and she placed a hand over her mouth.

"It's not as bad as it looks."

Her eyes welled with tears and she wrapped her arms around him, mindful of the bandage on his arm. Her warmth, her touch...it felt good.

After a minute, she stood back and wiped her cheeks dry. Peter filled two glasses with wine, and they retreated to the balcony to watch the sun set. The storm clouds had dissipated a couple hours earlier. Peter hoped that was a good omen.

The conversation was casual and light, even awkward as both tried to avoid any subject that might spark an argument. More than once, Peter thought he noticed Kate looking at him expectantly.

"I've had a lot of time to think," he said.

"Me, too." She raised her eyebrows.

"And I…I want you to know how much you mean to me."

She placed a hand on his.

"I… " His mind started to spiral in circles again, his throat locking up just like the many times before.

As if on que, his phone rang. She pulled her hand back.

"Peter Savage." Then he didn't say anything, just looked at Kate.

Clearly it was a one-sided conversation.

In frustration and anger, she grabbed the phone. "Peter is busy right now. Call back later."

"Excuse me?" the voice said.

"You heard me. Find someone else to save the world for a change."

"Ma'am, I'm sorry to intrude. This is President Joshua Taylor."

Her eyes bulged and she handed the phone back.

"I apologize," Peter said.

Taylor was laughing. "She has some spunk. Put the speaker on. No reason she shouldn't hear what I have to say."

Peter did so and set the phone on a table between them. "Well, it's clear to me, Mister Savage, that you have a good woman there. Uh, what's your name, ma'am?"

She cleared her throat. "Kate. Kate Simpson."

"And you, Kate, have one extraordinary man. You two need to hang on to each other. Mister Savage, if you haven't already made Kate an honest woman, then you're a damned fool."

"Well, sir, I was just about to address that issue."

"Then get on with it. My business can wait another minute."

Peter dropped to a knee and took hold of Kate's hand. "Kate, will you marry me?"

"Yes, of course I will. Took you long enough to ask." Tears of joy ran down her cheeks.

"Okay," President Taylor boomed over the speaker. "Now that the important stuff is done, there is a small matter I wanted to discuss with you. In ten days, Governor Bingham is going to join me at the White House for a conference on Northwest issues. We'd intended to have this meeting when I was in Redmond, but, well, it didn't happen, for reasons you know too well."

"Yes, sir," Peter said.

"I want you and your fiancée to be on that plane. And bring your pooch—what's his name, Diesel?"

"Yes, sir. Diesel."

"I want all three of you here with Governor Bingham for a ceremony in the Rose Garden. On behalf of a grateful nation, I want to bestow upon you the Presidential Medal of Freedom. I have one for Diesel, too. Although this will be a first. I'm told a canine has never received the medal."

Peter and Kate chuckled at the thought of Diesel sitting at attention while a medal was placed around his neck.

"Now I just have one more thing to say before I go. And this is for you, Kate. I heard the pain and frustration and sense of helplessness in your voice. And you're right. Why is it that a handful of people are always the ones who are called upon to make a sacrifice? It isn't fair, but that's the way it is. And thank God we have those people, because if we didn't, the world would be a lot worse off. From the top of the control tower at Roberts Field, Governor Bingham watched as Air Force One was attacked by domestic terrorists. I thought I was going to die. Thought we all were going to die. And then a crazy man with his dog fired up an airport tug and drove right at those gunmen. According to what Governor Bingham saw, and what my security team reported, that made the difference. The gunmen hesitated and then tried to kill your fiancée. It allowed precious seconds for me and most of the crew to evacuate. Good people, innocent people, died, including Colonel Norton, the commander of Air Force One. But many more would have perished, including yours truly, if it wasn't for that selfless act. I'm living proof that one man can make a world of difference. Just remember that."

"Thank you, sir," Peter said.

The call ended with Peter's promise to visit the White House.

Kate threw her arms around Peter as she wept for the second time that evening.

He returned the embrace, liking the way it felt.

"I'm not perfect, Kate. But I love you. And I don't want to live my life without you. Not anymore."

She smiled, warm and giving.

And for the first time in a very long time, he felt hope… hope that life once again was worth living.

AUTHOR'S POST SCRIPT

BY NOW, YOU SHOULD HAVE FINISHED *Valiant Savage*. At least, I hope you have. But if you've jumped to this section without reading the preceding chapters, let me warn you that there are spoilers—or semi-spoilers—herein that will reduce the thrills and excitement of the plot. So it's you're call. But you've been warned.

I've already addressed the technical feasibility of handheld pulsed-energy weapons (Author's Notes). I chose to focus on industrial uses of lasers, and public reports of U.S. military development of laser weapons. However, as expected, other countries are also pursuing similar goals, and unconfirmed reports have recently surfaced of Chinese efforts to develop a laser rifle.

Many may view residents of the Pacific Northwest as a laid-back crowd that loves its beer and coffee. While that certainly describes yours truly, there is also a lesser known and more radical political mindset that is intent on either forming a fifty-first state—example, the State of Jefferson—or leaving the Union entirely. Secessionist activity crosses the border into British Columbia, home of the Cascadia Party. To this day, popular support for a new nation called Cascadia, approximately comprising British Columbia, Washington, and Oregon, remains strong.

The two seminal themes of *Valiant Savage* are the presidential assassination plot and the expansion of the young United States to the Pacific Ocean during the first three decades of the nineteenth century.

The assassination plot depicted herein was, indeed, inspired by the John Wilkes Booth conspiracy. American history tends to overlook the breadth of that plot. If it had succeeded, not only would Lincoln have been murdered, but Vice President Andrew Johnson and Secretary of State William Seward would have been also. The goal of Booth and his co-conspirators was to remove the influential leaders of government at a time, just days after the surrender of Lee, when Lincoln and his sympathizers had a precarious hold on power. With the government in chaos, Booth believe that a different Commander-in-Chief and cabinet would have resulted in a Federal government more sympathetic to the Confederacy. If the plot had succeeded, the United States might be a very different country today.

Captain Meriwether Lewis provides a strong historical cornerstone to the plot, and to General Denson's motives. Sadly, the final months of Lewis's life were tragic and ended in his death, as portrayed in the story. Did he commit suicide, or was he murdered at Grinders Stand on the Natchez Trace? Perhaps the truth will never be known.

This brings me to the beginning of the Monroe Doctrine and the Lewis and Clark Expedition (or the Corps of Discovery, as it was known at the time). To my thinking, this is a fascinating time in early American history when there was a perfect storm of international circumstances that resulted in unprecedented opportunity for the United States to expand its boundaries.

Specifically, were it not for the Napoleonic Wars and the

financial strain they wrought on the French coffers, France would not have been motivated to sell the Upper Louisiana territory to the U.S. If Spain had not been under pressure from Mexico seeking independence, Spain would not have relinquished its claims to the Northwest. And if Russia had not been threatened by Britain, along what is now coastal British Columbia and Alaska, Russia would not have surrendered its claims to the Pacific coast.

All of the above took place within the span of twenty-five years, and marked the beginning of the Monroe Doctrine of expansion from the Atlantic Ocean to the Pacific. While the Old-World colonial powers were regrouping as to their positions in North America, the government of the United States took every advantage of that fluid situation.

Sadly, no regard was given to the people who had the first historical claim to the North American continent, the indigenous tribes.

But that's the subject of another story.

ABOUT THE AUTHOR

DAVE EDLUND IS THE USA TODAY BESTSELLING author of the award-winning Peter Savage novels, and a graduate of the University of Oregon, with a doctoral degree in chemistry. He resides in Bend, Oregon, with his wife, son, and three dogs (Lucy Liu, Dude, and Tenshi). Raised in the California Central Valley, Dave completed his undergraduate studies at California State University, Sacramento. In addition to authoring several technical articles and books on alternative energy, he is an inventor on 114 U.S. patents. An avid outdoorsman and shooter, Edlund has hunted North America for big game, ranging from wild boar to moose to bear. He has traveled extensively throughout China, Japan, Europe, and North America.

www.PeterSavageNovels.com

THE PETER SAVAGE SERIES
BY DAVE EDLUND

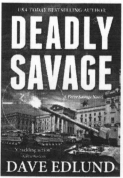